THE BURLINGTON AFFAIR

THE BURLINGTON AFFAIR

Carol L. Parrilli

iUniverse, Inc.
New York Lincoln Shanghai

The Burlington Affair

iUniverse, Inc.

For information address:
iUniverse, Inc.
2021 Pine Lake Road, Suite 100
Lincoln, NE 68512
www.iuniverse.com

ISBN: 0-595-33131-9

Printed in the United States of America

For Doris Stutsman,
My mother, my friend, my hero.
I love you, Mom.

Acknowledgements

No writer completes a book entirely on their own and I am certainly no exception. I have many people to thank for their contributions to *The Burlington Affair.* A special thank you to my mother, Doris Stutsman, for reading every page and giving her honest opinion. Thanks for the fox hunt, Mom. To my best friend, Terry Horton, the real life Chloe, who also did the initial editing; you inspire and encourage me every day and will forever be my "Queen of Word." To Robyn Davis, the greatest massage therapist in the world, who helped develop so many plot points while digging the knots out of my back. To Barbara H. Neilson, my extraordinary editor and friend; without you there would be no *Burlington Affair.* To my beautiful daughter, Alexis Spicer, who never let me give up the dream of seeing my work in print. And many thanks to Jessica Bryan and Michelle Grieco for proofreading my original draft.

I also want to thank Christine Reynolds, Assistant Keeper of the Muniments, Westminster Abbey; Clare Woodcock, Information Officer, University of Oxford; Julie Palfree, Dragon Antiques; the Cheltenham Spa Tourist Information Center and the Metropolitan Police Service of New Scotland Yard for graciously answering my emails and helping with my research.

CHAPTER 1

▼

Monday, September 17, 1002—10:00 AM
Meet Madeline Marlborough

Her feet were swollen, her head throbbed, and her back ached. Come to think of it, there wasn't an inch on her body that didn't hurt. Madeline was tired to the bone, but considering the turmoil of the past week, she was just happy to be home, back at her cluttered little desk. As she sat there, trying to gather enough energy to begin the final report on her tour group that had just returned from London, she thought, "If only I'd had a few more hours sleep…but, oh well, once I get this done, I'm free and clear for the next thirty days!"

For the past twenty-five years, Madeline Marlborough had been held in the highest regard by all the top, tour companies in the United States and could easily have worked fifty-two weeks a year, if she were so inclined. She also designed her own itineraries and had trekked through New Zealand with oil company executives, climbed the Great Wall of China with a group of dentists from Boston and barged through the canals of France with the directors of a charter airline. Indeed, Madeline had been leading groups to The Wakaya Club in Fiji, The Seychelles and Nepal long before such trips became fodder for the one-ups-man-ship at country club, cocktail parties.

After such a hectic pace for so many years, on her fiftieth birthday last August, Madeline finally accepted the fact that she wasn't getting any younger; and, as a special gift to herself, decided to arrange her schedule so that she worked for two months and then took a month off.

She looked around her office and smiled. To the casual observer, including most of her family and friends, her office was a complete disaster. There were piles of books, maps, brochures and file folders all over the floor. Rolling file cabinets encircled her desk chair like pioneer wagons around a campsite. Scattered on her desk were envelopes, some opened, some not, several calculators—the one with the big buttons was her favorite—her little black phone book, an opened box of diskettes, an array of colored highlighters, her phone and rolodex, a stapler and tape dispenser, several pads of Post-its®, a magnifying glass, a fingernail file, a half used box of AA batteries, three different kinds of white-out, an open box of jumbo paper clips, a dictionary, a bottle of Tums, her phone headset, several Papermate pens of various colors, copies of faxes and e-mails, her computer and various reference books and guides. Everything was *just* as she left it. It might look like total chaos to anyone else but Madeline knew where to find every tiny scrap of information. Her father's desk had always been piled high with stuff, too, so she figured she came by her little quirk honestly. A mess? Maybe to others, but to Madeline, it was just perfect.

Home was a charming, ranch-style house in Fort Collins Colorado, nestled in the foothills with the Front Range of the Rocky Mountains as a backdrop. This was Madeline's sanctuary and, as she watched her neighbor's two llamas grazing in the morning sun, she almost wished she could give up her job and never leave home again.

Dragging her attention back to the task at hand, Madeline tried to concentrate on her report, but her attention kept drifting back to her furry friends. She sighed, stretched her arms over her head and was ready to give up and go back to bed, when the shrill ring of the phone jolted her out of her jet-lagged stupor.

Instinctively, she reached out and picked up the receiver. After saying hello several times, she realized her headset was still plugged in, so she put it on and tried again in her most controlled, business voice, "Hello, this is Madeline."

"So! Did you get any sleep last night?" Chloe never announced herself, assuming whomever she was calling would somehow know it was her.

"Hi Chloe. Yeah, I finally tried that awful herbal tea you gave me. It was disgusting, but it worked. I slept clear through the night."

"Well, I should hope so."

"I'll tell you, I was so tired, by the time I pulled into my garage I just left the luggage in the trunk. Remind me to bring it in as soon as we get off the phone. Anyway, I went straight through the house, left my clothes in a heap on the floor, took three aspirin and crawled into bed. Of course, as soon my head hit the pillow, my mind woke up and ran a replay of the last few days."

"Well, duh, I'm not surprised."

"After a couple hours, I decided to give up and try your tea."

"And it worked, didn't it?"

"Yes."

"See, I told you."

Chloe Ambrose and Madeline had been best friends for thirty years, and were indeed, closer than many sisters. No matter where she was or what she was doing, Madeline always felt better after talking with Chloe. Instinctively, they seemed to read each other's thoughts and feelings, knowing what the other was going to say and do. After twenty-three years of marriage, Chloe's husband Mark was still amazed by the uncanny connection between them. They'd recently redone their kitchens and, unbeknownst to the other, had picked out identical cabinets and flooring, right down to the color and hardware. They had seen each other through so much; marriages, divorces, remarriages. Chloe always referred to Madeline's daughter, Victoria, as "their" daughter. She was Vicky's Godmother after all!

Knowing that Madeline was scheduled to return from Madrid on September twelfth, Chloe had been frantic when she couldn't reach her in the aftermath of the attack in New York City and the Pentagon. Calls to her hotel in Madrid were in vain. Phone lines were jammed and her e-mails couldn't get through for hours.

"Frankly, we were just happy to be home safely. Chloe, you wouldn't believe the reaction of the Europeans and how wonderful they were to us. Even people on the street."

"I gathered that from your e-mails, but how did you end up in London?"

"Well, we were on our way back to Madrid the afternoon of the eleventh for our farewell dinner at the Ritz. When we arrived at the hotel, Roberto, the concierge, was waiting for us on the front steps.

"After he told us about the Twin Towers disaster and that all the US airports were closed, I knew we were going to be stranded indefinitely. Since there are a lot more flights out of London to US cities than from Madrid, I suggested we spend a few days there. I called Robbie and you know the rest."

Robert MacDuff was head concierge at the Ascot House in London. Over the years, Madeline had stayed at the hotel many times with various groups and she and Robbie had become fast friends. As soon as she reached him, he told her to come immediately and he would handle everything.

"Ah, that sounds like Robbie," said Chloe with a smile.

"When we landed at Heathrow the next morning, Robbie had limousines waiting for us; by noon we were settled into our rooms at the hotel. Baskets of fruit and candy were in each room, with a letter from Lord Hargrove himself, extending his deepest sympathy and inviting us to stay as long as necessary as his personal guests. We ended up spending five days.

"We were all holding up pretty well until I took them to the Changing of the Guard at Buckingham Palace. When the band played the Star Spangled Banner, we all just lost it. There wasn't a dry eye anywhere."

Madeline paused, "You know what I really need right now?" It was more of a statement than a question. "I need a Chloe fix. Why don't you come out for a few days."

"Truth be told, I need a Maddie fix. Mark is at a seminar and when he comes back, I'll be on my way. In the meantime Maddie, you need some serious down time. You know, eat bonbons, read trashy books?"

"Sounds great to me," Madeline laughed.

"Have I forgotten anything?"

"I don't think so, Dr. Ambrose. I suppose that will cost me five cents."

"You should be so lucky, kiddo! My rates have gone up. That will be one thin dime, thank you "ma'am"! I'm the best you know. Oh, and Maddie, don't forget the luggage in your trunk. Talk to you later."

Madeline quickly wrote "Luggage" on a Post-its® note and stuck it on her computer. She leaned back in her chair, closed her eyes and smiled. Chloe always made her smile.

A few minutes later the phone rang again. Madeline opened her eyes and sighed as she looked out the window at the llamas standing by the fence, their comical faces peering at her through the boards.

"I'll let the machine pick it up," she thought, determined to give her report another go. However, recognizing Frank Crawford's voice, she reluctantly grabbed the receiver.

Frank was Managing Director of Global Tours in Chicago and, over the years, Madeline had led many groups for them. She clicked in her headset, "Hi Frank, I'm here. How are you?"

"Oh good. I caught you. Welcome home."

"Thanks."

"I heard you were stranded in Europe and wasn't sure you were back. A friend of mine thought he saw you and your group in London. I thought you were supposed to be in Spain. How on earth did you get to London and back to the States so soon?"

"Oh, Frank, it's a long story. Actually I just got back last night and I'm trying to bang out this report so I can sleep for the next three days."

There was an awkward pause as Frank cleared his throat and Madeline could practically hear the wheels turning in his head as he was trying to decide what to say next.

"Uh Madeline," he hesitated, "I'm in kind of a pickle here, and I was hoping you might be able to help me out."

Madeline sensed a little panic in his voice. "I'll try as soon as I've recovered. What's up?"

"Do you remember Ruth Winslow?"

Ruth was another tour director at Global. She and Madeline had worked several groups together. "Of course I do. How is she?"

"Well, that's why I'm calling. She had a heart attack last Thursday and they did a triple bypass Friday.

"She has a group scheduled to leave for London this coming Friday, on the twenty-first. Most of the passengers canceled, but nine of them still want to go."

Without missing a beat, Madeline continued, "And your company policy is, 'Departures are guaranteed with eight or more passengers fully paid.' Right?"

"Exactly."

Resting her forehead on her folded hands, Madeline groaned and closed her eyes. She knew she owed him a favor. She just wished he didn't want to collect now.

"Madeline, I know the timing couldn't be worse, but is there any way you can help me out? None of my other tour directors are available. It should be very simple. You'll have the museum guides in London and the theater tickets have already been sent to the hotel. You'll even be at the Ascot House. I know how much you like it there. I'll fax you the rest of the details. Please say yes Madeline, I really need you. I would take them myself, but I have to be a witness in court on Monday."

"Oh Frank. You're certainly right about the timing," Madeline sighed and slumped back in her chair.

"I know, I know, but I'll double your fee!" he pleaded.

She closed her eyes again and said, "You'll pick up the tab for Chloe to go with me. Right?"

"Chloe Ambrose? Absolutely, anything you want."

"Business class. Both of us," she added.

"I promise."

"OK Frank. Let me call Chloe and I'll get back to you. And Frank, you're going to remember me in your will. Right?"

"Of course, I'll remember you! Madeline you are a queen among women, a *goddess*," he exclaimed with great relief.

"Yeah, yeah. Goodbye Frank," she said, and clicked off.

She was suddenly exhausted again. "Caffeine! I need caffeine!" she said out loud. Looking back at her computer screen, she thought, "This report's going to have to wait."

As she pushed her chair back and stood up, her knees protested vehemently. Stretching, a huge yawn escaped and she walked down the hall, oblivious to the treasures from around the world that hung on the walls, turned left and crossed through the living room to her kitchen.

The little green light on the control panel of her dishwasher was shining brightly, indicating the wash cycle was completed. She hated to come home to dirty dishes and had long ago adopted the habit of hitting the start button on the dishwasher as she was walking out the door.

She opened the door and found the 4-cup pot just where she'd left it almost two weeks ago. Filling it with water, she poured it into the top of the coffee maker. Then she opened the freezer door of her side-by-side and rummaged around the top shelf for the hazelnut coffee beans. Scooping out a handful, she dumped them into the grinder, then poured the freshly ground beans into the filter. As she pressed the On button, the smell of fresh coffee was already wafting through the room.

Madeline was an excellent cook who never measured anything. Much to the consternation of people asking for recipes, she gave directions like a pinch of this and a handful of that, or use enough wine to cover the meat. How much meat? How ever much you have. Although it made her friends and family crazy, they eventually they stopped asking and simply adopted the theory, if you want a fabulous meal—go to Madeline's house.

She filled a mug with fresh coffee, added sweetener and laced it generously with hazelnut cream. She walked toward the living room, when she heard the phone ring again. This time Madeline let the machine pickup; a good decision considering it was someone trying to sell her a "free" trip to Las Vegas.

Setting her cup on the glass top coffee table, she nestled into the deep, soft cushions of her sofa, snuggled in the chenille throw she pulled from the back and reached for her cordless phone.

Chloe answered on the second ring.

"Hey Babycakes," Madeline said. "Did you ever get your passport renewed?"

"Are you in bed? You're supposed to be in bed."

"I know, I know. No, I'm not in bed, but I'm lying on the sofa, having a cup of coffee."

"Oh fine. That's good. Coffee will really help you fall asleep. Madeline, you can't lay down and drink coffee at the same."

"Come on, Chloe, is your passport up to date?"

"I got it back a couple of weeks ago. Why?"

"Well, Frank Crawford just called". Madeline related their conversation to Chloe.

"Are you nuts? If you don't slow down, you'll be the one having the triple bypass," Chloe yelled in the phone.

Madeline felt better already. Chloe was so predictable. "Well, are you coming or not? It's all expenses paid. You can't beat that. It'll be fun."

"So, when are we leaving?"

"I'm not sure, either Thursday or Friday. I don't know exactly what time and I forgot to ask Frank if we meet the group here or in London. I'll find out when I call him back." There was a momentary silence on the line.

"How long will we be gone?"

"About two weeks."

"I'm putting you on hold a minute while I call Mark to confirm he can handle the girls." The girls were Brodie Mae, a five-year-old Doberman Pinscher, and Molly, a beautiful Persian cat.

Chloe was back on the line in less than a minute, "All set Maddie."

Following a brief discussion about wardrobe, Madeline added, "I'll let you know the departure plans as soon as I talk to Frank." When she hung up, Madeline laid her head down and promptly fell asleep, the phone still in her hand.

Monday, September 17, 9:30 PM

She was floating in a deep, dark pool, the warm water caressing her aching muscles. Her body felt weightless and heavy, as if she were lying in a cloud covered with a lead blanket. The sound of distant church bells seemed to be getting louder. Coming out of a deep sleep, Madeline gradually became aware that the bells weren't church bells at all, but the insistent ringing of her phone. Fumbling around in the dark, she finally located the receiver, which had fallen out of her hand when she fell asleep.

"What?" she asked, her voice muffled in sleep.

"Madeline, is that you? You were going to call me back."

"Oh, hey Frank, sorry about that. I think I'm asleep. What time is it anyway?"

"It's late. Were you able to reach Chloe?"

"Yeah, she's good to go, so I hope you were you able to get those business class seats."

"Great!" he answered as the weight lifted from his shoulders. "I'll fax you all the passenger information and send all the documents overnight. You're a lifesaver, Madeline!"

Tuesday, September 18, 7:00 AM

Madeline awoke to the brilliant Colorado sunshine. With only two and a half days to get ready to leave again, she had not a moment to spare. As she stood in the shower washing her hair and going through her mental checklist, she worried about telling Vicky and her mother of the assignment. She knew they wouldn't be overjoyed, but she also knew their anxiety level would be relieved slightly knowing Chloe was going with her.

She also had to do laundry, although there wasn't as much as usual. However, she did need to wash her underwear.

Madeline had been fighting the "*Battle of the Bulge*" her entire adult life, yo-yoing up and down so many times that long ago she decided it was foolish to give away clothes that didn't fit. If they didn't fit now, they surely would at some point in the future. As a result, not only had she built her wardrobe to be prepared for all occasions, but she also had clothes in three different sizes. Now that her daughter had moved into her own home she made use of the closets in all three bedrooms, with a different size in each.

Corresponding with her different sized wardrobes, she also had complete sets of underwear in various sizes. She always traveled with the "good stuff", matching sets of bras and panties that were relatively new and in perfect condition. God forbid she was in an accident and taken to a hospital. Or what if she had to bunk in with one of her passengers due to a hotel snafu? And, if she had to send things to a hotel valet, she didn't want it circulated through the staff that she had cheap underwear!

In each of her three bedrooms, she reserved two dresser drawers exclusively for her lingerie; one labeled "Trip", the other, labeled "Home." The "Home" variety, was just the stretchy cotton kind she thought of as her solid comfort undies.

Rinsing her hair, she was still obsessing about bras and panties, pushing her real concern, talking to her mom and Vic to the back of her mind. She stepped out of the shower, wrapped herself in a soft bath sheet and toweled the excess water from her hair. Thank God for curly hair. No bothering with curling irons or hair dryers, all she had to do was shake her head and she was ready to go.

Getting dressed, she was pleasantly surprised to discover she didn't have to go to the size 16 closet. Having been wined and dined so lavishly in Spain and London, she was sure she'd put on some extra pounds, especially after drinking all that English *lager*.

"Hallelujah!" she shouted as she zipped up her size "14" jeans without having to lie down on the bed. As she began unpacking her garment bag, she set aside all the evening clothes with the exception of one basic black dress. This trip wouldn't be as formal as the last. Then she walked into her "14" closet and pulled a variety of mix and match pieces, all in her favorite colors. Her naturally curly, silver hair and fair skin looked best in vibrant jewel tones ranging from deep purple to ice blue.

Satisfied with her clothes, she moved on to shoes. She always told her clients, "Always think of your feet!" By all means, comfort was the name of the game. She had her sturdy walking shoes, Rockport oxfords and low-heeled pumps. She also packed her favorite tennis shoes and soft, cushy socks. Madeline never unpacked her make-up and toiletries case. She just replaced items as needed.

Clothes—√

Shoes—√

Makeup case—√

Next on the list was her Palm Pilot. She still marveled that such a small instrument could hold so much information. Without it and her laptop, she'd be lost. From the phone numbers of all her contacts around the world, to hotel managers and concierges, restaurants, airlines, car rental companies and favorite local guides, every bit of information was at her fingertips.

Palm Pilot—√

Briefcase—√

Cell Phone—√

Passport—√

Airline tickets—on the way.

Dressed in comfy cotton pants and a well-worn T-shirt, she headed for the kitchen to brew a pot of Earl Gray while she called her mother and Vic. Their reactions were exactly as she'd predicted; neither was happy about her leaving so soon and both were relieved Chloe was going along.

Taking her tea and the large blueberry muffin she had popped into the microwave, Madeline made her way through the house to her office where Frank's promised faxes were on her machine. Scanning the manifest, she knew this was going to be a very interesting trip. She knew nothing about them personally, but, despite all the turmoil, they were still determined to travel to England.

"I can't wait to meet these people," she called out to the llamas across the street.

CHAPTER 2

▼

Friday, September 21, Oak Brook, Illinois
The Travelers Trickle In

Joe Dalton rinsed off his razor and put it back in the medicine cabinet. As he closed the mirrored door, it seemed to melt into the vast expanse of mirror covering the entire length of the wall. Married twenty-two years, Joe and Marty had promised each other that someday, when they built their dream house, they would have a magnificent bathroom. He and Marty each had their own shower, lavatory, walk-in closet and dressing room. Between the two sides, a large Jacuzzi rested on a raised marble platform. Behind it, sliding glass doors opened onto a private balcony overlooking the garden. The walls were a pale mint green and the woodwork and cabinetry, bleached oak. In contrast, the floor was covered with deep green marble.

Closing the medicine cabinet, Joe caught a glimpse of Marty's reflection in the mirror as she shoved hangers back and forth in her closet., doing her familiar travel dance.

"Joe, what do you think? Leather or suede? I really like the suede, and it does fit better, but what happens if it rains? I don't want it to get water-marked."

"Marty, you can always send it out to the dry cleaners. They do have them in London you know. Of course, they have plenty of rain too, so you better take an umbrella."

"Well, it might be easier to take the leather and not have to worry about it." Taking both jackets, she walked toward him and held them up for inspection. "What do you think?"

"Marty, honey, I don't know. Just take both of them." Bemused, he looked at her reflection knowing she was completely oblivious to his advice. It was one of the quirks he loved most about his wife. He called it her travel dance. He actually admired her ability to focus, even though it meant she tuned him out in the process. Before he could say anything else, she returned to her closet, hung up the leather jacket and came back with the suede one draped over her arm.

"Are you almost ready? We have to leave in an hour," she said. Turning, she took her jacket and went into the bedroom to finish packing.

Joe smiled as she walked away, shaking his head and thinking, "How did I get myself into this?" He glimpsed his reflection in the mirror. The dark circles under his eyes belied his forty-eight years. He still had a full head of hair, but the rich brown color was now flecked with silver and his temples were nearly white. There were laugh lines around his deep blue eyes and the frown line in his forehead was getting more prominent by the day. His body wasn't too bad. He played racquetball three days a week to keep his six-foot plus frame in shape and played weekend golf for fun. Marty kept him on a healthy diet with only an occasional indulgence of his sweet tooth. Once a month she allowed him to have a super-sized hot butterscotch sundae, whipped-cream and chopped pecans included!

"All in all, not too bad Dalton," he told himself, "But how did I let her talk me into this trip? The last thing in the world I want to do, is go on a tour with a bunch of people I don't even know."

Joe was the President and CEO of Dalton and Sons, an investment-banking firm with offices in London, Tokyo and Sydney. The firm had been in his family for three generations and, as the oldest of three brothers, the chairmanship fell into his hands when his father retired four years ago. The only reason he finally agreed to go on this tour was because he would be able to do some business while they were in London. That, and the fact that his only daughter, indeed his only child, was going to spend her freshman year of college at Oxford rather than attend his alma mater, Northwestern. Of course he was proud of her and completely supported her choice, but secretly he missed her already and wanted to check out her living arrangements while there was still time for him to back out.

As soon as Kelly had received the acceptance letter from Oxford, her mother began planning. Marty thought an escorted tour of London and the English countryside would be the most efficient way to see the highlights. And traveling with a knowledgeable guide would guarantee they wouldn't miss anything important. She knew Joe wouldn't want to travel with a group, so initially she made reservations for just Kelly and herself. Ten days—highlights of London, Oxford, and the Cotswolds—in and out—mission accomplished.

Once the reservations were confirmed, Marty began her campaign to persuade Joe to come along. Although Martha Jane Dalton could be relentless when she wanted something, in the end it was Joe's love for his daughter that won him over.

Somehow his little girl had grown up and, like a lot corporate fathers, Joe had missed out on many of the important milestones in Kelly's childhood. After graduating from Northwestern University, Joe went on to earn his MBA before joining the family's investment banking firm. As heir apparent, and at his father's *instance*, he worked his way up through the ranks of the company, experiencing every facet of the business. Meeting his father's administrative assistant, Martha Jane Bradley, gave him even more incentive to work his way through the training process. By the time they married and Kelly was born, Joe was on the road much of the time, establishing his presence in the investment banking community around the world. When Kelly took her first steps, he was attending a conference in Sydney. On her first day of Kindergarten, he was attending a meeting in Zurich. And so it went until her Senior Prom. When she came down the stairs in her strapless black gown, he thought she was the most beautiful creature he had ever seen, but where was his little girl? Where was his cute pixie with the floppy curls? This exquisite young woman was nearly six feet tall with a figure that belonged on the cover of Vogue. Somehow his little girl had grown up, and it scared him to death.

It had taken him three weeks of late nights and long weekends to get his business commitments to a point where he could leave them for ten days. He was also planning to see two of his clients in London while the group was off sightseeing. He hadn't told Marty about that yet. He figured he would spring it on her at the last minute so she couldn't put up too much of a fight.

"Joe, are you ready?" Marty interrupted his thoughts. "Please hurry. The driver is waiting."

"I'm coming, I'm coming", Joe said. "Leave the bags. I'll bring them down in a minute."

"All right, but hurry. Airport security is going to be a nightmare and I don't want to miss our flight."

Friday, September 21, Green Bay, Wisconsin

"Sister, are you sure you remembered to call for the taxi?" Millie Talbot didn't trust her sister's memory these days. She tried to be patient. After all, Marjorie was her older sister and the only family she had left.

"Of course I did. I called last night. I even wrote down the name of the boy I talked to, Eddie Something-or-other," Marge snapped. She loved her little sister dearly, but ever since their retirement Millie had been driving her batty. She had managed perfectly well living on her own for the past fifty-five years, and she didn't need Millie hovering over her every move harping, "Did you remember to turn off the oven? Don't forget to take your pills."

Marge and Millie Talbot were as close as two sisters could be and as different as night and day. Marjorie was tall and thin, with a longish nose and pinched features that made her resemble an ancient bird of prey. Mildred, on the other hand, was short, round and soft, rather like a favorite teddy bear that had seen years and years of cuddling. Their personalities, however, were just the opposite of their appearance.

Marge, who had never married, was a warm and compassionate woman. Fiercely independent and active in the community, she liked to do things in her own time and her own way. She was a major organizer and fund raiser for the Senior Citizen's Center, Chairperson for the hospital auxiliary's annual blood drive, and served on the Board of Directors of the Green Bay Animal Welfare Society. Marge Talbot was the kind of woman who could walk into a room of people, assess the situation, delegate responsibilities, and have everything under control within minutes. No wonder the president of Door County Insurance Corporation had personally begged her to stay on as the Director of Human Resources past her self-announced retirement date. Their agreement of one year eventually turned into seven and she finally retired two weeks before her seventy-fourth birthday.

Millie Talbot, five years younger than her sister, had married her high school sweetheart right after graduation. She had been heartbroken when he left her two years later claiming she was smothering him to death. After the divorce, she returned to her maiden name and Marge found a position for her in the secretarial pool at the insurance company. Millie found her niche as an administrative assistant and never remarried. Her constant hovering and need to please made her the perfect match for the new recruit in the accounting department. As he climbed the ladder of success, eventually becoming manager of the department, she followed and, when he retired after forty years, so did she.

The sisters retired within a week of each other. The company threw a huge party for them where the president gave each a gold and diamond watch, a complete set of luggage and a gift certificate for the Global Tour of their choice. No mention was made of the considerable shares of stock he gave Marge when he took her to lunch three days before the party.

Marge and Millie had always wanted to see England, and after thorough investigation they decided on the deluxe *London and English Countryside* tour, departing September 21, 2001. After they retired, Marge decided it was silly for them to maintain two homes when they could live together and share expenses. Now, as the blue cab pulled up in front of their house, she was seriously questioning the sanity of that decision.

"Oh sister, please hurry. The taxi is here," cried Millie in a state of near panic. Her face was flushed and her heart was beating furiously as she opened the door and waived to the driver. She turned and scurried down the hall toward Marge's bedroom. "Have you got the traveler's checks and tickets? We don't want to forget anything," she said, gulping for air.

Marge was just locking her suitcase when Millie came charging into the room. "Millie, will you please relax? I haven't forgotten anything, and will you please stop calling me 'sister'? I'm not a nun," Marge said with exasperation.

"But you are my sister."

"Yes, I am well aware of that," Marge replied. "But my name is Marge. If you keep calling me sister, no one on this trip will learn my name. And they might think I really am a nun, and then we won't have any fun!"

Millie took a deep breath, thought for a moment and, as if a light bulb in her head had just turned on, said, "I never thought of it that way. I guess you're right. Well, sister, I mean Marge, I'll do my best. Now please hurry."

With that, Millie flew back down the hallway and opened the door just as the taxi driver was about to ring the bell. With the luggage stowed in the trunk and the two sisters installed in the back seat, the taxi driver slowly drove off, somehow knowing this was an important adventure for his two elderly passengers. Before they reached the end of the block Millie said, "Are you sure we turned off the coffee pot and unplugged the iron?"

"Millie!"

Friday, September 21, Otter Creek, Iowa

John and Delores Shepard drove south on US Highway 61, through the rolling hills of Iowa farmland. The corn had been harvested and freshly cut bails of hay were scattered across the fields. They drove in comfortable silence, each lost in their own thoughts. After September eleventh, they briefly considered canceling, but they had planned this trip for so long and were determined to go. Besides, this was the only time they could get away from the farm.

Red Hollings, their nearest neighbor, had offered to look after the livestock, collect the mail, and keep an eye on everything while they were gone.

"I talked to Red again this morning," John said. "He'll be by to feed the stock this afternoon."

"He's a good friend," Delores replied, remembering how their children had played together when they were younger. She and Ruth had been co-leaders of the local 4-H Chapter and traded duties as Room Mothers, and now, all five of their children were enrolled at the University of Iowa in Iowa City.

"It's too bad we don't have time to stop and see the kids, but I'd rather have plenty of time at the airport," John said.

"Me, too." Delores sighed and leaned her head back against the soft leather headrest of the new Lincoln Towncar. The casual observer, looking at their modest, unassuming manner, would never suspect the Shepards were financially comfortable. The farm was a huge, successful spread of dairy cattle, corn, soybeans and other crops, and Delores had received a sizeable inheritance from her maternal grandfather. Her mother had always dismissed John as not worthy and was constantly reminding her how far beneath her station she had married. Delores, however, felt she was the luckiest woman in the world. She had everything she had ever wanted; a beautiful home, happy, healthy children and above all, a husband who loved her beyond reason.

Reaching over, he took hold of her hand, and glancing over briefly, saw she was smiling. It warmed him down to his toes and made butterflies in the pit of his stomach. After twenty-five years, she was still the most beautiful woman he had ever seen.

As they came to the bridge they would take across the Mississippi River to the Illinois side, they saw signs directing them to the Quad City Airport.

"Do you remember when we used to come down here and watch the planes take off and land?" John asked

"I think it was our second or third date, wasn't it? And we had the most amazing time too," she answered with a chuckle.

"It sure has grown since then. Hey look, they even have valet parking."

John pulled up in front of the terminal building next to the valet parking sign. A young man in an airport jacket opened the door and said, "Can I help you sir? If you'll pop the trunk, I'll get your bags."

"Thanks a lot," John said as he pushed the trunk button on the control panel.

Delores waited as he came around the front of the car and opened her door. Once, when they first started dating, she opened the car door herself and he said, "How can I be a gentleman if you open the door before I can get around the car to do it for you?" She never did it again and he continued to be a gentleman to this day.

"What airline will you be flying today, sir?" the young valet asked. John and Delores looked at each other, then looked quickly away, trying very hard not to laugh. There were only three ticket counters in the small airport. United and American had their own, while Northwest and TWA shared.

"We're flying United to Chicago and connecting to London," said John, bemused by the young valet's intensity.

The boy was so sincere and was trying so hard to be professional. They made arrangements for the car, then followed him as he wheeled the luggage cart into the main entrance.

Surprisingly, there were quite a number of people lined up at the United counter. "Please have your tickets ready to hand to the agent, Sir," the boy said adding, "Can I help you with anything else?"

John handed him a generous tip. "You've been very helpful. Thanks again"

The boy stared at the twenty-dollar bill, turned beet red and stammered, "Thank you, sir and you have a wonderful trip." Then he turned around and practically ran back to the door as if wanting to make sure John didn't want change.

Remembering what it was like to young and broke, John couldn't help but chuckle. "Poor kid. Maybe he thought I was going to take it back."

Dolores shook her head and smiled.

Friday, September 21, Double-D Ranch, Shallowater, Texas

Jake Donovan was a big, bawdy Texan. He stood six feet six and weighed well over two hundred fifty pounds, a huge man who would have looked right at home playing Center for the Dallas Cowboys. His parents had scratched out a meager living on a little dirt farm just north of Lubbock. He and his two younger brothers knew what it was like to be hungry. Jake learned at an early age his size was sometimes the only protection they had against the bullies of the world. He also learned, if he could make the bad guys laugh, he could avoid using his fists. Over the years he developed the ability to talk himself into or out of just about any situation. This skill came in very handy when, at sixteen, he negotiated a job on a ranch and acquired his first two head of prime Texas Longhorn.

Jake had been the star quarterback on his high school football team. The local cattle baron, J. T. Dobbs, who was a big team supporter and a friend of the coach, often stopped by to watch football practice. One afternoon Jake was standing on the sideline, catching his breath after a series of plays, when J.T. came up and asked him how things were going.

Never one to pass up a great opportunity, Jake said, "Goin' great, Sir. You comin' to the game Saturday?"

"Sure am, kid. Told coach if y'all kick Central's butt, y'all are invited to celebrate out at the ranch. Got a big barbecue goin' Sunday. Don't take nothin' to make it a little bigger."

"We're gonna kick their butt all the way back to Sweetwater, so you better be ready," Jake answered with all the bravado of a cocky teenager. "Can I tell the guys? Some of 'em never seen your place before."

"You better ask coach first," J.T. said as he turned to leave.

"Hey, Mr. Dobbs," Jake said, not wanting him to get away. "Ain't it about time for your roundup? Sure would like to see that." What he really wanted was to get on J.T.'s good side and, hopefully, land a job.

J.T. knew Jake didn't have two nickels to rub together, as Coach Jenkins had discussed Jake's situation with him and asked him to help the boy out. J.T. and the coach had been friends a long time and had a mutually philanthropic deal between them. Jenkins would find a worthy kid with nothing but dirt in his pockets and J.T. would supply the funds, usually in the form of a job, to keep the kid in school. "I imagine we could work something out," J.T. replied with a grin. "We'll talk about it later, after you win that game tomorrow."

And so began the friendship between Jake and the rancher. Jake's team won the football game, and at the barbecue J.T. had offered him a chance to help with fall roundup. As payment for his hard work, Jake was rewarded with a pair of cattle from J.T.'s stock and a permanent job helping around the ranch. With J.T. as his mentor, Jake learned the ranching business and made it his life's work.

Underneath his teenage macho exterior, Jake was a hard worker, both at school and the ranch. When the time came for college, J.T. helped Jake find scholarship money. He did well at Texas A&M, spending his summers working at the ranch and, after graduation, returned to the Double-D as J.T.'s right-hand man. In the meantime, J.T.'s only child, Susan had grown up into a lovely young woman. She was a tiny little thing, quiet and shy, about as different from Jake as a girl could be, but she could ride like the wind, rope like the best wrangler, and understood the ranching business as well as any man. She was her father's daughter alright and Jake couldn't help falling head over heels in love with her.

Now, twenty years and two children later, Jake wanted to surprise Suzie for their anniversary. She always wanted to see the world, but between raising children and running the ranch, there never seemed to be any time. This year, however, was special. Twenty years deserved something more than a trip to Las Vegas. Jake enlisted J.T., who had retired and moved to Dallas, and his own parents to stay with the boys and take care of the ranch.

Their twentieth anniversary party had been quite an affair. About a hundred of their friends and family had been there when Jake took Suzie's hand and led her to a table with a strange looking package sitting on top. It looked like some kind of statue wrapped in anniversary paper and topped with a huge white bow.

As she studied the package, completely baffled by what it could be, Suzie asked, "Jake, what did you do?" For a moment she thought it might be a birdbath for the garden. If it was, she was going to kill him.

"Now Suzie-girl, don't look at me like that." Jake couldn't keep his feet still, rocking back and forth on his heels. He was as antsy as a little boy. "Go on and open it."

"If it's that birdbath…," she said as she removed the bow.

"Just rip it! Hurry up!"

She gave Jake a puzzled look, then tore into the paper. At first she couldn't tell what it was. It *wasn't* a birdbath. Jake had mounted porcelain miniatures of Big Ben, the Houses of Parliament and Westminster Abbey on a board painted to look like their actual locations. The streets were painted to look like cobblestone and the water of the River Thames, which flows behind the Parliament building, was done with a pallet knife. Little trees surrounded Parliament Square and a little white boat was making its way up the river. Attached to the top of Big Ben was a tiny banner that read "I Love You, Suzie".

With a questioning look, she turned to Jake. As their eyes met, he handed her an embossed leather wallet. With tears in her eyes, she opened it to find two airline tickets, luggage tags and an itinerary that began "Welcome to London". Suzie was speechless. She had always wanted to go to Europe, but they hadn't even talked about it for years. She figured they would have to wait until they retired.

"Well," Jake said with exasperation, "do ya like it?"

Suzie jumped in the air, threw her arms around his neck and kissed him as hard as she could. With her feet a least a foot off the ground, he held her there and kissed her back. As the crowd began to cheer, he swung her around in a big circle, then gently set her down. With a sheepish grin he said to everyone, "I think she likes it," and for once in his life, he couldn't think of anything else to say.

The party had been August eighteenth. Following the events of September eleventh, they were afraid Global Tours might cancel their trip. They truly believed what their President and fellow Texan had said, "Get on with the business of your lives. If you have plans to travel, travel." They were thrilled when their travel agent called to advise them their trip would continue, as planned.

At eight-thirty on the morning of September twenty-first, J.T. drove them to the airport in Lubbock, where their flight to Chicago was scheduled to depart at Noon.

Friday, September 21, 6:25 PM

When United 928 departed from Chicago's O'Hare Airport that evening at six-twenty-five, all nine members of Global Tour's *London and the English Countryside* group were aboard. None were aware of their fellow tour members as the Global luggage tags that would have identified them, were attached to bags now residing in the cargo hold. And none had the slightest inkling of the bond that soon would be forged amongst them.

CHAPTER 3

$\blacktriangledown$

Thursday, September 20, 2:45 PM
Denver To London, The Journey Begins

Madeline had arranged to meet Chloe in the British Airways departure lounge at DIA early Thursday afternoon. For once, the flight from Seattle was actually on time and, as Chloe made a beeline for the concourse, she heard a familiar voice say, "Hey, little girl. Want a walnetto?"

Startled, Chloe did an about face to find Madeline right behind her. She threw her arms around Madeline's neck and hugged her tight. "Oh, I'm so glad to see you, you wretched woman. I thought we were supposed to meet at…"

"I know, I know," interrupted Madeline. "Traffic was light, so I got here a little early. You look great."

Never one to mince words, Chloe shot back, "Well you don't. Those circles under your eyes look like someone used you for a punching bag."

Coming from anyone else, Madeline would have been offended, but this was Chloe.

"I mean it, Maddie," Chloe continued, "I'm worried about you. You push yourself too much. You look like a raccoon on speed. Honey, you're not twenty-five any more."

"Many thanks for the reminder," Madeline said with a wry smile.

Linking arms, they headed down the concourse, chattering away as if they hadn't seen each other in years. Arriving at the cocktail lounge across from the British Airways gate, they sank into comfy leather chairs and ordered drinks, a Bloody Mary for Chloe and coffee with Bailey's for Madeline.

"I owed Crawford a favor and, besides, I have you along to keep me company. There are only nine people in the group, so it shouldn't be too hectic."

"What are they like? Do you have profiles on them?"

"At this point I've only got their names and passport numbers. Not much to go on. No pictures, medical information, nothing. I loathe the way Global handles this part of the booking process and I really don't like meeting a group without knowing more about their personal information beforehand."

When Madeline organized her own groups, she always asked for copies of their passports along with the other profile information, so she had a pretty good idea of what her group members looked like in advance. Since passports are valid for ten years, the pictures were often out of date, but it was still better than nothing. She also liked to have a record of their passport information just in case one was lost. That had happened several times over the years and it also turned up a few surprises, the most memorable being an incident a few years ago, when one of her clients had failed to tell her he wasn't an American citizen. All Madeline's conversations had been with his wife and when Madeline asked her about citizenship, she obviously thought the question pertained only to her. When Madeline received copies of their passports, the husband's was from Iran. Since the trip was going to Italy, he needed a visa.

Although Madeline always asked that profiles and passport copies be in her office at least thirty days prior to departure, some people were always late, which caused a huge problem. Without enough time to obtain the visa by mail, the man and his Iranian passport had to drive two-hundred-fifty miles to the nearest Italian Consulate and apply in person. To add insult to injury, he had to overnight in Los Angeles because the Consulate required twenty-four hours to process the visa. Since then, Madeline did everything in her power to avoid a repeat performance.

"So, what *do* you know?" Chloe asked.

She dug around in her purse and pulled out a name list, which she handed to Chloe. "Here, see for yourself."

Chloe looked at it and furrowed her brow. "Well, I guess we'll know soon enough."

"I guess," Madeline sighed. "When we meet them at Heathrow, I'll hold up a sign saying Global Tours and hope they find us."

Chloe glanced across the concourse just as the British Airways agents arrived to begin checkin. "Thank God we already have our boarding passes," she said. "It took me over an hour just to get through security in Seattle."

The thing Madeline liked best about flying business class was the seat size. It allowed plenty of squirm room and best of all, the seat fully reclined with a wonderful footrest.

Once airborne, Madeline and Chloe opened their British Airways gift bags, eager to find the warm fuzzy slippers, earplugs, sleeping mask, toothbrush, toothpaste, and lotion inside. They kicked off their shoes, donned their slippers and leaned back in their chairs. Madeline promptly fell asleep.

Chloe found dinner delicious. The filet mignon was cooked just the way she liked it, medium rare, with a buttery Béarnaise sauce. The Merlot was excellent and dessert was a thick brownie covered with chocolate ice cream, hot fudge and whipped cream. Savoring every mouthful, she sighed to herself, "Ah, Divine decadence." Finishing off with a nightcap of Grand Marnier, she put her feet up and closed her eyes.

Friday, September 21, 8:30 AM

Madeline awakened to find the sun shinning and the flight attendants busily serving breakfast. Glancing over at Chloe, she saw that she was still sound asleep. "Chloe, wake up," she said, gently shaking her arm. "We must be arriving soon."

"What? Ok, Ok. I'm coming," Chloe said as she tried to stand up.

Madeline laughed and grabbed her arm. "No, not quite yet. Your seatbelt is still fastened."

"What? Oh yeah." Chloe sank back in her chair as a cheery, young flight attendant approached with a coffee pot in her hand. "Good morning, ladies. Are you feeling better? Would you like coffee? Breakfast?"

"Yes, yes and yes," said Madeline.

Coffee cups in hand, they watched as the flight attendant made her way back to the galley to get their breakfast. Madeline shook her head, "It should be illegal to be so young and perky so early in the morning. She's thin too. I hate her."

"I know. It's disgusting," Chloe whispered back.

September 21, 10:05 AM

The rest of the trip was uneventful, and they touched down at Gatwick airport right on schedule. As they emerged from the Customs Hall, looking for the Britrail sign, Madeline spotted a familiar shock of red hair wading toward them through the sea of people waiting for incoming passengers.

Madeline had met Robbie MacDuff ten years ago when one of her clients held a board meeting at The Ascot House. Robbie, who was the night concierge at the time, had been invaluable, obtaining nonexistent theater tickets, last minute dinner reservations and even a personal shopper for the CEO's wife. Madeline was convinced Robbie possessed some kind of magical power, for he always knew precisely who to call and what to do in order to fulfill any request a guest might have, regardless of how outrageous that request might be.

"Robbie. What are you doing here?" Madeline cried with a mixture of surprise and delight.

"Well, I've come to fetch ya now, haven't I, Lassie?" he answered in his thick Scottish brogue.

Robbie had grown fond of Madeline over the years and, after what had happened during her last trip, wanted to do whatever he could to make this one easier for her. It was to have been his day off, but he knew Madeline was returning to the hotel, so he decided to drive down to the airport and surprise her.

The sight of him always made Madeline's heart skip a beat, or four. Robert MacDuff was a big man, tall and broad shouldered, with a full head of beautiful red hair flecked with silver, and the kindest, deep, green eyes she had ever seen. When he was wearing his kilt, as he did when he was working, he looked like a noble Scottish laird, who would have been right at home on the back of a great stallion, leading his warriors into battle. Today he wore snug, faded jeans, a polo shirt, and a pair of sleek Oakley sunglasses.

Madeline dropped the handle of her suitcase and reached up to give Robbie a hug. He wrapped his arms around her, held her for a second, then let go. "Oh my," she said, half teasing. "I could get used to this."

"And here I am, thinking I just got rid of you," he teased back.

Madeline feigned a stricken look. Robbie took her hand and, with a flourish, bowed and kissed it. "I'm only teasin' ya Darlin'," he said with a devilish smile.

A voice chimed in, "Hey, what about me? This is all quite entertaining, but people are beginning to stare."

"Oh!" Madeline exclaimed, having momentarily forgotten about Chloe. "You remember Chloe, don't you?" she asked as she let go of the hand Robbie was still holding.

"Of course I do." Robbie leaned forward and kissed Chloe's cheek. "It's good to see you again, Chloe. And you're looking wonderful I might add."

Walking to his car, Robbie turned to Madeline and said, "I took the liberty of changing your schedule a bit so you don't have to go out again this afternoon. The people from Global Tours will be joining you for afternoon tea in your suite."

"Oh Robbie, thank you."

"My pleasure. Actually, they were falling all over themselves to accept the invitation."

"I'll bet. Afternoon tea at Ascot House is an event."

The Ascot House was more like a private club than a hotel. Located just off Hyde Park, the entrance looked like a private residence, with white columns and a portico topped with flowering vines. Flowering shrubs also lined the black iron fence that surrounded the property. The small marble-clad reception area resembled the entry hall of a grand, Edwardian mansion. On the left was a beautiful, English drawing room with floor to ceiling windows that looked out on a formal, rose garden. A gilded antique desk was used for guest registration. Arriving guests were served either tea or champagne, depending on the time of day. To the right of the entry was an elegant oak paneled drawing room that served as a library and common room. Three magnificent Waterford crystal chandeliers hung from the towering ceiling of the entry hall, the center one over a round marble table festooned with brilliantly colored fresh flowers. At the far end of the hall, a rose colored, marble staircase took guests to the upper floors. On the right, a lift was discretely tucked away at the foot of the stairs.

Lord Clive Hargrove, owner of the hotel, was a distinguished looking gentleman of, perhaps, seventy. He had snow white hair that ringed his bald pate like a halo and a thin mustache and goatee to match. His sharp eyes twinkled behind little round spectacles and, except for his modern Saville Row clothing, he looked like he had just popped out of a Dickens novel. Ascot House had served as his family's London residence since it was built in 1742. It had been renovated several times over the years and the façade had been remodeled in 1907. Lord Hargrove thought it silly to maintain such a huge residence for his small family and turned the property into an all-suite, luxury hotel in 1983, keeping an apartment for himself. As it turned out, the family had a real flair for the hotel business. His elder son, William, now served as General Manager and his younger son, David, was Master Chef of the hotel's restaurant, La Violette, named after their sister, Violet.

Upon their arrival, Lord Hargrove personally greeted them at the door. "Ms. Marlborough, how wonderful to see you again," he said as he took her hand and escorted her through the doorway. "Your flight was lovely, I trust?"

"Actually, it was. I slept all the way from Denver. You remember Chloe Ambrose, don't you?" she gestured towards Chloe who was following with Robbie.

"Of course. Mrs. Ambrose, how nice to see you, again," he smiled, giving Chloe a formal nod.

Madeline turned to go to the reception desk, but Lord Hargrove took her elbow and said, "Not necessary, my dear, not at all. We've seen to everything".

Madeline and Chloe followed Lord Hargrove into the lift. As the doors were closing Robbie said, "Go ahead, Lass, I'll be along shortly."

Lord Hargrove led the way down the second floor hall and, unlocking the door, said with a slight flourish, "I trust this will be satisfactory," He was quite proud of his establishment and, other than his own, this was his favorite suite. Although Madeline had requested this suite for her VIPs many times, this was the first time it had ever been reserved for her.

"Your luggage will be up directly," Lord Hargrove said, all business again. "And I've taken the liberty of ordering refreshments."

Handing Madeline the key, he gave her hand a little pat and closed the door behind him. Madeline and Chloe walked down the short hallway that opened into a large, sunlit common room with a bedroom at each end. To the left was an opulently decorated living area, fusing French chic with English warmth. A pair of overstuffed sofas had a large square coffee table between them. The antique desk, equipped with a phone, fax and data port was flanked with bookcases. The large TV was discreetly hidden in an armoire just to the side of the fireplace. The other side of the room was used as the dining area. The table for four could easily be extended to accommodate eight. The matching sideboard held a complete china service, silver and crystal. Directly ahead was a glass alcove that overlooked the rose garden.

"Isn't this beautiful," Chloe exclaimed as she looked around. "I thought the suite we had last time was fabulous, but this is," she hesitated, looking for the right word. "Wow!"

"I know. How generous of him" Madeline said as she set her purse down on the desk. "I can't believe Lord Hargrove gave us this suite. It's the most lavish in the hotel. I can't believe it's available. It's always occupied."

Chloe didn't hear her. She was busy poking around, opening drawers and doors. She found the wet bar in the dining area behind a pair of louvered oak doors and the guest bath just around the corner. She yelled from the bathroom, "My God, Maddie. They even have flowers in here!" Fresh flowers were every-where, on the coffee table, the desk, the dining table, the sideboard, and, as Chloe had discovered, even the bathrooms. "This has got to be a full-time gig for some lucky florist."

Opening the door at the far end of the dining area, Chloe discovered a bed-room, lavishly decorated in soft shades of blue and white. The king size bed had a headboard that extended up the wall and over the bed to form a canopy, covered with blue and white brocade. The walls were covered with pale blue silk, and heavy draperies matching the canopy framed the large window. A bleached oak armoire and desk, along with several chairs and tables completed the ensemble. The adjoining bath, had a long vanity and mirror, a glassed-in shower and a deep-jetted tub, and of course, a beautiful vase full of flowers.

The doorbell rang. When Madeline opened the door, there was Robbie, followed by a bellman pushing a luggage trolley. Behind him was a waiter whom Madeline recognized from the restaurant. "Roger. How good to see you again."

"Thank you, Madame," he said with a little bow. "Welcome back to Ascot House. I'll just see to your lunch." With another bow, he opened a door half way down the hall to reveal a full kitchen. Somehow "Madame", spoken with an English accent, didn't bother Madeline at all.

Madeline peeked in and saw Roger open the door to the dumb waiter. The smell of coffee wafted through the kitchen and followed her into the living room. Robbie was busy directing the bellman to deposit Chloe's luggage in the blue bedroom, Madeline's in the green. The green bedroom, on the opposite side of the suite, was identical to the blue room, but decorated in shades of pale green and white.

As he led Madeline to one of the sofas, Robbie said "Come, sit a moment," and, rather than sit on the opposite one, sat down beside her. He shuffled through some papers until he found the one he wanted.

Casting furtive glances at her from the corner of his eye when he thought she wasn't looking, he continued matter-of-factly, "The Global people will be arriving at three and I've ordered afternoon tea for three forty-five. Roger will be up to serve and clear. He'll make sure they don't linger. I know their museum guide and she does prattle on, doesn't she? Drive you batty, that one, if you give her half a chance. Well, don't you worry, lassie. Roger will have the lot off your hands by four o'clock without any clue they've been rushed along. Right?"

Madeline looked at him and nodded. Their eyes held for a second, then she looked away and he forged ahead. "Here is the guest list and suite assignments," he said, handing her the paper. "Do you know Miss Dalton's age? I didn't have another two-bedroom available, so I've given her the suite just across from her parents."

"No," Madeline replied, shaking her head. "That should be fine. I would think if she were very young, it would say two adults and one child. The information Global gave me only shows them as a party of three.

"No Matter. If she is too young to be on her own, we can always set up an extra bed in her parents drawing room or she can use the pull-out sofa."

Just then, Chloe opened her bedroom door and, looking across the common room, saw them sitting together on the sofa. She smiled, knowing how fond they were of each other, easy and comfortable with genuine respect. She could also tell, by his actions and the look in his eyes, Robbie's feelings toward Madeline were growing more personal. Robbie was a good man with an obvious attraction to Maddie, but whether or not Maddie would venture out from behind her professional veneer long enough to test the waters of their mutual affection, was entirely another matter.

Madeline had been alone almost sixteen years, far too long in Chloe's estimation. She knew Maddie was happy. She had her daughter and her work. But that rat husband of hers had left a void in her heart that only grew bigger as the years passed by. Robbie could, and appeared to want to fill that void, if only Maddie would let him. Chloe also knew Maddie would never act on any personal feelings she might have.

"You two look cozy," Chloe said, deciding to help things along as she headed toward the dining table.

Madeline and Robbie both jumped up immediately, papers fluttering everywhere. He reached, then she reached. He leaned, then she leaned. Trying not to laugh, Chloe turned her back to them so they couldn't see her.

"Well, I'd best be off. Leave you ladies to settle in," Robbie said with a formal, yet slightly flustered air.

There was no response from Madeline, so Chloe teased, "It appears Madeline has lost her voice. You have to stay for lunch, Robbie. You were so nice to meet us at the airport. It's the least we can do. Besides," she added, gesturing toward the sideboard, which was laden with silver trays, several chafing dishes and a tureen, "it looks like David has outdone himself again and sent up enough food to feed the Royal Guard."

Her composure back intact, Madeline finally spoke, "Oh yes. Please Robbie, stay. You can catch us up on what's been happening in London."

"Well, when you put it like that ladies, I could hardly refuse," Robbie said with a grin. "I'd be delighted."

David Hargrove was truly a kitchen magician. There would be no counting calorie points today. First was a creamy potato soup, flavored with garlic and herbs. Next came a chilled spinach salad with mandarin oranges and slivered almonds. The main course was a delicate mixture of chicken, vegetables and wild rice, served in a puff pastry shell. All this was complimented by a chilled Chardonnay. Dessert was a richly smooth crème brulee.

Leaning back in her chair, Madeline laid her napkin back on the table. "Oh my," she groaned, "I really shouldn't have done that. I know I'll be paying for it later. I'll be right back." She disappeared into her bedroom, then reappeared with a bottle of Tums ceremoniously resting on a small porcelain soap dish she'd found in her bathroom.

"Mint, anyone?" she asked with a straight face.

They all burst into laughter, but no one refused the offer. Robbie glanced at his watch, suddenly aware of how much time had passed. He stood up and said, "Look at the time. I'm afraid I've dallied long enough. I'll leave you to freshen up and I'll ring after you've had your meeting."

September 21, 3:00 PM

Madeline and Chloe met the three representatives from Global Tours promptly at three o'clock and went over the general itinerary. Madeline made a few changes to the order of the sightseeing route. Contrary to the published tour, Madeline requested doing the stops in reverse. She always had her clients go to The Tower of London first thing in the morning, when the lines weren't so long, especially at the Jewel House. St. Paul's Cathedral would remain in the middle and they would arrive at Covent Garden around noon, have a look around, then have lunch at Rules, the oldest restaurant in London.

At three forty-five, precisely on schedule, Roger arrived with afternoon tea, accompanied by scones, cream and jam and toasted teacakes. Within twenty minutes, he served, cleared and manipulated their guests right out the door, without ever seeming to rush, leaving Madeline and Chloe sitting on opposite sofas, with their feet up on the coffee table between them.

"Oh, he's good," said Chloe, obviously impressed by Roger's little show.

"I know. He's elevated waiting tables into an art form," Madeline added. "Don't you wish you could import him to handle those obligatory parties where you wish everyone would just go home and leave you alone?"

"Good thought. Wouldn't that be heaven? Do you think he would give us a group rate?"

Madeline chuckled. "Maybe, I don't know. But I do know that if we don't get up and start moving, we're going to crash right here."

Somewhere between a groan and a whine, Chloe answered, "Do we have to? Can't we sit here and grow roots or something?"

"No, we're going to take a walk. It will be good for you. And anyway, pain builds character."

"Yeah, Yeah," Chloe muttered as she slowly stood, retrieved her purse and headed for the door.

It was a perfect afternoon, the crisp fall air combining with the warm sun to make it ideal weather for a walk through Mayfair. As they neared the corner,

Chloe put her arm through Madeline's and asked, "OK, fess up, what's with you and Robbie?"

CHAPTER 4

▼

Saturday, September 22, 7:45 AM
A Tale of Two Airports

Senior flight attendant, Jane Turner, made one last check of the cabins before going to her seat to buckle-up for the final descent. The flight may have been routine, but Jane couldn't remember when she'd had so much fun. Between the two little, old ladies in row 14 and Texas Jake, who was facing her now, she'd been in stitches all night.

As she pulled down the jump seat, in preparation for the descent into London's Heathrow Airport, Jane smiled. She could always tell the first time flyers to Europe. They were the ones glued to the windows, trying to catch their first glimpse of foreign soil. Fortunately it was a clear morning, so the view was spectacular.

"Janie girl" Jake drawled, "You sure my hat's not gonna get bumped around up there. Took me three years…"

"I know, Jake," she laughed, "It took you three years to break in that hat". She was trying her best to imitate Jake's accent. "And a man's hat is his crowning glory."

"That's right, honey. Some kings wear crowns. I got me a good Stetson and I'll take mine over a bunch of rocks any day."

"Better wait until you see the Crown Jewels. You might just change your mind," Jane tossed back.

Stretching out his long legs, Jake tapped her toe with the toe of his snakeskin boot. "Nah," he drawled. "That little old pile of rocks don't hold a candle to my Stetson." Then he winked at her.

Jane glanced over at Jake's wife, Suzie. So tiny she looked like a little girl sitting beside him, Suzie caught her eye and with an elaborate roll of her eyes, shook her head and returned her attention to the view outside her window.

When they boarded the plane in Chicago, Jake, with tongue in cheek, had made a major production out of finding the right spot for his hat to reside during the journey. No one had any carry-on luggage, so there was plenty of room in the overhead compartments. Jane had come down the aisle while all this was going on and helped make a little throne out of blankets, then watched as Jake ceremoniously laid his precious hat on top. Concerned at first he might be trouble, it didn't take long for her to realize that most of Jake's "show" had been his way of lightening the mood of the other passengers. Clearly, the man had a heart as big as Texas and everyone he talked with had a smile on their face when the conversation ended. Jake had told her about the anniversary surprise for his wife. Suzie didn't say much, but Jane noticed that every time she looked at Jake, her eyes were full to overflowing with love.

"Jake, are there any more men in Texas like you?" she asked, in jest.

"Why honey, my back forty's chock full of 'em," he teased. "Now, come to think of it, they probably ain't as purty as me, but I reckon they'll do just fine. Y'all will just have to come for a visit and find out for yourself."

Suzie, who'd been half listening to their conversation, finally had to throw in her two cents. Feigning outrage she implored, "Jake! Behave yourself. Miss Turner, don't you believe a word he says. My husband's view of himself is highly inflated. I swear, if his head was any bigger, that hat of his surely wouldn't cover it."

"Now Darlin'," Jake laughed as he took Suzie's hand. "Don't tell her that." Jake winked at Jane again. "I just love it when she gets jealous. Proves she loves me". Then, with a flourish, Jake planted a kiss on Suzie's hand and Suzie went back to her window. The wheels were about to touch down at Heathrow.

On the other side of the plane and back a few rows, Millie Talbot was bursting with excitement as she tugged repeatedly at Marge's sleeve. "Oh sister, look. I think I see Big Ben. And that must be Westminster Abbey. Oh sister, do you think we might see Queen Elizabeth. Wouldn't it be wonderful? And look there, I'm sure that's Trafalgar Square!"

"Millie, calm down," admonished Marge as she made an attempt to retrieve her sleeve from Millie's grasp. "That couldn't possibly be Big Ben. We're not even over the city. We're coming into the airport and Heathrow's too far west to see anything yet. And Millie, please remember, don't call me sister."

Millie, as usual, paid absolutely no attention. She was much too busy looking down at what she was sure were London's major sights. In reality, they were just passing over Reading and she was mistaking the local priory for Westminster.

Marge momentarily rested her head against the back of the seat, wishing she could have one more cup of coffee and a few more hours sleep.

Compared to the chaos that reigned while they were trying to leave the house, the flight had been relatively quiet. Of course, there *was* that little incident at the airport.

Friday September 21, 3:00 PM

Marge and Millie checked their luggage and stood in line waiting to go through security. Marge carried her book in her purse, while Millie had a small bag with her embroidery hoop and the cross-stitch she was planning to finish on the flight. When they reached the front of the line, Marge went first, putting her purse on the conveyor belt and walking through the metal detector. Millie followed. Marge retrieved her purse and waited for Millie to pick up her bags. As Millie reached down, a security guard stepped in front of her, took both bags and said abruptly, "Do these bags belong to you Ma'am?" As Millie nodded her head he said, "Please follow me."

Leading Millie to a table where two more guards were waiting, Marge tried to follow, but was intercepted by a big, burly man with a badge pinned to his shirt. "Not you, Ma'am. You'll have to wait over there."

"But she's my sister!" Marge exclaimed.

"Look lady, I don't care who she is. You'll have to wait over there," he jabbed the index finger on his left hand toward the concourse, motioning her to move along.

Millie turned back for a second. When she saw that Marge wasn't behind her, she started to panic. The guard behind the table said, "Ma'am, we need to look in your bags. Do you have any objection?"

Before she could answer, a female guard approached her from behind. When she spoke, Millie jumped and gave a little shriek. "It's OK Ma'am. I just need to run this wand over your clothes and pat you down. All right?"

By now, Millie was really panicked. Tears were running down her cheeks and she was gasping for breath. "Oh my God," she cried. "What's wrong? What did I do? Are you going to arrest me? Oh, please, I didn't do anything."

Now the guards were beginning to panic, too. They were afraid she might faint, or worse, have a heart attack. "Ma'am," the female guard said, trying to lead her to a chair. "It's alright. No one is going to hurt you. Why don't you come and sit down for a minute and catch your breath."

As she became more hysterical, the two guards standing behind the table looked at each other nervously. One turned to the other and growled, "There's no way she could be a terrorist. Just check her bags and get her out of here."

Millie sat down, still shaking, when the supervisor came up and offered her his handkerchief. "Ma'am, we certainly don't mean to scare you. Something in one of your bags set off the alarm in the x-ray machine. We just have to find it and then you'll be on your way."

Still trembling, Millie looked up at him and accepted his handkerchief. "Well, I don't know what it could be," she sniffed, dabbing her eyes. She grabbed his hand and he knelt down beside her. "Those people made me feel like a criminal," she continued, her voice now tinged with a combination of anger and indignation. She looked at his nametag. "Walker? Is that your name? Well, Mr. Walker, I've never..."

"Mr. Walker," called one of the guards searching Millie's bags. "We found it!"

They both looked up to see him holding a tiny pair of embroidery scissors.

"My embroidery scissors? All of this over my embroidery scissors?"

Mr. Walker got up and went over to have a look. Coming back to Millie, he knelt down again. He really was sincerely sorry the poor little thing was so distressed. He could imagine how his grandmother would feel if she were detained and frisked. "Ma'am, again, I'm truly sorry we upset you. It's our responsibility to make sure everyone is safe," he said, looking back over his shoulder and pointing at the line of people moving through the security check. "Your little scissors are what set off the alarm. You can't take scissors, pocket knives, knitting needles, nail clippers or anything sharp on the planes."

"Well, then I won't use them," Millie exclaimed.

"No Ma'am. You can't take them at all. We're going to have to keep them."

"But I would never hurt anyone," Millie exclaimed, astonished and angered that he would think she could do such a thing.

"Of course you wouldn't," he reassured her. "But we still have to keep them. I hope you understand."

"Well, I don't understand. Can you tell me how am I going to finish my English Rose? I have to finish it. It's a gift for our tour director. You're always supposed to have a gift for the tour director, you know." She nervously patted her hair, still babbling, "Well, I'll just have to wait until you give them back. I'll have to finish it in London. I hope you know this is really most inconvenient. Now, it that all?"

Mr. Walker stood and took Millie's hand to help her up. "Not quite, Ma'am. I'm afraid we just have to run this wand over your clothes. If you could just hold out your arms," he said, praying she wouldn't object.

Millie raised her arms while the female guard passed a metal detecting wand all over her body. She was outraged, but decided to say nothing. Finally, she retrieved her bags, minus the scissors, and went to find Marge.

Saturday, September 22, 8:10 AM

Jane had heard at least three versions of Millie's story throughout the night, each a little more embellished than the last, and funnier as well. As the wheels touched down, she thought to herself, "I love my job."

September 22, 8:30 AM

Passports and Customs declarations in hand, the passengers from United 928 filed off the plane and followed the signs to London Heathrow's Customs and Immigration hall directing them to either the line for EU passport holders or foreign visitors. A few were wide-awake, but most were a little bleary-eyed. Joe, Marty and Kelly Dalton were at the front. The immigration inspector looked at their passports, asked a few questions, affixed his stamp, wished them a pleasant visit, and they proceeded to baggage claim.

Other passengers soon began to congregate, each laying claim to their spot around the carousel. For a group of tired travelers, everyone now seemed to be in a hurry, wanting to be first to drag their bags off the conveyer belt. Everyone, that is, except a huge man wearing snakeskin boots and a Stetson.

"Don't know why these folks are in such a big hurry," Jake drawled, as he leaned up against a large column, arms crossed over his chest. "If they don't look just like my cattle at round up, I don't know what does. Wonder if they really think a few seconds makes that much difference."

"They do look a little like cattle, except mine are the dairy variety." A man came and stood next to Jake, the same amused expression on his face. "John Shepard's the name," he said, extending his hand.

"Jake Donovan." Jake shook his hand. "Pleased to meet you. Suzie, come meet John Shepard." Suzie, who had been completely hidden by her husband, came around him and shook John's hand.

"And this is my wife, Dolores," said John, completing the introductions. "Something tells me you're from Texas."

"You would be right. Our spread's just north of Lubbock. Where you from?"

"We have a farm in Iowa, mostly corn and soy beans, and a few dairy cattle."

A red light began to flash over the luggage carousel, signaling the arrival of United 928's cargo. As the conveyer belt started and a variety of suitcases, duffel bags, baby strollers and boxes spilled onto the carousel, the herd began to jockey for position, some armed with luggage carts, and others with only their fortitude. Joe Dalton's bags were some of the first to appear and, as he pulled them off, he handed them back to Kelly, who then handed them to her mother who put them on her cart.

While the Donovan's and the Shepard's were watching with interest, Jake observed, "Now, they have the right idea, their very own conga line. Why didn't we think of that?"

Just then Suzie tugged on Jake's arm. "There are those two old ladies from the plane." Suzie pointed at Marge and Millie Talbot, who were getting bumped around and looked quite distressed. "You'd better go help them before one of them gets hurt."

Spotting them in the crowd, Jake turned to John, "Come on, Partner. Let's ride to the rescue."

"Right behind you,"

The big Texan waded into the fray, followed by the farmer, who was pretty big himself. It was like the parting of the Red Sea, no one was about to contest the king salmon making their way upstream. They got to Millie just in time to hear her say, "Oh sister, what are we going to do?"

Jake arrived at Millie's side and said, "Ma'am, you look like you could use some help."

Startled, Millie turned, her nose just above Jake's huge belt buckle, and screamed. Then she stumbled over his boot and began to fall. Without thinking, Jake scooped her up in his arms and carried her out of the crowd. Marge turned to see her sister being carried off by a giant in a ten-gallon hat. "Now you see here, you Neanderthal! Put her down!" she shouted, as she ran after them, purse raised, ready to do battle.

John ran after her, trying to explain. "Sister, Sister, it's all right. We just wanted to help you with your bags."

Marge stopped dead in her tracks, turned and hit him with her purse. "Well, why didn't you say so." She hit him again, thoroughly exasperated.

By that time, they had reached the spot where Suzie and Dolores were standing. Everyone was talking at once when two security guards, guns drawn, appeared yelling, "Halt! Police! Stay where you are!" Two more guards joined the circus. The entire Customs Hall was silent, all eyes watching as the little group of Americans was escorted to a secured office for questioning. As they disappeared behind the door, the rest of the passengers quietly returned to the business of retrieving their luggage.

While the Dalton's were watching this curious drama, Kelly noticed several suitcases with Global Tour luggage tags making their third trip around the carousel. "Daddy," she said quietly. "Look at all those bags with the same luggage tags as ours. Nobody is picking them up."

Joe turned towards the carousel. He counted six large suitcases and six smaller ones he assumed were carry-ons that had to be checked.

Marty, who was manning their cart, said, "I'm going to go for help. Kelly, you stay here with your Dad." She looked at Joe who nodded in agreement. "Turn your cell phone on and I'll call when I find out what's going on." She pivoted the cart around one hundred eighty degrees, and pushed it to the partition that said "Nothing To Declare".

September 22, 10:00 AM

In anticipation of the scheduled eight-thirty arrival, Madeline and Chloe had been waiting outside the Customs Hall since eight o'clock. People had been streaming through the exit doors of the Customs Hall since nine-fifteen but, as of yet, there was no sign of anyone from her group. Chloe went to the service desk to check the posted information and asked the woman behind the counter, to page the members of the Global Tours group.

September 22, 10:10 AM

Martha Jane Dalton pushed open the doors of the Customs Hall with the front of her cart just as the announcement came over the loudspeaker: "Members of Global Tours group *London and the English Countryside*, please meet your party outside the Customs Hall exit." The crowd had thinned considerably, so she easily spotted Madeline. Wheeling her cart towards Madeline and Chloe, "Hi," she called, "I'm so relieved to see you. I'm Marty Dalton. I think we have a real problem in there." She nodded her head toward the Customs Hall.

"I'm Madeline Marlborough and this is Chloe Ambrose. What's going on? What's happened?"

As they helped Marty with her cart, she told them about the scene with the cowboy and the elderly women. She also told them about all the luggage with Global Tours tags that her husband and daughter were guarding.

Madeline left Chloe to take care of getting the Dalton's luggage to the bus waiting outside, while she and Marty went to the security office. Checking their cell phones so they could stay in contact with each other, Madeline said as they left for their assignments, "God bless modern technology."

Marty called Joe to let him know she'd found the Tour Director and they were on their way to the security office. Joe said, "Good. Kelly and I pulled all the luggage with Global tags. The security guard said, as long as we stay right there, we can keep all the luggage together."

Marty relayed Joe's information to Madeline as they walked through the door marked, Airport Security. "Good morning sir. My name is Madeline Marlborough and I think you may have my missing children."

Following much explanation and many phone calls later, Madeline's little tribe was released and were escorted back to the Customs Hall where they found the Daltons, sitting on their luggage. By the time they all exited Customs to the main terminal, they were talking and laughing like the best of friends.

Madeline introduced herself, Chloe and Marty, then said, "My goodness. You've had quite an adventure. I imagine you've seen enough of airports for awhile."

"Little lady, you don't know the half of it," Jake laughed as he patted the white hair of the elderly woman glued to his side.

"Oh Jake," cooed Millie Talbot, blushing.

"Looks like there's a story here," teased Madeline. "I can't wait to hear all the juicy details, but let's get out of here first. The bus is right outside and we have hot coffee, tea and scones for everyone."

At the sound of the word coffee, Marge Talbot dropped everything, even her purse, and threw her arms around Madeline. Hugging her tight, Marge exclaimed, "You blessed child!"

September 22, 12:30 PM

Following the calamity at the airport, the ride into London was blissfully calm. Everyone had coffee or tea and buttered scones while Madeline handed out room keys. She explained to the Dalton's that no more two-bedroom suites were available, so Kelly had been assigned the suite across the hall. As Kelly was almost nineteen, and would be living in England soon, her parents actually thought it was a great idea for her to have her own independence.

They approached the city on the M40 Motorway, which resembled the expressways in the United States, except for one significant difference; they were driving along the left side of the road. Not only were they on the opposite side of the highway, the driver was seated on the opposite side of the bus. As they exited the motorway and came to their first roundabout, the bus made its way around by going clockwise.

"It tends to make you feel slightly off balance, doesn't it?" Madeline remarked, adding, "It's not unusual to have five or six streets emerging from a roundabout. Also, every time you reach an intersection, the name of the street changes. We're going to be turning onto one of the only continuous straight streets in London and you'll see that it's name changes eleven times before it reaches the other side of the city."

As they circled another roundabout, Madeline continued, "At this end, the street is called Holland Park Avenue. If you'll look to your left, you'll see the Holland Park Underground Station." The bus slowed as the proceeding car turned left onto Ladbrook Grove. "As soon as the car in front of us gets out of our way, you'll see our street changes names to Notting Hill Gate. The Portobello Road Market is a magnet for collectors of virtually everything. I'm afraid we've missed the street market, Saturday morning, but you will have time on Tuesday afternoon if you want to come back and have a look at the permanent shops."

As they continued, Madeline pointed out the landmarks and Hyde Park on their right. At Cumberland Gate, they turned right, passed Marble Arch, where they turned onto Old Park Lane, and finally turned left into the fashionable section of London known as Mayfair.

"We'll be arriving at Ascot House in just a minute. The staff is waiting for us and will show you to your suites. Don't worry about your luggage, it will be delivered to you. Ah, here we are now." The bus, which was nearly as wide as the street, came to a stop in front of a brick building, surrounded by flowering shrubs. Above the door, black letters spelled out Ascot House, the only indication it might be a hotel.

"Are you sure this is the right place?" asked Jake.

"I know," Madeline answered with a grin. "It doesn't look like a hotel, does it? It doesn't feel like one either. It's really more like a private club, but be assured, they are expecting us." Looking at her watch, she added, "We're running a little late, so why don't you all go to your rooms and freshen up. Let's meet in the restaurant at two o'clock."

As the weary travelers climbed the stairs to the hotel entrance, the double doors were pulled opened from the inside, and as they crossed the threshold, contrary to the normal check-in procedure, Lord Hargrove, Robbie and the reception staff stepped forward to formally greet them. Madeline didn't know they were going to do this. She had called Robbie from the airport to let him know about their delay. The smile on her face and the look in her eyes told him she was pleased.

Madeline introduced everyone to Lord Hargrove. "Lord Hargrove, I'd like to meet Mr. and Mrs. Dalton and their daughter Kelly."

"Welcome to Ascot House," said Lord Hargrove, shaking Joe's hand. Then, with a twinkle in his eyes, he took Marty's hand, bowed, and lightly kissed it. Marty flushed. She didn't know whether to curtsy or not. Fortunately, before she could decide, Lord Hargrove passed her off to Robbie.

Each staff member took one family, personally escorting them to their rooms. Exclamations of "Isn't this beautiful," "How lovely," and "Damn, it's big enough to ride my horse through here," floated down the halls.

Madeline and Chloe went with Robbie to the dining room. Except for the few diners still lingering over dessert, the room was empty. David Hargrove was just coming out of the kitchen when he saw Madeline, smiled, and walking toward them said, "Had quite an adventure this morning, did you?"

"David, I'm so sorry. I hope I let you know in time," Madeline said.

"Not to worry. The soup can easily simmer all day and I wouldn't have started the entrees until they were ordered, regardless. I'm going to put you in the private dining room. It's a bit more cozy than here." David Hargrove was enormously proud of La Violette, and with good reason. His exquisite French cuisine was considered the best in Great Britain. David found his calling while still a teenager, and, with his father's blessing, trained with the greatest chefs in France. When he returned to London, La Violette was born. His reputation swiftly grew, as word of his culinary prowess spread throughout the country. Today, the menu changes constantly, depending on the availability of the produce of the season, and most importantly, David's inspiration of the moment.

As Robbie, Madeline and Chloe made their way to the lobby, Chloe headed directly toward the lift, deliberately leaving Madeline and Robbie alone. As the doors closed, she looked out and called in a little voice, "Toodles. I'm going upstairs. See you later."

Ignoring Chloe's obvious attempt to throw them together, Madeline continued with the business at hand, "I've only got a minute. I need to go over the orientation packets one more time before lunch and I want to change clothes."

"Lord Hargrove wanted a word with you. I don't see him about," Robbie said, his eyes scanning the room. "I think he wanted to ask if he could speak to your group again, before you begin your meeting. Why don't I tell him you couldn't wait. I know he'll understand. He can ring you if there is anything else."

"Wonderful. Oh, and Robbie, with the day we've had, I'm sure everyone will want room service for dinner. Would you let David know?" As she turned toward the lift, she smiled, "Thank you, again, for everything," then quietly added, "We'll talk later."

CHAPTER 5

▼

Saturday, September 22, 2:00 PM
Bon Appetit! And On To The Abbey

The private dining room of La Violette was exquisite. Pale blue silk covered the walls which were framed with white molding at the floor and ceiling. Heavy silk damask drapes of the same blue were pulled back at the floor to ceiling windows to reveal a breathtaking view of the rose garden. Two glistening crystal chandeliers hung over the long dining table, elegantly set for twelve. A rope of white flowers accented with shades of yellow and bronze, extended down the length of the table and a matching garland was draped across the white mantle of a fireplace located at the far end of the room. Each place was set with blue and white Wedgwood china, complimented with the Hargrove family sterling, Waterford crystal goblets, wine glasses and crisply folded white linen napkins with the Hargrove family crest facing the chairs.

Madeline and Chloe were first to arrive, carrying the orientation materials for their presentation to the rest of the group following lunch. Just as they leaned over to stash their parcels in the corner near the fireplace, Lord Hargrove came through the door, giving the elderly gentleman a perfect view of their posteriors.

Deliberately clearing his throat, he said with a flourish of formality, "Ladies, may I be of assistance."

Face flushed with embarrassment, Madeline sprang up almost knocking Chloe over, to see his lordship peering at them over the rim of his spectacles. They stared at each other for a second, then all three burst into laughter. "Well, we all have our good sides," Madeline laughed, trying to catch her breath.

"And you got two for one," Chloe added. "How lucky is that?"

"I am a most fortunate man, indeed," replied Lord Hargrove twinkling as he took each lady's hand and gave them a little squeeze. "I trust everything is to your liking. After your harrowing morning, I thought something a little special was in order."

"A *little* special?" Madeline exclaimed, gesturing around the room. "This is absolutely beautiful."

Lord Hargrove walked to the fireplace and removed a stray leaf that had come loose from the garland. "I've taken the liberty of selecting the wine, a Chardonnay from my private cellar," he said while he discreetly put the leaf in his pocket. Genuinely fond of Madeline, he continued, "Your groups are always filled with such interesting people. I thought I would join you for lunch, if it wouldn't be an intrusion. I'm especially curious about the gentleman from Texas. He's larger than life, isn't he?"

"Indeed, he is," she replied. "We would be honored and I know the group will be thrilled."

Madeline was touched by Lord Hargrove's gesture. A quiet man by nature, he usually left the operation of the hotel to his children, but he had always gone out of his way to make her feel welcome and personally acknowledge her guests.

"The honor is mine, my dear," he flushed slightly. With a straight face, and a bemused tone in his voice, Lord Hargrove teased, "I understand one of your number would like to ride his horse through his suite. It is my duty to discourage him from this endeavor."

"Well! Here's your opportunity," she exclaimed cheerfully as she spotted Jake coming through the door. "Jake," she called sternly, "His Lordship would like a word with you."

Jake wasn't sure what to do. His normally cocky grin vanished as his mind went racing back over everything he'd done since he arrived. He hadn't broken anything, at least he didn't think he had and he couldn't imagine any other reason the owner of the hotel would want to talk to him.

Jake approached cautiously. "Sir?" he said, towering over the proper little man standing in from of him.

It was all Chloe could do not to giggle as she thought, "This is David and Goliath in reverse."

"Young man," his lordship spoke with grave seriousness. "I understand you have equestrian designs on the interior of my humble abode. In my grandfather's day I believe it was permissible, as his father was known, on occasion, to prance his noble steed up the front stairs and into the hall. Unfortunately, the ladies objected, so that sort of behavior is no longer allowed. Whilst you are here, we will be happy to accommodate your stallion in the stables and have him brought round whenever you wish to ride."

Poor Jake was really confused. Then Suzie began to laugh, softly at first, followed by Chloe, who couldn't hold it in any longer. They were soon joined by the Shepards, who had followed Jake and Suzie into the room, and finally by Lord Hargrove, himself. "Dear boy," he chuckled, "you must think I'm a dottering old man."

Suzie caught her breath long enough to poke her husband with her elbow. "Don't you remember what you said when we walked into our room?"

The lightbulb suddenly went on. The old man had gotten him! "Well hell," he said, chagrined. "That room's big enough to have a rodeo in. I just bet your great granddaddy thought so too."

John Shepard nodded to his lordship. "I think you'd better let him keep a horse up there in case he has to rescue another damsel in distress." Marge and Millie Talbot arrived in time to hear John's reference to a rescue. "Of course, if you're not up to it, Sister Margaret can fill in for you. She swings a mean purse."

Marge glared at Millie, then turned and smiled at John Shepard as she touched his arm. "I'm so sorry. I hope I didn't hurt you. I'm so embarrassed. I've never hit anyone in my life—with or without a purse!"

"Marge, I thought you did a fine job," Dolores Shepard interjected and continued laughing at her husband. "I've wanted to do that a few times myself. I only wish I'd had a video camera. The kids will never believe us."

The Daltons finally arrived and Madeline, who had gone into the kitchen, to double check room service arrangements with David, returned to find everyone laughing and talking. "I hope all of you are hungry. I just had a preview of our lunch and the Master Chef, our host's son, has outdone himself. Lord Hargrove will be joining us, so please, let's be seated."

Lord Hargrove sat at the head of the table, with Madeline, Chloe and the Dalton's on one side and Suzie, Jake, Millie, Marge, John and Dolores on the other.

When everyone was seated, Roger and another waiter entered with silver trays of crystal champagne flutes which were formally placed before each guest. Bottles of Dom Perignon were opened and after the glasses were filled, the waiters fell in line behind Lord Hargrove's chair. David Hargrove, resplendent in his spotless white chef's suit, complete with tall, crisp white hat, came to stand beside his father. William and Violet Hargrove entered from the main door and joined the family, while Robbie and his staff congregated at the foot of the table.

When Lord Hargrove stood and began to speak, a hush fell over the room. No one had any idea what to expect. "Friends, welcome to our home. Welcome to our family." Gesturing around the room he continued, "Your courage and determination to defy those who attacked your country by getting on an airplane and coming to our shores, makes us all extremely proud. I know I speak for the British Commonwealth and the entire European community when I say, you are not alone. Our hearts go out to our American cousins who lost loved ones on that horrible day. Together, we will not allow their sacrifice to be in vain. By coming here, you send a powerful message to those who would try to destroy you, that they are already defeated. And to that end…" he picked up his champagne flute. "Someone once said that living well is the best revenge, and while you are here, we intend to see that you live very well indeed."

Lord Hargrove and his children raised their glasses and shouted "Here! Here!" while the rest of the staff broke into applause. Everyone at the table then raised their glasses and returned, "Here! Here!" There wasn't a dry eye in the house. The staff began to circle the table, stopping to personally thank each guest.

Madeline was overcome. Tears streaming down her face, she turned to Lord Hargrove. "I don't know what to say. Thank you."

"No my dear, it is I who thank you." He leaned down, kissed her cheek, then handed her his silk handkerchief. Everyone was smiling now, so he sat and tapped his spoon on his crystal goblet. The waiters disappeared into the kitchen and returned just in time to hear his lordship say, "Let the feast begin."

And what a feast it was. They dined on such delicacies as chilled strawberry soup, white asparagus, bits of pheasant in a creamy wine sauce, served on a bed of wild rice, and fresh lemon sorbet. Dessert was a choice of crème brulee or pots du crème accompanied by coffee, tea or espresso.

When the table was cleared, Lord Hargrove said his good-byes while Madeline and Chloe distributed the orientation packets. Madeline's eyes roamed the group, looking for signs of fatigue. She was pleasantly surprised to see everyone alert and ready to go. She'd been particularly concerned the elderly Talbot sisters might not be able to keep up the pace, but Millie was flirting shamelessly with Jake, and Marge had already opened her folder eager to investigate the contents.

Madeline took Lord Hargrove's place at the head of the table and exclaimed, "Well I'm stuffed. How about you?"

Everyone nodded in agreement, with an occasional moan for added effect.

"I know some of you are thinking a nap would be wonderful right about now, but I warn you, if you take a nap this afternoon, you will wake up in the middle of the night. The best way to deal with jet-lag is to stay awake until after dinner. Then you'll sleep through the night and your internal clock will adjust to the time difference much faster. Tomorrow morning you will be well rested and ready for a full day. Now, if you'll please open your folders and take out this afternoon's itinerary. We'll go through it quickly and be on our way."

"This morning, I didn't think I was going to make it, but I'm feeling fine now," said Marge, glancing down at her empty espresso cup.

"Yup, God bless the coffee bean," Jake answered tapping his empty cup. "This stuff'll grow hair on your toes!"

"You'll see I've given each you a city map of your own to keep with you at all times," Madeline continued. "I've highlighted the major landmarks around the city. Remember when we were driving in from the airport, how the street names keep changing? I think it's even confusing to the locals, because they always give directions in terms of the nearest landmark. The trick is, if you ask someone on the street for directions, they will tell you it is so many minute's walk. For example: you are standing in Trafalgar Square and ask someone for directions to Westminster Abbey. They will tell you it's a seven-minute walk across the square and down the road. Of course you have to remember they are telling you how long it takes *them* to walk. It always takes me longer. The trick is to remember that you go from landmark to landmark, not street to street. Oh, and don't forget, always look left before you cross the street. Since childhood, we've all been taught to look right, then left. If you do that here, you might be hit by a bus.

"We'll be concentrating on those sections of central London which are highlighted on your map. The names in blue are the names of the various districts or neighborhoods that make up the city. Right now, we're in Mayfair. Covent Garden is located between Soho and Holborn, and Westminster Abbey and Parliament are in Westminster."

"What are the round red things with the lines through them?" asked Kelly Dalton.

"Those are the Tube stations. The correct name for the subway is Underground, but virtually everyone refers to it as The Tube. If you'll turn your maps over, there is a tube map on the back.

"London has one of the best subway systems in the world and it is extremely easy to use. Most Londoner's don't own cars. They don't need them. Look at the map. Do you see the different colored lines?"

Everyone nodded. "Each color is a different line, dark purple is the Piccadilly Line, yellow the Circle Line, green the District Line, and so on. You can go to any Tube Station, look at the map, and figure out how to get anywhere in the city. Wherever you see a black circle is a stop. Double black circles indicate where you can transfer from one line to another. Here's a little trivia for you, did you know that during the Blitz, thousands of people used the tube platforms as air-raid shelters? They would camp down there all night, safe from the bombs that were falling up above. I don't know if the tunnels could withstand today's weapons or not. I hope they never have to find out.

"I've included a list of some of the more popular shopping areas and landmarks along with the nearest tube stop. You'll want to take it with you when you go shopping Tuesday afternoon."

Glancing at her watch, Madeline said, "This afternoon we were supposed to take our orientation tour, but we're running pretty late. I've asked our driver and local guide to do an abbreviated version, then drop us off at Westminster Abbey. We can have a look around and take the tube back. It will be good practice. Inside your folder you'll find your four-day tube pass. You'll use the same pass for all four days. I'll show you how it works when the time comes…Please make sure you don't lose it."

Looking around the table, Madeline concluded, "If no one has any questions at this point, why don't we adjourn and meet in the lobby in fifteen minutes."

Chloe pointed to her feet, prompting Madeline to remind them, "Oh yes, if you're not wearing comfortable shoes, be sure to change. We won't be walking too far, but let's not ruin any feet today as we'll be walking quite a bit tomorrow."

Everyone gathered their belongings and headed for the lift. The men decided the stairs would be faster. As they hit the first step, Kelly bounded past them, "Come on Dad. I'll race you," she called back, taking the stairs two at a time.

John and Jake looked at each other, then at Joe. They all laughed and John commented, "You've got a beauty there, Joe."

"Thanks," he replied, "we think she's pretty special. Now if we could just bottle that energy of hers." They all laughed, again, as they disappeared around the corner.

Chloe went up to their suite to get their purses, while Madeline found the local guide, Molly McBride, at the reception desk talking to Robbie.

Molly was a striking young woman, about twenty-five Madeline guessed, with sable colored hair drawn up in a ponytail and big brown eyes. She was tall, but not nearly as tall as Kelly Dalton. Madeline hoped she and Kelly would get to know each other so Kelly would have at least one friend when she returned to England to go to school.

"Hello Molly" Madeline said shaking her hand. "I hope Robbie has filled you in as to why we're so late."

"How are you, Madeline? Robbie's just been telling me the saga about your morning. Quite an interesting way for your passengers to bond isn't it. I do hope there were no ill effects."

Within ten minutes, everyone reconvened in the lobby and followed Molly out to their waiting mini-coach, which seated only twenty passengers, all in window seats. Once everyone was seated, Madeline asked, "Do you all have your London Transport Visitor Travelcards? We'll need them later." Satisfied all were prepared, she took a seat in the back across from Chloe.

Molly, who was in front with the driver, took the microphone. "Good afternoon. My name is Molly McBride and I welcome you all on behalf of Global Tours and the London Visitor's Bureau. I will be your local guide whilst you visit our fair city and our driver is George Black. Together we hope to show you the highlights of London. If you have any questions please don't hesitate to ask." She surveyed the faces before her, saw smiles all around, then continued.

"This afternoon, we're going to take a short drive, then have a walk round Westminster. I know you're all tired, so we won't tax you overmuch."

As they passed alongside Grosvenor Square with the Roosevelt Memorial in its center, she continued, "The US Embassy is just on the other side of the square. I urge you to take a walk past and read some of the cards and please take pictures of the flowers and memorials to share with your friends and families. They might be able to take comfort in seeing the outpouring of support and affection from my countrymen."

They drove south along Park Lane to Hyde Park Corner, then turned onto Piccadilly. "To your right is Green Park which was once part of Henry VIII's hunting grounds. Like St. James's Park, it was opened to the public by Charles II in the 1660's. In the 18th century, the park was a favorite site for duels. So beware gentlemen, if your affections stray toward one who is taken, you may find yourself challenged to appear at dawn with your second."

Everyone laughed and Jake leaned forward, saying over the top of Millie's head, "Now you boys best behave around my best girl here or I'll have to call you out. That goes for you, too, George. I'll be watching!"

"Oh Jake," Millie said, color rising in her cheeks, obviously pleased by Jake's attention.

Marge hadn't seen Millie glow like this since she was a young girl. It was all in fun, but it warmed her heart to see her sister having such a good time. She'd decided to forgive Millie's faux pas, calling her "Sister" at the airport, leading John Shepard to think she was a nun. The catastrophe had turned out to be hilarious and now John's calling her "Sister Margaret" was a running joke between them. This was going to be a wonderful trip!

Marge turned her attention back to Molly who was saying, "If you will look on the corner just on the right, you can see the Tube Station. It's Green Park, and is the closest stop to your hotel. Now, just beyond, on the right, is the famous Ritz Hotel.

"Just ahead, on the left is the most famous shopping mall in London, the Burlington Arcade. It was built in 1819 by Lord George Cavendish to protect his garden from the rubbish bawdy Londoners of the day liked to throw over his garden wall. Today it houses thirty-eight shops that specialize in traditional British luxuries. I'm especially fond of the shoemakers at number twenty-two. Of course, *you must mind your manners.* You are not allowed to sing, whistle, shout, run or open your umbrella. Any such infraction will have the Beadles escorting you out to the street."

"The Beatles?!" exclaimed Kelly Dalton. "I didn't think any of them still lived in London."

"No, no, Kelly. Not the Beatles...Beadles. The Beadles were, or rather are, the oldest police force in Britain. Long before Scotland Yard, two or three hundred years, the Beadles maintained law and order in London. I think they were originally a private company. I mean, if a nobleman was robbed or threatened or something, he could hire his own Beadle to investigate. As far as I know, the Beadles at the Burlington Arcade are the last of their kind. They wear top hats and formal coats, quite proper you know, and ceremoniously open the gates at nine o'clock every morning. Also, at five-thirty in the evening, they ring the Burlington Bell to signal the end of the day, after which the gates are closed again.

"Here we are at Piccadilly Circus. This is probably the most famous intersection in London. Straight ahead of us is Shaftesbury Avenue, heart of the theater district. To our left is Regent Street. We'll just circle around and go south past Horse Guards."

As the coach began to circle the roundabout, George slammed on the brakes to avoid hitting a tourist, bringing the bus to a screeching halt.

"Everyone alright?" Madeline called out. They were a bit jostled, but everyone was fine.

Molly bent down to have a short conference with George. She forgot to turn off her microphone, so everyone heard George blurt out, "Stupid sod. Paying more attention to his bloody cell phone than where he was going. Good way to get yourself killed, isn't it? Cell phones. Bloody nuisance they are!"

Molly quickly realized everyone had heard George's outburst. "Please people. The traffic in this part of London is always busy. If you are walking, please pay attention to the signals and only cross where it is specifically allowed and please follow the signs that say, Look Left. This wasn't planned, but it certainly proves the point."

At The Mall, they turned right, passed Buckingham Palace, then circled back on Birdcage Walk, coming to a stop opposite the Cabinet War Rooms.

Molly stood and said, "We're going to leave George for now. We will see him again in the morning. If you will follow me, Westminster Abbey is just down the street."

George stepped down and waited by the open door to help the ladies down the stairs. As he helped Marge down, she patted his hand and told him he'd done a splendid job avoiding the man with the cell phone. "Thank you, Madame. I hope I didn't frighten you." George stood just a little taller as he assisted the remaining passengers from his coach.

Chloe took Madeline's arm as they approached the Abbey. "How are you doing?" she asked quietly.

"They're nice, aren't they?"

"Yeah, they really are. And funny too. That Jake is too much. I wish I could have seen him pick up Millie and cart her off to who knows where. I wonder if we could get a copy of the security camera's tape?"

"Somehow I don't think so," Madeline replied. "Do you believe John Shepard actually thought Marge was a nun and then she turned around and slugged him? I think that's priceless. Look at them. Jake's walking with Millie, John with Marge. and Suzie and Dolores are looking more and more like us."

"It's a good thing because I'm afraid they've lost their husbands to the Talbot girls."

"I'm a little worried about the Dalton's," Madeline said, glancing in their direction. "They seem a little out of the loop, not quite as down home as the others."

"They're not stand offish really. I can't quite put my finger on it," said Chloe. "Kelly's a beautiful girl. What I wouldn't give to be that tall." Chloe had always been a good judge of character, so the fact that she didn't have a read on them yet either, confirmed what Madeline was feeling.

They joined the others at the Abbey's West Front Towers and listened as Molly told the group about the famous church.

"We'll be returning tomorrow morning for a complete tour of the Abbey, but it doesn't really feel like you're in London until you've seen her and Big Ben, does it?" Looking for Madeline, she continued, "I know Madeline has a particular fondness for the Abbey and probably knows more about it than I, so Madeline, why don't you give us a few bits of it's history before we go in."

Madeline was passionate about history and architecture and felt it was her mission to educate her clients, whether they wanted it or not. She made her way to the front of the group and as she was speaking, her little audience inched closer and closer to her, completely drawn into the world she painted with her words.

"The thing you have to remember is that we Americans are mere babies in the context of history. The towers in front of us were built around 1740, thirty-six years before our Declaration of Independence, and the actual church is even older. Edward the Confessor, who was a Saxon king, founded the Benedictine abbey in 1065 and rebuilt the old minster church that was already here. Harold was the first English king to be crowned here in 1066. Later the same year, William, Edward's Norman cousin, defeated Harold at the Battle of Hastings. Try to remember the year 1066. You'll hear it referred to as the Norman Conquest or hear references about William the Conqueror. Many of the major cathedrals and fortress castles began construction either in 1066 or shortly after, and the British monarchy, as we know it today, traces directly back to the coronation of William the Conqueror. Every monarch since, with the exception of Edward V and Edward VIII, has been crowned here at Westminster Abbey.

"Over the years, there have been additions and some alterations to the original design, but most of what you see now, was built in the medieval period between the 13th and 14th centuries, long before America was even discovered.

"All the abbeys and cathedrals are built in the shape of the cross and lie lengthwise, facing east. We're at the west end or the foot of the cross. The public entrance was located here for many years, but now this entrance is used only for those attending a memorial or special service.

"I see some of you eyeing the Book Shop. Don't worry, we'll stop here tomorrow or you can even order books and videos online when you get home. That way you don't have to carry them. I always seem to go overboard buying books and then I'm stuck having to lug them around.

"If you'll follow me we'll go around to the entrance which has been moved back to the North Transept, where it was in medieval times. I guess you can tell I'm nuts about English history. I'll try not to bore you to death, but I truly believe understanding the three W's, who, why, and when, makes seeing these wonderful places you've read about in history class or seen in the movies, much more meaningful."

As Madeline began walking, she explained, "It's near closing time and we only want to look around for a few minutes. If there is a service in progress, we won't be able to wander too far, but you'll be able to get a good feel for the place. Oh, and be sure to look down. A lot of famous people are buried under the floor, even one of my shirttail relatives. Molly's arranged for the entrance fee to be waived."

Madeline opened the heavy, wooden door and led the group inside. She was right, a sign was posted saying, "Service in Progress". She pointed it out to everyone, then motioned everyone to follow her to the left, away from the entrance. They looked about in awe as they gathered around her. Even Jake couldn't think of anything to say.

"I know, it's incredible, isn't it?" Madeline whispered. "If you circle around to your left, you can see the Chapel of St. John the Baptist and the Lady Chapel. Go on around. Poet's Corner is in the South Transept." She pointed to the opposite side of the church. "I think it's alright to walk about, but please don't cross in front of the High Alter or the worshipers. Go on around." She looked at her watch. "Let's meet back here in twenty minutes."

Everyone checked their watches, nodded in agreement and set off to explore. The Dalton's however, stayed behind. Joe wanted to ask Madeline about her relative. "Do you really have someone buried here?" he whispered.

"Oh yes," she whispered back. "His name is George Graham and he is in a double grave with his uncle, Thomas Tompion. Tompion was the royal clockmaker to King George I and the greatest of all English clockmakers. Two of his clocks are in the Royal Collection at Buckingham Palace. My boy Graham was his apprentice and became his partner in 1711. In 1713, after Tompion died, Graham went on to invent some of the first astrological equipment. Their grave is on the south side of the nave, near David Livingstone. I don't know if we can make it all the way up, but if you want, we can certainly try."

The Daltons seemed very interested and followed Madeline around the east end of the abbey where she pointed out the places of interest, but, when they got to Poet's Corner, they were reluctant to move on. Kelly especially was enthralled with the monuments to Shakespeare and Dickens. Madeline assured them she would show them the tomb when they returned.

Everyone reconvened at the appointed time and together they left the building. Once outside, everyone started talking at once. Marge said, "I remember watching Queen Elizabeth II's coronation on television in 1953."

"I just had no idea it would be so immense, John said in awe. "Even in the movies, you can't grasp the size, and did you see the vaulting in the ceiling?

"How did they ever build something like this in the Middle Ages?" asked Marty.

"I can't get over the graves," said Dolores. "There must be someone under every stone and in the walls too."

"Did you see the dates on some of those tombs?" asked Suzie. "We found one that said 1389."

"I gotta tell you, I'm sure impressed," added Jake.

One of the goals with all her tours was to make history come alive for the group and it tickled Madeline to see how quickly these people were getting into it. She looked at Chloe, then Molly, and smiled.

Molly was back in the lead as they left the Abbey and crossed the street to Parliament Square where they stood and watched Big Ben as it struck five o'clock. They turned left and walked along Parliament Street which turns into Whitehall. As they passed Downing Street, Molly pointed out Number 10, the official home of the Prime Minister. The street was blocked off due to the threat of terrorist activity, but they all thought it was fun to at least pass by. As they continued past Horse Guards, headquarters of the Household Division, Molly said, "There has been a changing of the guard here since 1649, when Horse Guards was the entrance to the Palace of Whitehall. We'll try to get back here tomorrow morning for the Queen's Life Guards ceremony at eleven."

At last they arrived at Trafalgar Square and Nelson's Column, one of London's most famous and recognizable landmarks. "Lord Nelson commanded the British troops at the Battle of Trafalgar and defeated Napoleon's navy off the coast of Spain in 1805."

Madeline was starting to get a little weary and she knew the rest of the group must be exhausted. "We're almost there," she reassured them. "Do you see the Underground sign around to your right? That's where we're headed."

On the way down the stairs she told them, "OK, now we're going to use your four-day *Tube* passes. The scanner in the turnstiles reads the magnetic strip on the back and will begin ticking off the validity since this is the first time we've used them."

She and Molly demonstrated how to put their passes into the turnstile and retrieve them at the other end of the machine and Madeline showed them their location on the large map and pointed out the two train lines that run through the Charing Cross station. They were going to take the Jubilee Line, marked in gray, to Green Park. The signs were quite easy to follow. As it was Saturday, the train wasn't crowded. Everyone found a seat and Madeline watched as they all visibly wilted before her eyes. She knew they would sleep through the night!

They reached Ascot House a few minutes before six o'clock. Before saying good night, she suggested they order a light supper from room service. They could either have breakfast in the dining room, or, if they would like to have it sent up, they could mark the breakfast cards in their suites and hang them on the doorknob. They were to meet in the lobby the next morning at ten o'clock. As they dispersed to go to their suites everyone opted for the lift.

Madeline looked around, but Robbie was nowhere to be seen, so she thanked Molly and arranged to meet her at nine o'clock the next morning.

"You know Chloe," Madeline said as she unlocked the door to their suite, "It turned out to be a good day, even after the fiasco at the airport. They're a good bunch. I'm really glad I took this assignment. It's going to be fun."

CHAPTER 6

──────────── ▼ ────────────

Sunday, September 23, 8:45 AM
We're Off To See The City

Madeline took a quick glance in her bathroom mirror as she called out, "Chloe, are you about ready?" Satisfied she looked good even though her hair was still wet, she hurried through her bedroom and into the dining area thinking, "Thank God for short curly hair."

Chloe opened her bedroom door, "I'm not altogether with it this morning," she groaned, leaning her head against the doorjamb.

Astonished, Madeline said, "I don't believe it. I'm good to go and you're still in your robe? Well, you're in luck. There's hot coffee on the table. I think Robbie figured we'd forget to fill out the breakfast card. He called earlier and told me there was a surprise in the dumb waiter. Isn't he a gem?"

"Oh, you think so?" Chloe perked up a little, "Maddie, the guy's crazy about you."

"Now don't get carried away, Chloe. He's just being thoughtful. Anyway, he must be at least ten years younger than I am. I'll see you later. I have to meet Molly downstairs."

"I don't get it. What's with you? And who cares about ten years anyway?" Chloe called after her, but Madeline was already out the door.

Chloe shook her head as she poured herself a cup of steaming coffee. Robbie had never actually come out and said anything, but Chloe knew he was smitten and she couldn't understand why Madeline was completely oblivious to his affection for her. The way he looked at Maddie when he knew she wasn't paying attention was like a great big Scottish puppy dog. OK, so she'd never actually seen a Scottish puppy dog, but he must look like one. Chloe was sure there was more to it than just professional courtesy.

Last night, Robbie had taken them to a small Italian restaurant in Soho owned by a family from Florence. Papa was the chef, Mama ran the dining room and their two sons served as waiters. The pasta was delicious, the Chianti smooth and the conversation delightful. They ate and drank, laughed and talked until nearly midnight. By the time they left, they had become fast friends with Vito, Angelina and their boys, promising to return as soon as possible.

When they got back to the hotel, Chloe again tried to maneuver it so Maddie and Robbie could be alone, but before she could duck into her room, Robbie said good night and left. Subtlety was just not going work, she decided. She was going to have to draw them a blueprint, hit them over the head, or something else just as dramatic. Maddie was so astute at everything else, how could she be so totally obtuse when it came to her own love life?

September 23, 9:00 AM

Madeline entered the dining room and saw Molly was just being seated. As she made her way to the table, she saw everyone in her group, except Joe and Marty, having breakfast. Kelly was sitting with the Talbot sisters having an animated conversation and, as Madeline passed, Millie called out, "Madeline dear, do join us. Kelly was just telling us about her encounter this morning with her neighbor's poodle."

"I'd love to," Madeline paused, "but I don't want to keep Molly waiting. You'll have to tell me all about it later."

Madeline was pleased to see how comfortable Kelly was with older people, which was not always the case with teenagers. There had been trips in the past where teens had not been so great.

"You're looking chipper this morning. Did you have a good time last night?" Molly asked as Madeline approached the table.

"Oh yes. We had a wonderful meal at a tiny Italian place just off Leicester Square. How about you?"

"Nothing special. Just made sure everything for today was tip top and ready to go," answered Molly.

"Great. Everyone is looking forward to returning to the Abbey. They all want to see where my ancestor is buried."

"Well, I've changed things a bit round," Molly explained. "I was able to get an appointment at St. Paul's this morning, so I moved Westminster to tomorrow. I hope you don't mind. St. Paul's is normally closed to tours on Sunday, but they agreed to squeeze us in between services. Lovely of them, isn't it? It will save us jumping about."

"So we'll go to the Tower first, then St. Paul's." Madeline was drawing a map of the route in her mind. To her, maps were not just lines on a piece of paper. When she looked at a map, she was actually there. She could visualize buildings, rivers, streets, bridges, even moving from place to place. This ability was quite useful, especially when clients mistakenly thought they could drive from Paris to Rome in one day. "Molly, where had you planned to go for lunch?"

"We have reservations at Shepherd's," Molly answered.

"Why don't you see if you can change it to Rules. It would be more in keeping with the atmosphere of The City, and we can have a look around Covent Garden afterward." Madeline had always liked London's oldest surviving restaurant and it was so close to Covent Garden, which was always fun.

By the time Chloe arrived in the dining room, Madeline and Molly were in deep conversation so she joined the Talbot sisters and Kelly. "I only have time for coffee," she told the waiter as she wrapped two scones in her linen napkin and stuffed them in her purse. "Don't worry, I'll bring the napkin back later."

"Of course, Madame," he smiled, his expression never changing, as if guests did this sort of thing all the time.

"Hey, you made it. I was beginning to wonder," Madeline teased as she found Chloe on her way to the lobby. They joined the others and Madeline noticed that Marty Dalton was talking to Kelly, but she didn't see Joe. "Hi Marty," she said. "Where's Joe? Is he about ready? We need to leave in a few minutes."

"I'm so sorry," Marty began, a slight sound of embarrassment tingeing her voice. "I didn't even know until this morning he had scheduled a business meeting, but he said he would try to meet us for lunch."

"I'm afraid we've changed things around a little. Can you call him and let him know to meet us at Rules, not Shepherd's?"

"I'll call his office and leave a message. If he doesn't find us, too bad. He can fend for himself." Marty was miffed at her husband, and Kelly was beginning to fidget uncomfortably. "I just can't believe he would drag those poor people out for a meeting on Sunday."

"Mom, it must have been important or he wouldn't have done it. You know Daddy doesn't do things like that just to be mean," said Kelly in her father's defense.

"Don't worry about it," Madeline said, attempting to smooth their rumpled feathers.

Molly returned from changing the restaurant reservations and she and Madeline ushered everyone out the door to the coach where George was waiting. Once everyone was seated, Molly began.

"Good morning. I trust you all had a good rest and recovered from your jetlag. If you've had a look at today's itinerary, we've changed it a bit round. We'll still be going to the Tower, but then we'll stop at St. Paul's. The verger has agreed to take us today rather than tomorrow. It's quite nice, actually. It will save us hopping about."

"All right, George," she said, leaning toward him. "Let's be off."

Standing at the front of the bus, like a teacher addressing her students, Molly began, "We talked a bit yesterday about Edward and William and the Norman Conquest. How many remember the year?"

"1066," they answered in unison.

"Well done!" Molly exclaimed. The group looked quite pleased with themselves.

"Indeed, 1066 marked the beginning of modern Britain, but the country is actually much older. Julius Caesar's army invaded England in 55 BC. When he reached the Thames, there were only a few tribesmen about, but when the Romans invaded the second time, about 90 years later, a small port and community had been established. The Romans built the first bridge over the river and placed their headquarters, which they called Londinium, on the north bank. They occupied Britain until the fall of the Roman Empire in the 5th century, when the Saxon's came back to power. By the time William arrived, in 1066, London was a thriving city of 50,000 people.

"Edward the Confessor is responsible for dividing London into two areas; The City, the center of commerce and Westminster, the center of Government. Today London is divided by invisible borders into neighborhoods that still include Westminster and The City. This morning, we're going to visit The City."

"I thought we were going to the Tower of London," said Millie, dismayed.

"Quite right," Molly interjected. "We are indeed. The Tower is on the far side of The City."

"Oh…Good…" Millie was still confused.

"Don't you worry, Darlin'," Jake reassured her, leaning forward to pat her arm. "Wherever it is, that's where we're going."

"Quite right," Molly said again. Jake's attentions had apparently alleviated Millie's concern, so she continued. "If you look to your right, you can see Wellington Arch. Yesterday we took Piccadilly from this point. Today George is going on around to Constitution Hill and along the other side of Green Park. Are you getting your bearings now?"

There were a few murmured agreements and heads nodded. Dolores Shepard was following along on the map she had unfolded in her lap.

They continued along the Mall, past Trafalgar and on to the Strand, with Molly pointing out the sites along the way. When they reached Fleet Street, Madeline and Chloe turned to each other and both sang "The demon barber of Fleet—Street. Attend the tale of Sweeny Todd."

Kelly exclaimed, "Oh, I loved that show! Is it still playing here?"

"I'm not sure," Madeline answered, impressed she had recognized the Sondheim lyrics from *Sweeny Todd*. "We'll find out."

They continued past St. Paul's, where Molly reminded them they would return later. As they neared the Tower, Molly said, "Most first-time visitors think The Tower of London is just that, a tower. In fact, it is an entire fortress, containing several towers, a chapel, the Jewel House, the Queen's House and many other buildings, including the residence of the forty Yeoman Warders."

"Aren't they the Beefeaters?" asked John.

"Yes, they are one and the same, but please don't use the name in front of them."

"Why not?" Kelly wanted to know.

Marge answered from behind her. "From what I've read, it's an insult. Is that true Molly?"

"Yes. The Yeoman Warders were created by Henry VII to guard the Tower. Legend has it that, in times of hardship and famine, the Yeoman Warders were given extra rations of meat so they would remain loyal to the throne. Supposedly, the poor, starving peasants would spit at them and call them 'Beefeaters' behind their backs, but that's rubbish, isn't it? No documentation has ever been found to support the theory. The nickname stuck, however, but you can see why they're offended. Call a Yeoman a Beefeater and you'll make no friend of him.

"If you'll look just ahead, on your left, you can see Tower Hill, where most public executions were held." The coach then turned right and drove along the outer wall of the compound and came to a stop at the entrance. Molly took care of the tickets and soon they were walking across the bridge that once spanned the moat, now a grassy area, toward the Bell Tower.

"Did any of you watch Masterpiece Theater's production of *The Six Wives of Henry VIII*?" Madeline asked. "Remember when Henry wanted to divorce his first wife, Catherine of Aragon? She was the daughter of Isabella and Ferdinand of Spain and a devout Catholic. The only way Henry could be free to marry Anne Boleyn, was to either trump up charges and have Catherine executed, or divorce her."

The group was hanging on Madeline's every word because she had a way of telling historical tales that brought them to life. Even Chloe, who had heard the story many times, was listening with rapt attention and Molly was only too happy to defer. She only wished she possessed a thimbleful of Madeline's way with words.

"Well," Madeline was on a roll now. "Henry didn't want to kill Catherine, she was Mary's mother after all, and she was well loved by his subjects, so offing her wouldn't have been politically correct. He just wanted her out of the way so he could marry his mistress. You see, Henry needed a male heir and Catherine had only been able to produce a daughter and several miscarriages. In order for Anne's child to be legitimate, he had to marry her, so Henry decided the best answer to his problem was divorce.

"Then things really got complicated. Up to that point, England had been a Catholic country, like most of Europe, but the Pope would not give permission for Henry's divorce and decreed that any children born to anyone other than his lawful wife, Catherine, would be illegitimate and could not inherit the throne. So Henry said, 'OK—fine', dissolved the Catholic Church, and declared himself to be supreme head of the Church of England, and a Protestant.

"The whole point of this story is that Sir Thomas More, who was one of Henry's best friends and a devout Catholic, refused to acknowledge the validity of the king's divorce which meant he also refused to accept the Act of Succession. Poor Sir Thomas was imprisoned right here in the Bell Tower in 1534 and was executed a year later, and for what? We all know what happened to Anne. Henry caused all this trouble, set Catholic against Protestant which is still a struggle today in Northern Ireland, killed off a close friend and Anne only lasted a thousand days. She was beheaded in 1536. And to top it off, Anne gave birth to another girl, Elizabeth. When you look back at it, Henry really screwed up!"

As the group proceeded past the Bell Tower, on the way to Traitor's Gate where they would meet their Yeoman Warder guide, a hushed reverence settled over them. Madeline made Henry and his entourage seem so real, they half expected to see him walking down the path.

Reginald Grey, their Yeoman guide, was waiting for them at Traitor's Gate. He, too, had many stories to share. "Prisoners were brought to the Tower by boat," Reginald continued, "and entered the compound through the gate below. One of the most famous prisoners was Princess Elizabeth. After Henry died, his young son died as well and the throne passed to his eldest daughter, Mary, a Catholic. Mary abolished the Protestant faith and returned the country to Catholicism. The struggle for power between the two religions became so intense that Mary ordered her younger half-sister imprisoned in the Tower. Later, after Elizabeth became Queen, she visited the Tower and insisted on passing through

Traitor's Gate. "What was good enough for Elizabeth the Princess is good enough for Elizabeth the Queen", she is supposed to have told the Constable.

"Elizabeth carried on the tradition of imprisoning family members when she reinstated the Protestant Church and later had her cousin, Mary Queen of Scots, a Catholic, arrested and held in the Tower. Mary wasn't executed there, however. She met the block in 1587 at Fortheringay Castle.

"Bloodthirsty bunch, weren't they?" commented Dolores.

"Indeed Madame," answered Reginald, "however, only seven were executed here on Tower Green. The rest met their fate outside the walls at Tower Hill. Of course there were those who died from torture or illness. And there was that nasty business of the two Princes."

The group continued through the compound, Reginald telling them about points of interest. They were curious about the ravens they saw hopping around the Green. Reginald told them about the legend. "If the ravens ever desert the Tower, the kingdom will fall. To ensure that won't happen, each raven has one wing clipped so they can't fly. But don't feel overly sorry for them. One of the Yeoman Warders is designated as the Ravenmaster and his sole responsibility is to care for the birds."

At last they arrived at the Jewel House. At one time or another, the Crown Jewels have resided in both the White Tower and in the Martin Tower. Today they reside in the Jewel House, which is part of the Waterloo Barracks.

They entered the main floor gallery to see a multitude of glass cases containing the Royal collection of gold shields, swords, and other regalia belonging to the Royal Family. At the back of the room, they descended the stairs to the underground vault where the most important pieces are displayed. A long glass case holds the treasures, and as they passed by on moving walkways, Reginald explained, "Most of the pieces are only used during the coronation ceremony and date from 1661 when the monarchy was restored after Cromwell's demise. The Imperial State Crown, however, is used all the time. The crown was made in 1937 for George VI and is set with more than 2800 diamonds, 273 pearls and such significant stones as Edwards the Confessor's sapphire and the Black Prince's ruby. The Stuart sapphire is set in the back of the rim and the Second Star of Africa, cut from the Cullinan diamond, at the front. With all the gold and jewels, the crown is so heavy, Her Majesty can only wear it for short periods of time. Before her coronation, she had to practice many times to increase the strength in her neck and shoulders in order to bear the weight. The collection also includes the Jeweled State Sword, The Orb and The Scepter, which holds the largest cut diamond in the world, the 530-carat First Star of Africa."

As the group moved along the case, their murmurs became more audible, "My God, I can't believe they're real." "Did you see that? It's the size of an egg." "TV just doesn't do them justice." "Y'all would have to have a neck like the Hulk to wear that thing."

Madeline smiled at their universal reaction. No matter how many groups she brought here, the response was always the same.

Their excitement was evident as they walked back through the compound, left Reginald at Traitor's Gate with many thanks for his wonderful stories, and headed for the gift shop.

"How much fun is this?" Chloe said as she put her arm through Madeline's. "They're like little kids in a candy store."

"I know, they're so cute." Madeline whispered. "Look at Marge and Millie. They're debating whether to get one or two sets of miniature Crown Jewels." She let go of Chloe and went to see if she could help.

Meanwhile, Jake and Suzie bought a beautiful porcelain replica of The White Tower, along with books and videos for their boys. They were even tempted to buy a full suit of armor. The dilemma of how to get it home was solved when they decided on a Child size set instead.

Dolores fell in love with a miniature pin of the Scepter. It was gold with a tiny diamond in place of the Star of Africa. When she turned away to look at a display of books, John signaled the salesgirl and quietly bought it for her.

Marty bought a large coffee table book and had it shipped home along with a video. Kelly didn't really need to buy anything. She was returning for school in a few weeks and was much more interested in clothes than souvenirs.

Molly, who was waiting with George, was surprised that after fifteen minutes they were all returning to the coach. After they were all on board, she switched on the microphone and said, "I'm impressed! Did you clean them out?"

Laughter filled the coach as they pulled out and headed for St. Paul's Cathedral. Marge turned around and asked Madeline, "Isn't Petticoat Lane supposed to be somewhere around here? I couldn't find it on my map."

"Yes," Madeline told her, "its just north, near Liverpool Street Station. However you can't find it on your map because it isn't there. If you look on your map you'll find Middlesex Street. Middlesex Street is Petticoat Lane. I've always had an issue with the mapmakers over this one. Most tourists have heard of Petticoat Lane, but the maps only show Middlesex Street. If you didn't know they were one in the same, you'd never find it. Anyway, you really have to get there before noon, and besides, I think Portobello Road is a better market."

"Oh, I did find that. Didn't we go past Portobello Road?" asked Marge.

Madeline nodded. "On the way in from the airport. It's in Notting Hill. I'll show you how to get there when we get back to the hotel and maybe you can go on Tuesday."

"Oh good," said Dolores, whose ears had perked up at the mention of another place to shop. "We'll go with you."

As the coach stopped in front of St. Paul's, Marge and Dolores were busy discussing their plans for Tuesday. They followed their friends up the massive stairs of the West Front to the entrance, where the verger met them. "Welcome to St. Paul's," he said as he led them inside. "We're just between services, so I'll show you as much as possible in the time that we have."

They gathered around and listened as he told them, "There has been a church on this site since the 7th century. Obviously, this building was constructed much later. It's a bit of a miracle really that St. Paul's has survived at all. It has burned down three times and was even destroyed once by an army of Norsemen. The last time it burned was during the Great Fire of 1666 that destroyed most of London. The present cathedral was designed by Sir Christopher Wren and constructed between 1675 and 1710. We did suffer some damage during World War II, but thankfully all has been restored. If you will follow me, we'll go to the crossing so you can get a better look at the dome."

He led the little group up the Nave, pointing out the massive arches that opened into a mammoth space beneath the central dome. Standing in the center, he gestured up and around, "This is the second largest dome in the world. Only St. Peter's in Rome is bigger. On a clear day, you can climb the inside of it to the Golden Gallery for a magnificent view of the City. I'm afraid it's closed today, but perhaps you can return during your stay. I must warn you though, be prepared to climb 530 stairs. I haven't been up there since I was a boy, although I dare say you two gentlemen and the young lady should be able to manage it."

Jake, Kelly and John looked at each other as if to say, "Who me? Nah, I don't think so."

"No?" the verger asked, amused at their reluctance. "Perhaps just the Whispering Gallery then," he said pointing up to the rim just above them, "it requires only 259 stairs."

The rest of the tour was very interesting. They saw Wren's Tomb and the model of his original design, carved in 1672, and everyone was moved by the memorial to the Americans who lost their lives during World War II.

They lunched at Rules, and spent the rest of the afternoon browsing through the shops of Covent Garden and enjoying the street performers. Eventually, they returned to Ascot House with enough time to rest and change for dinner. Madeline reminded them to meet in the lobby at seven o'clock and bring a jacket or sweater. Dinner was going to be casual, but they were returning to the Tower of London for The Ceremony of the Keys and the breeze was picking up.

Monday, September 24, 8:00 AM

The next morning, at breakfast, Joe Dalton, who had never shown up for lunch the day before, made a point of apologizing to Madeline for his absence. "I really thought my meeting would only last a couple of hours. I had to see the head of our office here and I didn't want to miss today."

Madeline, sensing his discomfort, figured Marty had been on his case. "Joe, don't worry about it. I completely understand. Sometimes business just won't leave you alone."

At that moment Robbie signaled her from the doorway. "See what I mean?" The look on Robbie's face told her it was important.

Leading her toward the reception room, he told her, "Global just called. Apparently Molly's had a mishap this morning. I don't know exactly what happened."

The lilt of Robbie's brogue always made her smile.

"They want you to ring them straight away." He took her to a desk, held the chair and commented about the ornate phone, "It's a bit old fashioned, but works all the same."

When Madeline met her group in the lobby, she announced, "Molly's under the weather, so I'll be wearing two hats today."

"Wonderful," said Marge, digging in her purse. "I've got my map right here."

"We're right behind you, fearless leader," Jake teased. "Hey Chloe, ya think she's got any more stories?"

"More than any of would ever want to hear. I guarantee!"

Their first stop was Buckingham Palace. "Did you know there have only been forty monarchs since William the Conqueror?" Madeline was now in Molly's place at the front of the coach. "In nine-hundred and some years, only forty. Next year Queen Elizabeth will celebrate her Jubilee. Fifty years—and there have only been three who have reigned longer."

"How do you know this stuff?" asked John, amazed at the way Madeline pulled information from thin air. "Did you stay up all night memorizing facts and figures?"

"No. I can testify she didn't," Chloe chimed in from the last row. "Madeline is a veritable font of trivial information. I swear, her brain is like an encyclopedia of European history."

"You mean it's not just England?" Jake wanted to know.

Raising her hand to her forehead, Chloe did her best Talula Bankhead impression, "No, Dahling! She can bore you to death with the whole continent! For God's sake don't encourage her, she'll go on forever! We'll never get off this wretched bus!"

Laughter erupted as everyone jumped on the horror bandwagon. There was a momentary pause until Madeline said in mock apology, "OK, OK. Guilty as charged. May I continue now?"

With a straight face, Millie said, "That's all right dear. You go right ahead. Some of us are listening." Then she clapped her hands and giggled at her little joke, which made everyone laugh even more.

Madeline watched them having a wonderful time at her expense and thought how rare it was to have a group with such great chemistry. These people, who had absolutely nothing in common, were already developing a kinship; becoming friends. Even Joe Dalton was beginning to get with the program!

Madeline continued, "You know, we're actually lucky to be in London right now. The Palace is only open to the public in August and September while the Queen is in residence at Balmoral. It's only been recently that Buckingham has been open at all. In 1992, there was a terrible fire at Windsor Castle. Since Windsor is a Royal residence, and the property of the Queen, she didn't want to ask for public funds to restore it. But cost was staggering, even for her, so she opened Buckingham Palace and used the proceeds from ticket sales to pay for it."

"Now that was a good business decision," said Joe.

"I thought so too," Madeline replied.

When they arrived, everyone disembarked and waited for Madeline to get their tickets. Returning, she motioned them to gather around and said, "This really is our lucky day. The Queen's Gallery is displaying the Royal Faberge collection."

"I've seen pictures of the eggs," said Dolores. "They're beautiful."

"Well, wait until you see the miniature furniture made of gold and jewels!" Madeline exclaimed. "The whole collection is amazing and Her Majesty owns more Faberge pieces than anyone in the world!"

After touring the palace and Queen's Gallery, the group returned to Westminster Abbey, where Madeline showed them the grave of her ancestor, George Graham.

Before they went to lunch, Madeline explained, "Lunch at Shepherd's can be an exciting experience when Parliament is in session. It's just across the river and so popular with the MP's and House of Lords, that they installed a division bell.

When it rings, it means a vote has been called and they have ten minutes to get back. Don't be surprised if it goes off and half the patrons get up and walk out."

The afternoon's itinerary included a visit to the National Portrait Gallery and a drive around Hyde Park. At the lower end of the park, Madeline had George turn at Queen's Gate and drive past the Natural History Museum, The Victoria and Albert Museum and Brompton Oratory. "We don't have time to stop, but I want you to at least see where they're located."

As they were driving up Brompton Road, Madeline feigned surprise. "Oh my goodness," she said in a breathy English accent, clutching her bosom. "I do believe, can it be, God's blood, it's Harrods!" Then, back in her normal voice and with mischief in her eyes, she yelled, "Let's go!"

George stopped the coach right across the street from the most famous department store in the world. Madeline gathered her flock together on the curb and said, "We don't have much time, but we have to go in, even if it's only to see the food halls. If we get separated, take a taxi back to the hotel and get a receipt. Remember, you should try to get back in time for Afternoon Tea at four o'clock. We're going to see *Noises Off* tonight and won't have dinner until after the show. We need to meet in the lobby at six-thirty." The light changed, everyone looked left, then crossed the street giddy as school children running to recess.

CHAPTER 7

▼

Tuesday, September 25, 2:00 AM
The Bard and Mr. Bumbles

It had been a good day, a wonderful day. *Noises Off* had been hilarious. They laughed about it all through dinner and on the way back to the hotel. Everyone was looking forward to tomorrow. Madeline was too, so why was the old feeling of foreboding creeping into her consciousness, threatening to overwhelm her?

Without warning, it descended and covered her like a shroud, isolating her in her loneliness, making it difficult to breathe. Tears slowly trickled from the corners of her eyes and ran into the hair at her temples, Madeline had no idea why the specter had chosen this moment to visit her again. It had been over a year. Why now?

Returning just before midnight, Chloe teased her about having a late night rendezvous with Robbie. But Madeline hadn't seen him all day. She hadn't expected to.

Robbie was a great guy, clever as well as funny and easy on the eyes too, but Madeline didn't want to get involved with him. She didn't want to get involved with anyone.

Every man she had ever loved left her. Her grandfather died, her father had always been cold and distant, then he died too. Starved for affection, she went from boyfriend to boyfriend, never finding the love she craved. Her first husband was a heartless cretin who only wanted her to put him through law school and he died in a car accident the year after their divorce.

And then she met Jeff. God how she'd loved him. After living together for a year, Jeff wanted to get married, but Madeline had been so afraid of rocking the boat, she almost said no. She finally relented and, with Chloe as her Matron of Honor, she married the love of her life.

They had been blissfully happy and the birth of their daughter made their world complete. At least Madeline thought it was complete. The night before Christmas, just after their twelfth anniversary, Jeff announced he was leaving and Madeline's world blew apart. Completely blindsided, she began to doubt herself, her judgement, everything she'd ever thought to be true. If it weren't for her seven-year-old daughter, her work and years of therapy, she wouldn't have made it.

It had taken a long time to put her life back together and she didn't want to risk her hard won peace of mind by investing herself in another relationship. However, the fates exacted a price for her solitude.

Loneliness, like depression, could take on a life of its own. During a therapy session shortly after Jeff left, the doctor pulled out a third chair and told her to place her depression on it. Thereafter, there were three entities in those sessions, Madeline, her doctor and her depression. Over the course of two years Madeline learned to tell the difference between the truth and when the depression was distorting the truth.

She often thought it would have been easier if Jeff had died. At least then, the love would have stayed intact and their friends would have rallied around her in support. The reality was the love died a dismal death and their friends didn't know what to say to her. Eventually they stopped trying to say anything at all. Chloe was the only one who didn't desert her, but she lived two thousand miles away in Seattle. Even her mother lived a thousand miles away.

From early childhood, for reasons she had never been able to identify, Madeline had always been afraid to be alone. The worst thing that could ever happen to her was to be left alone, and yet, that is exactly what happened. She was left alone and responsible in a huge city, with no family or friends.

The depression didn't magically disappear, but she learned to recognize it and deal with it. Loneliness is altogether another matter. She learned to be alone. She even learned to like it. She relished her liberation and the ability to control her own destiny, raising her daughter without interference and carving out a life of her own choosing. However, loneliness still found a way to occasionally pay her a visit.

Lying in bed, Madeline knew she had to stave off the darkness that enveloped her. Was merely the thought of opening her heart so terrifying that it had bubbled to the surface again? Maybe the possibility of a relationship with Robbie made her vulnerable to attack? If this were true, she would just have to go into defense mode. Eliminate any possibility of a commitment and the pain would go away.

"Oh Maddie," she thought to herself, "how sick is this?" Throwing off the covers, she got up and went into the bathroom. Looking in the mirror, she could see her eyelids were already puffy, so she soaked a washcloth in cold water and pressed it against her eyes.

After a few minutes, she regrouped, soaked the washcloth again, squeezing out the excess water and took it back to bed with her. "I don't have time for this," she said, "I have to work."

September 25, 8:30 AM

"Do you believe it's Tuesday already?" Chloe asked Madeline, as she took another sip of her breakfast coffee. "I can't believe we go to the country tomorrow. Where do you want to go this afternoon, or do you already have plans? Listen, I can go to Notting Hill with Marge and Millie, so you can have some free time. What's Robbie doing?"

Madeline glanced around the dining room, making sure no one could overhear, "Chloe, I love you to death, but please give it a rest. Nothing is happening between Robbie and me and nothing's going to."

"Why not?" Chloe's exasperation was showing. "You're both single."

"Look, I know the attraction goes both ways…"

"And if you would just give yourself half a chance. Damn it Maddie, the man is standing right in front of you."

Desperately trying to keep her own exasperation in check, Madeline hissed, "I can't have a fling with Robbie. Robbie is not fling material. Yes, he's a wonderful man, and yes, I'm a little attracted to him. Chloe, he's a colleague. I have to work with him and I'm not about to jeopardize our friendship."

Chloe signed, noticing, for the first time, Maddie's eyelids were a little puffy and recognizing the haunted look. She knew what had happened. They had been down this road before. She touched her index finger to her lips and gave Maddie a silent kiss of encouragement. "Mads, are you OK?"

"Yeah, I just had a rough night."

Marge and Millie approached with their city map already partially unfolded. "You were going to show us how to get to Portabello Road," Marge said as she handed Madeline the map.

Spreading the map out on the table, Madeline dug through her purse and pulled out the yellow highlighter she always carried with her. "This is where we are now," she said, marking the Tube station at Green Park, "and this is where you're going." She circled Notting Hill Gate, then flipped the map over to the Tube Map side and marked the stations they needed. "From Green Park, take the

Jubilee Line one stop to Bond Street, then transfer to the Central Line and go four stops to Notting Hill Gate. See, it's pretty simple." Looking up, she asked, "Are Dolores and John still going with you?"

"As far as I know," replied Marge. "But either way, we'll be just fine," she said confidently, folding the map and tucking it back in her bag.

"I think Chloe and I would like to join you and I know a great place to have lunch."

Delighted that Madeline and Chloe were going with them to Notting Hill, Marge and Millie started out to the lobby and ran into Dolores, who was coming out of the Ladies Room. "Good morning, ladies," said Dolores, "have you got your shopping shoes on?"

"We certainly do," replied Millie, barely able to contain her excitement, "Madeline and Chloe want to come too."

The three women made their way to the lobby where, except for Joe Dalton, everyone else had congregated.

"I've got the credit cards," Marty was telling Madeline as she patted her handbag. Turning to her daughter, she winked, "And we intend to see he is properly punished, don't we honey?"

"Oh boy, we sure do!" Kelly laughed, gleefully rubbing her hands together.

"Good for you," chuckled Madeline. "In fact, I'll just bet you all have that dreaded "Credit Cards Burning a Hole in your Pocket" disease. The Globe Theater is our only stop this morning, then you are free to boost the British economy. Just be sure you're back here by seven o'clock this evening for our farewell dinner. Then tomorrow we're off to the Cotswolds."

Molly was still unavailable, so Madeline was again in charge of the microphone. "I detest these things," she said, referring to the microphone. "Can you hear me without it?"

"Can you hear me now?" chirped Chloe, "Can you hear me now?"

Marge and Millie were sitting right in front of her and everyone else nodded in agreement, so Madeline put the microphone back in it's holder. "We're off to Shakespeare's Globe Theater. The original Globe was built in 1599, during the reign of Queen Elizabeth I.

"Don't look at me like that," she said, shaking her finger at them and grinning. "I know it's more history, but this is good stuff. Trust me!"

"I swear, you're more determined than a dog diggin' for a bone," Jake fired back, which brought another round of chuckles.

"Anyway," Madeline continued, "Will was born in Stratford-upon-Avon in 1564. We'll get to see his home on Thursday. Now that was only seventy some years after America was discovered. History is a little fuzzy about his childhood, but we do know he married Anne Hathaway in 1582. He was only eighteen years old and she was twenty-six. We also know they had three children. We don't hear about him again until 1592. What happened in between and how he got to London is anybody's guess.

"Documents show that *Henry V* was performed five times in rotation with thirteen other plays in March, 1592.

"Have you all seen *Shakespeare in Love*? They must have taken a few liberties with the dates. Christopher Marlow was murdered in 1593 and *Romeo and Juliet* wasn't written until 1595, but, for the most part, I thought the movie gave a pretty accurate picture of the times.

"Will definitely was an actor as well as a playwright and poet, and Richard Burbage and Will Kemp were also members of The Chamberlain's Men. Remember when Ben Afleck made his first entrance? He and the acting company had returned from touring the countryside, that part was true. The theaters in London were closed because of the plague in January of 1593, so actors had to tour the villages and towns outside the city in order to make a living. Shakespeare stayed in London and eked out a living by writing poetry and sonnets for wealthy aristocrats, and performing for Her Majesty at Greenwich.

"When the theaters finally reopened in the spring of 1594, Will was back in business. Here the movie again jumbles the dates. Richard Burbage's father held the lease for The Theater. He didn't move to The Curtain until 1597, when he lost the lease on the original building."

Once again Madeline had drawn the group into her story and they were listening as if she were relaying yesterday's gossip hot off the press. "Now this is the good part." Wild applause filled the bus.

"The landlord of The Theater only owned the land, not the building, and there was nothing in the lease that said the building couldn't be taken down, so that's exactly what they did. Burbage, his brother and their workmen dismantled The Theater and took the timbers across the river to be used in the construction of The Globe."

As she finished her story just as the bus pulled up in front of The New Globe, Madeline's little audience applauded even more enthusiastically. They went inside and were met by their guide, Robert, a member of the acting company. Taking over from Madeline, he told them the original Globe had burned down in 1613 when a prop cannon fired a shot into the thatched roof during a performance of *Henry VIII*. It took nearly four hundred years before it was rebuilt.

As they stood in the center of the pit, where commoners stood to watch the plays, Robert told them The Globe was recreated using the same materials, techniques and craftsmanship used four hundred years ago. Madeline gazed up at the open sky and imagined what it must have been like to see Shakespeare perform in one of his own plays. The roof covered only the tiered seats, allowing the sun to light the stage. And if it rained? Oh well, you'd have to come back another day. She recalled the scene in the movie where Will and Viola are under the stage while a fight is going on above. There really was a trap door and there was a balcony too. She turned around and looked up at the tiers. There were three levels, much higher than she expected. Robert was saying the new theater was about ten feet taller than the original at forty-five feet, but the same diameter, one hundred feet.

As they left the theater, Robert encouraged them to visit the exhibition next door, housed in the shell of The Inigo Jones Theater. Shakespeare's Globe Exhibition tells the story of the recreation of The Globe. Madeline thanked him, waited until he left, then polled the group. It was unanimous. Shopping won.

Returning to Ascot House, everyone except Marty and Kelly decided to go to Portobello Road. Kelly wanted to shop for clothes so she and her mother were going to Knightsbridge, Bond Street and The Burlington Arcade.

"Good Luck," Madeline called to Marty and Kelly, and led her merry band out the door and down the street to Green Park. They followed the same route she had shown Marge and Millie earlier and arrived at Notting Hill Gate in short order. Madeline's favorite pub, Mr. Bumble's, was just off Pembridge Road, so they walked past the Gate and Mercury theaters and went into the pub for lunch.

The green façade of Mr. Bumble's wrapped around the corner of the street. There were green and white awnings above the windows and "Est. 1887" over the door. A plaque of the famous Dickens character was mounted on the wall.

Madeline first discovered Mr. Bumble's while on a site inspection trip in 1983. She and a colleague were exploring Notting Hill, saw it, loved the name and stopped for a pint. They had such a wonderful time, they stayed until the closing bell, when Alfie, the barkeep, poured them into a taxi and sent them back to their hotel. Today, no trip to London would be complete without a visit to Alfie and Mr. Bumble's.

Alfie greeted them as they walked in the door. "Maddie, me luv!" he exclaimed as he gestured to the odd assortment of men and women leaning against the bar, "Look who's here. It's Maddie come to visit us again. And who have ya brought with ya this fine day?"

Madeline stood on the bar rail, leaned over and gave him a big kiss on the mouth. Turning beet red, he bellowed, "Ah lads, even after all these years, she still loves me. Ain't life grand?"

"Oh I do Alfie, you know I do, always," Madeline answered, tickled she made him blush. "And you look so well in red."

When she first met Alfie, he was a wild young buck, working for his Uncle, earning just enough to keep himself in women and ale. About fifteen years ago, he married the pretty little girl from the bakeshop across the street and now they owned the pub. Alfie manned the bar and Hester reigned over the kitchen.

Hearing the commotion, Hester came bustling out from the kitchen to investigate. As soon as she saw Madeline, she broke into a run, pulled off her apron and gave Madeline a big hug. "Maddie, this is glorious. Let me look at you." She held Madeline at arms length, then hugged her again. "Glory me, it's been at least two years, hasn't it? You should've rung up, I would've fixed something special."

The mention of food made Madeline remember her group. She turned back to see them staring at her in amusement. "You'll have to forgive me, I've known Alfie and Hester forever. They are dear friends," she looked back at Alfie and shouted, "and they have The Best Pub in London." At that, everyone in the pub cheered.

Madeline made introductions all around. Everyone in the pub was thrilled to meet a real, live cowboy and, of course, Jake was only too happy to play the part. Hester remembered Chloe, who had come in with Madeline a few years ago. Alfie was busy drawing stout and lager. When he asked Marge if she would rather have a half-pint, she straightened her shoulders and said, "Hell no! I'll have a full pint and maybe even another." Poor Alfie didn't know if she was offended or not, but when Millie marched up and said, "Me, too" then giggled, everyone, including Alfie, howled with laughter.

They left the smell of beer and cigarettes and followed Hester to the back of the pub, where tables and chairs were set up for the lunch crowd. The closer they got, the stronger the aroma of fresh baked bread, beef stew, cottage pie, and bread-and-butter pudding.

Lunch was a joyous feast. They sampled everything on the menu and decided English cooking wasn't really bland after all. Many of the pub regulars came back to greet them. They pulled up chairs, rearranged the tables, and, with everyone laughing, talking and cheering each other on, the back room of Mr. Bumble's soon resembled King Arthur's roundtable. Jake was a huge hit. Everyone wanted to see his snakeskin boots and try on his hat. With tongue-in-cheek, he told them he had killed and skinned the snake himself and had his blacksmith make the boots. Marge and Millie were the darlings of the day, with young and old alike, flirting shamelessly. John Shepard was embroiled in a good-natured political debate with the local grocer about farm subsidies, and Hester gave Suzy and Dolores a tour of her kitchen.

They could easily have spent the rest of the day at the pub, but the power of the pesky credit cards, being too irresistible, they bid their new friends farewell with the promise to return whenever they were in London. They followed Madeline out the door and off to Portobello Road where, in contrast to the pub, nothing much was happening as the Street Market is only in full swing on the weekends. When Suzie asked where they could find the best selection of china and crystal, Madeline told her about two wonderful shops in Regent Street, Lawleys and the Waterford-Wedgwood shop. Everyone jumped on the bandwagon and piled into taxis for the ride to Regent Street.

Madeline rode with Suzie, Marge and John, while the others followed close behind. Quiet little Suzie was saying, "I sure never expected to meet such nice folks."

"I didn't either," answered Marge. "This is the first tour we've ever taken. Are they all like this?"

"Dee and I have been on several, and I have to tell you, this is the first time I've been slugged by an outraged nun." John winked at Marge and she gave him a big smile and an elbow in the ribs. "Seriously," he continued, "we've never had so much fun. This has been just great. And Madeline, I know we give you a hard time, but your stories are incredible."

"You make those old kings and folks seem so real. I can just see those boys takin' that theater down and sneakin' them boards across the river. I bet that ol' landlord was madder than a dog in a cat fight."

"I'll bet he was too," answered Madeline. "And no, this kind of chemistry doesn't happen that often."

"How did you learn so much about history?" asked Marge. "Did you study it in college?"

"No. Actually my degree is in music education and theater, but European history has always fascinated me. Europeans live their history. They never tear anything down. They'll build over, under or around an historical site in order to preserve it. I've always loved the stories, but they didn't come alive for me until I came here for the first time and ended up talking with the vicar in a little parish church in Yorkshire. He told me about every stone in the place, and when we came to a headless statue, he went on and on about how horrible Cromwell was, and "just look what he did". You would have thought what happened four hundred years ago, had happened yesterday. To walk where they walked and stand where they stood made it all come alive for me. I try to bring their history to life for all my clients."

September 25, 3:00 PM

Laden down with shopping bags, Marty and Kelly Dalton walked into the Burlington Arcade. With just a few more needed items, all of which could be found at the Arcade, Kelly was on her way to becoming the best dressed girl at Oxford.

Kelly wanted a pair of English riding boots. Her feet were long and narrow, just like the rest of her and it was difficult to find ready-made boots that fit. Madeline had steered them to Edward Green and Company at Number 12, Burlington Arcade, where the best boots in London could be hand crafted to fit any foot.

Next on the agenda was a Burberry coat. Madeline had told them Berk's, at Number 20, carried them and it would save a trip to the main store in Haymarket. They also wanted to stop at The House of Cashmere at Number 8 and at N. Peal, which was also in the Arcade.

At Berk's, Kelly found just the coat she wanted. They didn't have it in her size, so her measurements were taken and the store said they would have the coat delivered to her hotel. She didn't find anything in her colors at the House of Cashmere, so they decided to see about the boots, then go to N. Peal.

They went into Edward Green and were greeted by a gentleman who invited them to sit down while finished up with another client. Until she sat down, Marty didn't realize how exhausted she was, her feet throbbed and the shopping bags were becoming unmanageable. Her face was beginning to take on an unnatural pallor. When the clerk returned and told them their consultation would take approximately forty-five minutes, Kelly took pity on her mother and said, "Mom, why don't you go back to the hotel and put your feet up. I can finish up here and take a taxi back later."

"I was just thinking the same thing myself. I'll never make it to dinner tonight if I don't get off my feet for awhile. I'll take the bags with me. You take Daddy's credit card. If you have any problems, call me."

September 25, 4:30 PM

As Madeline and her weary band of shoppers returned to Ascot House, the doorman greeted her, "Madame, I believe Mr. MacDuff has a message for you."

Madeline and Chloe found Robbie in the reception room sitting at a desk near the windows overlooking the rose garden. He saw them approaching, got up and crossed the room to greet them. "Did you have a bonny day then?" he asked. "I'm thinking you could do with a sit and a wee dram." As he led them to the two wingback chairs facing his desk, he nodded discretely to a young woman standing nearby, who quickly brought champagne flutes and a chilled bottle of Piper-Heidsieck.

Resplendent in his red and white dress plaid, Robbie looked every inch the Scottish laird. Filling their glasses while continuing, "I had a ring from Le Pont de la Tour about twenty minutes past," he began, leaning casually against the corner of the heavy rosewood desk. "If they can move your dinner reservations an hour later, you can have the tables with the best view of The Tower and Tower Bridge. I thought we could have cocktails and Hors d'oeurvres here, then you could be on your way. I said we'd ring them."

"I don't see why that wouldn't work," said Madeline. "Did you clear it with David?"

"Aye, he was most pleased actually. Wants to do something special."

"Wonderful," Madeline and Chloe said in unison as they raised their glasses in thanks.

"I'll call the restaurant and accept their offer."

As Madeline rose from her chair, Robbie touched her arm. Chloe saw the gesture and made a hasty exit.

"Maddie girl," he said softly, "have a drink with me later."

She looked up. His green eyes were even darker than usual and turbulent, like a stormy sea. It was a look Madeline had never seen there before and it caught her by surprise, searing into her soul and leaving her breathless. For a moment she couldn't speak. She nodded, handed him her empty champagne flute and fled. As she hurried up the stairs, her heart pounding, she thought, "What am I doing? What is happening? What the hell am I going to do?"

CHAPTER 8

▼

Tuesday, September 25, 2001 6:30 PM
Where in the World is Kelly Dalton?

Kelly Dalton was absolutely terrified. She had no idea where they were taking her or why. How, she'd asked herself repeatedly, could a Tuesday afternoon shopping expedition have turned into such an unfathomable nightmare within the course of an hour?

She should have known something was wrong, but when the man called her by name and told her about her mother's accident, she'd gone with him willingly. All she could think about was her mother, lying unconscious in an unknown London hospital. It never occurred to her to ask him for identification.

A sudden wave of pain washed over her entire body. Her shoulders and arms ached from being tied behind her back and the rope binding her wrists cut into her skin. The gag was so firmly stuffed in her mouth she couldn't move her jaws or swallow and saliva was beginning to trickle down her chin. Her blindfold was so tight, her head felt like it was in a vise and, with her knees and ankles bound, she felt so claustrophobic that every breath was a struggle. If she didn't marshal her thoughts and calm down, she knew she would suffocate.

Now lying in a heap on the car floor, going God knows where, Kelly forced herself to return to the sequence of events that brought her to this horrible state. When the well-dressed man had approached her as she was leaving the Burlington Arcade, he told her about her mother's accident and said he'd been sent to drive her to the hospital. Because of the braid on his cap and his dark jacket and driving gloves, she'd assumed he was a chauffeur. He'd been so kind, helping her into the back seat of a plush, black limousine, while assuring her he would get her to her mother's side as soon as possible.

Oh, how she wished she'd returned to the hotel with her mother. Maybe she could have prevented the accident. She had paid no attention as to whether the privacy window was up or down until, groping for answers, she'd leaned forward to ask how long was the drive to the hospital.

When she pushed the button to lower the dividing window, nothing happened, so she leaned forward and tapped on the glass. The driver looked in his rear-view mirror, smiled and merely shrugged his shoulders. Feeling increasingly anxious and determined to get some answers, Kelly leaned forward again, this time knocking loudly against the window. Again, the driver looked in his rear-view mirror and smiled, only now his smile was more like a smirk and there was a hard look in his eyes he hadn't shown before. He quickly averted his glance while reaching up with his left hand to adjust the mirror, completely cutting off any eye contact with her.

Instantly it hit her. It was *deliberate*…The *"Chauffeur"* had intentionally locked her in the back seat. But, why? Beginning to panic, she frantically tried to lower the rear windows. Nothing happened! They, too, were locked.

Sickening pulses of fear began to throb in her stomach and Kelly began to shake uncontrollably, as she looked out the window and saw an endless row of warehouses surrounded by miles of chain-link fence.

The car slowed down, the driver turned left, passed through a gate, drove along the side of the building to the back, and came to a full stop in front of a large garage door. A quick call on his cell phone opened the door and the car proceeded into the cave-like interior. Straining to adjust her eyes to the darkness, Kelly thought, either there were no windows or they had been boarded up; the only light coming from the open door. As the car inched slowly into the black hole, she could barely make out two shadowy figures waiting for them.

She thought she was going to throw up.

Squinting to see through the tinted windows, Kelly leaned against the left door, nearly falling out when it suddenly opened and one of the men reached in and pulled her out of the car. When she screamed, he slapped her hard across the face. As she stumbled backward, he grabbed her roughly by the arms, held her upright and snarled in an ugly voice, "Shut-up or you'll be sorry". Without warning, the second man grabbed her from behind, yanked her arms and proceeded to tie her hands behind her back, while her first assailant forced a wad of rags into her mouth.

She couldn't distinguish the features of either man in the shadows, only that the one who hit her was thin and the one who bound her, was stocky. As a blindfold was being tied over her eyes, she heard the limo drive away, then felt what she thought must be duct tape binding her knees and ankles.

Everything was happening so fast. Kelly couldn't catch her breath. Her heart was pounding so fast she thought it was going to explode through her chest. The next thing she knew, she was shoved viscously onto the back floor of another car. Wedged between the front and back seat, unable to move, her ribs crushed against the driveshaft hump.

"Throw this over her. Can't be havin' anyone see our little package. Hurry up. We gotta get outta here!" Kelly felt a heavy, musty smelling blanket land on her.

The car bolted forward and, after what seemed like an eternity, slowed slightly and made a sharp turn to the right, spitting stones and debris with such force, there was no mistaking the sound of gravel. She might not be able to distinguish her captor's conversation, but, with her ear pressed against the floor, Kelly could definitely tell when the car left the highway and turned onto a country road.

A few minutes later, the car slowed down again and this time swerved to the left onto another road which made no sound, but was deeply rutted, like a dirt road or path. As the car bounced over ruts and holes she was pitched up and down, her ribs thrown against the driveshaft casing, ready to snap like twigs.

Finally, the car stopped so suddenly she was dislodged, her head crashing painfully into the door-handle. She could hear her assailants yelling as the door opened and quickly realized they were arguing about whether to pull her out by her head or feet. Rough hands grasped her ankles and began to tug. Due to her trussed up state, they had quite a struggle, but finally succeeded in hauling her from the car. She could hear water splashing and a damp mist fell on the exposed skin of her arms and legs. She heard a creaking door, then felt herself falling as she was half-dropped, half-thrown onto a hard mattress.

The rope around her wrists was removed, quickly replaced by a handcuff on her right wrist only and, while her left hand was free, her ankles and knees were still bound. She was stunned when they took off the blindfold and she saw her right wrist was chained to an iron loop embedded in a stone wall.

Kelly could make out the silhouettes of the same two figures she'd seen at the warehouse, but the light from the doorway was too faint to see their faces. Bending over her, so close she could smell the stench of his rancid breath, the thin one pressed a knife blade to her cheek and said, "OK now, little missy, if yer a good girl and keep yer trap shut, I might even take that gag outta yer mouth." She could hear the sneer in his voice.

Heart pounding, brain screaming, she nodded her head silently as tears rolled down her cheeks.

"Right then, not a word, or I'll slice that pretty face so's even yer dad won't know ya," he said as he lowered the blade, stuck his fingers in her mouth and scooped out the saliva soaked rag. It was all Kelly could do to keep from vomiting the rising bile in her throat. She swallowed several times, then began to cough.

Turning, he said to his partner, "Don't just stand there, you sod. Get her a drink."

A few sips of cold water later, Kelly eventually got herself under control. Her captors went outside, shutting the door behind them.

Just enough light filtered under the door, allowing her to see she was in a small room with a dirt floor. Menacing shadows danced on the walls and the sour smell of decay overwhelmed her. It wasn't rotting garbage, but decaying wood and vegetation. The air was cool and damp, and again, she thought she heard the sound of splashing water.

What did they want with her? What were they going to do to her? Were they going to rape her? Were they going to kill her?

Suddenly the door opened, interrupting her torturous questions. The thinner of her two jailers walked towards her holding up a cell phone and pressed it to her ear. "Someone wants to talk to you," he said tauntingly.

"You have reached Joseph Dalton at the Ascot House Hotel…".

Kelly's anguished wail pierced the darkness, "Daddy!"

September 25, 8:00 PM

The cocktail party was a huge success. Once again they were in the private dining room which had been set up as a buffet with conversation areas. The large table had been replaced with several small, round ones. Kelly had not yet appeared, but her parents didn't seem concerned, as Marty was sure she had just lost track of time while shopping.

However, when the time came to depart for the restaurant and Kelly still hadn't arrived, her father called her room. No answer. She was probably in the shower. Joe apologized for the delay, suggesting the others go ahead and he would wait for his tardy daughter.

The fine hairs at the nape of Madeline's neck began to tingle. She could feel it. Something was wrong. She pulled Chloe aside and whispered, "Go with them to dinner and don't alarm anyone. I have an awful feeling."

"Feeling about what?" Chloe whispered back.

"I don't know, but I'm staying here until I find out." She nudged Chloe towards the door.

"Is everything OK?" Dolores wanted to know.

"Yes, of course. Everything's fine. Wouldn't you be a little late if you had free reign with your dad's credit card?"

Everyone laughed. "Chloe's going to take you on to the restaurant. They are holding a special table for us. I don't want them to give it to anyone else. You hold the fort and we'll catch up with you."

Madeline could see that Joe and Marty were beginning to worry, after Joe had called again and still got no answer. "Wait here, I'll be right back," she said as she went to find Robbie and tell him what was happening.

She and Robbie returned to the lobby to find the Dalton's waiting for the lift. When it arrived, all four entered and Joe pressed four.

They arrived at Kelly's door. Joe knocked. No answer. He pounded on the door again and yelled, "Kelly Dalton, you open this door right now!"

Still no answer. A sick feeling was slowly pooling in the pit of Madeline's stomach. She closed her eyes and said, as calmly as she could, "Robbie, please open the door."

He pulled out his master key, and, in what seemed like slow motion, inserted it into the lock. You could feel the tension in the air. The sound of the moving tumblers was like an explosion. Robbie threw open the door. They were met by total silence, no sound of a shower or hair dryer. Robbie turned and cautioned them to wait. If Kelly had had an accident, he wanted to shield them as long as possible.

He entered the room with Joe right behind him. Nothing. Joe and Robbie ran to the bedroom, while Madeline and Marty checked the bath.

Nothing.

It was clear, Kelly wasn't there. In fact, it didn't look like she had been there all day. The bed was just as the maid had left it, without so much as a wrinkle. The fresh towels in the bathroom had not been touched.

A feeling of dread invaded the empty suite, stunning the four of them into silence. Madeline was the first to react. "Now, let's not get ahead of ourselves. She could have been held up at the bootmaker. We don't know anything yet."

Madeline could see tears beginning to well in Marty's eyes. She took her by the shoulders and said with determination, "Marty, look at me. She's all right. We'll find her."

Marty nodded as the tears trickled down her cheeks.

Robbie was already calling the front desk to see if there were any messages from Kelly. He looked at Joe. "A message came in for your suite. It should be on the…"

Before he could finish, Joe was already out the door and across the hall. They ran after him into the Dalton's suite. The red message light of the phone on the desk was blinking. Joe picked up the receiver and listened. After a few seconds, he blanched, clutched his chest and pitched forward, his full weight landing on Madeline.

Marty screamed and rushed to her husband who was still clutching the receiver. Robbie grabbed Joe under the arms and held him up, so Madeline could escape. She pried the phone out of his hand and was about to put it back in the cradle when Robbie shouted, "No!"

He walked Joe to the bedroom, helped him sit down and returned to Madeline. Taking the receiver from her, he entered a code into the phone and waited. The message replayed and what he heard would haunt him the rest of his life.

An anguished voice screamed, "Daddy!" Then a muffled male voice laughed and added, "I've got your girl, daddy. Wait for instructions. If you call the police, she's dead."

CHAPTER 9

September 25, 8:45 PM
Madeline Takes Charge

Robbie's green eyes ignited with another emotion unfamiliar to Madeline. Rage. She lowered her voice and asked, "My God, what is it?"

Putting his hand on her shoulder, his voice cracked as he replied, "She's been taken."

Madeline looked at him in horror, not wanting to believe what she was hearing. "Taken? What do you mean, taken?"

"Maddie, the lass has been snatched. Kidnapped."

Madeline felt as though she'd been punched in the stomach. She'd sensed something was wrong, like a car accident or a mugging. But kidnapped? She never anticipated this. "Robbie, what did they say?"

Robbie entered the replay code again and, holding the receiver to her ear, he said, "Here, listen."

Hearing the message for herself was surreal. It was hard to grasp this was really happening. Robbie took the receiver from her and entered the codes to permanently save the message, then immediately dialed the house doctor. Although Joe was still conscious, it was clear he needed medical attention. They left the door open for the doctor and went to the bedroom.

Joe was sitting on the bed, still unable to speak, while Marty was near hysteria. Madeline took her hand and led her to the chaise lounge. Marty sat as Madeline kneeled in front of her and clasped Marty's hands in hers. "Marty, she's only been gone a couple of hours. We have to think. Did you notice anything unusual while you were out today? Was someone following you? Can you think of any reason why someone would take her?"

From across the room, Joe uttered his first words, "Why would anyone take Kelly? How would anyone even know who she is?"

With that, they heard a voice calling from the living room, "Is anyone here?"

"We're in the bedroom, Gerald," answered Robbie.

Upon entering the room, Dr. Gerald Stone couldn't immediately tell who was his patient, as looking from one person to the next, they all seemed to be in various stages of distress.

"Thank you for coming," Robbie said as he quickly made introductions and brought the doctor back to Joe. "He's had a bit of a collapse. May have had some chest pain."

"I'm OK," Joe insisted, "just had the wind knocked out of me."

"Don't worry sir, I should have a listen all the same. Nothing to fool with, chest pain, is it?"

The doctor proceeded to examine Joe and finally announced, "Your heart is in tip top condition, although your blood pressure is elevated. Had a bit of a fright then, did you?"

"They received some distressing family news," Robbie answered, not elaborating.

"Of course, understandable. Mrs. Dalton, you look done in as well. Could I have a listen? Always better to be safe."

Marty nodded and Dr. Stone repeated the same procedure. She was obviously shaken, but otherwise fine, so he took his leave, saying, "Please call me if you need anything further."

Robbie and Madeline escorted Dr. Stone to the door. "Thank you again Gerald," said Robbie.

"Yes, thank you so much," added Madeline. "Is there anything else we should do?"

"See they get something to eat and again, don't hesitate to call if there are any other problems."

Relieved the Dalton's were not in any serious danger, they closed the door and walked back to the living room. "What are you thinking?" asked Robbie.

"I think we need to stay calm and figure this out," she replied. "Kelly hasn't been gone that long. Somebody has to know something. Can you make a tape of that phone call?"

"Aye, and I can program the system to record any incoming calls. He said he would call back with instructions."

"I think it was a man too. Why don't you go take care of the phone while I get them talking. They may remember something."

"I'll be back," said Robbie as he headed for the door.

Madeline went back into the bedroom and found Marty and Joe sitting on the bed, hands clasped, staring at the floor, looking completely lost.

"Come on," Madeline said, "we need to talk."

They got up, followed her into the living room, and sat at the dining table. Madeline poured four glasses of water, as she knew Robbie would return, and sat down across from them.

The look of despair that had settled over Joe and Marty was gut wrenching. Madeline was also at a loss. Nothing in her thirty years of professional experience had prepared her for this. She'd dealt with misdemeanors such as drunk and disorderly clients, pick-pockets and medical emergencies, but never anything of this magnitude. She did know, however, the longer they waited to do anything, the colder the trail would get. She also knew they needed help.

Gently she asked, "Are you alright?"

"Hell no," Joe lashed out. "Of course we're not alright! Our daughter's been kidnapped! How could we be alright?"

His outburst startled Marty and she began to cry again.

"Joe, I know you're upset," said Madeline, "we all are and we're going to figure this out together."

"I'm sorry Madeline, I know you're trying to help. It's just that some bastard's got Kelly. Why would anyone take her? What do they want?"

"That's precisely what we have to figure out, and Joe, we're going to need help. We have to call the police."

"No, absolutely not! They'll kill her. You heard him."

Madeline could see Joe wasn't ready to listen to reason, so she tried another approach. "OK, no police, for now. Marty, think. What happened after you and Kelly left this afternoon?"

Marty took the tissue Madeline offered, wiped her eyes, blew her nose and answered, "I don't know. We went shopping."

"Yes, I know, but start at the beginning and tell us everything. You might have seen something that can help us."

"OK. We left the hotel right after you did," Marty began. "The doorman got us a taxi and we went back to Harrods. Kelly found a pair of riding pants she liked and a jacket. We looked at boots, but nothing fit, so we went up to the restaurant and had lunch. Nothing unusual."

"Uhum. Then what happened?"

"We left Harrods and walked down the street to Escada and the other designer boutiques. Even the boots at Gucci didn't fit. Kelly's feet are long and narrow, and she has such a high arch." Marty's voice broke and her eyes began to well up with tears again.

Just then Robbie and room service arrived. Joe and Marty both insisted they couldn't eat, but Madeline urged them to do their best, adding, "You won't be any good to Kelly if you let yourselves fall apart." They began to pick at their plates, pushing around bits of chicken and green beans, unable to force down much, if anything.

Robbie had made a copy of the message and played it several times on the portable tape player he'd brought back with him. "I know the voice is muffled, but do you recognize it at all?"

They listened several times, but nothing sounded familiar. "Robbie," Madeline said, "Marty was telling us what happened this afternoon." She filled him in on the first part of the story, then asked Marty to continue.

"We were striking out with the boots, so we decided to try Bond Street. We were trying to flag down a cab without much success, when a nice man offered to help. He was looking for a cab as well, but said he would take the next one."

"Wait a minute," Madeline stopped her. "What did he look like?"

"I don't know, average, well-dressed, like a businessman."

"Did he have a lapel pin or an insignia on his jacket, or did he wear a hat of any kind?" Robbie asked.

Marty was trying her best to remember. "No he didn't have a hat," she answered tentatively. "I don't remember whether there was a pin or not. Is that important?"

"Some gentlemen wear their family crest on their lapel. Even their service staff sometimes wear the insignia. It's a carryover from the old days. If you could recognize the crest, it might help us identify him."

"Well, I don't remember anything like that. It all happened so fast. He was there, the taxi arrived, he gave the driver instructions, and we were off."

Joe looked at his wife. "So he knew where you were going?"

"Joe, he was just trying to be nice. He asked where we wanted to go. I told him Bond Street and that was that. I never saw him again."

Madeline had been taking notes all along. She looked up and asked Marty, "Do you have any idea how old he was?"

"Maybe forty-five or so, about our age," she replied.

"Good, that's good." Madeline was pleased. "Go on Marty, you're doing a great job. See, you're remembering a lot more than you thought you could. What happened next?"

Encouraged, Marty continued, "We walked down Bond Street, bought a few things and ended up at the Burlington Arcade. We ordered Kelly's Burberry coat at Berk's, and finally ended up at Edward Green, which was a good thing because my feet couldn't walk any farther. They said the consultation would take at least forty-five minutes, so Kelly suggested I take the shopping bags and come back here. She was going to take a taxi back as soon as she finished and meet us downstairs in time to leave for dinner."

"What time did you get back here?" asked Madeline.

"It was a little after four," Joe answered. "I had only been here a couple of minutes when Marty got back. I remember because I teased her about spending so much money and it was only four o'clock."

"The Arcade closes at five-thirty," muttered Robbie. "She would have finished at Edward Green by five and was going to take a taxi straight away, which means she must have been taken between five and five-thirty. Someone had to have seen something."

"Do either of you have a recent picture of Kelly?" Madeline asked. Both Joe and Marty carried her graduation picture in their wallets. "Good," Madeline said, taking the photograph from Joe. "We'll take this to the Arcade first thing in the morning. I'll bet anything the Beadles will remember her."

"Aye, they will for sure." Added Robbie.

"I'm going with you," Joe said, pushing his chair back from the table.

"No, you can't," said Madeline. "You need to be here when the kidnapper calls again. Maybe you can recognize the voice or get some useful information out of him. And make sure you demand to speak to Kelly. You need to make sure she is OK and listen for any clues she might give you."

Joe went to the bar, poured himself a shot of Glenlivet, tossed it down, then asked if anyone else would care to join him. There were no takers, so he poured himself another shot and walked to the sofa.

Marty looked up and cried, "How can you all be so calm about this? We have to do something! Dammit Joe, Kelly could be dead and you're drinking scotch!"

"What do you want me to do?" Joe exploded, his anger and frustration past the boiling point. "You think I don't care? Christ, Marty, she's my daughter, too!"

Marty burst into tears again, ran into the bedroom and slammed the door.

"My God," cried Joe, his hand shaking so much the scotch sloshed out of his glass onto the floor, "What are we going to do?"

The agony in his voice slashed through the air like a dagger. Madeline and Robbie both went to him at once. Robbie gently lifted the shotglass from his hand while Madeline put her arms around him. At her touch, Joe did what he couldn't do in front of his wife. As sobs of anguish wracked his body, Madeline held him like a little boy, rubbing her hands over his back, and murmuring words of encouragement.

Marty quietly opened the bedroom door and saw her distraught husband in Madeline's arms. Her heart broke as she went to them. Madeline gently disengaged from Joe's grasp and Marty took her place. Together, Marty and Joe silently rocked back and forth, sharing their fear and grief.

Robbie was standing at the bar, disposing of Joe's leftover scotch, when he turned and saw Madeline coming toward him. She looked drained, about to collapse, and he went to her with outstretched arms. She gladly fell into his warm embrace. Robbie felt so solid and substantial, she was grateful he was there.

"Maddie darlin'," he whispered into her hair, "it will be alright. You'll see."

"I'm so frightened for them." Madeline pulled back and looked up into Robbie's eyes. "We have to help them," she whispered. "We have to convince them to call the police."

"Aye," he answered, then pulled her close again. "I've a friend at the Yard. Let me have a go once more. I'll make them see reason. Darlin', your group will be back soon. Have you thought what you're going to tell them?"

"No. We're supposed to leave for the Cotswolds in the morning. I'll think of something."

CHAPTER 10

September 25, 8:00 PM
Sticks and Stones and a Cast-Iron Bracelet

As the chill of evening seeped into her dark damp prison, Kelly Dalton began to shiver. She was sitting on a makeshift mattress in the corner of the room, her right arm handcuffed to a short chain which had been screwed into the wall, level with her shoulder. As long as she remained upright, resting her arm on her bent knees, the handcuff didn't cut into her wrist. However, her ribs were so bruised from her torturous ride on the floor of her kidnapper's car, that every breath brought a new wave of pain. She wanted so badly to lie down, but the position of the chain would have left her suspended by the wrist at a forty-five degree angle.

She turned her head and looked up at the ceiling, grateful for the dark. She was trying to keep her imagination in check and, if there were bats hanging from the rafters, she didn't want to know about them.

The sound of her father's voice was still clear in her mind. She knew that when he heard the message threatening to kill her, he would go ballistic. But then what? He couldn't do anything except wait for the next call and patience, especially where she was concerned, wasn't his strong suit. And what about her mom? Had she really been in an accident, or was that just a story designed to lure her into her captor's trap?

She could hear her two jailers moving around outside, but it was difficult to make out their conversation because there was the incessant sound of splashing water. It had a rhythm to it. Splash—beat—splash—beat, going monotonously on and on. She had no idea where it came from, but decided she could either let it drive her to distraction or she could just go with it. Resting her head against the wall, she focused her attention on the water, her breathing automatically accepting the rhythmic pattern. Inhale-beat, exhale-splash. She became one with the sound and mercifully drifted off to sleep.

"Keyes," yelled Thomas Stout as he came around the side of the old mill, "What about supper then? I've a powerful hunger and it's past time."

"Shut it, you stupid idiot," hissed Henry Keyes. "Didn't I tell you to keep your voice down? You never know who might be about."

"Sorry," muttered Stout, "I forgot."

"You won't do it again, if you know what's what," Keyes shouted.

"I can't say nuffink if me mouth's full of somethin' good to eat," Stout said, sulking.

"Food is all you think about, Stout. If I hear 'I'm hungry' one more time, I swear I'll break every tooth in your head. You'll get fed when I decide it's time."

Henry Keyes was determined that this time he was going to get it right. This time he was going to be rich. He knew what the villagers of Greysmeade thought of him. Since childhood, they'd written him off as a lost cause, but this time he'd show them he could score big. Hadn't he found this hiding place, and hadn't he tricked the little rich girl inside and gotten her here from London in broad daylight?

Nobody knew about the abandoned mill. The building had been empty for hundreds of years, remote and unapproachable, disguised by centuries of overgrowth. But he had found it and it was his secret place.

The only reason he'd cut Stout in on the deal was to watch the girl while he was going about his business. Once he had the money, he would take care of Stout. Besides, Stout was a bit dull in the head and he'd never guess what was in store for him.

At the age of eight, Keyes had been orphaned when his brutal father had been stabbed to death in a pub brawl and, since there was no one to care for the boy, the local authorities placed him in a foster home. Foster care proved to be a disaster and finally, after he ran away from the third home, he'd been shipped off to a facility for incorrigible children, located in a remote part of Wales. He escaped when he was fourteen years old and lived hand to mouth until he returned to Greysmeade as a young man of twenty-five, determined to make a name for himself and establish himself as a successful pillar of the community.

He'd made a name for himself alright, going from job to job, cooking up one get-rich-quick scheme after another. Even though he had no education, he did have a certain glibness that allowed him to convince people his schemes could work. He was persuasive, but he didn't have the staying power to follow through. In the beginning, people were willing to give him a chance, but, after enough of them lost money, he had no choice but to move on. The night before he left, four years ago, he stood a round at the village pub, vowing to return when he'd made his fortune.

His luck proved to be no better in London than it had been in Greysmeade. However, after one particularly botched scam, he did have the good sense to get himself arrested and convicted of burglary under an assumed name. Ironically, going to jail proved to be the best thing to happen to Keyes since he was eight years old. He met his ticket to the gravy train at Wormwood Scrubs, as he befriended the old man in the neighboring cell and discovered his path to a pot of gold.

"Do you think they'll have bangers and mash down the pub tonight?" Stout whined, interrupting Keyes' thoughts.

"Food again. Is food all you think about?" Keyes shot back.

"Yes, specially if I'm hungry. I need me dinner," he whined, "its way past time to eat. Now when can we go?"

"You're going to stay with the girl, and you'll get your food when I'm ready," Keyes answered as he walked the few remaining steps to the door.

Throwing open the door to the millhouse, Keyes aimed his flashlight toward the huddled figure in the corner. She was sitting half-upright, still asleep, her arm suspended from the chain on the wall. Not wanting to awaken her until he could put his hand over her mouth to keep her from screaming, he cautiously crept forward.

"And how are we doing in here dearie?" he shouted, raising his other hand and shining the light in her face.

Kelly awoke with a jerk, her eyes wide with terror, her scream muffled by the hand over her mouth.

"Here now," he taunted malevolently, "Don't go thrashing about like that. That cuff'll slice your wrist and then where would we be? All that blood over you, and you cold as a stone. No, that wouldn't be nice at all."

Kelly remained completely motionless and didn't utter a word. "There now, that's better. You're going to behave if I take my hand away, right?"

At that she tried to nod her head, indicating she would follow orders. Slowly, as he removed his hand, a moan escaping her lips as she closed her eyes against the pain in her ribs. Her tethered arm had slipped off her knees while she'd slept, and as it began to come back to life, she sucked in a breath.

"Could I please have a drink of water," she asked, barely above a whisper.

"I think that can be arranged," Keyes taunted, imperiously enjoying his position of power.

Stout had been standing at the door watching when Keyes called out, "Don't just stand there. Fetch the little lady a drink."

Stout went out and soon returned with a cup of water and handed it to Keyes who placed it in Kelly's free, unshackled hand. The cold water eased her parched throat, but made her shiver again. Her mini-skirt and short sleeved sweater were no barrier against the cold.

"Getting a bit chilly, is it?" said Keyes. Looking up at Stout, he ordered, "Get that blanket out of the boot and be quick about it. We can't have our little missy freezin' to death, now can we?"

Returning to the car, Stout grabbed the old wool blanket Keyes had requested, then opened the boot, rummaged around and found a dirty towel and a large piece of plastic tarp. Quite pleased with himself, he returned to the millhouse.

As Stout entered the room, Keyes barked, "I said a blanket. What do you think you're going to do with this?" he asked, indicating the tarp.

"I don't know. We can use it for something." Stout started to sulk again when Keyes didn't appreciate his find.

"Bleedin' idiot," Keyes mumbled as he grabbed the blanket and went back to Kelly. Throwing it at her, he commanded, "There, now stop your shiverin'."

Because of the cuff and chain, Kelly awkwardly wrestled the blanket around her shoulders and found herself sitting crossed legged, wrapped like an Indian chief. If the situation weren't so grave, it would have been funny. A small laugh escaped her lips and cost her a slap so hard, her head jerked back and hit the wall behind her.

"Think I'm funny, do you? I'll show you what's funny." He drew back and prepared to hit her again.

"N-no. I-I'm sorry, I wasn't laughing at you." Kelly pleaded, bringing her free hand up to shield her from another blow. Tears streaming down her face, she sobbed, "It was m-me and how funny I must look."

This was more than Stout had bargained for. "She didn't mean no harm," Stout said, as he came forward to replace the blanket, which the blow had knocked from Kelly's shoulders. As he reached down, he turned to glare at Keyes over his shoulder. "You said she weren't supposed to get hurt," he accused, and, in a voice even Stout didn't recognize, he continued, "You said soon as we got the coin, she'd go back to her dad, good as new."

Furiously, Keyes stormed out slamming the door behind him.

Turning back to Kelly, Stout muttered, "Sorry 'bout that," as he pulled the blanket back around her. Keyes had taken the flashlight, so Stout fumbled around in the dark, but he was careful not to hurt Kelly.

Surprised he was trying to help her, Kelly whispered, "Thank you."

Gently patting her on her on the head, just like a puppy, Stout said, "He shouldn't a koshed you like that. Got a bloody foul temper, he has."

"Can I ask you a question?" When Stout didn't reply, she continued, "Why am I here? What do you want?"

"Well, now that's two questions, ain't it?." He answered, then thought for a minute. "Let's see now. Why? 'Cause I got no job and me kids need to eat. And what do we want? The blunt you're dad's gonna pay to get you back."

Keyes stormed back into the room and yanked Stout up by the hair. "Get out here" he screamed and viciously shoved Stout out the door. Slamming him up against the parked car, cursing all the while, his spittle flying in Stout's face, Keyes screamed, "What the fuck are you doing? I didn't cut you in to be her bleedin' nanny. You keep your bloody nose out of my business. Once more and I swear, I'll slit both your bloody throats."

Keyes's free hand had been around Stout's throat and, when he abruptly let go, and in disgust, turned away, Stout sucked in a deep breath and coughed several times. "Jesus Keyes, I didn't mean no harm," he sputtered.

Keyes spun around. "No names," he growled. "If she finds out our names, we'll have to kill her." With deadly calm, he continued as he opened the car door "I'm going for something to eat. I'll bring yours back. Guard our pot of gold with your life."

"The torch," cried Stout. "At least leave me the torch."

Keyes responded by pulling the door shut and starting the engine. He pulled away, not turning on the car lights until he reached the main road.

Left in the dark and rubbing his throat, Stout went back inside.

"Are you alright?" asked Kelly.

"Yeah," he answered, touched by her concern. "But we can't be talkin', somebody might hear. Bad for our health."

"OK," she whispered. After a few minutes listening to the splashing water in the otherwise total silence, she whispered again, "Where is this place? What's that splashing water?"

"This here used to be an old flour mill," he whispered back.

Greystone Abbey was founded by Benedictine monks in 1136 on a parcel of land several miles from the village of Greysmeade. Built of Cotswolds limestone, the complex grew until, by the thirteenth century, it was one of the largest and wealthiest abbeys in Britain. The monks also built a mill downstream, using the river's current to turn the water-wheel, which in turn, ran the gears and millstone to grind grain into flour. In 1536, following his split with Rome, Henry VIII dissolved England's religious houses and confiscated their riches to finance his foreign policy. The monks fled and, over the years, while local peasants took stones from the abbey to build their own cottages, the mill remained intact, completely forgotten.

Keyes stumbled on the mill quite by accident when he ran away from his second foster home. He'd been hiking through the forest, looking for a place to hide, when he discovered a huge mound at the river's edge. Upon further exploration, he realized it wasn't just a mound, but a stone building, covered with debris that had washed downstream. A little digging, and he found an opening. Inside was a large room with rotting wood, two large flat stones at one end and open space at the other. Eventually he went back to town and was placed in another home, but he never forgot his secret place.

Over the years Keyes had excavated the doorway and installed a proper door, as well as repairing the roof, then camouflaging it again with dead tree branches. Every time he had come back to Greysmeade, he'd checked on his hideaway and so far, no one had found it. It was still his secret and the perfect place to hide his kidnap victim.

"The millwheel don't work proper," whispered Stout, "but the river keeps going, it does. Sounds kinda nice, I think."

Silence descended again, but Kelly's brain was on fire. She lined up the facts as she knew them. She knew she was being held in an abandoned mill. She thought to herself, "If he had been talking about Henry VIII, what had Madeline said?" She had to concentrate and remember. They had been at the Tower of London and Madeline talked about Henry VIII having a fight with the Pope and getting rid of the Catholic Church. "Madeline said it all happened in fifteen something-or-other, so that means this place is five hundred years old. No wonder it smells so bad!" she thought to herself.

She was being held in a five hundred-year-old abandoned mill that used to belong to an abbey. That meant there had to be a castle or an abbey ruin nearby.

No one knew about this place, so it had to have been covered up, probably with five hundred years of muck carried down the river. Somebody had to know about the river, and if the creep who'd hit her had gone to get something to eat, there had to be a village or town nearby.

Now all she had to do was figure out which village or town and convey it to her father as soon as they contacted him.

She knew the man watching her now wouldn't hurt her. He was only interested in getting enough money to support his family. She also knew she had get him to talk. He might slip and give her more information.

When she heard his stomach growl she whispered, "I'm getting awfully hungry. What about you?"

"Lord have mercy," Stout said out loud.

September 25, 11:00 PM

Kelly and Stout waited in the dark, seemingly for hours, until Keyes returned with their dinner. The menu of cold, disgustingly greasy fish and chips made her stomach churn, but Stout didn't seem to mind. He wolfed down everything in his bag, then devoured her leftovers as well.

Not knowing their names, Kelly began to think of them as The Boss and Frank. Clearly the Boss's strongest personality trait was a nasty disposition, which erupted into violence at the least provocation. As he had already hit her twice and she didn't want it to happen again, Kelly decided her best protection was to play along and do nothing to provoke him. The other man reminded her of the character Frank on *ER*, the stocky, ex cop, desk clerk, who was crusty on the surface, but a nice guy underneath. At least he was nice to her when the Boss wasn't around.

As they washed down their meal with warm beer, which Frank seemed to enjoy very much, the Boss' cell phone rang. He answered it, then went outside, only partially closing the door. Frank seemed as curious as she was, so they both sat there, silently listening to the one-sided conversation.

"Yeah, everything's fine....Yeah, I brought 'er back fish and chips....Did you call him yet?—Well why not? The sooner you call him, the sooner we'll get...—OK. OK. Whatever you think.—She ain't goin' nowhere.—No, I didn't hurt her none, just let her know who's who.—I won't, I tell ya.—I'll keep my end.—Right then. Let me know."

When The Boss returned, he shined his flashlight first at Kelly, then Frank, barking orders, "Take her outside to the river and let her wash up." He tossed Frank the key to Kelly's handcuff, then pulled a gun out of his pocket, saying, "And don't even think about trying to get away."

When they returned from the river, the Boss ordered her back to her makeshift bed. Praying they would leave the handcuff off for a while, Kelly sat down and waited, knowing it was useless to attempt an escape. She had no idea where she was, and then there was the little matter of a gun pointing at her head.

The Boss ordered Frank to reattach the handcuff and, as if being chained to a wall weren't bad enough, he told Frank to tape her ankles together as well.

Knowing what happened the last time she riled him, Kelly sat silently and waited for someone to speak. The next thing she knew, they had pulled her feet around and forced her to lie down, her arm suspended from the wall at a forty-five degree angle. The Boss was shining his flashlight on her feet and she lifted her head long enough to see Frank place a stake in the dirt floor a few inches from her toes. Panic began to pool in her stomach as he pounded the stake into the floor and tied her feet to it. He did the same thing to her free hand and, when she finally tried to protest, the Boss slapped a piece of tape across her mouth, threw a blanket over her and they left.

As she heard the car drive away, tears slid from the corners of her eyes. Terrified and alone, she did the only thing knew how to do, fight back.

If she was going to make it out of this alive, she had to figure out what was going on. Looking for any new piece to the puzzle, she began to replay the phone conversation she'd overheard. Maybe the Boss wasn't really the boss after all. Whoever was on the other end of that cell phone conversation might be the true mastermind. She tried to remember the Boss's exact words.

"Did you call him yet?" If he meant her father, it must mean the other guy was supposed to call her Dad. "The sooner you call him, the sooner we'll get…" Get what, the money? And then the Boss backed down. He must be taking orders from the cell phone man. Otherwise, why would he say, "Whatever you think."?

The more Kelly replayed the one-sided conversation in her mind, the more she was sure the Boss was only taking orders. Was the Boss really smart enough to have dreamed up this plot all by himself? And how could he have known her father? Had he worked for her father's company? She didn't think so. No, she was sure somebody else was in charge.

Her mind recycled this new information and, as her breathing gradually adopted the rhythm of the river, she drifted off to sleep.

CHAPTER 11

▼

Tuesday, September 25 10:45 PM
We Won't Leave, Don't Ask Us

Sighing as she left the comfort of Robbie's arms, Madeline said, "Chloe and the others will be returning from dinner soon and will want to know what's happening with Kelly."

"I can see the wheels turning behind your bonny eyes," said Robbie. "What are you going to tell them?"

"I'm supposed to be taking them to Oxford in the morning. Obviously Joe and Marty won't be going."

"What about you?"

"They'll have to go on without me," she answered. Madeline looked at the Daltons, who were huddled on the sofa talking quietly, and added, "Chloe will have to take over for me. She's traveled with me enough times, she knows the drill."

"Aye, Chloe's a good choice. You'd best be off. They'll be returning any minute. I'll have another go with the Daltons. We've got to have help from the Yard."

"Thank you," Madeline said as she stood on tiptoe to kiss him on the cheek. At that precise moment, Robbie turned his head and their lips met. It was just a light brush but, rather than startling them, it felt right, each one giving the other the reassurance they needed and the knowledge they were in this together. Instinctively, Robbie caressed Madeline's shoulder as she touched his cheek with the palm of her hand.

"Go on now Luv. Everything will work out," Robbie whispered as he took her elbow and guided her toward the door.

"I'll be back," she promised, opened the door and walked down the hall toward the lift.

She thought about how she was going to present the slight change of plans. Really, the only difference was Chloe would be in charge. Their itinerary could continue as planned. Local guides were already arranged in Oxford, Blenheim Palace, and the other stops. The hotel was confirmed and Chloe had been there before. Everyone already knew George, the coach driver. "Yes," she said to herself, "everything will work out just fine."

Madeline reached the lobby just as Jake and Millie came through the front door. "Perfect timing," she said.

As the others came in and began to gather around her, Jake threw an arm around her shoulder and said, "No offence Darlin', but you look like you been rode hard and put away wet."

"Something like that," Madeline said shaking her head and smiling wearily. "Did you have a wonderful dinner?"

"Oh yes," chirped Millie. "The view was unbelievable with The Tower and bridge all lit up."

"It was beautiful, but what's the story with Kelly?" asked Marge.

"Why don't we all meet in my suite in fifteen minutes. We can put our feet up, have a nightcap and go over the plans for tomorrow."

Sensing something was very wrong, Chloe immediately knew Madeline was trying to avoid public disclosure and, from the look on Jake and John's faces, their radar had gone off, too. Whatever Madeline had to tell them it needed to be said in private. "That's a great idea," she said, herding everyone toward the lift. "Get comfy and we'll see you in a few minutes."

While the others waited for the lift, Madeline and Chloe took the stairs, followed by the two men. At the second floor landing, Madeline turned and quietly said, "We'll see you in a few minutes," and proceeded down the hall, not giving them a chance to question her.

"This can't be good," said John as he and Jake continued up the stairs.

As they walked into their drawing room, Chloe turned and said, "Maddie, you're scaring me. What's happened?"

Looking years older than she had the moment before, Madeline turned to face her friend. "Kelly's been kidnapped."

"What did you say?"

"Kelly's been kidnapped."

"My God. Are you sure?"

"Yes. The kidnappers called Joe and Marty's suite."

"Are you sure this isn't a hoax?"

"I only wish it were."

Madeline told Chloe everything that had happened. "I need you to take the group on to the Cotswolds tomorrow. I can't leave the Daltons, Chloe."

"You know I'll do whatever you ask, but are you sure anyone's going to want to leave?"

A knock on the door interrupted them. Chloe went to answer it while Madeline walked toward the fireplace. Suzie Donovan entered first and looked up at Chloe as their eyes met and silently acknowledged the gravity of the situation. The others followed Chloe into the drawing room and saw Madeline looking into he fireplace.

As they took their seats, Madeline knew six pairs of eyes were staring at her back, waiting for an explanation. She turned to face them. "Thank you for coming," she began. "I appreciate your not pressing me for information about Kelly when we were downstairs."

Marge softly asked, "What is it, Madeline?"

"What's happened?" added her sister.

"Has she come back yet?" Dolores wanted to know.

Madeline answered. "Kelly is still missing."

Everyone erupted with questions. "What are we going to do?" "Have you checked the hospitals?" "Have you notified the police?" "How are Joe and Marty?"

Madeline raised her hands, trying to quiet them. "Let me fill you in and then I'll answer all your questions."

Looking around the room, Millie raised her hand like a schoolgirl.

"Yes Millie," Madeline acknowledged.

"Where are Joe and Marty?"

"They're in their suite with Robert MacDuff, the concierge," Madeline answered.

"They must be out of their mind with worry," said Marge.

Everyone murmured in agreement. "Yeah, what do the cops think?" asked Jake.

"Of course, Joe and Marty are worried," Madeline told them, trying to tap dance around the actual truth. "We're doing everything we can to find her."

Jake leaned his hands on the back of the sofa. "OK folks, time to call up the posse. You in?" he asked, looking around the semi-circle.

"You bet." "Absolutely." "Where do we start?"

"No, wait," Madeline cried. "Wait a minute. Everything is under control here. First of all, I'm going to stay and work with the Daltons. My friend Robbie is the best concierge in London. Trust me, he knows everyone in the city. We'll find her. And second, Chloe will go with you to the Cotswolds tomorrow. All the local guides have been arranged and Greystone Manor is expecting you. The only change in your schedule is Chloe will be charge. I'm going to stay here and meet you later."

After two beats of stunned silence, all hell broke loose.

"If you think for one minute we're going off on a sightseeing trip while our poor girl is out there somewhere in who knows what kind of trouble...I don't think so!" said Marge.

"That's right," added Millie, standing beside her sister, looking every bit the angry terrier. "We're going to stay here and help!"

"Absolutely! Who the Sam Hill cares about the Cotswolds? They aren't going anywhere. We need to find Kelly right now." Dolores was adamant. She turned to look at her husband who nodded in agreement.

"The vote's in and you're outnumbered, so you might as well give in," Jake said. "We're stayin', we're helpin', and that's that."

"No, wait a minute," Madeline cried again, "you have to leave tomorrow. Everything will..." John interrupted emphatically, "We don't HAVE to do anything."

Astonished by the intensity of their reaction, Madeline looked at Chloe, only to see "I told you so" written all over her face. Madeline knew they would be disappointed, but she never expected this. Mutiny was definitely in the air.

Jake had had about enough. "Ok most honored Tour Director, have we made it clear? You can let us help, or we will damned well find her on our own."

With Jake's threat hanging in the air like a hammer, Chloe went to Madeline's side and said, "Maddie, you have to tell them Kelly's been kidnapped."

"It's too dangerous," Madeline whispered. "I don't want anyone else hurt."

Suzie Donovan, who had been silently observing the pandemonium, leaned forward and quietly said, "There's more to this, isn't there? Kelly isn't just missing."

Madeline glanced at Chloe who took her hand and gave it a squeeze of encouragement. "They have to know the truth."

"OK," Madeline said, raising her hands again. "No more interruptions. Just let me sit down and I'll explain what's happened."

"Come, sit down dear," Millie said in a motherly tone, patting the cushion beside her, "We're all friends. Please tell us everything. We only want to help."

Madeline allowed herself to be led to Chloe's chair. She sat down, accepted the glass of water Marge gave her, took a drink and looking at Suzie, said, "You're right. She isn't just missing." With that, she looked at the group and said, "Kelly's been kidnapped."

An audible gasp filled the room. "When we first checked the Dalton's suites, nothing in Kelly's room had been touched, so we knew Kelly hadn't been there since before we all left to go shopping. We went across the hall to Joe and Marty's and the message light on their phone was blinking. There was a voice mail. Kelly screamed for her father and then a muffled voice said they had her and if Joe called the police, they would kill her. And before you ask who "they" are,—we don't know."

Jake, now more determined than ever, announced, "That does it. We're stayin'. Don't you understand Madeline? Nobody gives a crap about sightseeing. We've got to do everything we can to find that child. Where do you want us to start?"

"No, Jake," Madeline implored, "don't you see? We have to keep up the pretense that everything is business as usual. The kidnappers said if we call the police, they'll kill her and we have to take them at their word. To me that means, if we tell anyone, she's dead. We just can't take that chance."

After the initial shock of Madeline's news subsided, John asked, "But why Kelly? Why would anyone take an American teenager? I could see a diplomat's kid maybe."

His questions got everyone else thinking. "Maybe it's not political," speculated Marge. "Do Joe and Marty have any idea who could be behind this?"

"They say they don't, but they're so upset right now, they don't know what they might know. I agree with Marge. I don't think this is political, and if it isn't, it's personal. Someone has been watching us. How else would they know when Kelly was alone? I know you all want to help, but right now, the best way to do that, is to carry on like nothing is wrong."

"OK," said John. "Suppose we go along with your plan. How do you explain Joe, Marty and you staying in London?"

"Well, obviously Joe and Marty have to stay here and wait for the kidnappers instructions," answered Madeline.

Chloe decided it was time for those nightcaps. She went to the bar, called out the choices, took their orders and suggested they move to the dining table. Suzie and Dolores came to help mix drinks and pour wine, while the others made their way across the room.

While drinks were passed out, Madeline looked around the table.

"Is that a smile I see there Darlin'?" asked Jake.

"I was just thinking. In all the tours I've led, and as bad as this whole situation is, I'm so lucky to be here with all of you. You know, in all my experience, I've never encountered such a remarkable group of people. I'm so proud of you. Who would have thought such a diverse group could become so completely devoted to one another after three days. I hope Kelly knows how much we all care about her."

"Madeline, do you really think we're being followed?" asked John.

"What other explanation is there? Marty left Kelly at the bootmaker a little before four o'clock. The Arcade closes at five-thirty, so she couldn't have been alone for more than an hour and a half. Whoever took her must have been watching her, waiting for the right opportunity."

"Madeline, do you think this was a random act by some terrorist? asked Dolores.

"I don't think so," Madeline replied, "because they called Joe, not a government official. If it had been a terrorist, they would have notified a news organization or the Prime Minister or some other public outlet to claim responsibility. They didn't do that. They called Joe directly."

"I see what you mean," said Jake, taking the glass of bourbon and water Suzie handed him. "But I still don't cotton to the idea of leavin' tomorrow. We're gonna need all the help we can get. Besides," he squared his shoulders, "I've never walked away from a fight in my life."

"Jake," said Chloe, drawing everyone's attention to the other end of the table, "think of it as providing a distraction. We need to make our departure as big of a production as possible so whoever is watching will have no doubt we are out of the way and that nobody but her parents know about the kidnapping. Then they can go ahead with their plan. It may even buy Kelly more time."

"Chloe's right," said Madeline. "As far as my staying is concerned, I can say I need to do something at the home office and I will catch up with you later. Greystone Manor isn't very far from London, only a couple of hours."

"And don't forget, we have cell phones," Chloe reminded them.

John shook his head and said, "Yes, but the problem with cell phones is, it's too easy to tap into a conversation. You could use them to feed the kidnappers false information, but a public phone booth will be more secure to let us know what's really happening."

"Good point," Madeline said as she pushed back from the table and stood, signaling the conclusion of the meeting. "OK, so we're all in agreement?" She could tell Jake was still unhappy. "I promise I will let you know everything that happens here and I really thank you all for your cooperation. Don't think of this as deserting the ship. You may even be helping to keep it afloat a little longer. And, please, be careful. Don't talk about any of this in a public place where you might be overheard."

After Chloe took everyone to the door, she returned to find Madeline in her bedroom pulling on a pair of jeans. Flopping down on the bed, she asked, "What's going on? Where are you going?"

"I have to go back upstairs. I left Robbie trying to convince the Dalton's to call Scotland Yard. We've got to have outside help." She slipped her bare feet into her old Birkenstocks, shoved her room key into her pocket and headed for the door.

Chloe jumped up and followed Madeline down the hall. "Is there anything I can do?"

"Yes. You're going to get a good night's sleep so you can lead your group tomorrow." As they reached the door, Madeline turned and pulled Chloe into a bear hug. "Wish me luck."

"You know I do."

"I'm so glad you're here."

"Me, too and Maddie, don't worry. It'll all work out. I don't know how, but you'll figure it out. I love you."

With her hand on the doorknob, Madeline looked at her best friend, smiled and said, "Love you too."

CHAPTER 12

▼

Tuesday, September 25, 11:30 PM
Who You Gonna Call? Scotland Yard!

Madeline knocked on the door of the Dalton's suite, and when Robbie opened it, she beckoned him out into the hall. "How's it going in there?"

"Not all that well I'm afraid. A stubborn lot they are. And your meeting?"

"Well, they're not happy about it, but they've agreed to go tomorrow as scheduled. Robbie, I had to tell them the truth."

"Ah, Maddie girl, you shouldn't have done that." He closed his eyes and shook his head in dismay.

"I had to," insisted Madeline. "They were refusing to leave and Jake was ready to call out a posse and ride to the rescue. I didn't have a choice."

"Do they realize how much danger could be waiting for them?"

"Yes, when I told them the truth. I told them they were being followed, so they had to keep up the pretense that everything's alright. They're all in agreement now and will be on their way to the Cotswolds in the morning."

"And if the kidnappers find out you're still here, what excuse are you going to use?"

"I'm going to say I have some business to take care of here and will meet them later. Now, what's happening in there?"

"They're sitting on the sofa, staring at the telephone, waiting for it to ring."

"And they won't budge on calling the police?"

"Just as I get one of them leaning that direction, the other panics again and then they both refuse."

"Mmm…"

"I see those wheels turning again Maddie girl. What are you thinking?"

"Come on. Let's go try another approach," Madeline replied, leading the way back into the Dalton's suite where Joe and Marty were indeed, sitting on the sofa.

"How are you holding up?" asked Madeline as she sat down in one of the chairs across from them.

"I don't really know," Joe answered shaking his head. "This whole thing just doesn't seem real. I keep expecting her to walk through the door, looking guilty because she stayed out too late. I just don't understand anything that's happening."

"Neither do I," Madeline answered, shrugging her shoulders.

"No one does," said Robbie as he circled behind Madeline and sat in the other chair.

"But, let's think about what we do know," she continued, leaning forward, resting her elbows on her knees and clasping her hands together. "We know Marty left Kelly at the bootmaker a little before four o'clock. Marty, had the consultation begun before you left or was Kelly still waiting?"

"She was still waiting. The clerk, or whoever he was, was finishing up with another customer."

"OK. We know the Arcade closes at five-thirty, so assuming her consultation actually took forty-five minutes, she couldn't have been alone for more than a half-hour. Robbie, can you tell what time the kidnapper's message came in?"

"Aye, they rang at seven-forty-five, just before we came up to check the suites."

"Why do you think she was taken before five-thirty?" Joe asked. "She could've been waiting for a cab or could have walked to another store."

"I don't think so," replied Madeline. "I don't think this was a random act. I hate to say it; I think this is personal."

"What am I missing here? I'm not a wealthy man," snapped Joe, running his fingers through his hair in utter frustration.

Marty touched his arm, trying to calm him down. "Listen to her," she said to him, "Madeline's only trying to help."

"Joe," Madeline said, trying to draw his attention back to practical matters. "You're a banker, right?"

"Not exactly, at least not in the traditional sense. My firm deals with investment banking, not the general public. We don't handle checking accounts or mortgages like First National Bank. Investment banks help companies, even governments, issue securities and help investors trade securities and manage their financial assets."

"More of a stock broker then," added Robbie, thinking how clever Madeline was to distract Joe by talking about his business.

"That's part of it, yes," Joe continued. "But our clients are small to mid-size companies, not individual investors. We help our clients manage their financial growth through investing in individual securities, setting up retirement plans for their employees, Venture Capitol, Mergers and Acquisitions, that sort of thing."

"Forgive me for saying," Robbie interjected, "but the last couple of years have been pretty hard on your investors, haven't they? Everybody's losing money right and left?"

"Well, there you go," said Madeline matter-of-factly, "we have ourselves a motive."

"What do you mean?" asked Marty. "Where is there a motive?"

Madeline stood up and began to pace, thinking out loud. "If we assume the motive for Kelly's disappearance is not political, then it stands to reason that it has to be personal. And, if whoever is behind this doesn't have an axe to grind with you personally and financially, then it must have something to do with your business and its finances."

Madeline came back and standing in front of Joe and Marty asked, "Are you sure you can't think of…No, wait," she thought a minute, "Who knew you were coming on this trip?"

"Our families, and some of our friends," answered Marty. "I imagine Kelly told everyone she knew. She was really excited about it."

Joe got up and walked toward the bar. Madeline called after him, "Joe, your office had to know, didn't they?"

"Yes, but originally just Marty and Kelly were supposed to go on this tour."

Madeline asked slowly. "Joe, if Marty and Kelly were originally supposed to make the trip alone, when did you decide to come with them?"

"About a month ago, I guess," he answered, getting a drink of water and returning to the sofa.

"And when were your meetings here set up?"

"I'm not sure exactly. Probably right after I decided to come."

"Who arranged those meetings for you?"

"My assistant coordinated everything with the London office. But Madeline, these people have been clients of the firm for years. I can't believe they could have had anything to do with this. For God's sake, Lloyd McPherson's grandfather knew my grandfather."

"Who else did you see?" asked Robbie.

Joe thought for a minute, then answered, "I had a meeting with Paul Rushton on Sunday morning. He and his staff anchor our Venture Capitol group here in London."

"Was it just him, or were there others?" Madeline wanted to know.

"No, it was the whole staff, Paul, his assistant and eight others. We discussed the pharmaceutical research companies here in the UK and in northern Europe we are considering for investment. His people had new research on a lab in The Netherlands and another one in Germany. That's why the meeting ran over and I couldn't get away to meet you for lunch in Covent Garden."

"Joe," Madeline said with urgency, "Don't you see? The problem is, too many people knew you were coming to London, both here and at home, and any one of them could have cooked up a plan to extort money from you. Maybe your personal bank account's not huge, but you've got the company's. The question is, who wants money from you and why? Joe we need help! And we need it now! We have to call Scotland Yard!"

"You heard what they said. They'll kill Kelly if we call the police." He stood and walked to the fireplace, raised his folded arms, leaned against the mantel and cried in despair, "What am I supposed to do?"

Marty looked on in silence as tears trickled down her cheeks.

Robbie went to Joe and rested a big hand on his shoulder. "We've got to call the Yard. There's no way we can track down that many people, and we need to have the voice tape analyzed. There might be something in the background we can't' hear. I have a good friend at Scotland Yard. There really isn't any other choice. Please let me call him."

Joe looked at Marty who nodded once, then looked back at Robbie and quietly said, "OK."

September 25, 11:55 PM

Despite the late hour, Robbie used his cell phone and dialed Chief Inspector Paul Graham at his home. His friend was most likely in bed, but Paul had been a police officer for many years and was used to having his sleep disturbed.

After several rings, a voice answered, "Graham here."

"Paul, its Robbie," he said in his thickest brogue, "It's been a long time. And how are ya this fine evenin'?"

He'd had lunch with Robbie only a few days ago and Robbie's country brogue didn't come out without a reason. Paul knew immediately something was wrong. "Robbie, you old dog, good to hear from you. It has indeed been a while."

"Aye," said Robbie, "Why don't you come meet Violet and me for a pint. We can catch up."

"The usual pub?"

"Aye, 405 Ascot."

"I'm on my way."

Putting his phone away, Robbie turned and said to his audience of three, "He'll be here straight away."

"Are you sure?" Marty asked.

"Oh yes," Robbie reassured her, "I told him to meet me here at the hotel, Suite 405. He knows to make sure he's not followed and to come in the restaurant door and use the room service lift. He may even come up in the dumb waiter."

"Oh," her eyebrows shot up, "That was in code!."

"Aye."

Wednesday, September 26, 1:25 AM

Paul and Robbie first met twenty years ago when they were both fresh from school and new to London. They met one night when a fight broke out in a neighborhood pub. Robbie and Paul teamed up to force the fight out into the street, saving the pub from severe damage. The owner had been so grateful he offered them free beer for a year. The young men often took advantage of the offer and had been fast friends ever since.

Chief Inspector Paul Graham was a wiry man, a good head shorter than Robbie. Dressed in jeans and a black turtleneck with a stocking cap covering his light brown hair, he could have passed for a common laborer between the ages of thirty and fifty instead of an Oxford educated gentleman.

A soft rapping on the door signaled Graham's arrival. "Thanks for coming," Robbie said as he opened the door and they clasped hands.

"I take it this is serious," Paul said.

"Aye, I'm afraid it's worse, a kidnapping. Come, meet the poor lassie's parents."

Entering the suite, Robbie announced, "Mr. and Mrs. Dalton, I'd like you to meet Chief Inspector Paul Graham, Specialist Operations, New Scotland Yard."

Paul shook hands with Joe and Marty. "And this is Madeline Marlborough, their tour director," Robbie continued, while Paul crossed to shake her hand as well.

Paul spotted the tape recorder on the dining table and walking toward it said, "If we could sit at the table, I'll be wanting to take some notes." After everyone was seated, he continued, "Robbie, why don't you start at the beginning."

After almost an hour, Paul sat back and flipped through his copious notes. It was now, almost three in the morning and everyone's exhaustion was visible. They sat in silence, waiting for him to speak.

Finally Paul put down his notebook and folded his hands, his voice breaking through the silence deliberately, "I agree with Madeline and Robbie. I think this crime is personal rather than politically motivated. Everything you've said points me away from a terrorist act.

"So, what happens now?" asked Madeline.

"The first thing we need to do is get this tape to our laboratory. They will be able to eliminate the distortion and isolate any anomalies in the background noise. We also need to secure the phone lines into the hotel and here in your suite. When the kidnappers call back, we'll be able to trace the call and also get a more sophisticated recording."

Turning to Joe he continued, "I'll also need a list of everyone in your offices, both here and in the States who could have known you were coming to London and a complete client list."

Joe snapped to attention and blurted out, "If the kidnappers find out, they'll kill Kelly."

"Every kidnapper makes the same threat, but very rarely do they ever carry it through. A dead hostage is of no use to them, especially if money is the prime objective. Please trust me, Mr. Dalton. No one will know we're here."

"How can you do all this and make them think we haven't called the police?"

"When will they call again?" asked Marty.

"The second call always comes within the first twenty-four hours. I'll have one of our technicians install the recording equipment, and," he added, looking at Robbie and Madeline, "If one of you would stay until I return…"

"Of course," said Madeline. "Joe, why don't you and Marty try to get some rest. We'll take care of everything out here and wake you immediately, if anything happens."

They tried to protest, but Madeline was insistent. "You're going to need all your strength tomorrow, or rather today. You can't help Kelly if you can't think straight."

Reluctantly, Joe got up and said to Marty, "Honey, you go on. I'll work on the list for Inspector Graham and join you in a few minutes."

"Alright," Marty said, "and thank you, all of you." She stood, walked slowly to the bedroom, went inside and closed the door.

Joe found a piece of paper and began writing, while Paul retrieved the tape of the kidnapper's call and his notes. On the way to the door, he indicated he wanted a word with Robbie and Madeline.

"I don't think the next call will come until morning," he told them, "but if it does, record it, same as this one," he patted the pocket of his jeans. "And Robbie, there's a mole somewhere amongst your staff. Someone had to keep tabs on the Dalton's activities and inform the kidnappers when it was safe to strike."

With a deep sigh Robbie said, "I was afraid you were going to say that."

"We'll need to come up with a story to explain our presence in the hotel," Paul continued. "Additional maintenance and housekeeping staff usually works best. Nothing high profile. We'll need to move about as anonymously as possible."

"Right," said Robbie, already forming a plan. "I'll leave uniforms and a housekeeping cart for you in the kitchen. How many will you need?"

"I'll ring you when I get back to the Yard."

Pulling a business card out of his pocket, Robbie wrote out the security code needed to open the back door of the hotel's restaurant and handed it to Paul.

"I'll be back," said Paul as he turned toward the dumb waiter. "Be careful."

CHAPTER 13

▼

Wednesday, September 26 3:00 AM
Cough Up The Cash

Within the hour, Chief Inspector Paul Graham returned to Ascot House with two of his best technicians and a deputy inspector. The tape of Kelly's kidnappers had been safely delivered to the Specialist Operations' sound laboratory at New Scotland Yard. Punching in the numeric security code, Paul quickly surveyed the premises to make sure they were alone, then held the rear door of La Violette open while his crew silently carried their equipment into the kitchen.

Spotting the housekeeping cart Robbie had left for them, they found staff uniforms; maintenance coveralls for the men and a housekeeping uniform for Deputy Inspector Helen Bainbridge. If, as Paul suspected, there was a mole amongst the hotel staff, they would be able to blend in. Quickly changing their clothes, they stashed their sound equipment, fiber-optic phone cable, laptop computers and tool boxes in the bag of the cart, then used their street clothes as camouflage. The four agents from Specialist Operations, Division Seven, moved stealthily through the kitchen to the service lift.

They found the fourth floor hall completely deserted and, in the pre-dawn silence, the three maintenance men followed the housekeeper to the door of suite 405. A light tap summoned Robbie who opened the door

"All quiet?" asked Paul as they entered the Dalton's suite.

"Nothing yet," confirmed Robbie.

"All right gentlemen, lets get our equipment in place whilst we still have time," Paul said to his men. Turning back to Robbie, he added, "This is Deputy Inspector Helen Bainbridge. She will stay here in the suite so we can come and go as necessary."

The men took their equipment from Helen's cart and went to work. Reaching into the laundry bag, Paul pulled out three cell phones and, handing them to Robbie explained, "These are secure lines for you, Madeline and Mrs. Ambrose. They'll allow you to safely speak to each other, as well as to Helen and myself. They also have tracking devices allowing me to monitor your whereabouts. The small key with the raised star is the panic button. If you're in trouble, press it down hard, until it locks, and the tracking device will lead us to you. The keyboard can also be used for instant messaging if you're unable to speak for any reason. Don't worry about accidentally hitting the panic button. It takes quite a bit of pressure to activate."

Robbie took the phones, immediately tried the panic button and was satisfied it would be difficult to set off by mistake.

Robbie looked up as Paul continued, "We'll also need access to your communications office or wherever the main phone box is located, so we can get everything wired before your morning staff arrives at seven-thirty."

Pausing, Paul took a good look at his friend, "You're dead on your feet, old man. Helen is here now. Why don't you catch a few hours rest."

"Thanks, I will. The main phone board is in the reservations office behind La Violette's private dining room." Taking a card from his pocket, Robbie jotted down some numbers and handed it to Paul. "Here's the security code to unlock the door. Actually, the office doesn't open until eight o'clock. Will that give you enough time?"

"More than enough. What time does Mrs. Ambrose leave with her group?" Paul asked.

"They're scheduled for breakfast at eight o'clock and departure at nine."

"Perhaps you can catch her before breakfast and show her how to use the phone. Madeline will stay here, correct?"

"Yes," Robbie answered unable to stifle a yawn. "You'll let me know if the call comes in?"

"Of course."

"OK. I'll be down in the staff suite if you need me. See you in a couple of hours."

Robbie let himself out and walked toward the lift, hesitated, then turned and decided to take the stairs instead. Reaching the second floor, his tired body automatically gravitated toward Madeline's suite where he found himself at her door, his hand raised, ready to knock. Suddenly, the door opened and Madeline, with a startled look on her face, ran right into his chest.

"Oh my God, Robbie," she cried, trying to maintain her balance. "You scared me to death! What are you doing here?"

He was as startled as she and threw his arms around her to keep her from falling. "I just came to see if you were up," he sputtered, trying to catch his breath.

"Of course, I'm always up at four in the morning. Did Paul get back yet?" Her balance restored, Madeline let go of Robbie and looked up and down the hall. Even though it was deserted, she grabbed his hand and pulled him into the suite. "I know it's almost daybreak, but we shouldn't risk being seen."

Robbie followed her into the drawing room and headed toward the sofa in front of the fireplace.

Sitting beside him, Madeline asked, "Any word yet?"

"No, all's quiet, and to answer your first question, yes. Paul and his people are upstairs installing their high-tech toys as we speak. He even brought some for us," he said pulling three slim cell phones from his breast pocket. "There's one for you, one for Chloe and one for me. Paul and Helen have the other two."

"Wait a minute," Madeline said, shaking her head. "Who's Helen?"

"She's Paul's deputy inspector and will stay with the Daltons around the clock so the rest of us can come and go without leaving Joe and Marty alone."

"Good. What's the deal with these phones?" Madeline asked as she examined the ordinary looking instrument.

"They're equipped with a secure line between the five of us and they also have a tracking device. We can be in constant contact with each other without being overheard and Paul will be able to monitor our whereabouts, so if anything looks unusual, he…"

"…can call out the cavalry?" Madeline asked, raising an eyebrow.

"Aye," answered Robbie with a weary smile. "And if Chloe and her charges run amok, we'll know where to find them."

The smile vanished from Madeline's face, replaced by a worried frown. "God, Robbie, Kelly's a strong girl, but she has to be scared out of her mind. I hope they haven't hurt her."

Robbie took Madeline's hand and tried to reassure her, "Don't borrow trouble Maddie girl. Paul's convinced they only want money, and, if that's the case, they would be foolish to harm her."

Putting his arm around Madeline's shoulder, she relaxed against his side as they sat in exhausted silence, each lost in their own thoughts, and each drawing comfort and strength from the other.

Finally, Madeline muttered, "I just feel so responsible."

"Maddie, there's nothing you could have done. It's not your fault."

"I keep telling myself that."

"Well, believe it. Whoever's behind this would have snatched Kelly anyway."

"I know," Madeline sighed as she left Robbie's embrace and stood up.

Robbie stood up next to her, his shoulders rounded with fatigue. "We're nei-ther of us going to be any good to anyone if we don't get some sleep."

Madeline nodded her head in agreement.

As they walked towards the door, Robbie explained how to activate the panic button on the phone, so she could show Chloe in the morning, and told her he would call on the cell if he heard anything.

Reaching the door, his hand on the doorknob, Robbie turned and gave Made-line a quick kiss goodnight, the act so spontaneous it was as if he had been kissing her goodnight for years. "I'll meet you for breakfast and help see the group off to Oxford."

"Good," Maddie answered, adding, "Then we can decide on our own plan for the day."

He kissed her again, quietly closing the door behind him.

September 26, 4:45 AM

Paul Graham walked into the kitchen of the Dalton's suite and found Thomas Kent putting the finishing touches on the wiring of the digital voice equipment they would use to record the next call from Kelly's kidnappers. "You're about ready then, are you Thomas?" Paul asked, pouring himself another cup of coffee from the half-empty pot on the counter.

"Almost," Kent replied. "Did Darby have any trouble with the main board?"

"None at all. SO7 can now hear every call coming into the hotel as well as those going out, and every call between extensions within the hotel. If our mole tries to pass any information, we should be able to intercept it."

Kent taped one last wire, replaced the cover on the back of the recorder and turned to the Chief Inspector saying, "Ready for a test sir."

"Right then," said Paul. He went into the drawing room to find that the phone and a set of earphones had been moved to the dining table where Helen was waiting. Paul took the headset signaling Helen to pickup the receiver. "Ready when you are."

As Helen lifted the receiver, a red light began to flash, indicating the digital recorder was working. She spoke a few words, then hung up.

Kent emerged from the kitchen with a smile, "Everything's working perfectly sir"

"Alright then," said Chief Inspector Graham, looking at his watch. "It's almost five o'clock. Now we wait."

Joe awakened to the sound of voices in the living room. Assuming Paul and Robbie were talking, he opened the bedroom door and saw Graham standing a few feet away, speaking to a maintenance man and a maid. As Paul heard the door and turned, motioning him to join them, Joe stepped out and quietly closed the door behind him so as not to awaken Marty who had finally fallen asleep.

"Were you able to sleep at all?" asked Paul

"I dozed a little," Joe answered, stifling a yawn. "Marty fell asleep a little while ago." Reaching into his shirt pocket he handed Paul a slip of paper, "I thought of a few more names," and nodding toward Helen and Thomas, he asked, "Who are these people?"

Paul was making introductions when there was a light tap on the main door to the suite. Using his passkey, Nick Darby entered and made his way down the hall to join the others. "Now that we're all here," said Paul, "lets have a seat around the dining table and I'll demonstrate the equipment."

Overwhelmed by all the electronics and looking a little lost, Joe sighed as he sat down. Noting the bewilderment on his face, Helen asked, "Would you like some coffee, Mr. Dalton?"

"Coffee would be great, black, one sugar. Thank you." "I'll get it," said Darby, disappearing into the kitchen and returning with a steaming mug and a plate of cookies. "Not exactly a proper English breakfast, I'm afraid," he apologized.

"Thanks, it will do just fine."

Joe looked around the table, amazed at the similarities between these four people. "So this is Scotland Yard?" he thought to himself. Joe wasn't sure what he'd expected, but they weren't it.

To Joe, Scotland Yard, just the sound of it, conjured up images of fearless, distinguished detectives on the trail of fiendish criminals like Jack the Ripper. Maybe he'd seen too many Sherlock Holmes movies because these guys didn't look or sound anything like Basil Rathbone. They were more like the computer geeks he knew in college. The three men were all about the same size. If you looked closely, Paul was obviously older, about my age, Joe thought, but they all could easily pass for the same age. They were ordinary, average guys; average height, average build, average everything. Looking at Helen, the word dowdy sprang to mind. Of course a little makeup might make a difference and the uniform only added to his first impression.

"Whenever you pick up the receiver," Paul was saying, "you'll see the red light flash, indicating the digital recorder is working. We'll also be able to hear everything through the earphones. The trick is to keep our caller talking long enough to trace the call."

No, they certainly weren't the movie version of super-sleuths. Joe took a sip of the strong coffee and focused again on Paul's instructions.

"It doesn't take as long to trace a call as it did in the past. We need ninety seconds from the moment you lift the receiver," Paul continued, pointing to the digital clock on the recorder. "The timer will let you know when it's safe to hang up."

"How am I going to keep this guy talking? Won't he be a little suspicious?"

"Not necessarily," answered Paul. "People who kidnap for ransom usually fall into two categories, those who are desperate for money and those who are out to punish the victim or the victim's family. In either case, the kidnapper needs to be in control. He will need to assure himself that you know he holds all the cards. If you play to that power, his ego will keep him talking. If you put him on the defensive, he will, most likely, make his ransom demand and hang up."

"Great," Joe muttered in frustration. "So what do I say to this guy to feed his ego?"

"Ask him about Kelly," Paul answered. "Say you want to talk to her to make sure she's alive. Depending on his response, you can even plead for her safety. Ask him what he wants. He may specify a ransom amount, or, if we get lucky, he may give us an idea of why he's kidnapped your daughter."

Closing his eyes, Joe shook his head and said, "I don't know if I can do this."

"We'll be right here with you," Helen reassured him.

"And, don't forget," Paul added, "I'll be able to hear the conversation as well, so I can feed you questions."

Joe took a deep breath, steadied his nerves, then said with resolve, "OK, what do we do now?"

"Now we wait," Paul answered. Glancing at his watch, it was almost six o'clock. Kelly had been missing nearly twelve hours and he was well aware the trail was growing colder by the minute. The analysts at SO7 had been working all night on the voice tape and the name list Joe had provided, but the background checks were more likely to eliminate suspects than pinpoint anyone in particular. The city would soon be awake and going about its business, allowing his agents to begin a canvas of anyone who might have seen anything, and hopefully, by monitoring the hotel phone system they would ferret out the staff mole.

The shrill ring of the phone jolted them to attention. Joe reached for the receiver as Paul put on the earphones and after the second ring, picked it up and said, "Hello?"

"So Dalton, did you sleep well?" Even though the voice was distorted, it dripped with sarcasm.

Joe could see the red light flashing and digital clock counting backwards, ninety, eighty-nine. He quickly looked at Paul who made a circle with his index finger, telling him to start talking.

"No," Joe answered, "of course I didn't sleep. You have my daughter."

"And a lovely thing she is too," the voice taunted. "So lusciously long and willowy."

Paul cautioned Joe not to lose his temper.

With a calmness he didn't feel, Joe asked, "What have you done with her? Is she alright? I want to talk to her."

Sixty-five, Sixty-four.

"In good time, Dalton. Your darling daughter is alive, maybe a bit uncomfortable, but still breathing, and as long as you follow instructions, she'll stay that way."

Fifty-one, Fifty.

Paul nodded to Joe in encouragement. The kidnapper was playing with him, a good thing because his malicious taunts were allowing the precious seconds to tick away, which they needed to trace the call.

"What do you want?" Joe asked.

"Your misery…and ten million pounds," the voice said, "a small price to pay, considering."

"Considering what?" Joe answered, staggered by the outrageous demand. "My God man, that's fifteen million dollars. I don't have fifteen million dollars."

Thirty-six, Thirty-five.

"Of course you do, you bastard. Think about it."

"Look, I don't know where you're getting your information, but there is no way I have fifteen million dollars."

Twenty-six, Twenty-five.

"Think outside the box, Dalton. You have twenty-four hours to figure it out. In the meantime, remember, your lovely, leggy daughter is under my control and I shan't hesitate to use her and kill her if you don't do exactly as I say. I'll call you with further instructions."

Eight, Seven.

"Wait! Let me talk to her," Joe shouted, stalling for time. "Please! You have to let me talk to her!"

One

"That can be arranged. Stay tuned," the voice laughed and hung up.

"Good work, Joe," Paul said, elated that Joe had kept the kidnapper talking long enough to complete the trace.

Joseph Dalton, his hand still on the receiver, laid his head on the table and cried.

CHAPTER 14

▼

Wednesday, September 26, 5:00 AM
A Clue and a Departure

Floating on the edge of the abyss between sleep and consciousness, Kelly thought surely she must be caught in the midst of a horrendous nightmare. It was like a horror movie playing through her mind, the same loop of film repeating itself over and over. Her mother was hurt and she was trying to reach her but the driver of the limo morphed into not one, but two men, a skinny nasty man, who tied her up and hit her, and his big fat partner. They were like the two guys in *101 Dalmatians* who stole the puppies, only instead of puppies, they had taken her.

Drifting up through the layers of fog, the movie disappeared, as she slowly became aware of her surroundings. The rustling sound in the space above her, made her cringe, her eyes shut tight, not wanting to know if there were critters up there. Even though she could feel the weight of the scratchy blanket covering her, she was cold and her exposed feet were freezing. Neither the mattress nor the blanket was long enough to accommodate her six-foot frame.

Fully awake now, Kelly realized her predicament was definitely not a bad dream. The burning pain in her right shoulder was all too real. She knew if she moved, the pain would only get worse, so she lay there, eyes still closed,

Hungry and shivering with cold, Kelly lay stretched out like a human sacrifice, staked, chained and unable to move. The fire in her right shoulder was beginning to creep up her arm toward her tethered wrist and hand, which were completely numb. There was nothing she could do until the Boss and Frank returned, so she applied the same strategy she'd used the night before and concentrated on solving the puzzle of why she had been kidnapped, where she was now, and how she was going to get a message to her father.

She finally opened her eyes and was surprised at how much she was actually able to see. It had to be morning because bright daylight was streaming under the door and, for the first time, she was able to get a good look at her prison. She rolled her head to the left, then raised up to look past her feet. She was in the corner of an oblong room, larger than she'd originally imagined. The walls were made of stone with a thatched ceiling overhead. The wooden door was in the middle of the opposite wall and the light from underneath illuminated several large, flat round stones that must have been used to grind grain. A pile of rotting wood was heaped in the far corner. Now that she thought about it, the room reminded her of the old Graue Mill in Hinsdale, Illinois, only on a smaller scale.

Kelly had visited the Graue Mill and Museum on a high school field trip. The mill is the only working, water-driven grist mill in Illinois and was a "station" on the Underground Railroad. Kelly remembered the huge buhrstones used to grind the grain and thought the stones in her prison were smaller versions of the same thing. Now, with the light shining in, she could see there was room at the other end of the building for a set of wooden gears to turn the stones, and Frank had told her the river was used by local monks to operate a mill.

That was it, her clue! If its ransom they want, like in the movies, they have to let talk me talk to Daddy, she thought. Somehow she had to mention the Graue Mill and pray he could figure out what she was trying to tell him.

September 26, 6:10 AM

Chloe knocked on Madeline's bedroom door. When there was no response, she knocked again, then slowly opened the door and saw Madeline, fully clothed, sprawled on the bed, mouth open, snoring like a truck driver. No wonder Maddie hadn't heard her knock. She smiled, walked to the bed and shook Madeline's shoulder.

"Maddie," Chloe said, "Wake up, it's after six and you need to get in the shower."

Madeline sat straight up and asked, "Have you heard anything? Did he call?"

"No, No, nothing yet, at least not that I know of. I hate to wake you, but you wanted to meet with the group before we leave for Oxford. Did you get any rest at all?"

"I think Robbie left around four. He brought us special cell phones to use. Let me get cleaned up and I'll show you how they work."

Chloe went into the bathroom, turned on the hot water, then left Madeline to shower and change. "Coffee's ready when you are," she said over her shoulder as she left and Maddie walked into the bathroom.

Looking far better than she felt, Madeline joined Chloe at the dining table. "Its amazing what a designer blouse will do for you, to say nothing of the clearance rack at Lord and Taylor," she commented as she sat down.

"Hey," Chloe said, passing her a cup of steaming coffee, "you look pretty good for only having two hours sleep."

Madeline, who considered herself the queen of bargain shopping, was wearing a black and white Ralph Lauren shirt and matching black linen pants she had found on the clearance rack at Lord and Taylor last season. They had been marked down several times and, with a coupon for an extra twenty percent off, the whole outfit, including shoes, was under eighty dollars.

Madeline sat down, grateful for the coffee Chloe had poured, and explained the features of the secure-line phone. "There's even a tracking device and a panic button. Graham thought of everything."

"I think I should let my group know about this," suggested Chloe. "You never know when one of them might need to use it."

"Definitely," replied Madeline. "At this point, I think we all need to know what everyone else is doing and where we are. I don't care if Chief Inspector Graham likes it or not."

Finishing up their coffee, they left for the dining room. As they got the to bottom of the stairs they met Jake and Suzie coming out of the lift.

Jake was about to ask if they had any news when Robbie came sailing across the hall. "Jake, hold the door please." While taking Madeline's elbow and steering her into the lift, he continued, "We'll meet you in the private dining room in a few minutes."

"I guess that answers my question," Jake muttered under his breath. Beaming broadly for anyone who happened to be looking and with his best cowboy flourish, he said, "Ladies, let's grub!" With Chloe and Suzie on either side, the trio headed toward the dining room.

As the lift started up, Madeline met Robbie's eyes with a questioning look. He blinked once, then glanced toward the security camera concealed in the upper right-corner ceiling panel, signaling her to keep quiet.

Getting off at the fourth floor, they silently walked down the hall to room 405, where Robbie used his passkey to open the door. Once inside Robbie turned to Madeline, fatigue showing in his speech, "Maddie girl, we canna say anathing in the lift until I clear the guard who monitors the security camera. I dinna think he's our traitor, but I have to make sure."

Madeline nodded in agreement asking, "Robbie, what's happened?"

"The second call came in about an hour ago and Paul wants to fill us in over breakfast."

Of the six people seated around the dining table, Madeline only recognized Graham, Joe and Marty. After Graham introduced his staff, Madeline went to the sideboard, and helped herself. "So you've heard from the kidnapper again," she said, bringing her cup of coffee back to the table and sitting down next to Marty.

"Yes we have," answered Paul. "The tape is being analyzed as we speak. Joe did an excellent job keeping our man talking long enough to do a trace. Unfortunately the call was made from a phone box at Victoria Station. Nonetheless, we learned a lot about the caller."

"How so?" Madeline asked curiously.

"Well, to begin with," Paul continued, "the second caller's voice was electronically distorted, while the first was muffled by a rag or some kind of cloth. I can't confirm it yet, but when the report comes back, I think it will say the calls were made by two different people, from two different locations."

"How can you be sure?" asked Robbie.

"The background noise," answered Helen Bainbridge.

"Right you are," Paul affirmed.

Joe looked up from his half eaten breakfast plate, paused briefly and shaking his head added, "And we also know this is personal, very personal, though for the life of me, I don't know how or why."

Paul relayed to Madeline and Robbie what the others had already heard and they agreed to meet again at eleven o'clock to share information.

September 26, 8:10 AM

Chloe, Jake and Suzie entered the private dining room of La Violette and found the Talbot sisters and the Shepards gathered in front of the sideboard at the far end of the room, filling their breakfast plates while chatting quietly. A uniformed waiter Chloe didn't recognize, was filling water glasses at the table and Roger, whom they all knew, was about to carry Millie's plate for her.

"Mornin' y'all," greeted Jake. "Somethin' sure smells good." Walking up to the new waiter, Jake extended his hand, "Don't believe we've met."

"Thornton, sir," said the young man with a curt bow of his head. He set down the water pitcher long enough to shake Jake's hand.

"Haven't seen you before," Jake questioned. "You new here?"

"No sir, I've been on holiday, visiting my family in Cornwall, and only just returned," Thornton answered as he picked up his pitcher and continued to pour.

"Thornton's been with Ascot House three years now," interrupted Roger, not grasping why Jake was giving his colleague the third degree.

"That's wonderful," Chloe chimed in, understanding perfectly what Jake was after. "It's nice to meet you," she continued, smiling at the boy as she passed him on her way to the sideboard.

When they were all seated, Jake waited until the waiters were gone, then apologized, "Sorry Chloe, but we can't be too careful."

"I know," she answered, "but we can't be so obvious either. Look, Madeline will be here in a few minutes and I'm sure she'll let us know what's happening, but don't make a fuss if she doesn't say anything right away. This might not be the best place to talk, so just play along with whatever she says."

"Don't worry," said Marge, "we'll put on a show if need be." The others nodded in agreement.

Roger and Thornton returned with fresh pots of coffee and tea and the conversation immediately turned to the group's imminent departure for Oxford. Chloe was just telling them about Oxford and Blenheim Palace when Madeline and Robbie finally arrived.

"Good Morning everyone," Madeline said a little too brightly. "I hope you're all ready for a fantastic journey to the Cotswolds. I have some business here in the city, so Chloe will be taking over for me and I'll catch up with you tonight." Looking around the room, Madeline could tell each person knew she was being deliberately vague. "Are all the bags down?"

"I think so," Chloe answered for the group.

"I left my camera bag upstairs," John interjected. "I'll go up and get it now."

"Why don't you all check your suites one more time," suggested Madeline, "and be sure to check the bathroom. I'm always forgetting my toothbrush or leaving my nightgown on the hook behind the bathroom door."

"Trust me," Chloe added with a laugh, "she's left a trail of lingerie all over Europe."

As the group began to file out toward the lift, Chloe, already assuming her role as their leader, reminded them, "Fifteen minutes, people. We'll meet you on the bus."

Madeline and Chloe walked out of the dining room, just as Violet Hargrove came running toward them. Out of breath, she exclaimed, "Oh wonderful, I'm so glad I caught you. Father wants to say good bye before you leave."

"He's such a dear," Madeline said with a smile. "Actually I wanted to talk to him anyway. I…"

Robbie was suddenly beside Madeline, his eyes giving a look of warning, "I'm going that way," he said, smiling at Violet. "I'll let him know you'll be meeting at the coach in fifteen minutes."

"Thank you Robert," Violet said formally, as she turned and walked toward the hotel offices.

Chloe grabbed Madeline's arm and pulled her into the Ladies Room, looking around to make sure they were alone and asked, "What the hell was that all about?"

"You mean Robbie and Violet? I'm not sure. I've only met her a few times. She's always been nice enough, but kinda distant, you know?"

"She's probably jealous because Robbie's got a thing for you."

"Oh Chloe!" Madeline exclaimed with an exasperated roll of her eyes.

"All right. I know." Not wanting to start an argument, she quickly changed the subject. "So, did a second call come in?"

Madeline nodded her head. "Let's take a little walk, stretch our legs before the long bus ride."

"Good idea," said Chloe as she opened the door.

Once outside, Madeline told Chloe everything she knew about the last phone call and ransom demand. Reaching the end of the block, they pulled out their cell phones, tested them to make sure they were working properly, promised to check in with each other hourly and returned to the mini-bus which was parked outside the entrance to the hotel.

As Madeline and Chloe arrived at the front gate, Lord Hargrove and Violet were just coming down the front steps, chatting with Jake and Suzie. Lord Hargrove wished the group a safe journey and, with thank you's and good-byes they boarded the bus.

Anxious to get them on their way, Madeline stepped aboard and announced that Chloe was now in charge and would answer all their questions. When she returned to stand next to Lord Hargrove, he questioned curiously, "You're not going?"

Waving as the bus drove off, Madeline replied, "No, I have some business here in London, I'll catch up with them tonight."

"Is everything alright?" asked Violet. "I noticed the Dalton family wasn't with them."

Madeline didn't know whether or not to tell them the truth. While they might be useful in tracking down the informer on their staff, the fewer people who knew about the kidnapping, the better.

"Mrs. Dalton wasn't feeling well this morning, so they decided to stay."

"Have you called Dr. Stone?" asked Lord Hargrove as they turned and went back into the hotel. "He should see her right away."

"Actually, he saw her last night and was going to look in again this morning," Madeline said.

"Please let us know if there is anything we can do, anything at all."

"Thanks, I will and I'll see you before I leave."

She went to her suite and found Robbie on the sofa, looking very haggard.

Smiling at him she said, "If I sit down, I'll never be able to get up again, and you sir, don't look any better than I do."

"Aye lass," he chuckled. "I feel like I've done battle with a lory and the lory won."

"Aren't they going to miss you downstairs?"

"Nay, I don't work until noon."

"OK partner," Madeline said, grabbing her purse from the desk, "I'm ready when you are." Their mission was to interview the Beadles at the Burlington Arcade. As Robbie knew several of the officers, as well as some of the shop owners, he had convinced Paul that he and Madeline would be able to get more information without stirring up the speculation an agent from Scotland Yard would inevitably create.

"We shouldn't leave the hotel together. Why don't you take a taxi to The Ritz? The lobby is always busy, so you can lose yourself in the crowd, then go out the side door and walk to Fortnum and Masons."

"Good. I wanted to buy some blended tea there anyway."

"Right then, by the time I take the tube to Piccadilly, you should have your tea. The Arcade is just across the street. I'll meet you at Number 12."

As Robbie turned and headed for the door, Madeline called, "Robbie, wait a minute. We've got another problem."

He turned back to her as she continued, "Lord Hargrove and Violet know the Dalton's didn't leave with the group. They wanted to say goodbye to everyone and the Dalton's were obviously missing."

"What did you tell them?"

"I said Marty wasn't feeling well. What if they decide to look in on her and find all those people and equipment? Shouldn't we tell them what's going on?"

Robbie thought a minute, then said, "No, not yet. I'll I'll tell Paul to alert Helen. If anyone comes to the door, she can say Marty is resting. The "Do Not Disturb" sign on the door should take care of the maids."

"Yes, but I still think at least Lord Hargrove should know, even if we don't tell the rest of the family. And what about room service? Won't they think something is suspicious, taking up meals for an army?"

"I know there are a lot of loose ends," Robbie said, his frustration beginning to show, "but we really need to be on our way. We can work out the bumps when we get back."

"Fine" Madeline said curtly. "Its just that I keep thinking of all the things that could go wrong," she said, brushing past Robbie, grabbing her purse, throwing the door open with more force than necessary as she headed for the stairs. When she saw the hall was empty, she shot back over her shoulder, "I'll see you later," then ran down the stairs.

"Madeline, wait," Robbie shouted after her, but it was too late. She was gone.

Robbie stood there, thunderstruck. He'd never seen Madeline lose her temper before and the last thing he wanted was to have Madeline upset with him. He wasn't even sure what set her off. "Bloody hell," he muttered to himself as he closed the door, "you bungled that quite nicely."

After all, he only had a few hours before he had to take over the Concierge Desk and he needed to accomplish as much as possible. Stepping into the service lift, he was still muttering, "Lord help me, I'll never understand women, not as long as I live."

CHAPTER 15

▼

Wednesday, September 26, 9:45 AM
Beadles, Brainstorms and Who is the Mole?

Robbie emerged from the Tube Station at Piccadilly Circus, certain no one had followed him. He'd taken the service lift to the kitchen, then ducked out the back door of La Violette, circled around the back side of the US Embassy and headed for Marble Arch. Morning rush hour had come and gone and the usually crowded streets were almost deserted. Even the Marble Arch Tube Station had been empty.

He glanced at the familiar TDK/Sanyo sign in Piccadilly Circus, then turned and walked toward the Burlington Arcade. Crossing Sackville, he looked across the street, trying to spot Madeline in front of Fortnum and Mason, while hoping as well, she had cooled down a bit. She was nowhere to be seen, so he continued past the arched entrance of the Royal Academy of Arts and entered the Burlington Arcade.

Upon reaching Edward Green and Company, Robbie found Madeline already in deep conversation with the store manager.

As he opened the door, Madeline looked up and said, "Oh good, you're here," and gestured for him to join her. "Robbie, this is Mr. Plum. He took care of Kelly yesterday and remembers her very well."

She was smiling which Robbie took as a good sign and the shop was empty so they were able to speak freely.

"Excellent," said Robbie.

Mr. Plum was a curious little man with a bent back and knarled hands, the result of many years laboring over his designer's table and cobbler's bench. He had been completely captivated with Kelly's sweet personality and by her long shapely feet.

"Lovely girl. Very tall. Narrow feet," said Mr. Plum as he peered over his spectacles and shook Robbie's outstretched hand. "We finished just before closing time and I'm sure she said she was going back to her hotel. She's going to stop by for her impressions after she gets back from the Cotswolds on the thirtyth." He rifled through his appointment book. "Yes, here it is. If she's pressed for time, she said she'd let me know. I can always take the impressions at the hotel."

Thanking Mr. Plum for his help, Madeline and Robbie walked out, into the narrow arcade. "Well, we were right about the time Kelly left the shop," Madeline said, looking up and down the corridor for a Beadle.

"Maddie, I…" Robbie began.

"Look," Madeline interrupted, "About this morning. Too little sleep and too much coffee…"

Before she could say any more, Robbie threw his big arm around her, kissed the top of her head and laughed, "You're a treasure my darlin' Kate, and if that Beadle over there dinna look so disapproving, I'd kiss ya senseless, I would."

"Kate?" she questioned, raising her eyebrow. "Oh, OK Petrucio, I intend to hold you to that promise, but I'm warning you, this is one shrew you'll never tame."

"Come, you wench, I see an old friend," Robbie said, pulling her toward the next shop where a Beadle, in his top hat and long coat was standing by the door, his eyes scanning the crowd of shoppers. "Harold," Robbie called as they approached. Turning at the sound of his name, the officer smiled when he recognized his friend. "I was hoping you'd be on duty today."

"Well, Mr. MacDuff," the Beadle teased, "you're on the wrong side of town. Have you lost your way then?"

The two men laughed and shook hands, then Robbie introduced Harold to Madeline. "Madeline Marlborough, may I present Mr. Harold McKee."

"I'm afraid this isn't a social call, Harold. We need information," Robbie said in a hushed voice.

Handing Kelly's photo to Harold, Robbie said, "Do you recognize this young lady?"

"She would have been here yesterday afternoon," added Madeline.

Studying the photograph, Harold nodded his head in recognition. "Yes. I remember her quite well. It was just about five-thirty, time to lock the gate. She stopped me and asked if it would be easy to find a taxi, when a chauffeur shouted out her name. I think he called her Miss Balldon or Dalton. I was about to reprimand him for shouting. We don't allow shouting here you know, but he said the young lady's mother had been in a traffic accident and he'd been sent to drive her to the hospital."

"Do you remember what the man looked like or what he was wearing?" Madeline asked.

Trying to recall if there were any distinguishing marks on the chauffeur's uniform, Harold answered, "The whole incident happened so quickly. Now that I think about it, I don't know if he was wearing a uniform or a dark suit. I know he definitely wore a chauffeur's cap and said he'd been sent to drive the young lady."

"Can you describe him, Harold? Was he tall, short, thin? Anything you can remember would help immeasurably," Robbie asked.

"I'm afraid nothing else stands out. He was average height, average…no, wait. His shoes. They were quite scruffy looking, as if he'd never cared for them at all. I remember his shoes because they were not only in sharp contrast to the rest of his attire, but no chauffeur would have unpolished shoes."

Madeline looked down at Harold's shoes and then at Robbie's, both so highly polished she could almost see her reflection.

"Did you see the car?" Robbie asked.

"I'm sorry, no I didn't, but George Fellows locked the gate last night. Perhaps he saw them leave. I believe he's posted at the entrance today as well."

Following Harold to the front entrance, they found Mr. Fellows was indeed at his post. He told them a late model black limousine had pulled up in the no parking zone in front of the entrance at five twenty-five the previous afternoon. The driver told him there was an emergency and asked him to watch the car while he found his passenger. Returning shortly with a very tall young lady, he helped her into the back seat and drove away.

"Were there any markings on the car, anything that would indicate it's origin?" Robbie asked.

Mr. Fellows couldn't think of anything, "No, nothing exceptional, although the car was disgracefully dusty. It must have been a genuine emergency, otherwise the limousine would have been properly washed."

Looking at his watch, Robbie realized it was nearly time for their meeting with Paul back at the hotel.

"Thanks to you both," said Madeline, bidding farewell to the two Beadles. "You've been very helpful."

"Aye, you've given us more than you know," added Robbie, taking Madeline's arm and leading her out of the Arcade.

Preferring to err on the side of caution, they didn't want to arrive back at the hotel together, so Robbie hailed a taxi for Madeline and, after making sure she was safely on her way, headed back to take the Tube.

September 26, 8:00 AM

Joe Dalton sat down on the bed and stared at the phone in front of him as if it were a monster. He knew he had to pickup the receiver and call his father, but his sense of dread was as acute as when he was waiting for the kidnapper's call. How was he going to tell his dad about Kelly? She had been the first grandchild in the family and Grandpa's little princess since the day she was born. And what about the ransom? He didn't have fifteen million dollars. The bastard told him to "Think outside the box". What the hell was that supposed to mean? Did he mean the company? Fifteen million dollars would bankrupt the firm and he wasn't even sure they could liquidate that much cash in twenty-four hours without borrowing from their client's funds. The monster Bell had invented stared back at him, not caring that he felt desperate, helpless and trapped in his hotel suite.

Joe needed to talk to his father, but all the phones in the hotel were being monitored by Scotland Yard and he wasn't ready for them to listen in, especially since he didn't know what his dad was going to say. Besides, he couldn't leave until he'd talked to Kelly. The kidnapper said he would arrange it, but didn't say when. Feeling more and more like a caged tiger, if he didn't get out of here and do something, he was going to go crazy.

Just then Marty opened the door and asked, "What are you doing in here?"

"We need to talk," Joe answered in a hushed voice. "Shut the door."

"Joe, what is it?"

"I need to talk to Dad. Maybe he can tell us who's doing this. But I can't call from here. All the phones are tapped."

"What could he tell you that we don't know already?"

"I don't know, but you heard what the kidnapper said. He doesn't just want the money, he wants us to suffer. There has to be a reason."

"Well then, call him."

"From where? As soon as I leave, Kelly will call."

"I'll talk to her and the conversation will be taped. You can listen to it when you get back," she said, putting her arms around his neck and pulling his head to her breast.

Joe threw his arms around her waist and clung to her, absorbing the warmth of her body. Marty wordlessly ran her hands over his back, comforting him as if he were a child. It had always been this way, when she fell apart, he was strong, and when he needed help, their roles reversed and she became a tower of strength.

"Joe," she whispered. "I'm sure they have phones at the Embassy, or you could take a taxi to one of the train stations. You can't go to Victoria. That's where he called from, but Paddington's closer anyway. I'm positive they have international phones. I'll wait here in case Kelly calls."

Joe looked up at her. "Good idea and remember, Kelly's a smart girl. She may try to give us a clue about her location."

"I'll get as much information as I can."

"I know you will," Joe said, lifting one hand to touch her cheek. "Marty, I love you, with all my heart I love you."

Marty cupped his face with her hands, bent down and kissed him, saying into his mouth, "I love you too."

When they went into the living room, they found Helen Bainbridge sitting on the sofa, reading a report.

"Where is everybody?" asked Joe.

Helen looked up and saw the anguished fatigue etched on their faces. Although she gave the appearance of control, rigid and at arm's length, in reality, she would never get used to the pain and anguish the parents and loved ones of the victim suffered. "How are you holding up? Can I get anything for you?"

"As can be expected, I guess. I don't know." Joe answered. "How do people get through this? Is there any news?"

"Chief Inspector Graham has gone to the laboratory to see the voice analysis. Kent and Darby are working on background checks of the names you gave us."

"I'm going out for few minutes, take a walk or something," Joe said, walking toward the door. "I need to clear my mind."

"Yes, of course. I understand how hard this is for you, but don't be gone too long, and remember, everyone is returning here at eleven."

"I'll be back long before that," Joe assured her as he stepped into the hall and closed the door.

Walking around the corner, hurrying toward the US Embassy, Joe had second thoughts about using their phones and decided instead to go to Paddington Station. He flagged down a taxi and, in less than ten minutes, was in the middle of the busy train station, looking for the international phones. Rather than prowl the entire station, he found the information desk where a middle-aged lady pointed him toward the bank of phones on the north wall, near the shower facilities. He found the phone booth designated for credit card calls, took a deep breath, went in and dialed his father's number.

As the phone rang, Joe went over in his mind yet again what he was going to say, but when Edward Dalton said, "Hello," he was struck speechless.

"Hello, is anyone there?" Ed asked, impatiently. Thinking it was another tele-marketing call, he was ready to hang up, when he heard a faint voice on the other end of the line.

"Dad?"

"Joey?" Ed asked. "Joey, is that you? I can hardly hear you."

His parents were the only people in the world who still called him Joey, and hearing the familiarity of his name erased his nervousness and filled him with relief. He'd always been able to count on his father's help and together, they would figure out what to do.

"Yeah Dad, its me. Is that better?" Joe asked, his voice now filled with confidence.

"Much better. Where are you?"

"At a phone booth in Paddington Station."

"What?"

"I can't risk being overheard or traced. Dad, you'd better sit down."

"I am sitting down. Joey, what's wrong? Something's happened, hasn't it?"

In that instant, Joe decided to get right to the point, so he plunged ahead, "Dad, its Kelly. She's been kidnapped."

In disbelief Ed said, "What? I didn't hear you."

"It's true Dad. She and Marty went shopping yesterday afternoon. Marty came back early and Kelly was supposed to meet us for dinner and never showed up."

"What happened?"

"Dad, there was a message from the kidnapper on the phone in our suite."

Ed Dalton felt like he'd been sucker punched and was on the brink of passing out. His mouth was working, but words wouldn't come.

"Dad, are you there?" Joe asked.

Regaining some if his composure, Ed finally answered,

"Who did this Joey, what do they want?"

"I don't know who they are, but what they want is ten million pounds. I was hoping you could help me with that part."

"Ten million pounds, that's fifteen million dollars."

"I know. Dad, I told the guy I didn't have that kind of money and he laughed at me and told me to 'look outside the box'. Dad, I don't know what that means. He gave me twenty-four hours to figure it out. Dad, you've got to help me," Joe pleaded in desperation.

"Outside the box," Ed muttered, thinking outloud. "Outside the box. Joey, did this guy say anything else?"

"Yes. When I asked him what he wanted, he said, 'Your misery and ten million pounds.' Dad, he knows me…"

Ed's mind was racing. "Not necessarily," he interrupted, "he may be trying to get to me through you." He'd made plenty of enemies over the years. What successful businessman hadn't? But why now and why in London? Then he stopped, dead in his tracks. His mouth suddenly parched, he choked out, "Andrews, Nigel Andrews."

"Who?" Joe asked, not familiar with the name.

"Nigel Andrews," his father repeated. "He owned the London branch before we acquired it."

"But Dad, that was twenty years ago. What could that possibly have to do with Kelly?"

"Joey, we acquired Andrews Investments Limited when Nigel Andrews was convicted of stock fraud and sent to prison. He had gambled away his client's money and thought he could repair the damage by flooding the market with phony securities. One of his clients was a friend of mine. He thought something shady was going on, so I looked into the situation for him and discovered the fraud. When I reported it, Andrews was arrested. The sentence was restitution of ten million pounds and twenty years in prison. Of course, he blamed me because I blew the whistle on his scam."

"Dad, I don't remember anything about this," Joe said, taking in his father's story. "All I remember is that we had the office in Sydney and opened another branch in London."

"Yes, you were busy in the States and I made the deal with British authorities in private. They sold everything Andrews owned, including his personal property, with the proceeds going to pay off the investors. I agreed to pay the rest in exchange for the company and a business license to operate in the UK. It was a win-win opportunity for us. The clients were happy and we acquired an established branch and its clientele."

"Nothing like a hostile takeover. But I still don't see what any of this has to do with kidnapping Kelly."

"I'm not sure that it does, but the kidnapper told you to think outside the box and the ransom demand is ten million pounds. It seems like to much of a coincidence."

"Do you think the box he's talking about is a prison cell?"

"I don't know. It's certainly possible and I think it's worth looking into."

"By the way Dad, what ever happened to Andrews?"

"I really don't know that either. It's been twenty years and I would think, if he's not out of prison, he will be soon."

"Dad, there's something else, a really big problem." Joe hesitated, then went on, "There has to be an informant, somewhere in our organization. Otherwise, how would the kidnappers know we were going to be in London?"

"Quite right," answered Ed. "I assume they told you not to call the police?"

"Yeah, he said he'd kill her if I did, but Dad, I had too. The Concierge at the hotel has a friend who is the Chief Inspector for the Kidnap and Specialist Investigations Unit at Scotland Yard. It's a division of SO7, Serious and Organized Crime. There are just too many things to investigate on our own. He's a good guy Dad, and I trust him."

"Good. What did the kidnapper say about delivering the ransom money?" Ed asked.

"He said he would call back with instructions."

"Joey, try to suggest a bank transfer instead of cash. It would take a pretty large container to transport that much in bills. If we could do a transfer, we might be able to cancel it once we get Kelly back, and, if he agrees, we'll know he's an amateur. Any self-respecting pro would know we could make the transaction disappear."

"I don't know Dad, I don't want to take any chances. Dad, if you can take care of the money end, I'll work on finding out about Andrews."

"Consider it done. How can I reach you?"

"I think it's better if I call you and, thanks Dad, for everything," Joe said, his voice catching.

"Joey, we're going to get Kelly back no matter what it takes." Ed said with tears rolling down his cheeks, "I love you."

"I love you too, Dad."

CHAPTER 16

▼

Wednesday, September 26, 9:10 AM
Ah, the Country Life

With all eyes on her, Chloe waited for the explosion. As their bus pulled away from Ascot House, she knew everyone was dying to know what was going on with Kelly. She thought about Madeline, who was running on a mixture of adrenaline and high-test coffee, neither of which was a good thing, but Maddie was an amazing woman and Chloe knew she would be all right.

Chloe glanced at her watch, counting off the seconds, five, four, three…The Tower of Babble erupted, six people talking at once. "Did Madeline hear anything?" "What the hell's going on?" "Why didn't Madeline tell us anything?"

"OK," Chloe shouted over the wall of voices, "Hold on and I'll tell you everything I know."

"Wait," Marge said, pointing at George, wondering if he could be trusted.

Chloe got the message and leaning forward said, "George, are you going to be with us for the rest of the trip?"

He peered at her in his rearview mirror, a look of disappointment on his face, "No Ma'am, I'm afraid not. I'll be getting ya to Oxford and Blenheim, then leavin' ya at Greystone Manor. The locals will be takin' over so's I can get back to London. Didn't Miss Madeline tell ya?"

"No, she must have forgotten," Chloe said, wondering if Maddie even knew about this change.

"I'm sorry, Ma'am."

"No, no, its alright. I was just curious. How long will it take to get to Oxford?"

Turning onto Bayswater Road, George answered, "Traffic's light this mornin'. Oxford's eighty-four kilometers, so, once we get on the Motorway, it'll be less than an hour."

"That's great," Chloe said, then added, "We need to have a little group meeting. Miss Madeline would never forgive me if I didn't bore them to death with the complete history of Oxford and the University."

George laughed and shook his head. He knew Chloe was teasing, but he actually enjoyed Miss Madeline's little talks.

"We'll move to the back so we don't disturb you," said Chloe, loud enough for everyone to hear.

Turning to reply, George started to tell her it wasn't necessary, but Jake was already out of his seat, so he kept quiet. "No need, doesn't bother me," he muttered.

Chloe made her way to the back of the bus, where John was helping Marge into her new seat. "I'm sure he's OK, but better safe than sorry," Chloe said, turning around and waiving to George.

"We all agree, dear," said Millie, nodding her head. "Now tell us everything."

Chloe looked at the expectant faces staring at her, Jake and John obviously anxious and frustrated because they would much rather stay in London and help with the investigation, than be shipped off to the countryside to play tourist with the ladies.

Marge and Millie were worried about Kelly, but seemed ready to accept their mission and maintain the cover story Madeline had devised. Suzie knew her job was corralling her husband. Looking at him, she could tell he was ready to jump ship and take matters into his own hands. Likewise, Dolores knew John was seething underneath his calm exterior. What if it was one of their kids in trouble? She knew if Jake bolted, John would be right behind him. No, the women thought Madeline's approach was best. If nothing else, they could convince whoever might be following them that the kidnapper's demands were being met and maybe buy Kelly some more time.

"I know you're not happy about leaving," Chloe began, "but we have to do as Madeline asked. We have to maintain the pretense that everything is going as scheduled."

"Surely they've heard something by now," Marge said.

"You're right, Marge, they have. The second call came through about six o'clock this morning. Joe kept him on the phone long enough for the police to trace the call."

"Where'd the call come from?" asked John.

"A phone booth at Victoria Station. That doesn't tell us much, but the fact it came from within the city is important."

"The asshole was gone by the time they got there, right?" grumbled Jake.

Suzie glared at her husband, letting him know she didn't appreciate his language.

"Yes, of course he was nowhere to be found," Chloe answered, "but the point is that Chief Inspector Graham thinks it was a different caller than the first one. Madeline said Graham thinks the voice analysis will prove the calls came from two different places."

"So? Big deal," said John. "What does all this mean?"

"I don't know, but it's another piece of the puzzle. They also now know this is somebody with a grudge against Joe."

"Joe?" asked Marge. "How do you know that?"

"Because, when Joe asked what he wanted, the guy said Joe's misery and ten million pounds."

They all gasped and looked at Chloe in disbelief. Finally Jake spoke, "My God, ten million…How much is that?"

"Fifteen million dollars," Marge said solemnly.

"I know he's a banker, but does Joe have that kind of money?" asked John, trying to grasp the enormity of the kidnapper's demand.

"Even if he does," Dolores asked. "How much time did they give him to get it together?"

"Hold on. There's more," Chloe told them. "When Joe said he didn't have that kind of money, the guy told him to 'Look outside the box,' and gave him twenty-four hours to 'Figure it out'." Chloe raised her hands and made quotation marks in the air.

"There's more going on here than just kidnapping a child for ransom," Jake surmised.

"Jake's right. This guy's playing some sort of sick game," John added.

"I think you fellas've hit the nail on the head," observed Suzie, nodding her head, along with the rest of them.

"So, what happens now?" John asked with a frown, looking at Chloe.

"As far as I know, Madeline is going to the Burlington Arcade to see if she can find anyone who saw Kelly. Hopefully, someone saw her leave. The Scotland Yard people are running background checks on the employees of Joe's company. Madeline says they've got the entire hotel wired. Every phone in the place is being monitored by Scotland Yard. They have to find out who is giving the kidnappers information."

"I'm all for circling back and turning the tables on those bastards," grumbled Jake, defiant to the core. "We could follow them."

"Them who, Jake?" Suzie said to her husband, with customary calmness. Suzie's logical approach to any situation was the perfect counterpoint to Jake's jump-in-the-fire, head-'em-off-at-the-pass mentality. "You don't even know who 'them' is. You'd get up on ol' Rusty and ride straight in the middle of a whole bunch of bee hives, tryin' to catch one little ol' bear, and get yerself stung to death in the process. See," she said confidentially to everyone else, "when Jake here jumps on his stallion, he thinks he's Superman in Snakeskin boots and a Stetson. Ol' Rusty sprouts wings and he and Super Jake ride off to save the world."

Suzie's colorful description gave them all mental pictures of Jake on a flying horse, kind of a cowboy Don Quixote. One by one, they began to chuckle and within seconds, burst into hysterical laughter, the tension broken.

"Can't you just see him?" Chloe sputtered, clutching her sides, tears streaming down her cheeks.

Jake took the ribbing with a sheepish grin, grateful his pint-size wife had a giant-sized sense of humor.

As the laughter subsided, Chloe turned serious again, and pulled the secure-line cell phone out of her pocket. "Listen up everyone. You all need to know about this. Chief Inspector Graham gave us this phone to use. It's a secure line, meaning nobody can intercept the signal and hear what we're saying. It will connect us with him, Madeline, Robbie and his deputy, Helen Bainbridge. It also has a tracking device that Scotland Yard will monitor. If anything happens to me, you all need to know how it operates."

Passing around the phone, Chloe explained the panic button and how to dial the other four phones. "Something else," she said quietly, "Graham is certain we will be followed. I don't know if you heard or not,but George won't be staying with us, he's dropping us off this afternoon then going back to London."

"What do you suppose that's about?" asked Dolores.

"Well, it could be something or it could be nothing but coincidence," offered Millie.

"Replacing our driver in the middle of the tour seems a little odd, don't you think?" added Marge.

"Yeah," Chloe answered, "I'm not exactly comfortable with switching either, but there's nothing we can do about it except be extra observant. Supposedly local guides are going to take us from here, but I've got to tell you, I don't like the idea of going off with someone I don't know."

A collective "Me either" came from the group.

"OK then, we've got to be extra observant. If any of you see or hear anything that seems remotely out of place, let me know at once, so I can relay it to Madeline. And if anything happens to me…"

"Nothing's going to happen to you Chloe," Marge reassured. "You're our fearless leader now."

"All right troops," Chloe said, assuming her role as commander, "we have an assignment to carry out." She turned and walked back to the front of the bus, the others following one by one.

They were traveling Northwest, along the M-40, nearing the Oxford exit. When everyone had reclaimed their original seat, Chloe announced with a flourish, "Ladies and Gentlemen. May I have your undivided attention, please? Madeline would never forgive me if I didn't educate you with at least a few facts about Oxford."

A mock groan came from the peanut gallery.

"Don't give me that. You know this is for your own good. Oxford is the home of one of the greatest universities in the world. And I know that because Madeline wrote right here." Chloe had to glance down at the cards Madeline had given her. "And furthermore, it says the town was settled by the Saxons in the Tenth Century." She looked up and added, "I think that's nine hundred something-or-other, isn't it?" and looked to Marge for confirmation.

"Yes, you're correct," Marge answered. "The century is always one number higher than the date. If something happened in the year 1194, it's considered the Twelfth Century."

"Wonderful," Chloe continued, "So, by the Twelfth Century, Oxford had established a reputation as a seat of learning and the first colleges were founded in the Thirteenth Century."

Looking up at her audience, Chloe beamed, "See how much you're learning. Pretty entertaining, huh? I'm not losing you, am I?"

"No, No. You're doing fine," the chorus replied. "Go on, we're listening."

"OK, thanks," she looked down again, flipping through her cards, stopping at one that sounded interesting. "Now this is pretty cool and something I didn't know. You know how our universities have a central campus and the various departments are in clusters, but are still part of the same campus? Well, Oxford isn't like that. Oxford has thirty-six individual colleges."

The bus was just exiting the motorway when Chloe continued, "It would take all day to see everything, so he's going to show us the highlights. We're going to stop at the visitor's center where a university guide will join us.

Everyone settled back as they made their way into town, still marveling at George's ability to negotiate the roundabouts. They soon arrived at the Visitor's Center and were joined by a handsome young man named Jeffrey who gave them his thumbnail version of the history of Oxford's most famous colleges.

September 26, 10:30 AM

"Good morning everyone. Welcome to Oxford," Jeffrey said as he took his place at the front of the bus. "I think you'll find the colleges of Oxford are much different than your American universities. Oxford's traditions are steeped in a thousand years of history. Sound's ominous, doesn't it? I must tell you, some students would like to chuck those old customs straight into the river. One college, Sheldonian, still holds its graduation ceremonies in Latin."

"Most of the colleges here were founded during the medieval period, between the 13th and 16th centuries. In those times, education was the elite province of the church. In fact, scholars had to take a vow of celibacy just like the clergy. I'm pleased to report, that is no longer the case!"

"Amen to that," chuckled Jake.

"The older colleges were even constructed like monasteries," Jeffrey continued. "in a square formation with a quadrangle in the center. Where your universities have open campuses, each of our colleges is self-contained. Students live and work in their own colleges, however they intermingle at sporting events and the like.

"If you'll look to your right, we're just passing Christ Church. Because of the name, most visitors think it is just that, a church. Actually Christ Church is the largest college here. It looks like one continuos building, doesn't it? You can't see the quadrangle from the street. You can't see any of the college's quadrangles. They are for the use of their students and are kept quite private, however, Miss Marlborough apparently has connections, because we've been granted permission to visit Christ Church's quad. You'll also be able to see several of the locations used in the first *Harry Potter* film. I do believe it should be released soon. I'm afraid our thirteen Prime Ministers, who attended Christ Church, will soon be overshadowed by the boy wizard and his escapades, although, I must say, the whole filming process was frightfully exciting."

The bus stopped in front of Tom Tower, the centerpiece of Christ Church. It was time to check in so, as they disembarked, Chloe took the cell phone from her pocket, stepped away from the group and dialed Madeline. When Jeffrey noticed and asked if anything was wrong, Marge ran interference and told him Chloe was just checking in with the home office.

"She'll only be a moment," Marge told him. "Perhaps we can wait over here." She gestured to a spot just outside the entrance to Tom Tower. "Why don't you tell us a little more about yourself."

"Does it feel like you're going to church instead of college classes?" asked Dolores. "It's so different from where my children go to college."

"Do you go here, or to one of the other colleges?" John wanted to know.

"I'm actually in my second year here at Christ Church. My concentration is Art History and Restoration, much to my father's regret. He wanted me to be a Barrister."

"You're not wearing a robe," Millie observed. "I know I've seen pictures of Oxford students wearing black robes. Why don't you have one?"

Jeffrey smiled, "We don't have to wear them all the time anymore, only on formal occasions such as Matriculation, examinations, banquets, that sort of thing."

Looking puzzled, Jake asked, "What the hell is matriculation? It sounds like a dental disease."

"No, no, nothing so horrible as that, "Jeffrey laughed. "Matriculation is the ceremony where students are formally admitted to the University."

A few minutes later, Chloe joined them. "Sorry about that. I just had to let Madeline know we're on schedule. She particularly wanted to know if Jake was giving you any trouble."

When everyone chucked at the inside joke, Chloe answered Jeffrey's puzzled expression by whispering, "Jake's from Texas. They're all a little eccentric."

It took Jeffrey a second to realize she was teasing him. Then he whispered back, "It's the hat, isn't it? Affects the brain."

"Yes," Chloe whispered loud enough for everyone to hear. "His wife tried to have it surgically removed, but the damage had already been done."

Jake screwed up his nose, squinted his eyes, then quickly took off his Stetson and plunked it on Jeffrey's head. Roaring with laughter, he threw a huge arm around the startled boy's shoulder, while Marge and John snapped as many pictures as possible.

Jeffrey reluctantly returned Jake's hat and led them into the lower chamber of Tom Tower, telling them the tower was built in 1681 by Sir Christopher Wren, who was also the architect of St. Paul's in London, and named after Cardinal Thomas Wolsey. Every night at precisely nine-o-five, the eighteen thousand pound Tom Bell is rung one hundred and one times, signaling the closing of the college gates. The number of rings is for the number of students enrolled in the original college, founded by Henry VIII.

One of the more famous graduates of Christ Church include Charles Dodgson (Lewis Carroll), who wrote *Alice in Wonderland* and *Through the Looking Glass*, while he was a mathematics student. *Alice* was actually the four-year-old daughter of the Dean. Dodgson was working in the library at the time and became friends with the Dean, his wife and three daughters, ages two, four and six. Dodgson would often visit the family and spot Alice's cat, Dinah, watching them from a chestnut tree. The Cheshire Cat and *Alice in Wonderland* sprang to life during a rowing trip when Dodgson was trying to entertain the fidgety little girls.

Shelley, the English poet, was also a student at Christ Church; however, he was expelled for writing a document, *The Necessity of Atheism*. Even so, the college still erected a monument to him.

Walking through the hallowed halls of Christ Church, the group could almost feel the college's ancient traditions seeping through the walls. As they neared the Dining Hall, however, students assembling for lunch were laughing and talking in sharp contrast to their reverent surroundings. Looking into the hall, Jeffrey pointed out the fact that students still eat at long tables while the professors sit at the high table at the far end of the room and, following tradition, grace is still said in Latin.

The sight of the dining room set off everyone's hunger alarm and they were relieved to find out the next stop was the Bear Inn, one of Oxford's favorite and oldest pubs. Built in the thirteenth century, the inn has been in continuous operation for eight hundred years. It has always been a place that provided a common ground for its patrons, regardless of their status. You might be sitting next to a blacksmith or a Duke, a university professor or a raja from India.

As they walked in and looked around, Jake slapped his thigh and commented, "Hey Suz, this is just like the Buck Snort Saloon, isn't it?" referring to the walls around the bar, which were covered with the remains of thousands of neckties and the names of their owners.

"A friend of ours in Colorado has a saloon back in a canyon just outside Denver," Suzie explained to the rest of the group. "If a guy comes in all gussied up, wearing a tie, its the barkeep's duty to cut if off. Kinda levels the playing field, if you know what I mean. He even cut the tie off the governor and a couple of senators."

"Really?" asked Millie.

"You bet," answered Jake. "They'll sure be surprised to fine out somebody else has been doing it for eight hundred years. I'm gonna go see if they've got a postcard or something we can take back."

While Jake went off on his quest, Jeffrey led the others to the back of the pub where they found a table, ordered pints of larger all around and dined on cottage pie and bread pudding.

September 26, 1:15 PM

After lunch, Chloe and the others said goodbye to Jeffrey and dropped him back at the Visitor's Center. On the road again, everyone wanted to know about the phone call Chloe made and about Madeline and her connections.

Quietly Chloe asked, "Did you see anyone that looked suspicious? I didn't." No one else had either. "OK then, so far, so good. Madeline was just on her way back to the hotel for the meeting..." she glanced over her shoulder to make sure George was occupied, "with everyone else." She didn't need to use names. They all knew the players. "I'll call her when we get to the hotel. She should know a lot more by then."

"So, how does Madeline have connections at Oxford?" John asked, changing the subject. "And didn't someone say she had connections to Blenheim Palace too?"

"I don't know all the details," Chloe began, speaking at her normal volume again, "but wait until you see this place, it's magnificent."

"I saw a documentary about the palace on television a few years ago," Millie offered, then wistfully added, "it must be wonderful to live in a place like that."

"Only if you've got good help." From Dolores' perspective, more rooms meant more work.

Marge looked at her sister and smiled. Millie had always been a dreamer. "When we were little girls," Marge said, "Millie always wanted to be a princess."

Beginning again, Chloe said, "Blenheim Palace got its name because one of Winston Churchill's ancestors, the first Duke of Marlborough, defeated somebody at the Battle of Blenheim."

"I think it was the French, dear," interrupted Millie. "If I remember correctly, on the special I saw, they made a particular point of saying the English were never very fond of the French, especially Louis the fourteenth."

"I seem to remember that too," agreed Dolores.

Chloe was becoming impatient, thinking to herself, they never interrupted Madeline this way. "OK, lets say it was the French. At any rate, the Queen was so grateful, she had the palace built for the Duke."

"So how does Madeline fit into the story?" asked John.

"I'm getting to that," Chloe groaned with good-natured exasperation. "One of the Duke's servants had a little fling on the wrong side of the sheets, and when the creep found out the girl was pregnant, he gave her some money and sent her to America. When she arrived, she called herself Mrs. Marlborough. If her son couldn't grow up at Blenheim, at least he could have the Duke's name. Madeline's father is a direct descendant of Mrs. Marlborough's son. Does any of this make any sense?"

"Now let me see if I've got this straight," said John, "The actual Dukes of Marlborough are named Churchill and the Butler's pregnant girlfriend adopted the name Marlborough, right?"

Chloe put one index finger on the tip of her nose, pointed the other at John and exclaimed, "Exactly! Well, I don't know if it was the butler, but close enough."

Blenheim Palace is only eight miles from Oxford, so by the time Chloe had finished her story, they had turned off the A-44, and were circling the roundabout, on their way to the Palace Car Park. To their right, across a small lake, they caught their first glimpse of Blenheim Palace.

"Whoa," Jake blurted out, "will you get a load of that."

"I told you," Chloe said, thrilled they were all so impressed. "They even have their own train to take you from the Palace gardens to the Butterfly House and the Marlborough Maze."

Everyone was indeed impressed as they drove through the twin columns of trees that led to the entrance at the East Gate where they were met by one of the palace guides.

"Good afternoon everyone. Welcome to Blenheim Palace. My name is Jane Wharton and I'll be your escort. If you'll please follow me, we'll just go through to the Great Hall. His Grace has been about this afternoon, so we might run into him."

This news sent Millie into a complete twitter. To see the Duke, perhaps even meet him, was beyond her wildest dreams. One hand went to her hair while the other clutched the neck of her blouse. She didn't know which to straighten first.

Seeing her obvious distress, Jake came up beside her, bent down and whispered, "Darlin', you couldn't look any prettier than you already do. That fancy Duke'll be the lucky one, if he gets to meet you."

Millie looked up and saw Jake's smile was genuine. He wasn't patronizing her or teasing, he really did think she was special. Blushing a pretty shade of pink, she lowered her eyes, "Oh Jake, do you really think so?"

"Course I do." He linked her arm through his and announced, "Come, my lady, His Dukeship awaits!"

Suzie didn't need to look back at her husband, she knew what he was doing. For all his bluster, Jake had a sensitive side, which made his antics all the more endearing. Chuckling knowingly, she followed Jane and the others through the door and down the long corridor.

As they walked along, Jane told them how John Churchill, the first Duke of Marlborough, led his troops to victory over the French in 1704. His victory kept Louis XIV from invading Holland and Austria and extending French rule over all of Northern Europe. As a reward for his services, Queen Anne gave the Duke the Royal Manor of Woodstock and promised to build him a palace to be named after the site of the great battle.

Construction got underway in 1705, but by 1712, the Duke had fallen from the Queen's favor and the 45,000 pounds owed to the architect and workers, was withdrawn. After the Queen died in 1714, the Duke made a deal with the workers and suppliers, and ended up paying for the rest of the construction himself.

The group made its way through the palace, oohing and aahing at the beautiful furnishings and artwork. Paintings by Reynolds, Sargent and Van Dyck, lined the walls of the Red Drawing Room, while the murals of Louis Laguerre, who only charged 500 pounds for his work, covered the walls and ceiling of The Saloon. The magnificent Long Library, fifty-five meters in length, houses the Willis organ and two marble sculptures of the first Duke and Queen Anne.

Sir Winston Churchill was born at Blenheim Palace in 1874 and proposed to his wife in Blenheim's gardens in 1908. John Shepherd was especially interested in the Churchill Exhibition since his father fought with the British in World War II and actually saw Prime Minister Churchill once.

At the end of the tour, Jane led the group outside to the Water Terrace Gardens, where she snapped four group photos, one with each camera, with the palace in the background. Time was running short. High Tea at Greystone Manor was served precisely at four o'clock and, if they left now, they would just have time to freshen up beforehand. Much to Millie's dismay, they had to leave without seeing His Grace.

CHAPTER 17

▼

Wednesday, September 26, 3:30 PM
Marge and Millie Raise a Ruckus

Greystone Manor is a Grade One neo-Gothic stately home and historic monument, and one of only two properties in England to retain the same family ownership dating back to the Norman Conquest in 1066. By the time the Domesday Book, a survey of every manor in England, was written in 1086, the Grey family had already been in residence at the manor for three generations. In 1972, when the upkeep on the property became a strain on the family coffers, Simon Grey, the current Lord of the Manor, and his father, William, did extensive interior renovations and turned the estate into a luxury Manorhouse Hotel. Today their guests enjoy the trappings of antiquity along with the comforts of a modern estate, complete with spa and stables. It is said Shakespeare was a frequent visitor to Greystone Manor, which is set in an idyllic spot in the heart of the Cotswolds.

As the bus from Global Tours passed through the tiny village of Greysmeade, Chloe consulted the cards Madeline had given her that morning and read the history of the village and Manorhouse to her group. No one paid the slightest attention to her. They were too busy looking at the little stone cottages and buildings lining the village's main street. Dolores and Suzie were already discussing their desire to come back and shop. Since nobody seemed to care anyway, Chloe gave up on her sermon and enjoyed the view along with everyone else.

About five miles beyond the village, George turned onto a gravel road that wound through a thicket of trees, eventually stopping at a gate. Above the gate was an ornately carved sign that read, "Welcome to Greystone Manor." Lowering his window, George spoke into a callbox discreetly concealed in a fencepost and the heavy gate opened automatically. As they drove through, the forest opened into a beautiful park. In the distance, they could see the Manor glowing in the afternoon sun, the Cotswolds limestone reflecting a warm yellow light. Beyond the house, across the road to the right, horses were grazing near the stables.

The Manor, three stories tall, with pointed gothic arches gracing the windows, turrets and roofline, boasted sixteen bas-reliefs carved around the exterior. The reliefs depict the Grey family history, including the exploits of Wilfred Grey who joined Richard the Lionhearted on his Crusade to the Holy Land in 1190.

The bus pulled around to the side portico where two bellmen were waiting to unload the luggage. As fond farewells and generous tips were bestowed on George, a feeling of uneasiness settled upon the group. With George's departure, they were now truly on their own.

Squaring her shoulders, Chloe put on her professional face and led the way through the beautiful Victorian Conservatory to the Reception Hall. Exquisite walnut panels imbedded with the Grey family crest lined the walls, while the recessed panels of the ceiling were sculpted in the Rococo style. A hand-carved walnut canopy, supported by matching columns, topped the reception desk where an efficient looking woman, wearing a pinched face and huge horn-rimmed glasses, looked up from the list she was reading.

"May I help you," she said to Chloe with a formal detachment so different from the staff at Ascot House.

As soon as the woman opened her mouth, Chloe knew she didn't like her. What a horrid little person, she thought to herself. However, she pasted on a pleasant smile and answered, "Yes, we're the group with Global Tours."

Focusing her squinty eyes and looking everyone up and down with obvious disapproval, the desk clerk asked in a scolding tone, "Ms. Marlborough, where are the rest of your people? Your reservation is for a party of eleven."

"Excuse me," Chloe shot back, her temper rising, "Ms. Marlborough was detained in London. I am Mrs. Ambrose. Someone from Global should have called you this morning with the changes."

The woman looked right through Chloe as if she weren't standing right in front of her and said, "Wait here," then turned and disappeared behind a wall that held the room keys and message cubbies.

"What the hell was that all about?" grumbled Jake.

"The woman's a bitch. That's all there is to it," said Marge. Everyone did a double take, never expecting a comment like that to come from the eldest member of the group. "Well, she is!"

Chloe turned around, "I totally agree with you Marge. There is no excuse for behavior like that."

"What she needs is an attitude adjustment," John added.

"No," said his wife, "what Old Stoneface needs is a swift kick in the behind."

"That's Ms. Stoneface," Chloe said, dripping with sarcasm.

Just then "Ms. Stoneface" reappeared, holding a piece of paper, which she placed on the desk. Arching an eyebrow, she announced, "Everything is in order. Tea is served promptly at four-o'clock. Dinner is served from seven to nine. Breakfast is served either in your room or in the dining room from six-thirty to ten."

She then proceeded to call the roll and distribute room keys. "Your luggage will be up presently. Have a pleasant stay."

"Yeah, right," Chloe mumbled as they walked to the lift, discreetly placed beside the Grand Staircase.

The lift would only hold four people at a time, so the Talbot sisters and the Shepards went ahead while the others cooled their heels, hoping Ms. Stoneface would disappear again.

Attempting to lighten the mood, Jake commented, "Ya know, if these elevators were any smaller, there wouldn't be room for my Stetson."

The women looked at each, amusement in their eyes, as Suzie drawled, "Honey, your Stetson's got nothin' to do with it. Your head's so big, you may have to go up by yourself."

"Suz, you killin' me here!"

Mercifully, the doors opened before he could say anything else and he, Suzie and Chloe got in and rode to the third floor.

When they arrived, they found they were at one end of a hallway with rooms on either side and a floor to ceiling stained glass window at the other end. The afternoon sun shining through the stained glass cast a shower of color on the walls, ceiling and floor, as if they were standing in the middle of a jewel box. All four rooms were on the same side of the hotel, overlooking the manicured lawn leading down to the riverbank.

Chloe opened the door to her room and walked in. Although it wasn't nearly as large as the two-bedroom suite she and Madeline shared at Ascot House, the room was large enough for two twin-sized four-poster beds and a large sitting area. The bedspreads and canopies were a pale yellow brocade which blended beautifully with the red and gold draperies and carpet. An antique desk and chair sat in the alcove made by the dormer windows, and bouquets of fresh flowers had been placed on the desk, the coffee table, and interestingly, in the fireplace. A beautiful portrait of a young woman in a flowing white dress, holding a basket of flowers and standing before the very same fireplace, hung over the mantle. Chloe stood on tiptoe and examined the painting, looking for a date. In the lower left hand corner was the inscription, "Elizabeth Grey, 1852."

Chloe couldn't resist. She laid her left arm on the mantle and assumed the position of the woman in the painting, only to catch her reflection in the full-length mirror on the opposite side of the room. "Not too bad," she thought to herself. "Give me a white dress and a few roses and I could be the picture of genteel womanhood."

Lowering her arm, she chuckled to herself as she went to investigate the bathroom. Sure enough, a bowl of fresh flowers sat on a narrow pedestal at the foot of the deep, claw-footed bathtub. A hand-shower attached to the faucet and the dormer window over the tub had a stained glass border depicting the ivy that wound its way around the outside of the building. The ivy theme carried over to the vanity where a porcelain vine crept up the pedestal and down into the bowl of the sink. Even the floor was tiled with an ivy motif.

Just then she heard a knock on the door. Marge had come to see if she was ready to go down to tea.

When Chloe opened the door, Marge asked if she could take a peak at the room. "Isn't this lovely? Our room is similar, but done in shades of pink and rose."

"Oh look," exclaimed Millie, who had followed her sister into the room. She fluttered directly to the fireplace, "It's the same woman, only in our room, she's wearing a pink dress. Can I look at your bathroom?"

Millie reminded Chloe of a human butterfly, flitting from one place to the next, chattering all the way. Calling from the bathroom she shouted, "Sister, come and look. Her bathroom has ivy instead of roses. Have you ever seen anything like it?"

"Actually, I haven't," Marge remarked to Chloe. "Have you? The porcelain decoration on the sink is quite unique."

"The only place I've ever seen anything like it was in the lady's room at the Paris Hotel in Las Vegas," answered Chloe.

Still discussing the décor, the three ladies took the lift to the main floor and managed to find the lounge where tea was being served. They were all relieved they hadn't run into Ms. Stoneface along the way.

Decorated in shades of blue and ivory, the elegant lounge had a large windowed alcove at one end where an older gentleman in a tuxedo was playing a rosewood grand piano. Several groups of richly upholstered sofas and chairs lined the perimeter, while an ornately carved rosewood table, festooned with flowers, sat in the center of the room under a gold and crystal chandelier. To the left,

French doors opened onto a large flagstone patio, where guests were taking advantage of the lovely weather, having their tea and pastries at white wrought iron tables.

As Chloe surveyed the gathering on the patio, she spotted a familiar cowboy hat, shook her head and laughed. "You know, Jake may look like a bull in a china shop, but you can always find him in a crowd."

"I know, isn't that comforting?" Millie gushed, already fluttering toward her Texas flame.

Chloe and Marge followed Millie and took the small table next to their friends. A smiling waiter instantly appeared with a silver pot of tea in one hand and a pitcher of hot milk in the other, cheerfully asking if they would like their tea with or without. They all preferred their tea black, which he found appalling, but still smiling, he finished pouring and said he would return with the pastry tray.

"My, he was pleasant," commented Chloe. "He must not be related to our friend at the front desk."

"I was almost afraid to call housekeeping to ask for extra pillows," said Dolores, "but they were really nice too."

"And we stopped by the Concierge desk," added Suzie, "The man on duty was very nice. He even offered to have the hotel van take us into the village if we want to have a look around."

"I think she just had a bug up her butt about something." As usual, Jake's observation cut to the heart of the matter, and had everyone in stitches.

September 26, 4:45 PM

John and Dolores were eager to explore the village, so they all decided to take the concierge up on his offer and by four forty-five were headed back into town.

The village of Greysmeade is basically a one-street town, much like the clabbered towns of the old west, except here, the buildings are made of stone, the roofs thatched, and they'd been standing since the fourteenth century, long before the New World was even discovered. Like all medieval towns, the street was very narrow, having been originally constructed for horse and carriage traffic.

A Village Car Park had been constructed on the edge of town, near the Blacksmith, to accommodate modern tourist vehicles and it was here the driver parked the van.

"I'll just wait here whilst you have a walk through our village," he told them. "The shops are open until six, so if you'll meet back here by half past, I can have you to the Manor in plenty of time for dinner."

As they passed the Blacksmith, Jake was surprised to see the forge fired up and the Smithy hard at work hammering a horseshoe, most likely meant for the mare tied to the nearby hitching post. Jake tipped his hat and smiled, the Smithy acknowledging his greeting with a nod of his head.

As they walked up the street they saw each shop had a wrought iron sign above the door depicting the type of wares for sale inside. The Tobacconist had a gentleman with a pipe; the Tailor, a spool of thread and needle; and the next a shop, named The Habit, with a horse and rider. From the quality of the jodhpurs, red riding jacket and English riding crop in the window; it was obvious The Habit catered to the well-heeled horsy set.

There was a shop with nothing but buttons, millions of buttons in all shapes and sizes, made with everything from silver to bone. The group almost lost Millie there, so intrigued was she with the unique objects, until she spotted the needlework shop next door.

"Oh this is wonderful," she exclaimed. "I have to go in here. Why don't the rest of you go on. I'll catch up with you."

She was already opening the door, when her sister warned, "Millie, don't buy another pair of scissors. Remember what happened in Chicago. The airline people will only confiscate them again."

"I know Marge," Millie answered pointedly as she closed the door.

"Just watch," Marge said to the others, "she'll come out of there with a pair of scissors, you wait and see. She just won't listen."

The group continued up the street, past the pub and antique store, then crossed and started down the other side where the jeweler had an impressive array of timepieces in his window. The Apothecary was directly opposite the pub, a convenient location prompting the observation that a person could get sloshed over lunch, cross the street for aspirin and be over their hangover before dinner.

John and Dolores needed more film, so they went in, only to find an Apothecary, unlike drugstores back home, dispense prescription and over-the-counter preparations of a medical nature, while sundries like film are sold at the Tobacconist.

It was almost time to return to Greystone and Millie had yet to make an appearance. "God only knows what she's doing in there," said Marge, with an exaggerated sigh. "You can only buy so many pairs of scissors. I'll go light a fire under her." Marge crossed the street and went into the shop. Carrying a shopping bag in each hand, she emerged again, followed by her sister.

"My God," observed Chloe from in front of the Apothecary, "How much stuff did Millie buy?"

Millie also had two shopping bags and, by the look on her face, was arguing with Marge who was not happy. Two stone steps descended from the shop to the sidewalk, and as Marge stepped from the lower, she turned to say something to Millie, lost her balance and tumbled into a woman who was passing by on her way home from the market. Distracted by her sister's fall, Millie also wobbled and started to go down.

In a split second, all three women were in a heap on the sidewalk. Apples and potatoes were rolling into the street, needlework canvases spilled from Millie's bags, and the scissors that started the whole drama rested on the bottom step.

As soon as they saw Marge stumble, Jake and John broke into a run, followed by Suzy, Dolores and Chloe. The proprietor of the shop also came to help, as did the manager and two customers of The Habit.

In a barrage of cries and a flurry of hands, help arrived. Cushioning the landing of the elderly sisters, the poor local woman on the bottom of the pile caught the worst of it. Jake and John helped the other ladies up while Chloe checked the woman's injuries and Dolores chased down the escaping produce. Nothing appeared to be broken but her left ankle was beginning to swell, as was her right elbow, so Suzie ran into the pub for some towels and ice.

"Oh sister," wailed Millie, "I'm so sorry. This is all my fault. Are you all right?"

"I think so…just got the wind knocked out of me," Marge gasped, trying to catch her breath.

The local woman, whose name was Emma, was more concerned for the elderly women than herself. When Chloe wanted to call an ambulance, she protested, "Heavens no, what are they going to say? Use ice and take aspirin. I don't need a hospital to tell me that."

By now a crowd was gathering. Suzie came out of the pub carrying a bucket of ice and a few towels. No one seemed to notice the man who followed her, talking furiously into his cell phone. However, after she gave Chloe the ice, Suzie turned and watched him walk up the street toward the market. She couldn't put her finger on exactly why, but when she first spotted him in the pub she got shivers up the back of her neck.

Her attention was drawn back to the drama playing itself out on the sidewalk. Someone had produced three chairs, so at least the injured women were now sitting comfortably.

The barkeep brought three glasses of cold water while the pharmacist helped Chloe wrap iced towels around Emma's ankle and elbow. Jake ran to the Car Park to let their driver know what happened, while John and Dolores went to the market and bought replacements for everything in Emma's bag, returning to the scene just as Emma's husband arrived in his car to take her home. Chloe insisted on calling Emma's doctor before they left and was relieved when he said he would meet them at their home. She also insisted any expenses were to be charged to her at the hotel. They exchanged phone numbers, helped Emma into the car, put her groceries in the back and said goodbye.

By the time Marge and Millie were loaded into the Greystone van, everyone was in need of a stiff drink. Given their age, it was remarkable that neither sister was seriously injured. Marge would surely have a few bruises, but compared to a broken hip, or a broken anything for that matter, she was relatively unscathed. Since the other two women had cushioned Millie's fall, she was in great shape.

On the drive back to Greystone Manor, everyone was talking about the kindness of the local villagers, so none of them paid any attention to the old blue car that sped past them as they turned onto the Manor road.

Suzie had been half listening to the conversation, but her mind kept going back the strange feeling she'd had about the man in the pub. Her hand strayed into the pocket of her skirt, where Millie's scissors were presently residing. In the chaos, everyone had completely forgotten about them. Suzie found them on the stairs where they'd fallen out of Millie's bag, and picked them up. Now, as she felt them in her pocket, another shiver crept up her spine.

The driver had called ahead and, when they arrived, they were met at the door by the hotel doctor and Simon Grey, himself. Marge was a little embarrassed at all the fuss, but Millie, of course, was thrilled to meet Mr. Grey. Both women were ambulatory, so the wheelchairs sitting in the doorway weren't necessary. Instead, they walked through to the lift. Mr. Grey told the Talbot sisters to call him personally if they needed anything at all, then bid them a pleasant evening. After everyone agreed to meet for dinner, Dr. Fallcroft followed Marge and Millie up to their room, while Chloe went to check in with Madeline.

When Jake and Suzie reached their room, he took her hand and pulled her toward the bed, where he sat down, put his hands around her waist and pulled her between his knees. His eyes level with hers, he gazed into them with concern. "Ok Darlin', talk to me."

"Somethin's not right. I swear I don't know why, but sure as I'm standin' here, I know it's true."

"Hair on the back of your neck?"

"Uh huh."

"When did it start?" They'd been here before and he knew this was serious.

"When I walked into the pub. At first I thought it was because of what happened, but the more I think about it…I just don't know Jake."

"Honey, if it's makin' you stew about it, I'm thinkin' we better pay attention. You remember the last time? You knew the boys were in trouble before they ever left the barn. If they'd listened to you, Chuck might not have been in a cast for six weeks."

Two years before, a small crew of ranch hands was scheduled to repair the fence on the far west side of the ranch. Suzie began having an uneasy feeling during breakfast and by the time the horses were saddled the hair on the back of her neck was at full alert. She told Jake to reschedule, but the men insisted they needed to go ahead because bad weather had been forecast for the following day. About an hour's ride from the ranch, one of horses spooked and threw its rider. Chuck ended up with his left leg broken in two places and a new respect for Suzie's premonitions.

"When I went in, there was a man at the bar. The minute I saw him, I knew something wasn't right."

"Did he say anything?"

"It wasn't what he said. I didn't pay that much attention. I was too busy tellin' the barkeep what was going on outside, but I just got a feelin' about him."

"We gotta trust those feelin's Suz."

"I don't want to upset the applecart here unless we know more. I'm not even sure what this is all about."

"Lets go back to the pub after dinner. Maybe the barkeep knows somethin' about this guy or maybe we can find out if the locals know anything. If nothin' else we'll know if you get the same gut reaction again."

C H A P T E R   18

Wednesday, September 26 11:00 AM
A Tale of Two Tapes

Madeline walked into the lobby of Ascot House a little before eleven o'clock. Looking around, she didn't see Robbie anywhere, so she decided to stop by her suite before she went up to the Dalton's. As she opened her door, the cell phone in her pocket began to ring.

"This is Madeline,"

"Hi Maddie, why so formal?"

"Hey Chloe. Because I wasn't sure who was calling. This thing doesn't have caller ID. How's everything going?"

"We just arrived at Christ Church. Jake and John weren't happy about leaving London, but I think they'll be OK."

"Did anyone follow you?"

"I don't think so, but did you know George is returning to London when he leaves us at Greystone Manor?"

"What the hell…? I called Global this morning to let them know about the room changes at Greystone, but they didn't say anything about changing drivers." This was all she needed, as if she didn't have enough to worry about.

Sensing Madeline's frustration, Chloe said, "Maddie, it doesn't necessarily have to be suspicious. I don't think anyone is taking his place. George told me local guides would take over. It'll be all right."

"At this point," snapped Madeline, "everything sounds suspicious."

"Well, I blew that," Chloe thought to herself, then to Madeline, "So, um, where are you now?"

"I'm back at the hotel. Our meeting is at eleven. God Chlo, I didn't mean to jump down your throat. I'm sorry."

"Hey, I know you're exhausted. If you can't vent to me…."

"Yeah, I know, but I don't have to beat you over the head just because I'm tired. It just seems like this octopus has so many legs and the more we discover, the less we know. And meanwhile, the clock is ticking away.

"Any success at the Burlington Arcade?"

"Actually, we learned quite a bit. A man in a chauffeur's hat told Kelly her mother had been in an accident. Robbie's friend, Harold McKee, is a Beadle at the Arcade and heard the conversation."

"I swear, does Robbie know everyone in London?"

"It seems that way, doesn't it? Anyway, when Harold mulled it around, he didn't think this guy was really a chauffeur and neither did the Beadle at the front entrance."

"Why not?"

"The guy's shoes."

"His what?"

"Yeah, that's what I thought at first, but when I looked at Harold's shoes and Robbie's…Chloe, I could see my reflection. Harold said our so-called chauffeur's shoes were scruffy, like he never took care of them, and the Beadle at the front entrance said the limo was filthy. No respectable English chauffeur would have unpolished shoes and a dirty car."

"And if Kelly thought her mother was in an accident, I don't think she would have noticed the driver's shoes."

"Exactly. And we were right about the time. They left the arcade at five-thirty." Glancing at her watch, Madeline realized she was already late for her meeting. "I'd better get up to the Dalton's. Chloe, don't say anything to the others yet. Let's wait until I know more. Hopefully Graham found something helpful on the voice tapes."

"Sounds like a plan. I'll keep the troops in check and talk to you later and Maddie…please try to take it easy."

Madeline pressed the off button on her phone, smiled and headed for the door.

September 26, 11:10 AM

"Sorry I'm late," Madeline said as she walked into the Dalton's suite. "What did I miss?"

"Not a thing," noted Chief Inspector Paul Graham, "I just arrived myself."

Madeline took the chair next to Deputy Inspector Helen Bainbridge, directly across from the Dalton's. Graham was seated at one end, Robbie the other.

Retrieving a pen from her bag, Madeline looked up and asked, "Where are Darby and Kent?"

"Darby is monitoring the phone activity from the hotel, whilst Kent is still running background checks," explained Graham.

"Have you found anything?" Joe asked anxiously.

"We'll go into that later. First let me tell you what we've discovered from the kidnapper's tapes." Paul Graham was usually a methodical investigator, ferreting out one piece of information at a time, maintaining the detached calm necessary to combine those discoveries into a solution of the crime at hand. However, this time he was excited.

He pulled the tape recorder, a permanent fixture in the center of the table, toward him and inserted a cassette. "The first bit is the original message," he said, pressing play.

They had all heard it countless times, but listened patiently. Paul stopped the tape and explained how his sound technicians had removed the voices and punched up the background on the second cut. He pressed play again. "Do you hear it?" he asked.

Everyone listened intently, but weren't sure what they were supposed to hear. Paul stopped the tape and rewound it. "Listen again."

"Is that water?" asked Madeline. "Can you turn it up a little?"

Paul increased the volume and they listened for the third time. Madeline had been right, it was water, splashing water, and it almost had a rhythm to it. "It is water," she murmured, trying to decipher the other sounds.

Paul stopped the tape saying, "You're absolutely correct, it's definitely water and we've determined the source is outside. Did you hear a faint rustling sound? We think it's the rustling of leaves but, as there are no distinguishable insect sounds, they must be in some kind of shelter."

"So what does it mean?" Joe asked, not understanding, "why are water sounds so important?

"By itself, not much, but listen to this." Paul pressed play again and a different rendition came through the speakers, this time with the background noise and primary voice removed.

"There's another voice, isn't there?" observed Robbie.

"Yes indeed," answered Paul. "Putting all these bits together, the analysis proves there are two men holding Kelly in a location near running water and rustling leaves, both loud enough to be heard through an enclosure."

"So, what does that mean?" Joe asked, his inability to grasp the significance of this development threatening to destroy his patience.

"We think," Paul interrupted, speaking with confidence, "the location is outside London, in a forested area near a river or stream. The rhythmic splash could only be created with a good bit of water running over rocks or some kind of obstruction and no such condition exists within the city. Therefore, we can confidently assume Kelly is being held in the countryside."

Paul, removing the first tape and inserting a second, went on, "Now listen to the conversation you had this morning. We've removed the electronic distortion." When it was finished, he asked Joe and Marty, "Do you recognize the voice at all?"

Joe wanted him to play it again. The voice didn't register. They listened again, and a third time. Joe shook his, "I have no idea who he is."

Paul told him it was entirely possible he'd never met the man on the tape. The important thing was the voice on the second tape did not match either voice on the first. Furthermore, the background noises confined to the second tape, could be traced to the phonebox at Victoria Station.

"What all this proves," said Paul, "is there are three men involved, one in the city, two in the countryside and the man who made the second call is the mastermind."

"Aye," commented Robbie, "the second voice was educated, wasn't it?"

"Robbie," Paul asked as he returned the two tapes to an evidence bag, "What did you and Madeline find out at the Burlington Arcade?"

Robbie deferred to Madeline who told them about the chauffeur's story that lured Kelly into his car. They all agreed it was a clever ploy Kelly would never have questioned. Since they could confirm the exact time she left the Arcade, Paul put the location where she was being held somewhere within a hundred-mile radius of the city. It also confirmed the existence of a mole somewhere in the hotel. How else could the kidnappers know where Marty and Kelly were shopping? Someone had to have passed the information to a third party who followed the women to the Arcade. They must have been waiting for an opportunity to present itself and, when Marty left her alone, the kidnappers sprang into action.

"Have the phone taps here at the hotel produced anything yet?" asked Madeline.

"Not yet," answered Paul. "We're also investigating the possibility one of the staff or even one of the guests may have a connection to someone in Dalton's London office."

Listening to all the theories under discussion, Joe thought back to the conversation with his father and knew he had to share what he'd learned. "I talked to my dad a little while ago," he began.

"About the money?" Graham wanted to know. "Will he be able to help you?"

"He'll do whatever he can, but he had some questions and, frankly, so do I. Like how am I supposed to carry ten million pounds in cash? And when are we going to be able to talk to Kelly?"

"Mr. Dalton," interrupted Helen, "is that why you left the hotel earlier, to talk to your father?"

"Yes, so why is that a problem?" Joe immediately felt defensive. So what if he'd left the hotel? And so what if he'd wanted to talk to his dad where Scotland Yard couldn't listen to every word?

"Mr. Dalton, you shouldn't leave without letting us know," Helen responded, shaking her head. "How do you know you weren't followed?"

"I wasn't followed. I was very careful…"

"I'm sure you were, but these people know what they're doing."

"Where did you go Joe?" Madeline asked quietly, trying to defuse the situation that seemed to be building.

"Look I was going crazy cooped up in here. I just went for a walk." Joe looked at his wife, silently asking her to go along with his story. "I needed to talk to my dad anyway, so I went to Paddington Station and used one of their international phones."

"A good thing it wasn't Victoria."

"Ms. Bainbridge, I'm not so stupid that…"

"Joe, I'm sure you thought you took every precaution," said Paul, taking control again. "Our concern doesn't have anything to do with your ability to be careful. It has everything to do with our ability to keep you safe. I know its absolute torture sitting around here, twiddling your thumbs, waiting for the phone to ring, but that's precisely what we all have to do."

Looking at his watch, Paul continued, "Its been approximately five and a half hours since the last call, and remember what he said, 'Think outside the box.' He may not want the ransom in cash. We won't know until he calls again. As for speaking with your daughter, he said he could arrange it. He didn't say when. Frustrating as it is, we just have to wait. However, in the meanwhile, we must gather as much information as possible. The ultimate goal is to know who he is before he calls again."

Marty touched Joe's arm, offering what comfort she could. "You have to tell them what Dad said," she whispered. "It's the best lead we have so far."

Joe nodded, then related the conversation he'd had with his father, the Chief Inspector acknowledging the importance of this new information.

"We'll run Nigel Andrews through our data base. If he was released, we'll have an address for him."

Chief Inspector Paul Graham was actually smiling, a sign that gave Madeline and everyone else around the table a good measure of hope. "What should we do now?" she asked.

"We have to find our mole," Robbie said with determination.

"I agree," said Paul. "We have to stop information leaking from the hotel. And if you find the mole, you'll expose whoever is the outside link." Turning to the Dalton's, he added, "I know you hate staying in the suite, but there is really no choice. Your job is to wait for the next call. Do exactly as before and try to keep him on the line for ninety seconds. If you speak to Kelly, pay close attention for any clues she may give you."

As the meeting broke up, Paul indicated to Helen that she was to follow him and headed for the kitchen. As the other four walked toward the wet bar, Marty asked if Madeline had heard from Chloe.

"She called from Oxford," Madeline answered. "She said Jake and John put up quite a fight about leaving. They wanted to stay here and help with the investigation."

Marty gave a wistful smile and Joe said, "They're good guys. Please be sure Chloe gives them our thanks." He wondered to himself if they could have done anything anyway.

"I will," Madeline answered, "They are all very concerned about Kelly."

Madeline said she and Robbie would check in with them again later in the afternoon. On the way to the door, they stopped by the kitchen and conferred with Paul as to the next meeting time, deciding on four-o'clock.

September 26, 12:10 PM

Back in Madeline's suite, she and Robbie were discussing ideas as how to proceed with their assignment, when Robbie's cell phone rang. Paul's voice said, "Expect a package marked Confidential." After he clicked off, Robbie explained, "Paul got so excited about the Nigel Andrews lead, he forgot to tell me about the phone taps here in the hotel, so he's sending over tapes he wants us to hear and also the information his people gathered about our guests."

"Is someone covering for you at the Concierge desk?"

"Aye, my assistant will page me if anything needs my personal attention." He pulled his pager out of his pocket and showed it to her, "See, no messages."

"I just don't want anyone to get suspicious."

"Before I left this morning to meet you at the Arcade, I told my staff I was working on a special project. They know I'm back in the hotel and assume I'm doing something for one of the guests."

"Actually, you are," Madeline smiled up at him. They were sitting on the sofa, relaxed in each other's company, Robbie with his arm around Madeline's shoulders. They were just drifting off to sleep, when Robbie's pager began to vibrate.

"Damn," he muttered, not wanting to disturb Madeline, but needing to move her in order to reach the pager.

"Hmm, what is it?" Madeline asked as she leaned away from him, trying to stifle a huge yawn.

"My bloody pager." He pulled it out, looked at it, then put it back in his pocket and reached for the phone that sat on the end table nearest his elbow.

When he hung up the phone, he settled Madeline back against him and yawning himself, mumbled, "Package is here."

They didn't move. "I guess you'd better go get it," said Madeline as she snuggled closer to him.

"Aye."

They still didn't move.

"I could come down with you and have some lunch."

"Aye, that you could."

Their voices became fainter with every word and still they didn't move. Finally Madeline shook her head, pulled away from his embrace and sat up straight. "If we don't get up now, we never will and we can't afford to sleep away the afternoon," she said, reluctantly standing up.

"You're a cruel, evil woman, Maddie me darlin'," he sighed, opening his eyes and gazing at her with a look that half exhaustion, half desire. "We'll pick this up later?" he asked.

"Will we now?" she answered mimicking his accent.

He stood up and reached for her, however Madeline had other ideas. "Come on, babe," she laughed, ducking under his arm and walking toward the door, "Let's rock and roll."

"Maddie girl," he laughed and followed her, "you're such a damn Yank."

"Yeah, I know," she teased, "but you love me anyway, right?"

He was beginning to think he just might.

September 26, 12:30 PM

As they reached the bottom stair and stepped into the reception hall, Robbie turned toward the Concierge Desk and Madeline made for the dining room. She didn't see Violet Hargrove give Robbie a nasty look, then follow her. La Violette was very busy with the lunch crowd and the Maitre 'd was telling her there would be a twenty minute wait, when Violet appeared and said, "We'll be dining at the family table, if Ms. Marlborough will join me."

Startled, Madeline agreed and they followed the Maitre 'd to a large table near the windows, overlooking the rose garden.

"This is very nice of you Violet, thank you," Madeline said as the Maitre 'd draped a soft linen napkin across her lap.

"I'm so happy I saw you. I was ready for lunch and I do so hate eating alone. I usually go to the kitchen and see my brother, but the view here is much nicer than his pots and pans."

A waiter Madeline didn't recognize took their order. As he left for the kitchen, he sent the busboy to fill Madeline's coffee cup.

"Are you sure you wouldn't like a glass of wine? David just acquired a splendid Chardonnay from Australia."

"No thank you, wine at lunch always makes me sleepy, especially at sea level."

"That's right, you live in the mountains, don't you? Altitude really makes that much difference, does it?"

They chatted about the Rocky Mountains, the weather and the view of the rose garden. Madeline couldn't remember Violet ever talking so much. Granted, she didn't know her very well, but she always seemed to fade into the woodwork. Now she was animated and smiling, a remarkable contrast.

"And how are the Dalton's this morning? Mrs. Dalton feeling better I trust."

"I think so," replied Madeline. "I looked in on her this morning."

"I haven't seen their daughter lately, I so hope she is having a good time."

"Oh, I'm sure she is."

"Have you heard from Mrs. Ambrose?"

"As a matter of fact, she called from Oxford." "What is this, twenty questions?" she thought to herself.

"What a shame you couldn't join them. Did you finish your business here in town?"

"Unfortunately, no. I need to go over some other things this afternoon. Violet, if you need the suite, I'd be happy to move to a smaller room. Its way to big for one person."

"No, No. Don't be silly," Violet said, suddenly flustered. "I didn't mean anything like that. I was just curious. No need to move. No need at all. You're perfectly welcome to use the suite as long as you like."

Violet seemed relieved when the waiter brought their salads. "This is certainly an odd lunch," Madeline thought to herself.

September 26, 4:00 PM

The four o'clock meeting brought the astonishing revelation that Nigel Andrews was dead. Everyone at the table was stunned by the news, especially Joe and Marty.

"Andrews died of heart failure six months ago at Wormwood Scrubs," said Paul.

"Wormwood Scrubs?" questioned Madeline.

"Yes," Paul replied. "Wormwood Scrubs is the prison where Andrews was incarcerated. His cellmate found him dead in his bed. Pity, he was so close to his release."

"Pity for us," said Joe. "Now we're right back where we started."

"Not necessarily," interrupted Paul, "there's more. Andrews has a son, Clayton, whose last known address is a flat in Chelsea. Kent and Darby are checking it out as we speak. This could be the connection we've been looking for. Robbie, did you receive the package?"

"Aye and I've been looking at the guest dossiers all afternoon. I haven't found anything useful"

"What about the tapes?" Paul asked.

"I have them," Madeline announced, "I hope that's alright. We didn't think it was a good idea for Robbie to listen to them in his office. Anyone could walk in, so I took them up to my suite."

"Did you hear anything?" Marty asked hopefully.

"I'm not sure." She handed Paul a cassette tape. "There's nothing specific. Nothing sounded out of the ordinary to me, but there was a brief conversation that caught my attention and I think you should listen to it."

Paul put the tape in the machine and pressed play. They heard the phone ring, then a man answered, "Yes?" A woman's voice, barely above a whisper, said, "Hello Darling?"

"Everything on schedule?"

"Yes."

"Good. I'll get back to you." They both hung up.

"That's it?" asked Joe.

"Yeah, I know it's not much, but compared to everything else I listened to, I thought it sounded suspicious. What do you think?" Madeline asked, looking at Paul.

"We could hear the outgoing rings, so the call originated in the hotel. I'll get this tape to the lab right away. They'll be able to pinpoint the time of the call and which phone was used." Paul paused a moment, adding together the confirmed pieces of the puzzle. "This is good, very perceptive of you Ms. Marlborough. If you ever think of relocating?"

"I'm just happy we're making progress. So what now?" Madeline asked.

Lost in thought, Paul kept tapping his pen on the table. After a few seconds, he stood up and looked around the table. None of them had slept in the last twenty-four hours. Exhaustion was the only word to describe these poor people, Helen and himself included. "We all need fuel and sleep," he began. "I think a good dinner and as much sleep as possible is in order. I'll get this tape to the lab and Kent and Darby will track Clayton Andrews and anyone who ever heard of him."

Looking at his watch, he continued, "Its half past four. Let's meet back here at five tomorrow morning. If it is Andrews, he said he would give us twenty-four hours to figure this out, so he should call at six. If anything happens in the meantime, keep the secure phones on so we can reach each other."

Everyone stood, nodding in compliance with Paul's instructions. He went to Joe and Marty. "We're making substantial progress. Your father's information about Andrews is key. Use Helen's secure phone and call him again; he may have learned something else on his end, but make sure you speak in generalities. Someone might have tapped his phone."

Joe and Marty both nodded, and Marty reached out to touch Paul's arm. "We don't know how to thank you," she said, tears beginning to well in her eyes.

"Paul," Joe added, "that goes for me too. I'm sorry I've been jumping down everyone's throat. It's just that I…"

"I know," Paul said clapping his hand on Joe's shoulder and walking toward the door. "We'll catch this bloody bastard and Kelly will have a harrowing tale to tell her grandchildren, won't she?"

Once they were out in the hall, Robbie took Madeline's hand and teased, "Come lassie. This Scot is hungry enough to swallow you whole."

CHAPTER 19

▼

Wednesday, September 26, 6:00 PM
Dinner and a Nightcap

As daylight began to fade, Kelly estimated she'd been chained to her wall for twenty-four hours. Of course, after spending the previous night staked to the floor, the handcuff and chain were a piece of cake. She'd figured out if she leaned her back against the wall, with her right hand propped on her knee, the pain in her wrist was at least bearable.

The boys arrived that morning and untied her from the stakes in the floor, and although she was stiff and sore, the worst part was ripping the tape from her mouth. It felt like her skin had been torn off as well. Breakfast was two rolls, a large piece of cheddar cheese and a glass of water.

Stout had even brought her a toothbrush. When Keyes saw it, he cursed a blue streak. She'd never heard so many f-words in her life, but at least he allowed her to brush her teeth before she was chained up again.

The more she saw them, the more Kelly was convinced the two men holding her captive were working for somebody else. They're like two little kids, she thought, all they do is bicker. And they're not even smart enough to keep their names a secret. Keyes, the one who hit her, is never satisfied with anything, and all Stout thinks about is food. There's no way they could have dreamed up this plot on their own.

Thank God, it was Stout who stayed with her most of the day, while Keyes came and went, always waving his gun around and talking furiously into his cell phone. She asked several times when she could talk to her parents. Stout kept telling her, "soon", but the day was almost over and nothing had happened yet.

"Do you think The Boss will be back soon?" she asked.

"He said he was bringin' back supper," Stout answered grumbling, "We ain't had nuffink since breakfast. Hope he remembers today's when Nell makes Cornish pasties at the market. Makes me mouth water just thinkin' about 'em."

"Has he talked to my father yet? I know Daddy won't give him any money until he talks to me."

Stout felt sorry for the girl, but her constant questions were beginning to annoy him. "I keep tellin' ya, I don't know. I just follow orders."

They both heard a car approaching and Stout went to the door, opening it a crack, to make sure it was Keyes. Relieved to see the old blue car, he turned back to Kelly, "It's him."

If possible, Keyes was in a blacker mood than usual. Everything was supposed to be so simple; get the girl, get the money. After the last call, he'd even threatened to contact Dalton himself. Now the whole day had been wasted and he was no closer to getting his money than he'd been the day before. This whole plan was not working out. It should have been over by now and he should be on his way to Rio. With his cut of the ransom, he'd have enough to live large in tropical splendor for the rest of his life. "Only problem is," he thought to himself, "my asshole partner in London ain't following the plan. I don't know what kind of game he's playin', but I'm sick of it."

Kelly heard the car door slam and, when Keyes barged through the mill door, almost knocking Stout to the ground, she was stunned by his uncontrollable rage. Holding her breath, she thought to herself, "My God, what's he going to do to me now."

"Here," Keyes barked, thrusting a large, grease-spotted paper bag at Stout. "I don't want to hear no more complaining' about your belly."

Still staggering, Stout fumbled with the bag, almost dropping it, but the smell of food helped him recover quickly. "Pasties!," he exclaimed as he pulled one out and took a huge bite, nearly devouring the whole thing before he remembered Kelly. He walked over, plopped down beside her and offered her the bag.

Kelly had never seen a Cornish pastie, but figured anything had to be better than last night's dinner of fish and chips. The pastie she took from the bag looked like an Italian calzone or a turnover, and to her surprise, was still warm. She took a bite and found the inside was filled with meat and potatoes.

"Thank you," she said, her mouth filled with warm food, "This is very good."

"Well, don't you two look cozy," sneered Keyes and pulled out his gun.

"What are you doing?," Stout blurted out in defiance as he tried to get up.

Keyes shoved him back down and shouted, "Shut up and stuff your face, you fool. When I want you to know something, I'll tell you."

Keyes turned, ignoring Kelly completely, and walked back to the door, consumed again by his own problems. Impatiently, he walked back to Kelly and Stout."I got things to do."

"You said I could talk to my parents." Kelly blurted out, realizing immediately she'd made a big mistake.

Keyes grabbed her by the hair and jerked her forward so hard her chain went taught and the handcuff cut into her wrist. Kelly couldn't help crying out in pain. Infuriated, Keyes let go of her hair and backhanded her across the face. When she screamed, he took the gun in his other hand and swung it at the side of her head.

Kelly bounced from the blow, the back of her head thudding against the wall behind her, she collapsed and blood began oozing through her hair and trickling down her face.

Stunned at his loss of control, Keyes just stared at the girl. Kelly didn't move.

Finally, Stout whispered, "Jesus Christ Keyes, you killed her."

September 26, 9:00 PM

Jake and Suzie Donovan walked toward the Rose and Crown pub a little after nine o'clock. From the hustle and bustle of a few hours earlier, it appeared as if the good citizens of Greysmeade had indeed gone to bed for the night. However, as they soon discovered, the villagers weren't asleep, they were all in the pub, happily drinking and exchanging stories about their day, the main topic of conversation being the group of Americans staying at Greystone Manor. When Jake and Suzie walked through the door, they were greeted with cheers and a round of applause.

Astonished by their welcome, Jake leaned down to his wife and said quietly, "This is going to be easier than we thought." They were on a mission to gather information about the man Suzie had seen earlier. Jake was going to play Texas cowboy so Suzie could fade into the background to mingle and observe.

Many of the people they'd met that afternoon were there. Even Emma White was sitting at a table near the window, her foot propped up on a chair, left arm in a sling and a pint in her right hand.

While Jake and Suzie worked their way down the bar, talking and shaking hands, several people moved tables and chairs around, making room for them to sit in the middle of room. By the time they sat down, Charlie, the barkeep, had already drawn two pints, which were passed from person to person across the pub to their table. "Thank ya kindly my friend," Jake said and raised his glass, giving Charlie a nod.

Everyone wanted to know how the Talbot sisters were doing. "Those girls are feisty as any filly I've ever seen," Jake laughed. "They were holding court in the lounge when we left. Looks like Emma's a feisty one too."

Jake stood, gave her a devilish grin and raised his glass, "To Emma…"

"To Emma," shouted the rest of the room, joining the toast.

Emma White giggled and blushed. Usually quiet and shy, Emma was thoroughly enjoying her new status as celebrity for the day. Her husband, who sat by her side, looked on with pride and obvious adoration.

Jake was larger than life and the villagers of Greysmeade were enthralled to have a real live cowboy in their midst. One by one they all came to say Hello, several of the younger men wanting to try on Jake's Stetson. Smoke swirled through the air drifting up to the ceiling and Jake felt right at home when he pulled out a thin cheroot and struck a match on the sole of his boot.

The Rose and Crown had been the village gathering place for more than five hundred years. Over the centuries the pub had passed through many hands, but regardless of ownership, everyone from the local gentry to the village smithy had always felt welcome. The tables and chairs had been replaced, and the kitchen had been remodeled many times, but the bar itself dated from when the doors first opened in 1493.

"Anyone up for a game of darts?" Jake asked, spotting the dartboard on the back wall. He ended up with so many takers, he looked like the Pied Piper as he led everyone to the back of the pub.

Suzie chatted with some of the women, while keeping a watchful eye on the front door. She hadn't seen her target yet and didn't want to miss him. As news of their arrival made its way through the village, more and more people crowded into the pub, but she didn't see the man she was looking for.

Three games of darts and several pints later, Jake came back to sit with Suzie. It was getting near closing time and usually the crowd would have thinned to the last few hangers on. Thanks to the Americans, however, no one was in a hurry to leave and no one, other than Suzie, paid any attention when the door opened.

Suzie laughed as if Jake had just said something outrageously funny and threw her arm around his neck, pulling his head down to give him a kiss on the cheek. Instead she whispered in his ear, "He just came in."

Jake gave her a quick peck, then turned towards the door. In stark contrast to the throng of happy, though slightly inebriated, villagers, and looking even more sullen than when Suzie had first seen him, the man shoved his way to the bar. From the stench of his breath, it was obvious he'd been drinking heavily long before he arrived at the pub and, while people seemed to know him, they got out of his way as if they wanted nothing to do with him.

Jake stood up and reached the bar just as Charlie rang the bell for last call. Glancing at his watch, he laughed and said, "Things would just be startin' to jump back home." He cleverly maneuvered himself right next to Suzie's target, clapped a huge hand on his shoulder and bellowed, "The last round's on me."

A cheer went up from the crowd, but the man next to Jake, glared at him and mumbled, "Someday I'm standin' the last round," as he attempted to get a cigarette out of the crumpled pack he'd retrieved from his pocket.

"Let me help you with that," Jake said as he offered a light. "This place is great. Is it always so much fun?"

"Yeah, right," the man responded, wobbling so much he had trouble getting the cigarette to the flame.

"Nice town you got here. Lived here long?"

"What's it to ya?"

As Charlie started passing pints for him to pass on around the pub, Jake thought standing the last round hadn't been such a good idea after all. The noise level was so high Jake couldn't hear what the man was saying. The few words he did pickup were something about Brazil.

Jake was still passing back pints of beer when the first wave of people came up to say goodbye. He stooped down to let a short middle-aged woman kiss him on the cheek and shake hands with her husband. When he was able to turn his attention back to the man next to him, the stool was empty.

As they left the pub, Jake was kicking himself for letting the guy get away. "Dammit all Suz, I never shoulda bought the last round. That little snake slipped right through my fingers. I'm sorry."

"Don't be sorry Darlin', we got enough to go on."

"How do you figure we got anything out of that fiasco? The guy was drunker than a skunk, talkin' about South America."

"Jake," she answered patiently, "everybody knows him. Think about it. All we have to do is come back tomorrow and talk to the bartender. He'll tell us everything we need to know."

Jake grinned at her with pride, "You're really somethin', you know that?"

"Yep, that's me all right, Little Miss Detective. Come on Watson, let's head back to the ranch."

September 26, 11:30 PM

Jake and Suzie walked into the lounge of Greystone Manor to find the rest of their group having a nightcap.

"Hey," greeted Jake, "How Y'all doin'?" Suzie took a seat on the sofa next to Dolores, while Jake pulled up an armchair. Spying their glasses, he grinned, shook his finger at Millie and teased, "What have you got there, Darlin'?"

"Bailey's all around," answered John, "You interested?"

"Sure, why not? They threw us out of the pub. Craziest hours I've ever seen." John signaled the waiter to bring another round and add two more.

"So, what did you find out about our mystery man?" Chloe, who had been biting her tongue since they walked in, couldn't stand it any longer.

"You tell 'em Suz," Jake said, leaning back to enjoy his drink.

When Suzie finished, Chloe said, "We're supposed to have a free day tomorrow anyway, so we might as well make a little trip into town. Who wants to ride horses anyway?"

Everyone laughed when Jake gave a groan and slumped in his chair, pretending to be shot through the heart.

"So, what have Y'all be up to while we were playin' Sherlock Holmes?" asked Suzie.

"Well, John and I went for a walk in the moonlight," Dolores said, rolling her eyes as her husband tossed an arm around her shoulders and gave her a little squeeze. "No kidding, the grounds are really beautiful. We could hear the river gurgling, but couldn't really see anything. It was too dark.

"It might be fun to take a hike tomorrow," replied John, then looking at Marge and Millie added, "You girls up for it?"

"Only if I don't have a headache," answered Marge raising her glass to polish off her last drop of Bailey's. "This is my third one!"

Everyone laughed and agreed to meet for breakfast at nine the next morning rather than eight-thirty.

September 26, 9:30 PM

Madeline and Robbie sat at the dining table in Madeline's suite, wrinkled linen napkins resting beside their empty plates. They had ordered a simple dinner of roast beef, herbed potatoes and bread pudding from room service, along with a bottle of Cabernet which now, half-empty, rested on the table.

Robbie stood and stretched, raising his arms over his head, unable to contain a huge yawn. "I'm not really tired," he said, reaching for his glass and the wine bottle, "only oxygen deprived."

"Oh God, don't do that, it's contagious" Madeline said as she yawned back.

She followed him to the sofa where he filled their glasses again and they sat down facing the fireplace.

"All in all, I think this has been a pretty successful day," said Madeline as she kicked off her shoes, put her feet on the coffee table and leaned back against the pillows.

"Swing your feet around here, Lassie and I'll give 'em a good rub."

"Yes master," she said and groaned with pleasure as he began to massage first one foot, then the other. "You're a saint, Robert MacDuff, of the first order."

Madeline sank back against the padded arm of the sofa and closed her eyes for a second, then opened them again, looking at Robbie as a multitude of feelings raced across her face. "I just wish somebody had actually heard Kelly's voice."

"So do I, but I agree with Paul, it wouldn't be to the kidnapper's advantage to kill her. Paul still thinks she is alive." He stopped and shook his head, "And Andrews, if it is Andrews, is playing some kind of sick game."

"What is it? What are you thinking?

"Nothing. I'm just sitting here thinking, my stomach's full, I'm with the woman of my dreams, and we're talking about our poor lass like she was the pawn in a chess game."

"It's hard, isn't it?"

"Aye, the whole situation is unimaginable, and we still don't even know who's leaking information from here. Its just so hard for me to accept that one of our staff…" He couldn't finish.

"But we do have a good lead with Andrews. Don't borrow trouble Robbie. I just have a gut feeling we're on the right track." Silently reaching for her wine glass, she started to sit up, but Robbie beat her to the punch and handed it to her.

Madeline took a sip and leaned back again. They fell into a comfortable silence and when Madeline closed her eyes again, Robbie studied her face and thought how lucky he was to have found her. The soft lamplight shining on her silver hair made her lineless face all the more beautiful. He knew she was over fifty, but her face was as smooth as that of a woman half her age. Well maybe not half, but at least twenty years younger.

No, Madeline Marlborough was a natural and, as far as he was concerned, the most perfect match he'd ever met. The only problem was, she lived in America and he lived in London. "Well that's my next project," he thought to himself.

"We'll just have to move the Atlantic Ocean and half the North American continent."

She opened her eyes and caught him staring at her. "What do you see?"

"Ah Maddie girl, you've seen so much in your life, yet you've not so much as a wrinkle on your brow." He answered with awe.

She laughed, "You make me sound like Dorian Grey. Oooh, I've got a portrait in my closet that looks like a hag," she said doing her best imitation of a ghost.

Starting to apologize, he said, "I didn't mean it like that…I"

"I know," she chuckled, reaching for his hand. "Blame it on my genes. You should see my mother at eighty. It makes Chloe crazy. She keeps warning me my luck's going to run out and, when I turn into a prune, she's going to laugh at me all the way to the plastic surgeon."

"Well, you'll still be beautiful to me," he said quietly.

She pulled her feet from his lap and sat up. "Robbie, cut it out, you're going to make me blush," then patting her thigh said, "OK, put your feet up here."

"Maddie, you don't have to…"

"No way," she shook her head, patting her thigh again. "Turn about's fair play. Now get 'em up here."

As she began to massage his right foot, his reaction was much as hers had been and they fell, once again, into a comfortable silence.

Robbie's feet were long and lean, just like the rest of him and Madeline had to smile, wondering if the old wives tale was true about the size of a man's feet. She was about to make a smartass remark, when she looked up and saw he was sound asleep.

Oh Robbie, she thought, studying his sweet face. If only…If only what? Obviously a romantic relationship with him was out of the question. For one thing, he lived in London and she lived in Colorado. And then there was the age factor, she was at least ten years older. It might be OK if I never had to take my clothes off, she thought. My God, it would be like going to bed with the Pillsbury doughgirl! Her face might not look fifty-four years old, but the rest of her sure as hell did. No, she didn't even want to think about it.

Gently she slid off the sofa, trying not to wake him. She got an extra blanket from her closet, and when she draped it over him, careful to cover his bare feet, he didn't move a muscle. She kissed his forehead, turned out the light and thought, if only…if only…

CHAPTER 20

▼

Thursday, September 27, 5:45 AM
Coincidence? I Think Not!

Henry Keyes pulled up in front of the old mill. He was still fuming over the latest conversation with his recently acquired partner. He wished he'd never heard of Clayton Andrews, but it was too late now. Besides, he'd needed Andrews' contacts to get the necessary information to put his plan into action.

Keyes liked to think he'd befriended the old man in the next cell at Wormwood Scrubs, but it had actually been the other way around. Nigel Andrews had come to his rescue after an overzealous inmate had decided he wanted Keyes for his pet. Seniority had its perks and Andrews had been incarcerated at Wormwood Scrubs seventeen years before Keyes arrived. Andrews informed the randy fellow that Keyes was already spoken for.

When Keyes realized Andrews didn't expect any physical favors and was only trying to help him, they became friends. During the two years they spent in adjacent cells, Keyes repeatedly heard of Edward Dalton's betrayal. To escape hearing the same thing over and over, Keyes came up with the idea of plotting revenge. The old man relished the idea and not only wanted to retrieve the money he'd lost but also bring down the entire Dalton family. However, everything changed when Andrews died six months before his release.

Andrews planned to blackmail someone in Dalton's company for the computer system's security codes, but he died without revealing who or what he had on them. Without Nigel's contacts Keyes had no way to make the plan work, so he devised a new plan. He would simply kidnap the top official of Dalton's London office and collect a million pounds in ransom.

The only reason he'd contacted Clayton Andrews was to find out what he knew about Dalton and to make sure he didn't have any plans of his own. However, because Keyes was so aggressive, Clayton became suspicious and told Keyes he would blow his scheme sky high if Keyes didn't cut him in. Keyes had no choice but to agree. Soon the younger Andrews had assumed the role of mastermind and what Keyes had planned to be a simple kidnapping, now seemed to be much larger and more sinister. He wasn't sure what kind of game Andrews was playing, but he wanted it over and he wanted his money.

He opened the car door and stood up, his head pounding thanks to his previous night's drinking at the Rose and Crown. Andrews had called an hour before and demanded Keyes go to the mill and let Kelly talk to her father precisely at six o'clock.

Keyes opened the mill door to find Stout and Kelly fast asleep. When they'd discovered she wasn't dead, only knocked out, Stout insisted on staying with her through the night. Keyes was so relieved she was still alive, he didn't object. Stout didn't have the heart to stake her to the floor again. Of course she was still chained to the wall. "Time to wake up you two," Keyes said as he shook Stout's shoulder. "I even brought you a present."

Stout instantly awakened and whispered as he stretched, "Come on Keyes, let the poor girl sleep. I still don't see why you wouldn't unlock her hand. It's bloody unkind to keep her chained up like an animal."

Kelly began to stir, groaning from the tremendous pain in the back of her scull where she'd hit the wall. As she tried to sit up, she winced and cried out, so dizzy she thought she was going to be sick.

Keyes remembered the aspirin bottle in his pocket. "Hold her steady while I get some water," he told Stout. Quickly returning, he handed Kelly the cup and continued, "Here, take these." She hesitated. "They're just aspirin. Go ahead and take 'em. You want to feel better when you talk to your Daddy, don't you?"

Kelly swallowed the three pills and looked up at Keyes. She wanted so much to ask when, but remembered what that question had cost her the night before.

Keyes looked at his watch. Two minutes to six.

September 27, 2001 5:58 AM

Sitting around the dining table in the Dalton's suite, Graham, Madeline, Robbie, Helen Bainbridge and the Dalton's stared at the phone, willing it to ring.

Their meeting had begun at five, when Madeline rushed through the door desperate for a cup of coffee. Graham opened with two new pieces of information. "First, Andrews still resides at his flat in Chelsea, but when detectives arrived to question him, he wasn't there. We have officers staked out directly across the street and they'll question the neighbors if he doesn't return by eight o'clock.

"Why wait until eight?" asked Joe. "Are you afraid to wake them up?"

"If we wait until a civilized hour to question them, we'll obtain more information," replied Paul, raising his cup of tea. "We English need our morning tea as much as you Yanks need your coffee."

"Anything else?" asked Madeline, trying to diffuse a potential confrontation between Paul and Joe. Everyone's nerves were frayed and an argument would only draw their focus away from the real issue at hand.

"Yes, the lab analysis of the conversation you pinpointed Madeline, shows the call was made at half past ten yesterday morning from the phone in Robbie's office."

Everyone nodded.

"From my office?" exclaimed Robbie, "It's true then, the mole is one of the staff. The guests don't have access to my office. The gall to think someone would use my phone…"

Madeline interrupted adding, "We were on our way back from the Arcade. I remember because I had about twenty minutes before our meeting at eleven, so I went upstairs and checked in with Chloe." Turning to Robbie, she continued, "But I took a taxi and you took the Tube. You must have gotten back just before eleven."

"Correct," Robbie answered. "I arrived with no time to spare and came here directly. When we finish, I'll check the staff schedule and find out who was on duty yesterday morning."

The minutes were slowly ticking toward six o'clock. It had been twenty-four hours since the last call. Joe looked at his watch for the hundredth time, praying they would hear Kelly's voice.

When the phone rang, everyone jumped. As Joe picked up the receiver, lights began to flash, indicating the recording equipment had been activated.

"Hello, this is Dalton."

"Daddy?"

"Kelly. Honey are you alright?"

"I'm OK."

Joe could hear scuffling, knowing someone was trying to take the phone away from her. "Kelly, don't worry, everything will be fine. Be tough, Honey. You hang on. Don't give up."

"I will. And Daddy, make sure you tell Mom and Grandma Graue I love them."

The line went dead. Joe dropped the receiver and reached for Marty, half-falling into her arms as they held tightly to each other, weeping with relief.

"Thank God," said Madeline as she threw her arms around Robbie's neck.

"Splendid, absolutely splendid," said Paul as he quickly removed the tape and replaced it with another.

Helen picked up receiver and returned it to its cradle. "Wonderful!" she exclaimed.

Everyone was on their feet, laughing and hugging, thrilled to know Kelly was OK, when suddenly the phone rang again. Startled into silence, they sat down as Joe picked up the receiver.

"Hello, this is Dalton," said Joe. Even though his heart was still racing, Joe knew it was Andrews and that he had to keep him talking for ninety seconds.

"Did ET phone home?" asked the electronically distorted voice.

"Yes, thank God," Joe answered.

"You're welcome," he mocked. "I trust she was well?"

"Listen to me, Andrews, you better make sure she stays that way, or I swear I'll hunt you down and…"

"Ah, so you think you know who I am, do you?"

"You're Clayton Andrews, you bastard."

"If you say so."

Paul cautioned Joe not to give away too much and to stay calm.

Joe took a steadying breath and tried a new tactic. "Look Andrews, I'm sorry about your father's death, but why did you take Kelly? She didn't have anything to do with what happened."

"True," the voice said, "but she's the apple of her Grandfather's eye and your only child."

"What is it you really want, the money or revenge?"

"I'm entitled to both, don't you think? After all, your father swindled mine out of his company and left him to rot in prison."

"My father didn't swindle anyone. Your father's the one who gambled away his clients investments and then tried to cover it up."

"I'm holding the cards now and if you want to see your daughter again, you'll do what I say."

"Alright, I'll do whatever you want, but I can't carry ten million pounds in cash."

"Of course not, you fool. You're going to transfer nine million to a numbered account and deliver a million in unmarked, hundred pound notes. Surely you're strong enough to carry that much," he added sarcastically.

"Yes," Joe answered.

"Once I've confirmed the fourteen million's been received, I'll give you instructions where to drop the cash."

"Alright," Joe answered, "give me the number. And remember, it will take me a couple of hours to make the arrangements. I'll need to go to the office here and make some calls. Just make sure you don't hurt my daughter."

There was a click on the line. As Joe hung up the phone, Paul said, "Well done. We should have an answer on the trace shortly."

"Finally some progress!" Joe nodded, giving the account number to Paul. "You can track this number, right?"

Paul glanced at the number. "It's Swiss. Yes, we can trace it." Looking up, he smiled at Joe and Marty. "You did an excellent job, and now I'm certain the man behind the kidnapping is Clayton Andrews."

"Good, now all we have to do is find him," observed Madeline.

"Can you play back Kelly's tape?" asked Marty. "I just want to hear her voice."

"Of course," answered Paul. "The second call came so quickly, we didn't have time to listen, did we?"

At the sound of Kelly's voice, Marty clutched Joe's hand and listened intently, but when the short conversation ended, they looked at each other and simultaneously said, "Who's Grandma Graue?"

"What?" questioned Paul.

"Kelly doesn't have a Grandma Graue," Marty answered.

"We don't even know anyone named Graue," added Joe.

"Maybe she was trying to tell you something?" suggested Madeline.

"I'm sure of it," said Paul with a smile. "What a clever girl, your Kelly. Now think. The name Graue has to mean something."

After a moment, Marty shouted, "Graue, The Graue Mill! Joe, she means the Graue Mill."

Before anyone could ask the question, Joe pounded his fist on the table and said with jubilation, "That's it! She did it! She told us where she is!"

"You've lost me. Where is she?" asked Madeline.

"The Graue Mill is an old grist mill not too far from where we live. It was used as a station on the Underground Railroad during the Civil War and is now a historical monument. Every child in the area takes a field trip there at least once a year."

"A mill would also explain the water sounds from the first call," mused Paul. "We'll have to do some research to locate all the mills within a hundred mile radius, but this is crucial information. Excellent!"

Everyone now had an assignment except Madeline. Joe was going to his London office, Paul was returning to Scotland Yard, Helen and Marty would remain in the suite in case another call came through and Robbie was going to his office to check the previous day's personnel schedule. They were to reconvene at eleven.

As they walked down the hall to the lift, Robbie put his hand on Madeline's shoulder. "Thanks for tucking me in last night. I didn't mean to fall asleep on you."

"Oh, that's alright," she answered, a little embarrassed. "I was exhausted too. My head hit the pillow and I was out like a light. I didn't even hear you leave."

"I guess I woke up around three."

Stepping into the lift, Madeline, still felt a little awkward. "I'm going to go call Chloe and let her know what's happening. You'll let me know if you find anything?"

Robbie felt Maddie withdrawing from him and wished they could return to the closeness they'd shared the night before. He sensed her discomfort and, as the door opened on the second floor, he squeezed her shoulder and said, "Tell Chloe hello for me."

Madeline pulled her room key from one pocket and her cell phone from the other, letting herself in and dialing Chloe's number at the same time.

"It's about time I heard from you," Chloe scolded. "What's going on?"

"Good morning to you too," laughed Madeline. "I'm sorry I didn't check in last night. I was so tired I wouldn't have made sense anyway."

"Did you get any...sleep?" Chloe asked slowly, hinting that she might not have slept alone.

"Yes," Madeline answered in the same tone of voice, "and, for your information, Robbie slept on the sofa."

"I don't know about you," Chloe teased with a hint of exasperation in her voice.

"Yeah, Yeah. So, what's going on in the country?"

"No, you first,"

"OK, but where did we leave off?"

"Maddie, I haven't talked to you since you got back from the Burlington Arcade!"

"Well, things have been happening fast and furiously. Best of all, Kelly is still alive! And we know who's behind the kidnapping."

"Oh my God...My God, Maddie, that's huge!" exclaimed Chloe. "What did she say? Who is this guy? How did you find him?" she asked, her questions erupting one after the other.

"Kelly wasn't allowed to say much, but we know she is alright." Madeline paused, rearranging her thoughts. "I'm getting ahead of myself. Let me start at the beginning.

"Joe talked to his Dad yesterday to find out if he knew anything that could help the investigation. It turns out the London branch of their company was originally owned by a man named Nigel Andrews. Ed, Joe's father, found out Andrews had gambled away his investor's money and was trying to cover it up by dumping phony securities on the market and, when Ed blew the whistle, Andrews ended up in jail. Ed worked out a deal to take over the business and repay the investors."

"How does this have anything to do with Kelly?" Chloe asked, a little confused.

"I'm getting to that," said Madeline. "Andrews lost everything, his company, his money, his family, and then he died six months before he was supposed to be released."

"Dead? If he's dead, how could he have kidnapped Kelly? I don't get it."

"Chloe!" said Madeline, "If you'll quit interrupting me, I'll tell you."

"OK, OK, go on."

"Andrews has a son. He's the one who kidnapped Kelly, but he's in the city, at least we think he's still here, and Kelly is being held somewhere in the country."

"And you know that because?"

"Remember the two tapes from the very first calls?"

"Uhum."

"They came from two different places. The lab was able to filter out everything except the background noise, and one had city traffic sounds and the other had the sound of a river or stream and rustling leaves…Oh! I almost forgot. Kelly gave her Dad a clue."

"What did she say?"

"She told him to tell her Mom and Grandma Graue she loved them."

"So where's the clue?"

"Chloe!"

"Sorry."

"Kelly doesn't have a Grandma Graue. Joe and Marty think she was telling them that she's in an old grist mill. There's a historical monument near their home in Illinois called The Graue Mill."

Chloe was trying to digest all the new information when she suddenly remembered what the Shepard's said about their walk last night.

"Maddie, John and Dolores took a walk around the grounds last night and said they could hear the river going over rocks or rapids or something, farther downstream. They couldn't see anything because it was dark, but they could hear it. And there's something else. We went into town yesterday afternoon and Marge and Millie had a little accident."

"Are they OK?"

"They're fine. I'll tell you about that later. What I was getting at is when Suzie went into the pub to get ice, she saw a man at the bar who made her uneasy."

"Uneasy?"

"Yeah. According to Jake, she gets vibes from people or premonitions and most of the time she turns out to be right. Anyway, something about this guy made her uneasy, so they went back to the pub after dinner."

"What happened?"

"Well, this guy came in just as the pub was about to close. They didn't really get to talk to him, but Suzie got the same vibes as before, and they're convinced the locals know him. They're going back today to talk to the bartender."

"Chloe, you don't suppose…?"

"I'm thinking there's a possibility."

"Combine the whole water thing with Suzie's premonition…"

"And don't forget the trees," interrupted Chloe, her excitement building, "There are a lot of trees around here and dry leaves are all over the ground."

Madeline's mind was racing. What if…? "Chloe, I'm coming out there. Even if its only a remote possibility these pieces belong to the same puzzle, we have to follow the clues. If, by some miracle, we can find Kelly, we might be able to save the Dalton's fifteen million dollars. Scotland Yard has everything under control and Robbie is working on ferreting out the mole here at the hotel. They really don't need me for anything."

"Great! How soon can you get here?"

"What time is it now?"

"I've got seven-thirty."

"Me too. I have a friend at Hertz and if he can send a car to the hotel, it should take about an hour and a half. I should be there by nine-thirty. Let everyone have their breakfast and we'll meet in your room as soon as I arrive."

"Oh Maddie, I've got a good feeling about this."

"I do too. I'll see you in a little while."

CHAPTER 21

▼

Thursday, September 27, 7:45 AM
A Sleuthing We Will Go

As Madeline hurried down the stairs and through the lobby, she didn't see Robbie anywhere, so she decided it would be best to get on her way and call him from the car.

Her friend from Hertz had the rental agreement ready for her to sign, gave her the keys and she was pulling away from the curb in a matter of minutes.

Reaching for her cell phone, she dialed Robbie's number and waited for him to pickup. She knew he probably wouldn't be happy about her departure, but she thought putting some distance between them was a good idea. Remembering what might have happened last night, they could very well have ended up in bed. Madeline wasn't sure she was ready to take their relationship to that level. It had been so long since she had given herself to a man that the mere thought scared her to death. Besides, she rationalized, it wouldn't be fair to start something with Robbie when she knew nothing could come of it. My God, any relationship would be difficult for her, let alone one that required a transatlantic commute.

"MacDuff here."

"Hi Robbie, its Madeline."

"Just the person I wanted to talk to. How about going out to dinner tonight?"

"Well that's going to be a little difficult. I'm on my way out to Greystone Manor…" When there was no response, she plowed ahead telling him about her conversation with Chloe. "So you see why I need to be there."

"Aye lass," he finally agreed, "Much as I'll miss you, you're needed more at Greystone than here. If there is more to it than coincidence, you'd best find out what it is."

"If there is even a remote chance we could find Kelly, we have to investigate. Were you able to find the staff schedule from yesterday?"

"Aye, I found it. There are several possibilities, several women from housekeeping, the reservations staff and of course, my staff. I just can't believe one of my people could be involved with this. They have been with me for so many years, but you never know what a person will do if they are desperate enough."

As Madeline circled the roundabout at Holland Park and headed toward the motorway, she told him the traffic was moving quickly and estimated her arrival at Greystone to be about an hour. "I'll call you after our meeting. I'm really optimistic we're on the right track."

"I'll cover for you here. And Maddie, I think it's best if no one knows you've left the city."

"Good idea. I don't think anyone other than a few guests, saw me leave. Hopefully you can keep our mole in the dark."

"Drive safely and I'll talk to you in a little while."

Madeline clicked off and thought to herself, "Well, that was easier than I thought. Maybe I'm reading way too much into this thing with Robbie." Strangely though, she was a little disappointed.

September 27, 9:10 AM

The combination of Madeline's heavy foot and the light traffic brought her to the portico of Greystone Manor twenty minutes ahead of schedule. She gave her keys to the valet and went to find Chloe.

Walking through the ancient country house, Madeline was impressed once again at the way Simon Grey continued to improve the property. It had been three years since her last visit, and the carpet and furnishings were as fresh now as they had been then.

Walking into the dining room, Madeline spotted her group sitting in the alcove overlooking the gardens. As she approached, Jake stood up and gave her a bear hug, lifting her completely off the floor.

"If you aren't a sight for sore eyes," he said, setting her back on terre firma.

"Oh come on Jake, it's only been twenty-four hours," Madeline chuckled.

"And you wouldn't believe the mischief they've been making in that short amount of time," Chloe grinned and waved her finger around the table.

"So I've heard," Madeline said with a straight face, "You're all grounded!"

"Alright boys and girls. Roll call. My room. Fifteen minutes," barked Chloe, still grinning from ear to ear.

As Chloe and Madeline waited for the tiny lift to take them upstairs, Chloe whispered, "I ran into the Concierge this morning…"

Madeline looked directly at her and rolled her eyes to the left, cautioning Chloe to keep quiet as an unknown guest walked by. Chloe immediately got the message and clammed up until they were safely inside her room with the door closed.

"Sorry about that," she said, "But I wanted to tell you what I found out from the Concierge. I asked him if there were any good hiking trails in the area and he told me there is an abbey ruin about two miles west of here, on the north side of the river."

"Maybe Kelly mistook the ruin for a mill," Madeline offered, thinking this new piece of information would be a good place to begin their search. "How do we get across the river?"

"He said if we follow the path along the river, there is a footbridge. We can reach it by car as well, but we have to drive about ten miles out of the way and circle back to it on a dirt road."

They heard a soft tap on the door as Marge opened it, and the others followed her into the room. Marge and Millie sat on one bed, while Dolores joined Chloe on the other. Jake and Suzie turned the sofa around and John brought the desk chair for himself and the wing chair for Madeline.

"First of all," Madeline began, "Thank you for playing your part yesterday. If anyone was following you, I'm sure they thought it was business as usual."

"Oh my God," interrupted Chloe, "What about today? We were supposed to go to Stratford and Warwick!"

"It's alright. I called the local tour office from the car and told them we had to postpone today's sightseeing. I said Marge and Millie were under the weather and the rest of you didn't want to go without them."

"And they bought that?" asked Marge, raising her eyebrow.

"Well, of course they did," said Millie, answering her sister's question. "How could they know we're not your typical little old ladies?"

Everyone had to laugh for Millie was absolutely correct. The Talbot sisters were anything but typical.

The mood turned serious again as Madeline filled them in on everything that had happened back in London. "The more I think about it, the more I'm sure we're onto something. The pieces fit together too well to be coincidence."

"I'm sure of it too," Suzie concurred. "In fact, I'd bet Jake's Stetson on it."

"That's good enough for me," Jake said, slapping his hand on his thigh. "What do you want us to do?"

"You and Suzie are the only ones who have actually seen our mystery man, right?" asked Madeline.

"Yes Ma'am," answered Jake. "We were going to go back into town and see if we could scare up some more details about him."

"Is there a fast food place in the village?" asked Madeline. "We know another man is involved in this and there's Kelly too."

"You're right and it's been two days. Surely our mystery man would have to bring them something to eat," suggested Dolores.

"Or he could have taken supplies to the hideout before the kidnapping," John cut in.

"Either way, he would most likely have purchased those supplies at the village market," Dolores continued. "Remember John, when we went in to buy new groceries for Emma White? Wasn't there a take away counter back in the corner, beside the deli case?"

"You're right, Honey. There was even a chalkboard listing the daily specials."

"Good," said Madeline. Looking back toward Jake and Suzie, she asked, "Can you inconspicuously check out the pub and the market?"

"They can if we create a diversion," said Marge, bursting with enthusiasm. "Millie and I can stage a repeat performance of yesterday's fiasco. Everyone in town will come running. Then you two can slip into the pub and the market unnoticed."

"Only we can't use the needlework shop again," mused Millie. "It's right next to the pub."

"How about the button shop?" suggested Chloe. "It's closer to the other end of town."

"Perfect!" exclaimed Marge. "We can go in, stage an argument over something, then on the way out, I can fall down again."

"No sister. Let me fall down first this time."

"No, I should be the one to fall. You can do hysterical much better than I can."

"I suppose you're right," Millie began to acquiesce. "I am more theatrical."

Madeline shook her head at the elderly sisters, who were obviously delighted with their self-imposed assignment. Turning her attention to John and Dolores, she said, "Since you took a walk last night, it would make sense if you wanted to explore a little further today."

Chloe told them about the abbey ruin and footbridge. "If anything looks the least bit suspicious, don't get too close."

"Chloe and I will drive around to the back entrance and meet you," said Madeline. "It will save time getting back. Are we set then?" she asked. When everyone nodded, she added, "OK. Let's meet back here at noon. Be careful and Good Hunting." Looking around the room, she knew she'd been right to bring everyone in on the investigation.

September 27, 10:00 AM

Jake, Suzie and the Talbot sisters left Greystone Manor's courtesy car in the Village Carpark and parted company, the girls walking past the blacksmith while Jake and Suzie circled around and approached the main street from the other end of town, near the parish church.

As Marge and Millie proceeded past the Tobacconist and the Tailor, several villagers stopped to ask how they were feeling.

Opening the door to the button store, Millie whispered, "Everyone is so kind, I hate having to play a trick on them."

"We have a job to do," snapped Marge. "Don't wimp out now."

Millie glared at her sister with indignation. "I'm not a wimp, you…you tyrant."

This is great, Marge thought, we're not even through the door and we're arguing already.

As they entered the shop, Marge immediately recognized the woman behind the counter as one of those who had supplied a chair after yesterday's accident. She elbowed her sister and they both pasted on their best smiles.

"Good Morning ladies," said the clerk, "and how are you feeling this fine day?"

"We're quite well thank you," answered Millie.

"We wanted to stop in and thank you for your kindness yesterday," interrupted Marge.

Not to be outdone, Millie interrupted again, "Yes, everyone has been so kind and we wanted to look at your wonderful buttons too." Millie's eyes darted around the shop, and landed on a case of sterling silver buttons. "Oh look sister, aren't these beautiful?"

Marge and the clerk followed Millie to the glass display case. "I have some that are even better. Would you like to see them? I'll just fetch them from the back."

Without waiting for an answer, she disappeared behind a curtain and quickly returned with a stack of deep blue velvet cases. Laying them on top of the glass case, she opened the first to reveal an exquisite collection of intricate silver buttons shaped like flowers. There were several different sized roses, a daisy and a splendid bearded iris.

"Oh my goodness!" gushed Millie, "They are absolutely beautiful. Wouldn't this iris be perfect for my black dress?"

"I'm sorry I have only the one," apologized the clerk. "They're one of kind, you see, handcrafted by a silversmith in York."

"That's perfectly alright dear. I only need one. The jacket fastens right here," Millie said, indicating the hollow at the base of her throat. "How much is it?"

"It's rather expensive, twenty pounds, six, but it is a work of art."

"I'll take it," said Millie gleefully.

"Millie," cautioned her sister, "you realize that's about thirty-five dollars…for one button."

"It's a work of art. The lady said so," Millie replied, her head held high. "And besides, I want it. Go find your own button."

Marge wasn't sure if Millie was acting or not, but decided to assume she was and took the bait. "Fine Millie, it's your money, but don't develop buyer's remorse and complain I didn't warn you."

Millie gave her sister a rebellious smirk and ceremoniously handed the clerk her credit card. Not wanting to have any involvement in their argument, she quickly rang up the sale, placed the button in a small velvet box and prayed the sisters would leave before full-blown war was declared.

On the way out the door Millie whispered, "Wasn't that fun? Now say something really nasty to me."

Trying to keep a straight face, Marge whispered back, "OK, here goes."

But before Marge could say anything, Millie blurted out, "Don't you dare tell me what to do. It's my money and I'll spend it any way I see fit."

Picking up the cue, Marge shot back, "Well someone has to stop you from making a fool of yourself."

The argument got louder and louder, until it sounded like a first rate cat fight, each sister matching insult with insult, until Marge finally grabbed the package out of Millie's hand and whacked her in the arm with her purse.

Stunned, Millie wasn't sure what to do next until she saw Marge frantically rolling her eyes toward Millie's purse. Quickly catching the idea, Millie hit her back. Marge crumpled to the ground, careful not to hurt anything on the way down and Millie's shriek brought half the town running.

As soon as they saw the commotion at the other end of the street, Suzy darted into the market and Jake slipped into the pub.

From the back of the pub the barkeep, who was setting up for the lunch crowd, shouted, "You're a little early friend, we'll be open for lunch at eleven."

Jake strode back toward the kitchen and smiling said, "I may be from Texas, but it's even too early for me."

Looking up, Charlie greeted Jake warmly. "Well, when you're ready, it's on the house. You did a fine business for me last night. If you're not here for a pint, what can I do for you?"

"Got a question for you. Remember that skinny dude who came in just about closing time? What can you tell me about him?"

"What? Was he bothering you? Didn't steal nothin', did he?"

"Nah, he was too drunk to talk, let alone steal anything. I was just curious?"

"Not much to tell really. Name is Keyes, Henry Keyes. Good for nothin', if you ask me. Always cookin' up some plan to bilk people out of their hard-earned wages. Don't think he ever kept a real job in his whole life."

"He's lived here a long time then?"

"Off and on."

"What's his latest scam? He was trying to tell me about it last night, but I couldn't hear him over the crowd."

"He keeps saying he's going to hit it big this time, but he's said that a hundred times before and nothing's ever come of it. I don't expect this time will be any different."

"Well," Jake said as he looked at his watch, "I have to go meet the little lady, I thank you kindly for the information. If you wouldn't mind though, please don't say anything about our conversation to Keyes. I don't want him bothering my wife."

"What conversation? I was just telling you we don't open for lunch 'til eleven."

Jake reached up to tip his hat and remembered he'd left it in the car, so he shrugged his shoulders, thanked Charlie again and went out the door.

Once out on the sidewalk, Jake could see a crowd still gathered around the Talbot sisters and looking around, spotted Suzie just coming out of the market.

"Any luck?" she asked when she caught up with him.

"His name is Keyes and Charlie thinks he's a waste of a good barstool."

"Apparently he's a hungry waste. The girl at the take away counter says he's been buying enough food to feed an army. She said he comes in at least twice a day."

"Did she say what time he comes in? Maybe we could follow him."

"He's already been there this morning. Bought two loaves of bread, some ham and cheese and several bottles of water. Yesterday he came back in the evening and took every pastie she had."

"What's a pastie?"

"Cornish pastie. It's a hot pie filled with meat and potatoes."

Jake picked up his wife and swung her around in a circle. "Keyes is our man. He has to be. Come on." He grabbed her hand and they circled back around to the Carpark, then walked up the street as if they'd just arrived.

Making their way through the crowd of villagers gathered around Marge and Millie, they found Marge, once again sitting in a chair with Millie hovering around her, dabbing her tearstained eyes with a handkerchief someone had given her.

At first Jake thought that perhaps Marge had really been injured until he saw Millie wink at him from behind her hanky.

Suzy went to Marge's chair, "Are you alright? What in the world happened?"

"It's all my fault," wailed Millie, pretending to cry again.

"I'm OK," said Marge, "And it's not your fault. I shouldn't have badgered you." Looking up at Suzie, Marge made a silent appeal to get them out of here.

"Jake, honey, I think we ought to get them back to the hotel."

In true super-hero Jake fashion, he swooped in and scooped Marge out of her chair. "Don't you worry Sister Margaret, we'll get you back to Greystone in nothin' flat. You can have one of them fancy spa treatments. It'll cure whatever ails ya!"

Suzy thanked everyone for their kindness, put her arm around Millie's shoulder and guided her down the street following Jake, who refused to put his passenger back on the ground. When they reached the Carpark, Jake made a big show of putting Marge gently in the backseat, just in case anyone was watching. It was all they could do to maintain their composure until they were safely back on the road.

"We got 'im, girls! YEE ha, we got 'im," whooped Jake, one hand on the wheel and the other pumping air.

"And it's for sure everybody in town was watching you two, and not payin' a lick of attention to us. What on earth did you do to create such a commotion?"

"Oh my goodness," Millie said breathlessly, "We were wonderful, weren't we Marge?"

"Worthy of an Academy Award at least," Marge laughed.

"Oh sister, what a stroke of genius to hit me with your purse."

Astonished, Jake asked, "You hit her?"

"Well not very hard, but she really walloped me back."

"I had to make it look good, didn't I?" Millie chortled in her own defense. "I had to whack you hard enough so it wouldn't look too fake when you fell down."

"I was so afraid you wouldn't hit me back," laughed Marge, putting her arm around her sister's shoulder and giving her a squeeze, "but you came through like a trooper."

"I was magnificent, wasn't I?" Millie blushed.

"Judging by the size of the crowd you attracted, I'd say 'mission impossible' was definitely accomplished, but ladies," Jake said, about to burst if he couldn't talk about his and Suzie's discovery, "we got our man. I swear I'll eat my Stetson if Keyes ain't smack dab in the middle of this whole Kelly thing. Now all we gotta do is find him."

Giving voice to everyone's wish, Suzie said, "Hopefully John and Dolores' hike will turn up Keyes' hideout."

CHAPTER 22

───────── ▼ ─────────

September 27, 10:00 AM
The Lost Ruin of Greystone Abbey

The Shepard's left Greystone Manor by way of the conservatory and walked across the grounds, down to the riverbank. Fortunately Dolores had thrown their jeans in her suitcase, a last minute decision for which she was now very grateful. They didn't have hiking boots, but their well-worn walking shoes would suffice.

The manicured lawn, dotted with ancient shade trees, gently sloped down to the river where the trail Chloe had described was clearly visible.

Looking back at the Manor, Dolores said, "It looks just like a movie set, doesn't it?"

"Come on, Dee," John urged impatiently, "We don't have time to play Cecil B. DeMille."

"Will you please take a deep breath and slow down. If we're out for a leisurely stroll, we can't look like we're about to run the hundred-meter dash. Remember, if we can see the hotel, anyone watching can see us."

John knew she was right and he let her take the lead, following the trail downstream until the Manor was out of sight. Up to that point, the trail had been almost as well manicured as the hotel grounds, however, the terrain dramatically changed as the river turned sharply and plunged into a thick forest. Dried autumn leaves now covered the trail and crunched under their feet as they climbed the steep bank while the river rushed over the rocks below.

Dolores turned and shouted over her shoulder, "I don't think we're in Kansas anymore. You'd better go first."

The wind had picked up and between the rustling leaves and splashing river, John could barely hear her, but he got the message and climbed up beside her. "So much for the leisurely stroll, huh?"

Pointing ahead, Dolores shouted, "It looks like we keep going up while the river's cutting down through the ravine. I can't even see the trail anymore, can you?"

"Not really. It looks like some of it might have washed away. Maybe they've had a lot of rain."

"More like a monsoon," she answered, not thrilled with the prospect of delving into uncharted territory. "I'll bet the concierge hasn't been out here for a while."

"I think we'll be OK if we just follow the river."

"I think we should have driven with Madeline and Chloe."

Dolores followed her husband to the top of the incline and down the other side. Now the trail was invisible, overgrown with tall grass and dense vegetation. As they started to climb again, John tripped on a protruding tree root and almost fell.

"Are you alright?" Dolores asked hurrying up behind him.

"Yeah, but be careful. That root almost got me." John pointed out the danger spot and continued, "Looks like it gets pretty rocky up there, but I don't see any alternative do you?"

"No, not unless you want to try crossing the river, but it doesn't look any better on the other side and we have no way of knowing how deep it is."

John shook his head. "The current is moving too fast. Let's go on a ways. It can't be much further to the bridge and it may level out again."

"I hesitate to ask, but what are we going to do if the bridge is washed out?"

"Let's find it first, then we can worry about it. What is it you always tell the kids?"

"Don't borrow trouble?"

"Exactly!"

They started off again, climbing the next hill, which turned out to be steeper than the first one. Picking their way through the rocks and brush they finally emerged into a clearing and found the trail again.

"Look Dee," John said pointing to his right. "It looks like the trail went around the hills we just came over. We must have taken a wrong turn somewhere."

"I don't know where," she said with amazement. "John, look. Way up ahead. Could that be the bridge we're looking for?"

John turned to look where she was pointing. From his higher vantage point he could see something in the distance, about two hundred yards away, but couldn't tell whether or not it was the bridge. "Only one way to find out. Come on."

The trail was level and well defined so they ran ahead and were pleasantly surprised to find the little bridge in excellent condition.

Crossing the bridge was like stepping through Alice's looking glass. When Chloe said she and Madeline would meet them at the ruin, John and Dolores had expected to find a church with no roof. What lay before them was an enormous complex of half walls, towers and arches, resting on a carpet of thick green grass. Wild ivy cascaded down some of the walls and the morning sun cast eerie shadows of the sixty-foot high arches. Granted there was hardly any roof left intact, but this was certainly much more that just a church.

They didn't see or hear anything resembling human activity, but still they proceeded with great care. Walking along the outside of what must have been the monks quarters, they had gone about a hundred and fifty yards, when they finally rounded the corner and ran right into Madeline and Chloe.

"My God, you scared me to death!" whispered Dolores.

"I'm sorry," whispered Madeline in return. "We saw you coming, but didn't want to call out to you."

Understanding the situation, Dolores mouthed, "That's OK."

"Have you found anything?" John whispered anxiously.

"No, we just got here. What about you?" Chloe asked.

"No, we lost the trail for awhile and went through some rough terrain, but we didn't see anything," answered John. "In fact, I don't think anyone's been on that trail in a long time."

"Madeline, did you know about this place?" asked Dolores, in awe. "Its enormous."

Madeline shook her head. "I had no idea and I thought I knew every abbey ruin in England." Looking around the vast interior of the cathedral, she shook her head and continued, "This is every bit as large as Fountains Abbey. I can't believe I didn't know about it."

As they walked up the nave, Madeline pointed out the similarities in construction to Westminster Abbey. The nave had an aisle on either side leading up to the crossing tower and, while only the support columns and window arches remained, they could imagine what it must have looked like nine hundred years ago. Madeline was sure the architecture was the same style as Fountains Abbey, dating the construction somewhere between 1132 and 1247.

"Look at the arches of the cloister," she whispered, pointing to the area just to their right. A perfect square, at least a hundred feet on each side, was surrounded by an arched walkway. If the walls of the cathedral had been intact, the cloister would have been hidden from view, but with only the skeleton remaining, it could be seen perfectly. Some of the arches were still standing, but many were only partially intact, with grass and ivy seeming to sprout from the rock itself.

When they reached the crossing tower, with its outside wall still standing well over a hundred feet high, Madeline motioned them into the shadows where they couldn't be seen and whispered, "I don't think we're going to find anything in this part of the complex."

"They couldn't leave her here overnight without a roof," agreed Chloe. "Aren't all the ruins like this open to the public?"

"Yes," answered Madeline. "All the monastic ruins are under the jurisdiction of The British Trust."

"Surely our kidnapper wouldn't be stupid enough to use a public building for a hideout," John said.

"I'm thinking the same thing," returned Madeline. "But John, if we give up without searching the entire grounds, and it turns out we missed her, we'd never forgive ourselves."

"I know you're right, but searching every nook and cranny of this place will take all day and we're running out of time," John said echoing everyone's frustration. They were all getting more and more anxious as precious minutes slipped into history.

"Let's split up," Madeline suggested, "We can cover more ground. You two take the rest of the cathedral and the perimeter. Chloe and I will check the rest of the complex on the other side of the cloister."

"OK," said John, "We'll meet you back at the river. We need a signal, in case we find anything."

"I can whistle through my teeth," offered Chloe.

"Good," said John, already taking his wife's hand and heading for the opposite end of the cathedral, whispering over his shoulder, "So can I."

"Dammit, Chloe," Madeline growled. "Why do men have to be so impatient?"

"I don't know. It must be a testosterone thing."

"I don't really care what it is. We all want to find Kelly and we all know time is running out." She took a steadying breath, squared her shoulders and motioned for Chloe to follow her.

If this abbey were anything like the many others Madeline had seen, the most likely spot to hide someone would be the storage vaults, which were usually located under the monks quarters. The industrious monks would store everything from grain to animal pelts and sell their goods to merchants from Venice and Florence. If they could only find the entrance, they might get lucky and find Kelly as well.

Madeline and Chloe walked along the side of the cloister, passing what would have been the chapter house, finally coming to a stairway that lead down into the bowels of the abbey. Although steep and narrow, the stairway was shorter than Madeline expected and the two women emerged into the opening of a tunnel at least three hundred feet long. The vaulted ceiling, protected by the floors above, was perfectly preserved and natural light filtered through holes that had been cut into the walls along the side closest to the river.

Madeline and Chloe crept silently down the tunnel, careful to stay in the shadows. No sound could be heard, not even the wind.

Suddenly a sound broke the silence and both flattened against the wall. Madeline looked at Chloe and cautioned her not to move. There…they heard it again, about twenty feet away. Madeline motioned for Chloe to wait while she went ahead to investigate. Slowly she inched her way along the wall until she was right across from the source of the sound. She waited, then nearly laughed out loud. A rather large bird was trying to squeeze through an opening and into the nest it had built just under the ceiling.

Madeline reported back to Chloe, who was relieved to know they hadn't run into a monster or worse, and they continued their search. If the kidnappers had been looking for a sheltered spot to hide Kelly, this tunnel would have met all their criteria, but there was no evidence anyone had been here.

They returned to climb the stairway and found John and Dolores just in front of them, walking toward the river.

"OK kid," Madeline told her friend, "pucker up and blow."

At the sound of Chloe's whistle, John whipped around and ran toward them.

"Did you find anything?"

"Only a round bird trying to fit through a square hole," Madeline said shaking her head. "You?"

Dolores made a circle with her thumb and index finger. "Nothing," she said with dismay.

"I'm afraid we wasted a lot of time for nothing," said Chloe, obviously disappointed.

"There's one more building over there," Madeline said indicating a building about a hundred yards downstream. "Let's check it out and head back to Greystone. Jake and the others will be back soon."

They quickly walked to the last building on the abbey site, expecting not to find anything and they were right. The building was empty. Disappointment and frustration was visible on every face as they started to head back to Madeline's car, when she stopped abruptly.

"What is it?" Chloe asked.

"Listen. Do you hear it?"

"Hear what?"

"The river. Listen."

The four of them stood for a long moment, closing their eyes and concentrating on the sound of the river. Finally Dolores said, "It's louder downstream, isn't it?"

"Exactly," Madeline concurred. "Kelly told her father she was being held in a mill and a mill needs a river's current to turn the gears. The monks who built these monasteries were completely self-sufficient. Fountains Abbey has a mill downstream from the main complex and so do several others I've seen. Don't you get it? We've been looking in the wrong place."

"You really think there's something further downstream?" asked John.

"I do. John, you can make better time without us. Will you go check it out?"

"And if I find it?"

"If you find it, don't do anything. Just come back and we'll figure out what to do when we talk to Jake. We know there are two men holding Kelly. To me, that means at least one of them is with her all the time, and if he gets spooked, he might kill her, or you. Just see what you can see. Get the lay of the land. I'd rather have you and Jake go back together than have you go it alone."

"Be careful, Johnny. I love you," said Dolores, giving him a quick kiss. "We'll be right here when you get back."

John ran along the riverbank until he reached the edge of the abbey grounds. "This is like deja vous," he thought to himself as the river thrust into the deep forest. But unlike the edge of Greystone's grounds, a narrow path was visible, cutting through the trees.

Moving as quickly as he could, he made his way through the dense forest. When the path veered away from the riverbank, he thought twice about taking it. But the monks had to have known what they were doing, and Madeline was so sure they would have built a mill, he only hesitated a second, then followed the ancient trail at a brisk trot.

It turned out the path was actually a short cut. The river twisted and turned, while the path cut straight through the forest and caught up with the rushing water about a mile downstream.

He'd gone at least another mile when he stopped for a moment to catch his breath. As he stood there, bent over with his hands on his knees, he knew something was different, but what? Standing up, he turned in a circle, trying to find what had caught his attention. Nothing jumped out at him. Slowly he repeated the circle, all of his senses on full alert. Nothing. His eyes darted around and, through the filtered light, he was able to see the path had taken a small turn away from the river again. He couldn't see it, but he could hear it. "That's it! The river."

He stood frozen, like a statue, not moving a muscle, not even daring to breathe. The incessant splash of rushing water that had followed him all the way from the abbey had been replaced by a rhythm not produced by nature, splash—beat—splash—beat.

Slowly he moved forward, following the muffled, but steady sound. As he crept through the trees, trying very hard not to make any noise, the sound grew louder and louder. Suddenly he found himself at the river's edge.

Something was obstructing the river's progress. From his spot on the bank, it looked like a jumble of rotting tree trunks strewn over a large rock pile.

He darted back into the forest, using the trees as cover while he circled down-stream to get a better look.

"I'll be damned," he whispered under his breath. Madeline was right on the mark. It wasn't a rock pile at all, but a small stone building. The mill…Kelly's mill.

A kaleidoscope of emotions ran through the humble Iowa farmer. He didn't know whether to laugh or cry, shout with joy or scream with outrage. He'd found Kelly. He knew it as surely as he knew his own name and the hardest thing he would ever do in his life, was leave her there while he went for help.

Hidden in the trees, he could see the closed wooden door and the thatched roof. There was no outward sign anyone was in there, but John could feel her essence as surely as if he were looking straight into her eyes. He had to hurry now, but the thought of leaving her tore at his insides. What if it was one of his kids in there? What would he do? He would trust them to be smart and tough enough to survive until he could bring back reinforcements, which is exactly what he was going to do.

Just as he was turning to leave, something on the ground in front of the mill caught his eye. The sun was shinning down directly on a fresh tire track. It was all he needed to spur him into action. He walked quietly for about fifty yards, then broke into a run.

CHAPTER 23

▼

Thursday, September 27, 7:30 AM
Ransom Instructions and The Banker's Disguise

Until they knew who was leaking information and where it was going, and wanting as little movement in and out of the hotel as possible, Chief Inspector Graham insisted Joe stay in the suite rather than go to his London office. Joe was sitting on the sofa, talking into Helen Bainbridge's secure cell phone.

"Yes Dad, she's alive," Joe reassured his father. "Kelly's holding her own."

"Thank God, Joey," whispered his father, choking with emotion.

At the sight of her husband's tears, Julia Dalton felt her heart plunge into her stomach. "What is it Ed? What did he say?"

Unable to speak, Ed handed her the phone.

"Joey, it's Mom. Honey, what's happening with Kelly?"

"She's alright Mom. I just talked to her."

Relief replacing panic, Julia dropped the phone and threw her arms around her husband's neck.

"Mom? Dad? Are you there? Hello. Hello."

Overjoyed at the news their granddaughter was alive, Ed and Julia held each for a long moment, when Ed suddenly realized the phone was on the floor. He reached down with one hand to pick up the phone. Still holding Julia with the other hand, he could hear Joey's voice saying, "Hello. Mom? Where did you go?"

"Joey, we're here. Sorry about that, your mom got so excited she dropped the phone."

"I figured as much."

"What did Kelly say? Is she hurt?"

"I don't know. I only talked to her for a few seconds, but Dad, she gave us a clue where they're holding her."

"Where?"

"She said to tell her mother and Grandma Graue that she loved them."

"Who the hell is Grandma Graue?"

"That's exactly what we said. Dad, do you remember the Graue Mill out in Hinsdale?"

"We haven't been there in years, but I know where it is."

"Well, we think she was telling us she's being held in a mill."

"I'll be damned."

"Ed, what's he saying?" Julia asked impatiently.

"Kelly was able to tell them where she is," Ed told his wife.

"And?" she demanded impatiently.

"She's in a mill, like the Graue Mill," Ed said, dodging her hand. "Just wait and I'll tell you everything."

"Dad, there's more," interrupted Joe. "You were right about Andrews. The old man died before he was released from prison and his son, Clayton, is out for revenge."

"I'll be damned," his father said again. "I'm so sorry Joey, this is all my fault."

"Dad, how could you have known what was going to happen?"

"I should have remembered when Nigel was going to be released and I should have told you about it."

"Don't dwell on it, Dad. Besides, I need your help."

"Anything Joey, you know I'll do anything I can."

"I'm going to need a million pounds in cash. Can you authorize the bank here to withdraw that much?"

"Yes. What about the rest, do you only need a million now?"

"No he wants all of it, but I said there was no way I could carry that much cash. He wants the other nine million transferred to a Swiss numbered account."

"Good," said Ed, his mind racing ahead, thinking about how he was going to pull off the transfer and retrieval of such a huge amount of money. "Is Scotland Yard working on this?"

"Chief Inspector Graham is on it. He assured me that between his computer geeks and the ones from Interpol, they will be able to make the transfer look real, then retrieve the money. But Dad, there's an outside chance we may not be able to recover the cash."

"With Kelly's life at stake, do you really think I'm worried about a million dollars."

"Pounds Dad, a million pounds, more like a million and a half dollars."

"It's a small price to pay for our darling girl." Shaking his head and smiling, Ed added, "She's a real corker, isn't she? I'll bet none of us would have had enough composure to come up with a clue like that."

"I sure know I wouldn't have," answered Joe.

"Joey, I'm going to call Archibald Drake at the London Bank. It's the middle of the night here, but Archie can arrange all the transfers from there and I trust him. As president of the bank, no one will question his actions."

"So do I. I don't know him very well, but you've been friends a long time," said Joe.

"I'll ask him to bring the cash to you personally. Then he can work directly with your Inspector and Interpol to arrange the transfer of the rest."

"Great and Dad, be sure and tell him to come directly to our suite. We don't know yet who is leaking information to Andrews, but we do know it's someone on the hotel staff."

"Right. How is Marty holding up?"

"She's much better now that we've heard from Kelly. She's just anxious to have her back."

"Tell her we love her. You'll let us know as soon as you hear anything?"

"Absolutely."

"And Joey, we love you."

"I know Dad, I love you too."

September 27, 8:10 AM

Robbie hung up the phone, disappointed but understanding why Madeline had left the city. He'd never met anyone like her and if circumstances were different, he would have followed her. Madeline was everything he'd always wanted; strong, educated, funny, compassionate, down to earth, independent and passionate about her work.

It had been a short night. As a matter of fact, he'd only had a few hours sleep in the last three days. He got up from his desk, stretched and walked to the window. Staring out, but not really seeing the beautiful rose garden, he began to replay the previous night in his mind. If they hadn't been so tired, he knew they could easily have ended up making love. Would it have ruined their friendship, he wondered, or would it have taken them to a new beginning? Madeline was skittish, of that he was certain. And how did he really feel? Aside from the physical attraction, how far was he ready to commit?

His head was telling him this was not the time to be making life-altering decisions. He and Madeline were both under too much stress to think clearly. On the other hand, they had never needed each other more. But in what capacity? How did that song go? "So I'll be your friend, and I'll be your lover."

"Robert?"

"Hum? What?" Startled back to reality, Robbie turned to see Violet Hargrove poking her head through his office door.

"Are you alright Robert? Is anything wrong?"

"No, I'm fine, just enjoying the view for a moment. We never seem to take time to enjoy the beauty around us. Always too busy, aren't we?"

"How true," Violet answered. "I didn't see Miss Marlborough at breakfast. Did she go to join the rest of her group?"

"No, she actually had an early morning meeting. Something about her next group, I think."

"And how are the Dalton's this morning? I do hope Mrs. Dalton is feeling better."

"As far as I know, she is doing well. They're planning to stay a few more days. Something to do with business, they said."

Returning to his desk, Robbie sat down and asked, "Was there something you needed Violet?"

"No," she shot back. "I was just passing by. Carry on." Dismissing him, she huffed down the hall, careful to hide the vindictive clench of her jaw.

When he'd first joined the hotel staff, a dozen years ago, Violet had flirted with him shamelessly. She was a pretty girl, accustomed to getting anything she wanted, however, her aggressiveness immediately turned Robbie off. His subtle attempts to dissuade her only made her more blatant and he finally had no choice but to enlist William's help to convey the message that his sister would never be more than a colleague. Violet had never forgiven Robbie and, to this day, it was clear she was still angry. Fortunately, Violet wasn't really involved with the day-to-day operation of the hotel, although he noticed recently, she'd been around more than usual.

Robbie pulled the previous day's staff schedule off the printer beside his desk and began pouring over the names, hoping one of them would jump out at him, an obvious suspect. Everyone on the list had been with the hotel for years. They were more like a family than employees and he couldn't believe any of them could betray that trust.

Victoria Kent had been on the concierge staff at Ascot House for nine years, the last two, as Robbie's assistant. She always went above and beyond the call of duty, often at the expense of personal time with her family. Her children were now grown and settled, and she was a doting grandmother to her new grandson.

Obviously, she wasn't the culprit. "Well, I have to start somewhere," he sighed, picking up his phone and dialing the concierge desk.

"Concierge Desk, Victoria Kent here. How may I assist you?"

September 27, 9:20 AM

Archibald Drake strolled through the front door of Ascot House, certain nobody would guess the real reason for his visit. He was dressed in Bermuda shorts, a polo shirt and athletic shoes, carrying a sports duffel bag and two tennis rackets. His sun-visor and shirt were both embroidered with the emblem of the All England Lawn Tennis Club at Wimbledon. He looked about as far removed from an English banker as possible. Heading straight for the lift, he was surprised no one stopped him. No, he was more disappointed actually because he already had a cover story. If anyone stopped him, he was going to say he was there to pick up his doubles partner. As it was, however, he took the lift to the fourth floor.

After checking carefully to make sure the hall was empty, Archie purposefully knocked on the door and waited. He was just about to knock again, when a tall woman in a housekeeper's uniform opened it.

"May I help you?" asked Helen Bainbridge.

"Archibald Drake, here to see Joseph Dalton."

"May I see some identification, please?"

"That won't be necessary Helen," said Joe, coming down the hall behind her. "Tennis anyone? Nice outfit, sir. Let me carry something for you."

Tickled with his own cleverness, Archie handed him the tennis rackets as they walked into the living room. "Good disguise, don't you think? Didn't want to look like a banker."

"Mission accomplished, sir."

Joe ushered him into the living room where Marty, Chief Inspector Paul Graham and one of his tech-agents were waiting. After introductions were made and first names acknowledged, they all sat down while the Chief Inspector explained the tracking devices his associate was holding.

"Joe," Paul began, "We'll be using several different devices, enabling us to track both you and the money." He held up a round transmitter about the size of a dime. "This one emits a signal that can be followed via satellite. We can pinpoint your location anywhere in the country."

"Not to change the subject," interrupted Marty, "but what happened to the surveillance on Andrews's flat? Did he ever come back?"

"No," Paul answered. "I'm afraid that was a dead end. The last time any of his neighbors saw him was approximately four days ago. However, we did get a good description of him. It matches the photo on his driver's license, so we don't think he's colored his hair or grown a moustache. An all-points alert has been issued, but I really don't think he'll surface until it's time to pick up the ransom."

"You don't think he'll send someone to get it?" asked Joe."

"Not likely. Since he has someone else looking after your daughter, Andrews is the money man. He won't chance another party helping themselves."

While his associate attached the device to the inside of the duffel bag, Paul held up a thin wire covered with transparent tape. "This is also a transmitter which we'll tape to one of bills near the bottom of the stack, just in case Andrews transfers the money to another bag. And these are for you," he said pointing to a pair of glasses he'd placed on the table along with a tiny microphone. "There is a video camera in the right corner of the glass frame, so we'll be able to see exactly what you're seeing and the microphone will be sewn into your shirt collar."

Impressed by the electronic wizardry in front of him, Joe asked, "So, you'll be able to see and hear me, how do I hear you?"

Paul handed Joe the device saying, "I was getting to that. The earpiece is smaller than a standard hearing aid. Give it a try, won't you? It's best if you can wear it in your left ear. Alleviates any interference with the video."

"This is like something out of a James Bond movie," said Marty. "I keep wondering if you're related to "Q". He is the one with all the gadgets, isn't he?"

"Yes, "Q" is the one," Paul answered with a chuckle, "However, I assure you, our technology is the real thing. No special effects for a film here."

With the equipment in place, Paul and Archie left by the front door, each carrying a tennis racket, while the techno-geek used the back exit through the kitchen. Paul told Joe and Marty to wait with Helen. The money transfer to the numbered Swiss account and its subsequent retrieval had to be engineered in the Yard's computer lab. He'd be back as soon as everything was arranged.

September 27, 11:45 AM

As the minutes ticked by, Joe Dalton was becoming more and more nervous. The conclusion of this nightmare was rapidly approaching and, even with all the help from New Scotland Yard, it was ultimately up to him to rescue his daughter. There were so many things that could go wrong. Scenes of disaster raced through his mind like a never-ending newsreel. What if Andrews figured out the police were involved? What if he somehow fumbled the ransom drop? What if they killed Kelly anyway? What if he failed? Every time he thought of his only child, he broke into a cold sweat, terrified something would happen to her and it would be his fault.

Marty felt helpless. As if the kidnapping weren't enough, the endless waiting was taking a tremendous toll on everyone. Waiting for the kidnappers to call, waiting while other people investigated the crime, waiting for the ransom to be arranged, waiting for Andrews to call with instructions for the drop. She was sick to death of waiting and she didn't know how much longer she could keep from exploding. She wanted to scream, throw things, smash the china, anything to release the rage that festered inside her.

Joe had not stopped pacing the floor since Paul left to attend to the money transfer. His forehead was beaded with perspiration and he wore a look of anguished turmoil on his face. Marty knew it was useless trying to comfort him or even offer words of encouragement. Joe was treading on a thin edge and the best thing she could do for him was to stay calm. One way or another, this crisis would be settled today and Marty was determined to maintain a strong frame of mind. Contemplating the alternative was unthinkable.

Marty started toward the kitchen to refresh her iced tea and almost collided with Paul Graham, who was just returning from the Yard. Reaching out to keep her from stumbling, he said, "Sorry to have startled you. Are you all right?"

"I didn't hear you come in. I was going to get more tea." Cautiously, she asked, "Is everything set? Joe is wearing down a path on the carpet."

"Let's go into the living room. I'll fill everyone in."

Hearing them approach, Joe turned around. "Are we ready to go?"

"When Andrews accesses his Swiss account, it will show a transfer of nine million pounds completed at eleven ten this morning. I take it he hasn't called yet?"

"Nothing yet, sir," answered Helen.

"Should be any time then." Graham was as anxious as the rest of them. "Are you ready Joe? Do you have any questions about the equipment?"

"I'm OK," Joe said, looking anything but OK. "I just want to get going. This waiting is making me crazy."

"I know you're anxious to get under way…"

"What if I…"

The jarring ring of the phone silenced the room. Paul spoke softly, "All right, here we go. Joe, I want you take a deep breath. You need to write down his instructions accurately. Ready?"

Joe did as he was told, took the pen and paper Helen slid across the table and picked up the receiver.

"Hello, this is Dalton."

"You follow orders quite nicely, I must say. Daddy taught you well," mocked the voice on the other end of the line.

"You got your money Andrews, now where is my daughter?" Joe's voice had gone stone cold. "If you've harmed one hair on her head, I swear, I'll hunt you down if it takes the rest of my life."

"Getting a bit testy, are we? You would do well to remember who is in charge. Have you got the cash?"

"Yes."

"Go to the Tube station at Oxford Circus, the third phone box from the Regent Street entrance and don't try anything Dalton. You'll be watched." The line went dead.

Joe waived the paper where he'd written Oxford Circus—third phone—Regent's entrance, at Graham and shouted, "What the hell does this mean? He didn't tell me anything!"

Paul looked at the scribbled message. "He's telling you to go to this phone box where he'll call you with more instructions. Probably wants to make sure you're alone, not being followed."

Joe stood up, grabbed the bag with its two tracking devices safely in place, put on his video glasses and started for the door, when Paul grabbed his arm and spun him around.

"Not so fast, my friend. Let's just make sure you've got everything." Paul checked the microphone that had been sewn into his collar and, putting on a headset, told him to speak.

"OK," Joe said with frustration, "Does it work?"

"Yes, loud and clear. And your earpiece?"

"I hear you. Now I'm out of here."

"Wait," Helen shouted. Handing him the map she'd quickly drawn, she explained, "This is a map of the tube station. When you get downstairs, have a taxi take you to the Regent Street entrance. It isn't very far, and he will probably try to give you walking directions. Offer to pay him double and tell him it's an emergency. Go down the stairs on either side of the street. You'll see a bank of red phone boxes just here," she pointed. "I don't remember how many there are, but go to the third one and wait."

"What if someone's in there?" Marty asked.

Paul took her arm, trying to reassure her, "If the box is occupied, Joe will wait until they leave. If the phone is in use, it will ring busy. Andrews will call back, and Joe, don't worry. We'll be with you every step of the way."

Joe started for the door again, saying in a hoarse whisper, "I'll bring her back..."

Once in the hall, Joe decided not to wait for the lift and ran for the stairs, flying down four flights and out the front door. A young couple was just getting out of a taxi, so Joe jumped in, handed the driver a ten pound note and told him there would be another if he could get him to the Tube station in five minutes.

"Yes sir. Straight away, sir," said the driver stepping on the accelerator.

September 27, 12:30 PM

Dodging the midday traffic, the driver pulled up to the corner of Oxford and Regent Streets with twenty seconds to spare and, true to his word Joe handed him another ten pounds. "Thanks," he said scrambling out of the taxi hauling the heavy sports bag out of the back seat.

"Yes sir, thank you sir," the driver called, trying to decide whether his good fortune should buy him a hearty lunch or pay for a stop at the pub on his way home.

Joe hurried down the stairs and spotted the bank of phone booths exactly where Helen said they would be. They were all occupied, however, the woman in box number three was just leaving as Joe approached. She even held the door open while Joe wrestled with his luggage, having to stand it on end in order to fit both it and himself inside.

He didn't have to wait long. The phone rang and steadying himself, he picked up the receiver.

"Hello, this is Dalton."

"Very good," said Andrews with a sneer in his voice. "Right on time."

"Get on with it, Andrews. What's next?"

"Patience dear boy, patience."

"My patience was lost a long time ago. I've got your damn money. Now, when do I get my daughter?"

Andrews, delighted his sarcasm was fraying Dalton's nerves, continued in the same smarmy tone, "You're going to take a little trip first. You didn't think I'd be so stupid as to keep your darling daughter in London, did you?"

When Joe didn't answer, Andrews continued, answering his own question, "Of course you didn't. Go to Paddington Station and buy a ticket for Cheltenham Spa. There's a train leaving at one-o-three. Train schedules are posted in military time, so look for the departure at thirteen-o-three. By my watch, that gives you thirty three minutes, plenty of time."

"Chelton what? This is a wild goose chase Andrews," cried Joe, his temper rising.

"Chel-ten-ham Spa," Andrews said phonetically. "Charming little town. You should arrive there shortly after three o'clock. Go to the information desk. There will be an envelope waiting for you. And Dalton,"

"What?"

"Don't try sending the police. If you do, you can kiss Kelly goodbye."

CHAPTER 24

▼

September 27, 12:30 PM
The Mission of Madeline's Marauders

Madeline, Chloe, John and Dolores hurried through the conservatory of Greystone Manor, anxious to find the rest of their group. They couldn't wait to tell the news about finding the mill.

"They have to be back by now," said John, trying not to break into a run.

"Unless something horrible happened. My guess is they are either in the lounge or the dining room," Madeline said just before she spotted Jake coming toward them.

"Where the hell you been?" Jake asked through gritted teeth, trying to smile for the benefit of anyone watching. "We got back almost an hour ago."

"Couldn't be helped," answered Madeline, smiled back, linking her arm through his. "Where are the others?"

"They're holding the fort on the patio." Jake led the way through the lounge and out to the patio where Suzie, Marge and Millie sat at a large round table near the far edge. "We ordered you up some grub to save time. Hope we got somethin' you like."

Jake's grub was an array of chicken, beef and ham sandwiches, accompanied by shrimp salad, a vegetable tray and a luscious looking lemon torte. In answer to their wide eyed stares, he simply said, "Well, we gotta eat."

As they sat down and helped themselves, questions erupted around the table. Everyone wanted to know what everyone else had found. There weren't many guests dining on the patio and no one was sitting near them, so they were able to talk quietly without being overheard.

With a cocky grin, Jake announced, "We got him. We found out our mystery man's name is Henry Keyes and he's been up to something too."

"Well we got her," countered John, every bit as cocky as his Texas friend. "At least I think we've got her. For sure we found a mill."

"How do you know?"

"Because I saw what's left of the waterwheel."

The four who'd gone in to Greysmeade were astonished. "Oh John," Millie cried, "Do you really think so?"

"I'd bet my farm on it. I've never been one for the paranormal, but I swear, I could feel her in that place. I could almost smell her, the feeling was so strong." He went on to tell them how he'd hiked downstream from the abbey and first thought the mill was a pile of fallen trees. "I don't know what made me go further down and look at it from another angle, but I did and, sure enough, there was an old stone building hidden by the trees and I knew it was the mill."

"And you left her there?" said Jake trying to keep his voice down as he started to rise from his chair.

"Jake," Madeline interrupted, "I told him not to go in. We know there are two people holding Kelly and that means one is always with her. If John had burst in on them, he might have gotten both himself and Kelly killed. I thought it was better to come back and get you, so the two of you could go back together."

Jake felt a little better hearing Madeline's reasoning and sat back down. Pleased to be included in the rescue party, he turned to John, "Well, come on Farmer, eat up. We got us a damsel to rescue."

"Hold on Jake, we have to have a plan." Madeline was determined to keep the men in check. "We're not going to barge into a rescue attempt, only to have it backfire.

"She's right," said Marge throwing in her two cents. "There are eight of us here and we can all be useful."

"Yeah!" "Absolutely!" "We want to help too!" "You're not going to leave us behind!" Everyone chimed in on top of each other

"You boys are a little outnumbered," drawled Suzie in her quiet, all-knowing way. "You may be bigger and faster, but I'd wager we're a whole lot smarter, so sit yourselves back down and listen up."

Half-proud and half-annoyed, Jake grinned and sat back down as he leaned forward to listen while Madeline began to plot their next move.

Digging in her purse, she pulled out her secure cell phone, "The first thing we need to do is call London and let them know what we've got so far." Glancing at Jake and raising an eyebrow, she continued, "They may want us to wait until they get here before we go in with blazing guns."

"And we don't want to tip off the bad guys," added Suzie.

"Yeah," chimed in Chloe, "If they think they've been discovered, they could hurt Kelly or worse."

Summing up their collective assets, Madeline concluded, "OK, by my count, we have two cars and the hotel van at our disposal, two secure cell phone lines, two regular cell phones, two men and six women. A fair sized army, if deployed properly."

Turning her attention back to the cell phone, she dialed Paul Graham's number.

"Graham here," Paul answered.

"Paul, its Madeline."

"Wonderful, I was just about to ring you with an update. Andrews phoned and Joe left with the ransom money a few minutes ago."

"Shit!" Madeline blurted out.

Startled at her expletive, Paul asked, "Madeline, what is it?"

"Dammit Paul, we found her!"

"When? Where?"

"Not more than an hour ago. We discovered an abbey ruin and John Shepard hiked downstream and found a stone mill."

"But you didn't actually see the girl?"

"No, but with everything else we've found, Paul, it has to be Kelly. Too many things have lined up in place for it not to be her."

Madeline went on to tell the Inspector about Henry Keyes and the fresh tire track John had found, leaving everyone around the table in the dark as to why she was so upset.

"OK," said Madeline, "What do you want us to do?" She and Paul talked for a few more minutes, then punching the off button, she turned around to find seven worried faces staring back at her.

"Joe left the hotel about fifteen minutes ago with the ransom money," she began.

"Well hell," said Jake as if he were explaining two plus two to a bunch of first-graders, "We can go get the girl, head Joe off at the pass and everyone goes home happy."

"I wish it were that simple," Madeline replied, clearly disappointed and a little frustrated as well. "Graham says now that the drop sequence has begun, we have to let it play out. Andrews is watching Joe, and if anything interrupts him, he could go ahead and just kill Kelly."

"So what does he want us to do, sit here and twiddle our thumbs?" John asked, already furious. "Jake and I should go back to the mill and get her. Either one of us is twice the size of Keyes. And if the other guy is taking orders from Keyes, he's got to be a whole lot of cards shy of a full deck. I say we go get Kelly and worry about Joe and the police later."

"Yeah!" Jake stood up nearly knocking over his chair. "Exactly what he said."

As Jake and John simultaneously threw down their napkins and started to leave, Chloe jumped up in front of Jake, putting both hands on his chest and said, "Hold on you two." She sent a scathing look to John whose arm was in the firm grip of his wife. "I think we should do something too, but let's coordinate our efforts. OK?"

"The good Chief Inspector isn't going to like this, but you know what?" Madeline was now standing too. "I don't care! He's sending some agents out here, but if we wait that long, Keyes and his partner might try to move Kelly. And besides, we know where she is and they don't, so here's what we're going to do. Everyone go back to your rooms and bring anything that might be useful like a belt or a luggage strap."

"I have a rattail comb," offered Millie.

"Yes, anything like that would be great. We'll meet in Chloe's room in ten minutes, and don't forget to wear your walking shoes."

September 27, 1:10 PM

Madeline stood beside Chloe's bed, looking down at the array of paraphernalia everyone had collected. There were four belts—three leather and one elastic,—which Marge thought would make a good bungie cord. She also brought two cans of hairspray. Millie donated her rattail comb plus her new embroidery scissors, as well as the poker from the fireplace in her room. Dolores had a butane-fired curling iron and a luggage strap, while John supplied a straight edge razor. Jake had a cigarette lighter and the lance from the suit of armor he'd purchased for his son at The Tower of London. It wasn't very long, but it was made of sturdy wood and, when Jake broke off the rubber tip, he created a sharp point that could easily penetrate the enemy's skin.

Suzie brought a braided leather cord which held a silver Indian amulet. "It's not as effective as piano wire," she said as she wrapped the cord around her throat, "but if you snap it hard enough, this silver edge could bloody up someone's neck pretty good." She stuck out her tongue and made a face as she pretended to use the cord as a garrote and strangle herself. "You never know," she said with a grin, unwrapping it and placing it on the bed.

Madeline only had a change of underwear and a clean shirt, her toothbrush and a few cosmetics. Everything else was still at the hotel in London. However, Chloe had another curling iron and they had scoured the room and come up with a very sharp letter opener, a hotel umbrella that conveniently had a long pointed tip and their fireplace poker.

"This is wonderful," said Madeline as she assessed the arsenal of weapons before her. "Each of us needs to be armed with what we're comfortable using. We have four cell phones, so we can split up into groups of two."

"Chloe, you and I will drive the van and take Jake and John around to the Abbey. We'll keep one secure phone and the boys can take the other." She handed her phone to John. "Jake, you take your lighter and the lance. You'll also need the tying up stuff and the pokers."

"I think they should take the hairspray too," Marge said, taking a can off the bed and handing it to John. "Hairspray in the eyes is enough to subdue man or beast."

"True enough," Madeline, said, "But I think they're going to have enough to carry."

Marge took back the can, a little disgruntled, until Millie piped up, "Sister, we have our purse sized cans. Remember, I tucked them into your suitcase before we left home. Madeline, do I have time to get them?"

"If you hurry," she answered as Millie dashed through the door. "Dolores, your curling iron is brilliant. Will it fit in your purse?"

"I think so, and Madeline," she said, pointing to the umbrella, "There is a whole umbrella stand full of these right next to the door in the conservatory."

"Excellent, everybody grab one on the way out." She handed the letter opener to Suzie just as Millie fluttered back into the room, with two pocket-sized cans of Hard-to-Hold spray.

"Thanks, Darlin'" said Jake as he gave her a kiss on the cheek. "This just might come in real handy." John took the other can and put it in his pocket.

Madeline started to hand Suzie her amulet, but Suzie shook her head, "Jake's a whole lot better at this kind of stuff. I wish to hell I had my derringer," she mused as she took the amulet and tucked into Jake's shirt pocket.

Madeline continued handing out weapons until her troops were sufficiently armed. Turning back to Suzie again and, handing her the keys to her rental car; "You're still the only one other than Jake who has seen Keyes, so why don't you take Marge and stake out the market." Then, handing her one of the regular cell phones, "If you spot him, follow him and call us."

Suzie took the keys, "That OK with you Marge?"

"Absolutely. Grab an umbrella and let's go."

"Good hunting," said Madeline as they reached the door. "I'll call you as soon as we drop off the boys."

Jake grabbed his wife before she could get out of the door and gave her a hard kiss on the mouth, then closed the door behind her.

"Dolores," Madeline said drawing everyone's attention back to the business at hand, "You and Millie take the other car and park behind those tall trees by the road leading into the Manor. You should be able to see the highway from there as well as the entrance road. You'll be about equal distance from the road leading to the Abbey and the road leading into the village, so you'll be able to see what's going on in both directions. If you see anything the least bit suspicious, call me and likewise, I'll call you."

"We'll be ready," said Millie, all atwitter. "We won't let you down. Come on Dolores, we must get to our post!"

As Millie marched to the door, Dolores couldn't help but smile at her partner's brave enthusiasm and taking her husband's hand said, "Don't worry, we'll be fine."

"I know," answered John affectionately. "Just remember, if you have to give chase, this isn't Otter Creek. You'll be driving on the wrong side of the road." He gave her a quick kiss and she ran after Millie who was already at the lift.

The remaining four comrades looked at each other with solemn eyes, each determined to see their quest through to the finish. "Ready?" Madeline asked. She looked at Chloe, who for once in her life, didn't have a smart remark, and only nodded her head. Jake and John did the same. "OK, lets go."

September 27, 1:40 PM

Jake and John left Madeline and Chloe in the parking area of the Abbey grounds and headed toward the trail John had found earlier. The girls were going to circle around and try to find the road leading to the mill. John carried the cell phone and promised to call with an update as soon as they reached the mill, ensuring an unwanted ring wouldn't alert the kidnappers to their presence.

No one was around, so the men ran to the trailhead, then continued at a steady jog until they reached the river. John took the lead as they crept through the trees, pointing out the pile of logs gathered at the back of the mill. Jake nodded his head, seeing what John had meant when he said he could easily have missed finding the mill altogether.

Slowly they inched their way toward the stone building, listening for anything that sounded human. Nothing but silence. Jake got John's attention and motioned that he was going to circle around to the other side. Fortunately the sound of the river, splashing over what was left of the mill wheel, camouflaged his footsteps.

The ancient mill had no windows, so when Jake was set, the two men eased closer to the closed door, still not hearing any signs of life. John was first to reach the door and found it was not closed completely. Holding his poker in front of him like a sword, he mouthed to Jake, "On three." Jake nodded and preparing to strike, raised one hand and counted off with his fingers, one, two, three.

John's poker thrust open the door and both men sprang through the opening. John dove to the floor, rolled and was back on his feet in a second, while Jake leaped to the opposite side of the room, poker raised, ready to strike a lethal blow.

Both prepared to kill if necessary, the farmer and the cowboy, looked at each other in disbelief and shouted, "What the hell?"

The room was empty.

"Shit!" said John, throwing his poker on the floor. "We missed them."

Surprisingly, Jake kept his cool better than his partner. "Look here," he said moving to the mattress in the far corner. "This is where they kept her." Then he saw the chain hanging from the wall and vehemently spit out, "Those bastards had her chained to the wall like an animal."

John came to look and tripped over one of the stakes in the floor. Peering down to see what had caused him to stumble, the realization of what he was looking at, made his mouth go dry. "Jesus, man," he choked, "what did they do to her?"

Jake saw the stake and, looking around, found the other two at the foot of the mattress. "They had her staked out like a sacrifice." With a low voice, frigid as ice, Jake said, "They're dead. I'll kill 'em with my bare hands."

"Not if I get them first." John walked outside, unable to stay in Kelly's prison another minute. He looked at the ground and, finding what looked like fresh tire tracks, called, "Hey Jake, come here."

Jake emerged from the mill and squatted down beside John. Running his fingers lightly over the tracks, he said, "These are fresh, no more than thirty minutes, and look," he pointed to a group of footprints. "Two sets of shoes and a pair of skinny bare feet."

John put his hand over the footprint. "These are Kelly's. Remember, she had to have custom made boots because her feet are so narrow."

John pulled out the cell phone and dialed Madeline. When she answered, he told her what they'd found, or rather what they hadn't. "Jake says they can't be more than thirty minutes ahead of us. Where are you now?"

"We've circled in your direction, but I don't see any sign of a road." Madeline shook her head and whispered to Chloe, "She's gone."

"Madeline, Jake and I will follow the road out. It has to run into the main highway at some point. Keep driving and you'll see us."

"I'm nearly to Dolores and Millie now. I'll check with them and call you back."

"OK, but when you get to them, turn around. I know we're on this side of the hotel."

"Tell her to call Suzie," reminded Jake.

"And remember to call Suzie." John said before he punched the off button.

"Looks like we're gonna have to chase these bastards down," said Jake, going back into the millhouse to retrieve John's poker.

John met him at the door, took his weapon and the two men said together, "Lets go."

September 27, 2:20 PM

"Nobody was home?" asked Chloe as Madeline handed her the phone. "But she was there? They know it was her?"

"They're sure. Will you call Dolores and let her know? And ask her if they saw anything."

Chloe dialed the number and when Millie answered, Chloe gave them the bad news. "Did you see anyone drive by?"

"An old blue car went by, but there were only two people in it. It wasn't speeding or anything," Millie said, convinced it was nothing important.

"OK, I'll tell Madeline. Just stay put until we find Jake and John. Then we'll decide what to do next."

"Millie said they saw an old blue car drive by with two people in it, but they didn't look suspicious."

"Were they both in the front seat?" asked Madeline.

"I don't know. She didn't say. Do you want me to call them back?"

"No, not yet. Call Suzie and let her know what's going on. If they're on the road already, they won't be making a stop at the market."

Chloe dialed Suzie's number. "Hey Suz, its Chloe. Jake and John didn't find anybody, but Jake says the tire tracks are fresh."

"Damn," said Suzie, disappointed Kelly was still missing. "Jake's a good tracker. Could he tell how long they've been gone?"

"He said about half an hour. We checked in with Dolores and Millie. They saw an old blue car drive by, but..."

"What did you say?"

"They saw an old blue car, but it only had two people and…"

"It's them. Chloe, that was Keyes and whoever is workin' with him."

"My God, Oh my God!"

Madeline slammed on the brakes, jerking both women against their seatbelts and pulling over to the side of the road, grabbed the phone out of Chloe's hand. "Suzie, what is it? What's happened?"

"It was Keyes." Suzie, who was usually calm and grounded, was shouting frantically, "In the blue car. Keyes was in the blue car. I've seen that car before. I know it was him." The hair on the back of her neck was standing on end. The feeling was stronger than any she'd ever had.

"Suzie," said Madeline in the calmest voice she could muster, "I believe you. Do you know which way they went?"

"I don't know."

"Can you feel it?"

"Maybe if I'm on the same road."

"Come on back to the hotel entrance. We'll go pick up the boys and meet you there."

"OK, but Madeline, hurry."

CHAPTER 25

▼

Thursday, September 27, 2:45 PM
The Girls Capture a Kidnapper

Madeline's army of eight gathered in a circle at the intersection where the highway met the entrance road to Greystone Manor. They were pouring over the roadmap Marge had found in the glovebox, trying to figure out which route Keyes had taken.

"I'm thinking they're on their way to the ransom drop point," said Chloe, "I'll bet they're going to exchange Kelly for the money."

"Maybe," Madeline concurred. "We know they were headed this way," she said, pointing to the line on the map that corresponded with road next to them. "I wish we knew where Joe was going."

"Call Robbie," suggested Chloe. "I know you're pissed at Graham, but Robbie's there and probably knows something."

"There are so many little villages around here," said John looking at the map. "Even with three cars, we could drive around 'til dark and still not find them. Chloe's right, call MacDuff. He's bound to know something."

"Alright, I give up." Chloe was right on the mark, she was angry with the good Inspector. His keeping her in the dark was not an option as far as she was concerned. They were all in this crisis together and, if Graham had kept her in the loop, they might already have Kelly, the money and the kidnappers. At the very least, she and her troops wouldn't be running around the English countryside on a wild goose chase. And where was Robbie? He was probably in cahoots with his buddy to keep her in the dark. The big macho men probably thought they were protecting the poor little group of Americans. Well, they weren't little, they sure as hell weren't poor and she resented the implication they couldn't handle a couple of thugs. However, she did need information and it was obvious there was only one way she was going to get it.

Reluctantly, she took out her phone, and punched in Robbie's number. When he didn't answer on the first ring, she said under her breath, "Oh fine. This is just fine. Where the hell are you?" And when he picked up after the second ring, she didn't even give him a chance to say hello.

"What the hell's going on there, and why haven't you called me?"

"Me? I was wondering when I'd hear from you," he answered, sounding a little miffed himself. "I understand you told Paul you've found the girl. He's sending a battalion of agents."

"Too bad. He's too late," Madeline snapped back. "She's gone."

Robbie hadn't realized how angry she was. Better to back off a little, let her know he was on her side. "Maddie girl, I'm sorry. What can I do to help?"

Still fuming, she said, "Where's Joe? I know Graham's tracking him."

"He's on a train to Cheltenham Spa. Due to arrive there shortly."

"Cheltenham," she said to the group. "He's gone to Cheltenham Spa. Can you find it?"

Chloe found Cheltenham Spa on the map and pointed it out to Madeline.

"I know where it is," answered Robbie. Then realizing she wasn't talking to him, "Maddie, where are you?"

"We're standing in the middle of the road, trying to decide which way Keyes is heading. Oh, that's right, you don't know about him yet, or do you?"

Robbie didn't know, so she cooled down a little and quickly explained the situation, then asked, "Where does he go once he gets to Cheltenham?"

"Don't know. He's to pick up an envelope at the information desk. Presumably, with further instructions." When Madeline didn't answer, he asked cautiously, "Maddie, what are you thinking?"

Consumed with the map, Madeline distractedly replied, "I have to go now Robbie. I'll call you back." And with that, she clicked off and said to the others, "It looks like Cheltenham is about thirty miles from here, but our road isn't the most direct route."

"It's possible the exchange isn't going to be in Cheltenham," offered John. "I would think Andrews would plan it in a more isolated place."

"Me too," said Suzie. "It's going to be somewhere between here and there."

"Alright," said Madeline, formulating a plan. "We know we're looking for an old blue car. Any idea of the model?"

"I don't know," answered Dolores, wishing she'd paid more attention.

"Shit!" said Madeline for the second time that afternoon. "I forgot to tell Robbie about the car."

"We'll call him," offered Jake, hoping to take some of the pressure off their leader.

Chloe turned to him and mouthed the word, "Thanks."

"Sorry, I didn't mean to snap. It's just that every minute we stand here, Keyes gets another minute ahead of us."

"We know dear," Millie tried to offer Madeline some comfort.

"Yeah," Chloe said putting her arm around her friend's shoulder. "Let's get a grip. We're ready whenever you are."

Back to business, Madeline took the map and began to give assignments. "Suzie, I think you should take the main road here and follow wherever your vibes take you."

Nodding in agreement, Suzie unfolded her own map, marked their present location and drew a circle around Cheltenham.

Pointing to the map again, Madeline continued, "Dolores, you and Millie follow Suzie until you get to the cutoff for Shipton-on-Stour. Drive through the village and see if you find anything. We'll go around this way, through Chipping Campden and meet you in Moreton-in-Marsh. Please be careful. If you find the car, follow it and call me immediately."

September 27, 3:00 PM

"I still don't see why you won't tell me where we're going," whined Stout. "I got just as much right to know as you."

"The only rights you got are the ones I say you got," snapped Keyes. Stout had been whining non-stop since they'd left the mill.

Stout knew Keyes had a short fuse, but he just couldn't help himself, "And you didn't even bring any lunch."

That did it. Keyes had had enough. He slammed on the breaks, coming to a stop at the bottom of a hill and shouted, "Get out!"

"What?" Stout couldn't believe his ears.

"You heard me. Get out!" Keyes yelled even louder.

"You can't do that. I'm in this too Keyes."

"Not any more you're not," Keyes raged, reaching over Stout and opening the door.

"Keyes!" Stout panicked, not believing what was happening.

Before Stout could say another word, Keyes shoved him out of the car with such force, his round body hit the pavement with a thud and rolled down the embankment. Stunned, he sat up, trying to clear his head, only to hear screeching tires speeding away. By the time he scrambled back up to the road, all he could see was a blue spot cresting the next hill and disappearing down the other side.

What to do? Stout turned around, but the only things he could see were the rolling hills of the Cotswolds and a few sheep; nary another soul in sight. He didn't even know what villages were nearby. Keyes had been driving. He hadn't been paying attention.

Keyes, he thought bitterly. What a bloody bastard! Promised him a wad of cash. All he had to do was look after the girl. Bloody joke that was. Keyes'd treated her horrible, knockin' her around. Almost killed her, he had, throwin' her against the wall like that. "And leavin' me to clean up his dirty work," Stout muttered. The sheep in the nearby pasture stared back in silence.

"Bloody bastard didn't even bring us enough food to keep one person alive, let alone two," he grumbled as he started walking. "Then he has the nerve to chuck me out like I was rubbish."

Stout continued walking up the road, with no idea where he was going. He figured he'd walk to the next village or, if he was lucky, hitch a ride. "Then we'll just see what the constable has to say."

September 27, 3:08 PM

As the train pulled into the station at Cheltenham Spa, Joe turned his head slightly to the right and spoke quietly into his collar, "Is somebody there?"

"We have you Mr. Dalton," answered a voice in his earpiece. "The satellite puts you approaching Cheltenham Spa."

"Amazing," Joe said, still astonished at the pinpoint accuracy of the Yard's tracking equipment.

"According to our information, you should be arriving on track number two. Can you confirm?"

"Yes, you're correct." These guys were all business so Joe didn't think it would be wise to remind them there were only two tracks to begin with, and one platform between them.

"The Information Desk should be directly ahead of you as you enter the station."

"Right," said Joe. As the train came to a stop, Joe hoisted the heavy ransom bag onto his shoulder, disembarked, and walked quickly inside. Approaching the Information Desk, he said, "Hello, I'm Joseph Dalton. I'm here to pickup an envelope."

"Good afternoon," greeted the young woman behind the counter. "May I see some identification please?"

Joe pulled out his wallet and flipped it open to his driver's license.

She looked carefully at his picture and matched it to a photocopy of his passport she had pulled from under the counter.

"How did you get a copy of my passport?" Joe asked, trying to keep his temper in check.

"The gentleman who left the parcel gave it to me and said to check your identification carefully," she answered, aware that he was not at all pleased.

"And how long ago was that?"

She looked at the large station clock, just overhead. "Not more than a quarter of an hour, I should think."

"May I have my package?"

"Yes sir, of course," she said, handing him a large manila envelope.

Joe took the envelope and looked around for a vacant bench. The station wasn't particularly busy in the middle of the afternoon and he found a secluded spot in the northwest corner.

"Have you got the parcel?" asked his earpiece.

"Yes, give me a second." Joe sat down and after shoving the heavy bag of money between his feet and under the bench, he opened the envelope and poured out the contents; a key, a road map and a single white piece of paper.

"Joe? Paul Graham here. What did you find?"

"Looks like a car key, a map and instructions. Give me a second."

He quickly read the directions, then read them again. "Son of a bitch, he's got me chasing all over creation again."

"What do you mean?" asked Graham.

"There's apparently a red car out front. I'm supposed to take the A-40 out of town to the A-436, then the A-429. You guys have the most God-awful road system I've ever seen," he said, thoroughly exasperated.

"I know it can be confusing," replied Paul, trying to calm him down, "But you have to remember, some of our roads date back to the Romans," he mussed. "What's the final destination?"

"Let me get out to the car. I'm starting to attract attention." Joe got up, smiled at an elderly woman who was staring at him, pulled his bag out from under the bench, shouldered it and headed for the Queen's Road exit. Looking up and down the street, he spotted a red sedan parked just three spaces to his left.

He walked to the car, praying the key would fit. When the door opened, he breathed a sigh of relief, got inside, closed the door and started the engine.

"I hear the engine," said Paul. "Good. Now, where are we going?"

"A bridge. In the middle of nowhere."

September 27, 3:30 PM

Dolores had been following Suzie for about twenty minutes and finally felt somewhat comfortable driving on the left-hand side of the road. It wasn't so much a question of the steering wheel being on the right side of the car; it was having the bulk of the car on her left. Fortunately, traffic was light and following Suzie helped enormously. The undulating hills of the Cotswolds were beautiful and reminded her of home, but on a smaller scale.

"Dear," said Millie pointing at her window, "That sign has a picture of a circle with lines coming out of it. Must be a roundabout, don't you think?"

Dolores glanced to her left, saw what Millie was talking about and nodded her head. "I think you're right, but it looks like more than one road intersects. Help me watch for the sign to Shipston, will you?"

"Of course dear, but if we miss it the first time, we can always go around again."

"Yes, indeed." Dolores chuckled.

"Which way do you think Suzie will go? Remember, Madeline told her to follow her vibes."

"I don't know and I don't want to call her and ask. I wouldn't want to interfere with her cosmic connection, or whatever it is she feels. I don't really understand it, but she's certainly been right so far."

The roundabout was just ahead and, following Suzie, she didn't think twice about going clockwise rather than counter-clockwise.

"Look," cried Millie, "Suzie's taking our road. I wonder if she's on to something?"

Dolores felt her pulse quicken. "I don't know if I hope she is or isn't. I wish one of the men had come with us."

Suzie was completely focused on keeping herself open to her gift and was unaware she had taken the exit to Shipston and that Dolores and Millie were still following. Marge had intentionally kept quiet, not wanting to break her concentration. As she picked up speed, she glanced in her rear-view mirror and saw the other girls were still behind her. "I took the road to Shipston?" she asked, breaking the silence.

"Yes," Marge confirmed. "Your feelings are working then?"

"Yep, and they're gettin' stronger by the minute. We're gettin' close." And as they drove down the hill, the hair on the back of her neck began to tingle. "Somethin's over that next rise. I know it."

But when they crested the next hill, the only thing she saw was a bum trying to hitch a ride. She drove past him and down the other side. "No, this isn't right," she said, putting her foot on the brake. "We have to go back."

Dolores saw Suzie's brake lights and stopped behind her.

Millie jumped out and hurried up to her sister's window. "Sister," she said knocking on the glass, "What's going on?"

Marge rolled down the window and Suzie leaned over, "Tell Dee I'm goin' back. That bum knows something or has seen something."

"Oh my," Millie said overcome with excitement. She turned and started to leave, then turned back and shouted, "We'll follow you. Be careful," she called over her shoulder as she flew back to tell Dolores.

Both cars made a U-turn and drove back up the hill. Suzie spotted the hitch-hiker and, slowing down, stopped a few yards in front of him, with Dolores pulling up right behind her.

Seeing the two cars and, thinking his luck had returned, Stout rushed forward to Marge's window. She lowered it an inch, looking at his disheveled appearance. "Sorry 'bout that," he said, trying to brush himself off. "Took a tumble a while back. You giving me a lift then?"

Suzie grabbed the letter opener from the side pocket of the door, got out and walked around to the front of the car.

"Millie," said Dolores, getting the curling iron out of her purse and turning it on, "Get your hairspray and umbrella. We need to be ready if Suzie needs us."

Drawing the man away from Marge's window, Suzie pasted on a smile and drawled, "Looks more like you been wallerin' in a pig sty there, friend."

Stout turned and stepped toward the front of the car. "I was just tellin' your Mum I took a tumble a while back. You ladies American?"

Suzie nodded, drawing him a few steps further, so his back was completely turned toward her three friends. "How long have you been hoofing it?"

As soon as his back was turned, Dolores and Millie quietly got out of their car, armed with umbrellas, the curling iron and hairspray, and silently crept forward.

"Hoofin'?" Stout asked, not sure he understood.

"Walkin'."

"Oh," he nodded, "I get it. Seems like forever, what with the hills and all. Going' down's OK. It's getting' up the other side, nearly done me in."

Dee and Millie were poised and ready to strike at the rear bumper of Suzie's car, when Suzie asked their intended victim, "So, have you seen an old blue car go by?"

Stout, unaware of his peril, answered bitterly, "See it? I was in it."

Dolores sprang forward, shoving the point of her umbrella into Stout's back and yelled, "Freeze!"

Startled, Stout turned his head, just in time to catch a glimpse of a little old lady, before Millie let loose with a stream of hairspray, directly into his eyes.

Stout's hands flew to his eyes as he screamed with pain. Suddenly, he was being spun around and shoved, face first, against the hood of the car. Then he felt something burning hot next to his ear and the sharp prick of a knife against his throat. "Jesus, Mary and Joseph," he shouted, trembling with fear, "Please don't kill me."

Who would have thought four American women could successfully subdue a kidnapper, but that's precisely what they'd done. Marge had joined the others and she and her sister had their umbrellas firmly imbedded in their enemy's back, hairspray cans at the ready. Dolores held her hot curling iron a hair's breadth from his ear and face, ready to burn him if he moved, and Suzie was on his other side with her letter opener pointed directly at his jugular.

Suzie leaned in a little closer and feeling him shake, spoke softly with a voice cold as ice, "Now, you're gonna tell us exactly what happened and where Keyes is taking Kelly."

Whimpering, Stout felt the steady stream of hot liquid running down his leg.

CHAPTER 26

▼

Thursday, September 27, 3:45 PM
Sharp Curves and Chaos Reign

"Thanks Marge," said Chloe, still writing furiously on the crumpled piece of paper John had found in the back seat. "Hold tight. I'll let Paul know your location. His agents are in the area, so it shouldn't be too long. One of us will call you back."

She handed the phone back to Jake who was sitting in the front passenger seat next to Madeline. They continued driving through the village of Chipping-Campden. Beside Chloe, John had the road map spread out on his lap, pinpointing the exact location of Dolores and company. "I have them Chloe, they're right here," he said, jabbing furiously with his left index finger.

"Great, but don't poke a hole in it."

With his right hand, John pulled the other phone out of his pocket and handing it to her said, "Here, you make the call. Graham will recognize Madeline's number and be more likely to answer it."

"You're probably right," she said and, dialing Graham's number, leaned forward and said to Madeline, "Do you believe them? I'll bet that poor guy doesn't know what hit him."

"Maddie girl, where are you?" a voice answered in Chloe's ear.

Thinking she'd dialed the wrong number, she questioned, "Robbie? Is that you?"

"Chloe? Where's Madeline?"

Barely able to hear him above what sounded like the thawp thawp of a helicopter, she answered with urgency, "Madeline's right here. Look Robbie, I need to talk to Graham. It's an emergency!"

After his last conversation with Madeline, Robbie called Paul repeating his insistence that Madeline be advised of all developments in the investigation. When he told them Keyes and Kelly were on the move and Madeline's group had spotted the car and were giving chase, Paul decided Robbie should accompany him to the scene. That had been an hour ago.

"Chloe, this is Paul. What's happened?"

"What's happened? What's happened is we have one of the kidnappers, that's what's happened!" she replied in a patronizing tone, quickly telling him where to find them.

Chloe was relieved to know she'd been right about agents being nearby, and relayed the news to Jake. "Inspector," she then continued, "Where are you? Is that a helicopter I'm hearing? And where is the drop point?"

Sensing Chloe's lack of response to mean the inspector was reluctant to give up the information, Madeline said very calmly, through clenched teeth, "Chloe, give me the phone."

Controlling her building frustration, she seethed into the phone, "Inspector, you're going to tell me where Joe is headed and you're going to tell me right now," she added emphatically.

At that moment, she heard Robbie shouting over the noise of the helicopter, "Tell her everything. If you don't, I will."

Protecting Madeline and her group of tourists was clearly out of the question now that they had already captured one of the criminals, so bowing to the inevitable, he began, "Joe is on his way to the ransom drop, just as you suspected. The exchange is to take place on an old stone bridge between Moreton-in-Marsh and Stow-on-the-Wold. If you go approximately three kilometers south of Moreton, you'll see a gravel road leading west. The bridge is about seven miles from the main road."

"Is there a specified time?"

"No. Joe is to drive there and wait. Madeline, please don't interfere," he pleaded. "My people have it under control." Even as he said it, he knew his plea was futile.

"We won't interfere, but we'll be there just in case anything goes wrong. Inspector, you still haven't told me where you are and why Robbie is with you."

"We're just over Blenheim Palace, moving in your direction and frankly, I asked Robbie along to deal with you. Please," he said, trying again, this time showing his frustration, "Please let us handle this."

"Thank you Inspector," she bristled as she clicked off the phone and pulled over to the side of the road. "We're very close to the exchange point," she told the others. "Can you hand me the map for a moment?"

Handing her the map, John asked, "So they're going to exchange Kelly for the money?"

"Yes, I think so." Madeline replied, spreading out the map, the top edge flopping over the top of the steering wheel. "Graham didn't actually confirm it, but he did use the word 'exchange'.

"John, I see your marks," she studied the map for a second, "But there's supposed to be a gravel road here."

Leaning up to look over her shoulder, John replied, "If it's a country road leading to private property, it wouldn't be on a touring map. Back home the only place my back road's indicated is in the plat book at our county building."

"OK," Madeline said, handing him back the map as she eased onto the road, "If we get to Stow-on-the-Wold, we went too far."

They drove in silence for a few miles; everyone glued to the windows, trying to spot Keyes and his blue car. Breathing a small sigh of relief that they now had a destination, Madeline was grateful the height of the summer tourist season was over. Otherwise these little villages would be swarming with double-decker tour busses and battalions of people with cameras around their necks.

Passing through Moreton-in-Marsh, the tension inside the van was palpable. Madeline's fingers began to tingle as her grip tightened on the wheel. "The road's about three kilometers ahead on the right. Keep your eyes open."

Anxiously glancing at her odometer, the kilometers scrolled by in tenths, taking forever to reach one, then two and finally…

"There it is," shouted Jake, pointing just ahead. "Slow down."

Grateful there was no traffic in sight, Madeline put her foot on the brake and turned right.

"I think we're here first. There's no dust trail," observed John.

"You're right," Jake agreed, "Madeline, slow down so we don't kick up dust ourselves. Head for those trees up there," he added, gesturing to a thick stand of trees about two hundred yards ahead. "We're like sitting ducks out here in the open."

The rolling hills had given way to a fairly flat plateau, where a single car, especially a van, could be seen from quite a distance. Madeline slowly approached the thicket and pulled over. With the car still idling, Jake opened the door saying, "I want to look around." He walked ahead a few paces, then knelt down to get a closer look at the ground. Satisfied the gravel hadn't been disturbed, he returned to the van, got in and said, "Unless he's comin' from the other direction, Keyes isn't here yet. We need to find cover closer to the bridge. The Inspector said seven miles, right?"

"Kilometers," Madeline corrected, slowly stepping on the accelerator again.

As they moved forward, trees began to shade both sides of the road, becoming a dense forest, with a stream appearing on their right. Farther ahead, the trees now hanging over the road forming a canopy, the road narrowed, sloping downward, while the stream cut a deep ravine that fell away on their right. At the six and a half kilometer mark, John spotted a level place between the trees on the left side where they could watch the road without being seen and, while Madeline backed the van into position, Jake and John got out and walked ahead to find the bridge.

Madeline and Chloe got out to make sure the van was sufficiently camouflaged, then turned and watched the men disappear around the curve ahead. "I just hope to hell we're in the right place," groused Chloe, as she tromped back to the van and resumed her position behind Madeline.

Out of breath, the men returned. Jake opened the door and huffed, "Hell of a place to lose a horse."

"What!?" Madeline and Chloe asked together.

"That's as lethal a road as any I've ever seen," John agreed, adding, "Andrews is an evil son-of-a-bitch. I just hope he warned Keyes."

As the women became more and more anxious, Jake nodded, "You can be damn sure he didn't tell Joe."

"Tell him what?" asked Madeline. "What's up there?"

"The road from hell," answered Jake.

Leaning forward between the two front seats, John explained, "See where the road turns then seems to disappear? Well it does, almost."

Jake, turning to the others and nodding his head in agreement, said, "It goes straight down, makes a hairpin and goes down again. Take the first turn too fast and it's all over."

"Did you see the bridge? Is it even down there?" Chloe asked, her heart thumping with apprehension.

"Oh it's there alright," Jake answered raising his hands to draw an air map. "The stream over there runs down the ravine and empties into a river at the bottom, like a T. The road makes those hairpin turns, then one more turn at the bottom, and crosses the river."

"It's not very wide, the river I mean," continued John, "and the bridge is the same level as the road. This has to be a private road," he said, looking around. "There are no warning signs anywhere."

"Or someone removed them," Madeline thought out loud.

The silence in the van, combined with the stillness of the forest, was like a tightening shroud. The only sound was an occasional rustle of a leaf and the stream rushing through the ravine below. Waiting, not knowing what was going to happen was intolerable.

Suddenly Jake leaned out his window, signaling the others to keep quiet. "Someone's coming," he whispered.

Like a bat out of hell, the blue car sped past them, swerving around the curve, spewing gravel in all directions and plunged down the hill."

"He's going too fast!" yelled Jake. "Step on it, Madeline! Go!"

Madeline turned on the engine and the van tore threw the trees, onto the road. Slowing enough to safely make the turn, they reached the first hairpin just in time to see Keyes sail off the road and careen out of sight, into the river below.

"No!" Chloe screamed.

Her stomach churning, Madeline clenched her teeth, gripped the wheel, and continued down the hill, safely bringing the van to a stop at the river's edge.

Instantly both men jumped out and ran into the water, wading in chest deep, still able to stand as they reached the car. The impact had catapulted Keyes through the windshield and half onto the hood, his eyes unblinking in the stare of death.

Looking into the back seat Jake yelled, "Where's Kelly?"

John, who had circled around to the other side, shouted back, "There's a blanket on the floor, but I don't see a body." Pausing, he added, "And if we open the doors..."

"No, too much water and it'll sink."

Standing on the riverbank, Madeline could see the current was pushing the car downstream. "Is Kelly in there?" she shouted.

"No."

"What about the trunk?"

Jake and John looked at each other across the top of the car, "The trunk!"

The current was picking up speed as the two men fought their way upstream to the trunk of the car which, of course, was locked.

Chloe was already running back to the van. Returning with the two pokers they had taken from the hotel, she handed one to Madeline, saying, "Crowbars," then ran down the riverbank with Madeline right behind her.

As the two women waded into the water, pokers held above their heads, they could see the car was slowly sinking. Water was now pouring over Keyes's dead body and through the hole in the windshield, filling up the interior. By the time they reached Jake and John, the water was up to their armpits, but handing them the tools, they refused to go back to the shore.

"Get out of here, both of you," yelled Jake, getting the point of his poker into position. "You want to drown?"

Not waiting for an answer, the two men looked at each other and yelled, "Now!"

They had wedged the points of their pokers in the seam between the trunk and rear fenders, but even with both men jumping up and using their full body weight to push down, they only succeeded in bending the metal. The latch held fast.

In danger now of being swept away, they tried again with the same result. "You need to get closer to the latch and pry it away from the bumper," shouted Madeline.

"Can't get enough leverage," Jake said, shaking the water from his eyes.

"We've got to try!" Madeline was getting desperate. Water was beginning to lap over the top of the trunk.

"I think we can get it open if we all push," suggested John. "OK girls?"

"Absolutely!" they screamed in unison.

Jake and John positioned their pokers on either side of the latch, and with two sets of hands on each, all four sprang out of the water and came down with all their might.

The trunk popped open, hitting Chloe squarely on the chin, snapping her head back against John's chest, while, at the same time, water poured into the trunk, completely covering it contents.

Reaching in and feeling under several blankets, Madeline felt Kelly's bare foot. "Under here! She's under here!" she screamed, as she pulled with all the strength she had left.

Jake and Madeline tore off the blankets then Jake reached in and pulled Kelly out from under the water. As he cradled her limp body against his chest, Madeline ripped the duck tape from her mouth. "Is she breathing?" Jake asked.

"I can't tell. Let's get her out of here," answered Madeline. With fierce determination, they turned and headed toward the riverbank, daring the current to try and stop them.

The bank was overgrown and slippery, but Madeline scrambled up the side and found a spot where Jake could get out and lay Kelly down. Kneeling down and gently wiping the hair out of her face, Madeline bent over with her ear to Kelly's nose and mouth.

Her body sagged with relief as she turned to an anxious Jake and said, "She's breathing. Thank God, she breathing."

Jake knelt down beside her and ran his fingers down the side of Kelly's cold wet face. "The trunk must have acted like an air pocket."

"And those blankets must have cushioned her against the impact when the car hit the water."

Helping Chloe from the water and fearing the worst, John came up behind Jake and asked, "Is she…?"

"No," Madeline said softly, "she's alive." Then, turning around and seeing her friend, she exclaimed, "Chloe, you're bleeding."

Completely dismissing Madeline's concern, Chloe leaned over to look at Kelly. "We need to get her to a hospital."

Madeline began to work on the ropes around Kelly's hands while Jake and John untied her feet.

"I can take her," offered John when they were ready to leave.

"Nah," said Jake, picking up Kelly as if she weighed nothing at all. "You find the way back to the van. I've got her."

Trying to avoid overhanging tree branches, protruding roots and underbrush, John led the way back through the forest, followed by Madeline and Chloe, with Jake carrying his precious cargo. He felt her stir against his body and knew she was regaining consciousness. Without opening her eyes she murmured, "Daddy?"

"No honey," he replied, kissing the top of her head, "It's Uncle Jake. You're safe now. Just go back to sleep."

CHAPTER 27

▼

Thursday, September 27, 4:05 PM
Horses and Hounds and the Fox, Oh My!

"This is getting more ridiculous by the minute," Joe muttered into his collar microphone as he turned onto yet another gravel road.

"Mr. Dalton," an unfamiliar voice responded in Joe's earpiece. "This is Wilfred Landingham from Systems Operations. I grew up in Stow-on-the-Wold and know the road you've just taken. Indeed there is a stone bridge at the bottom the ravine."

"What ravine? I see some trees ahead. Is that what you mean?"

"No. Once you reach the trees, a ravine will appear on your right. The road will narrow and…"

"I'm at the trees," Joe interrupted as he drove past the thicket on his right, "and I see a stream. OK, I see what you mean about the ravine. How much farther to the bridge?"

"I was trying to warn you. Slow down and be careful. You'll come to a steep hill with several switchbacks. If you take the hill too fast, you'll end up in a heap at the bottom."

Slowing down, Joe drove in silence for a few minutes, concentrating on the road ahead. "Holy shit!"

"I take it you reached the hill, Sir."

"Hill? Don't you mean deathtrap? Don't you people believe in signs?" He came to a stop at the top of the hill, opened his window and leaned out, trying to digest what lay ahead.

"Of course we do Sir, but this is a private road, actually the back entrance to an estate. If you put your car in first gear, it'll spare your brakes."

Taking Landingham's advice, Joe downshifted into first and proceeded down the hill, only to stop again when he reached the first hairpin turn. "Somebody's already here."

"What's that Sir? We just put you on speaker."

"There's a white van parked by the bridge. The door is open, but I don't see any people. Do you think its Andrews?

"Sir, this is Agent Darby. The message from Andrews said you're to wait for him at the bridge. If he's arrived early, he'll be watching you, so press on, but proceed with caution."

Continuing down the hill, Joe parked across the road from the van, got out and quietly approached its rear windows. With pounding heart, he peered in the back window, hoping to find Kelly. Nothing.

Walking around the van, he said into his collar, "It's empty. No one is here." Closing the front door, he spotted a crest and exclaimed, "This van doesn't belong to Andrews, it's from Greystone Manor. Wait. I think I hear voices."

Ducking down behind the van, Joe raised up just enough to look through the windows to the trees lining the riverbank. A man suddenly emerged, but quickly darted back.

John Shepard thrust out his arm, catching Madeline in the ribs. "Wait. Somebody's there. I see another car."

Their little caravan came to a halt. "Do you think its Andrews?" asked Chloe.

"Either that or it's Joe. I'd say the odds are fifty—fifty and we don't have time to hedge any bets," said Madeline, running into the clearing before anyone could stop her. "Who's there?" she called.

"Madeline?" Dumfounded, Joe stood up and saw a woman, hair dripping wet, soaked clothes plastered against her body, running toward him.

"Joe? It's OK," she yelled to her companions, "It's Joe. Hurry!"

Flinging the door of the van open, she turned to Joe, "We found her. We found Kelly."

"Oh my God. Is she?"

"She's alive but she's hurt. We have to get her to a hospital." Madeline answered, climbing into the back of the van. "Help me put the seats down."

Working quickly, Madeline and Joe folded down the rear seat, and prepared the back of the van while Joe relayed the news to Scotland Yard. "Tell them Kelly is breathing, but I'm sure she has a concussion," Madeline reminded.

"Did you get that?" Joe asked.

"Affirmative," answered Darby in Joe's earpiece.

Jake carried Kelly to the open doors of the van, carefully handing her into the waiting arms of her father. Overcome with emotion, Joe didn't realize tears were streaming down his face as he rained kisses on his beloved daughter.

Her concern growing, Madeline said to Chloe, "She's too cold and we don't even have a dry towel."

Jake stepped around to the side door, reached in and parked a large hand on Joe's shoulder, "Hey buddy, you're the only one with dry clothes. Best git 'em off so we can warm up your girl."

While Joe got out of the van and stripped off his shirt and pants, Madeline and Chloe removed Kelly's wet clothes, handing them out to John. It took everyone's effort to maneuver the unconscious girl's six-foot frame into her father's clothes. They were then faced with another problem. The back of the van, even with the seat down, was only five feet long. Either they would have to bend Kelly's knees and turn her on her side, or come up with another plan.

Thinking out loud, Madeline said, "Joe, if you get in and sit with your back against the seat, you can pull Kelly up against you in a sitting position. That way your body heat will warm her back and you can keep her from rolling once we're moving."

Clad only in his shorts, shoes and socks, Joe climbed in, slipped into place and, with assistance from Jake and John, carefully pulled Kelly up far enough to close the doors. "Wait," he said, "her feet. Can you take off my shoes and socks and put them on her. Her feet are like ice."

Reaching in from the back, Jake did as Joe asked. Just as Jake was about to shut the door, they heard a car approaching from the opposite side of the bridge. Everyone turned to see a black sedan with heavily tinted windows come to a stop and, with only a brief hesitation, back up and turn around.

Simultaneously, Jake and John realized what was happening and ran for Joe's rental car. "It's Andrews!" they both shouted at once.

"The keys are in the car," yelled Joe.

Spitting gravel, the black sedan spun its wheels and roared down the road, disappearing into the forest on the other side of the river, with Jake and John not more than thirty seconds behind.

"Darby, are you still there?" Joe said into the collar of his shirt which was now wrapped securely around his daughter.

"We have you sir, but our monitor shows the money moving away."

"That's because it's still in the trunk of my rental car. We spotted Andrews. He didn't even try to get the money, just took off. Donovan and Shepard are following him."

"You should be hearing Graham's helicopter any second."

"Tell him there's no place to set down."

Hearing the unmistakable thawp-thwap of helicopter blades, Madeline jumped out and tried to wave them off.

"Here, talk to them," Chloe said, rushing around the front of the van and handing Madeline a cell phone. "I've got Robbie."

"Robbie," Madeline yelled.

"We see you Maddie, but there's no place to land."

"That's what I'm trying to tell you! You've got to help Jake and John. They've gone after Andrews."

"Which way? We can't see through the trees."

"Away from us, on the other side of the river," she said, both she and Chloe pointing.

The helicopter turned and started over the trees. "They won't get far. Does Jake or John have a cell phone?"

"No, we lost all but one in the river, but the ransom money is still in the trunk. You can track them that way."

As the helicopter disappeared from sight, Madeline hugged Chloe, "Where did you find the phone? I thought we'd lost all of them."

"It was on the ground near the rear tires. I must have dropped it when I came back for the pokers."

"Oh Chloe," Madeline said with great relief and threw her arms around her best friend, "What would I do without you?"

"Yeah, Yeah," Chloe answered, hugging her back. "Yuck, you're all wet."

"Very funny. So are you."

Pulling apart, they looked at each other and began to laugh. "If you aren't the sorriest sight I've ever seen," said Madeline, pulling Chloe toward the van. "Come on, let's get Kelly back up the hill."

September 27, 4:30 PM

"Son of a bitch," roared Jake skidding around a curve, narrowly missing a fallen tree branch that stuck out about three feet into the road. "I wish to hell I had my four-by-four truck. That sucker'll go over anything."

"There's no way you're going to get around Andrews until we clear the woods," said John. "Just stay behind him."

"Hey," Jake said, cocking his head toward his side window. "What's that?"

"You drive, I'll look!" yelled John searching what little he could see of the sky through the dense canopy of trees. "I see it! It's a helicopter. Looks like it's right over us."

"Is it the good guys or the bad guys?"

"I don't know. I only saw it for a second, but here, listen." John rolled down his window and leaned out only to catch a face full of gravel dust. Coughing and wiping his eyes, he rolled it back up. "Did you hear?"

"Yeah. I'll bet its Graham or one of his boys. I can't see Andrews paying somebody to pick him up in a helicopter, besides there's nowhere to land the damn thing."

"Look out, there's another turn up there," John warned.

When they came out of the curve, Andrews was right in front of them. "We're close enough to kiss his butt. Hold on Farmer, we're gonna give him a little smooch."

Jake floored the accelerator and rammed into the back of Andrews's car, propelling it forward and causing it to fishtail. Andrews quickly regained control and picked up speed, pulling about three car lengths ahead of Jake and John, when the forest abruptly ended.

There in front of them was a stately home about half the size of Greystone Manor, complete with formal gardens and a manicured lawn. Andrews raced up the road, taking out a number of flower beds when he turned sharply to the left circling the house. Jake didn't even bother with the road, cutting off the corner and driving straight through the petunias.

Overhead, the helicopter dipped as low as possible without hitting the building, and, as soon as Andrews rounded the house heading for the main entrance, set down directly in front of him.

Andrews slammed on his brakes, jumped out of his car, while frantically waving a gun, and screamed over whirring helicopter blades, "Stay back or I'll shoot."

Carefully stepping out of his car, Jake said, "You don't want to do that Andrews. Nobody's dead yet, but, if you kill one of us, it'll be cold blooded murder." He left out the news about Keyes and remained behind his open door, while John assumed the same position on the other side of the car.

Seizing the opportunity to move while Andrews's back was turned, Robbie and Graham ducked under the rotating blades, and with Graham's weapon concealed in his pocket, slowly approached.

"Jake's quite right," said the inspector, startling Andrews who whipped around, pointing his gun at Graham's head. "You don't want to add murder to the charges already against you. A peaceful surrender will go much better for you."

"Surrender? And die in prison like my father? Who are you anyway?"

"Chief Inspector Paul Graham, New Scotland Yard. Now put down the gun before someone gets hurt."

"You're just trying to distract me," Andrews said, making his way around to the passenger door of his car, "and it's not going to work." Pounding once on the window, he screamed, "Violet, get out here."

"Violet?" said Robbie, "I knew it!"

When no response came from inside the car, Andrews threw open the door, reached in and dragged his passenger out of the car and pushed her in front of him.

"Clayton? Darling? What are you doing?" screeched Violet Hargrove, not grasping the fact that her boyfriend was using her as a human shield.

Grabbing her around the neck and pointing his gun at Violet's temple, he yelled, "OK Inspector, either your chopper flies us out of here, or I blow her head off."

Suddenly Jake felt a familiar tremor in the ground. John felt it as well and glanced across the roof at Jake with a questioning look on his face.

"Stampede," Jake whispered.

"Here? Are you crazy?" the farmer whispered back.

Shrugging his shoulders, Jake thought maybe he was crazy, but there was only thing in his experience that could produce the vibrations, which were growing stronger. Thundering hooves.

Before anyone else realized what was happening, a red fox darted out of the forest and streaked across the lawn directly in front of Andrews and Violet, quickly followed by a pack of barking hounds. The thunder of twenty horses and their riders grew louder and, in the confusion, Andrews lowered his gun, as if he was trying to shoot at the dogs.

It was the opening they needed. Jake lunged at Andrews, tackling and throwing him to the ground, while John grabbed Violet, pulling her in the opposite direction. Graham ran to help Jake and quickly kicked the gun out of the way, as the riding party of red-jacketed fox hunters exploded from the forest at full gallop.

Completely caught off guard, chaos ensued as riders pulled their horses, trying not to trample the six people on the ground. A great black stallion reared up, his rider unable to control him, and came down, narrowly missing Jake's outstretched leg. When the horse reared again, Jake jumped up, ignoring the flailing hooves and spoke softly to him, "Whoa boy. You're alright. It's OK. Nobody's going to hurt you." Miraculously, the horse began to focus on Jake's voice and gradually calmed down.

As the pandemonium subsided an angry gentleman rode up and demanded, "What is the meaning of this? You could have seriously injured one of my horses or worse, one of my guests."

"And you are?" asked the inspector, getting to his feet and pulling a hand-cuffed Andrews after him.

"Sir Edmond Wakefield. This is my estate. Who are you and what are you doing here?"

"Chief Inspector Paul Graham, New Scotland Yard. As you can see, we've apprehended two suspects. Unfortunately, they chose your estate as an escape route."

Sir Wakefield swallowed his next remark as he saw the man and woman being led away. It was then he spotted the helicopter parked on the other side of his front lawn. Now, more curious than angry, he turned back to Graham, "I see. May I ask Chief Inspector, what was their crime?"

Since they had ruined his gardens and interrupted his hunting party, Graham felt he owed the gentleman an explanation and, without divulging too much information, replied, "They kidnapped an eighteen year old girl and kept her shackled like an animal in an old mill for two days."

"My God sir. Did you find her? Is she alright? Is there anything I can do?"

"Thank you, no. She's been rescued and is enroute to a hospital as we speak."

"Alright then. Carry on." Sir Wakefield tipped his hat to the Inspector and rode off to check on his horses and hounds and, of course, his guests.

Robbie had Violet Hargrove by the arm, her cuffed hands behind her, leading her to the helicopter. "I figured it was you, Violet. None of my people would do such a thing. What were you thinking? How could you betray your family like this?"

Jerking away from him, she turned and spit in his face. "Betray them? You bloody imbecile, they betrayed me years ago and so did you. I should be running the hotel, not my idiot brothers. But Father could never see it. His beloved sons are everything to him. Just because I was born a girl, I was relegated to the background. I was only an afterthought, a piece of window dressing. Well, this was my chance to pay him back, pay all of you back."

Violet turned and, with her head held high in defiance and her back ramrod straight, walked to the helicopter.

Robbie had always known she harbored a grudge against him, but had no idea of the extent she hated her father and brothers as well. She had always appeared to be a supportive member of her family's business, but obviously, that was not the case. How was he going to tell Lord Hargrove about his daughter's deception?

The helicopter, with Graham and his prisoners was ready to take off and, since there was only room for the three of them and the pilot, Robbie decided to return with Jake and John. They apologized again to Sir Wakefield for annihilating his flower garden and Robbie informed him a crew had been called to retrieve Keyes's body and the blue car from the river.

The three men retraced their route to the river, where Jake downshifted into first gear and drove up the hill. As they emerged from the forest, they spotted the hotel van parked near the thicket just off the main road. A helicopter with a large Red Cross on the side was just lifting off.

Shielding their eyes from the wind blown up by the propellers, they got out of their car and walked up to Madeline and Chloe.

Waving, Madeline shouted over the noise, "They're taking Kelly to the trauma center in Cheltenham Spa. Joe's going with her."

"Is she going to be OK?" asked Jake.

"I think so. She was awake and she knew who we were. She said she'd dreamt Jake carried her through a forest, but she was pretty fuzzy about everything else."

"Well I'll be damned," said Jake, slapping his thigh, then grabbing Chloe and swinging her in a circle.

"Aye, she's a brave lass, our Kelly. And so are you Maddie girl." He took Madeline in his arms and hugged her soundly.

Feeling a little left out, John cracked, "Ok you guys, enough of this lovefest. I want to see my wife."

"IEEE hah," bellowed Jake, jumping in the air and pumping his fist. "I can't wait to hear all about Suz and Dee and the senior umbrella brigade!"

CHAPTER 28

▼

Thursday, September 27, 8:30 PM
Party On!

"God it's great to feel clean and dry again," exclaimed Madeline as she opened the door of Chloe's bathroom at Greystone Manor and emerged wearing her best friend's clothes. Turning around for inspection, she added, "Not too bad, eh? You know, whoever invented elastic should be a candidate for sainthood."

"You look fine," said Chloe, "And you're not that much bigger than I am."

"Truthfully, I am, but thanks for not saying so."

"Are you about ready? This has been one hell of a long day and I'm starving."

"So am I," answered Madeline. "Did we even have lunch? So much has happened, I don't really remember."

Grabbing their room key, the two women headed out the door and down the hall to the lift, where they ran into Jake and Suzie.

"How's our fearless leader doin' tonight? You ladies are sure lookin' fine," greeted Jake.

"Have you heard anything from Joe?" Suzie asked.

"Actually, I talked to him a few minutes ago" Madeline said as the doors opened and they all entered the lift.

The lobby was bustling with people leaving the dining room, and when the foursome arrived, they found the others waiting for them at their favorite table in the alcove. Their little group were practically the only ones left, which suited them all perfectly fine.

Approaching the table and before anyone could ask, Madeline announced, "I just talked to Joe and Kelly is doing remarkably well." Sitting down, she continued, "She has quite a bump on her head, a cracked rib and some nasty bruises, but she'll make a full recovery."

"Oh that's wonderful," exclaimed Millie, along with everyone else.

"What about Marty?" asked Marge. "Was she able to get to Cheltenham?"

"Aye, that she was," answered Robbie who had joined them for dinner. "Chief Inspector Graham arranged for a helicopter to take her directly to the hospital. I imagine she arrived about an hour ago."

"Yes," added Madeline, "She was there when I talked to Joe."

The atmosphere at the table was giddy, everyone laughing and talking at once. Marge and Millie retold the story of how the four women had captured Stout, giggling with delight over his little accident. "Mr. Grey even said we could keep our umbrellas," said Millie, grinning from ear to ear.

They dined on pheasant, prepared in a delicate wine sauce, but by the time Simon Grey came to join them for coffee and desert, the adrenaline of the day was fading away, leaving everyone exhausted.

"I won't keep you long," said Grey, "but I wanted to congratulate you on your heroic rescue this afternoon. I understand Miss Dalton is doing quite well."

"She is, thank you," answered Madeline. "And thank you for the use of your vehicles. We would never have been able to track down the kidnappers without them."

"I don't know," he smiled. "Something tells me you would have found a way." As the others went back to their chocolate soufflé, he leaned down and told Madeline he needed a word with her in private.

Madeline told the others she would be right back and followed Simon Grey to the dining room door. "Is anything wrong Simon?"

"No, no of course not. I only wanted to let you know the constable from Stow-on-the-Wold called. His men helped the special agents recover the kidnapper's car from the river. Both the body and the car have been sent back to London, as has Mr. Stout. I also wanted to give you these," he added, handing her a stack of envelopes containing the Greystone Manor crest.

"Simon, what are these?"

"They're certificates for a complimentary four night stay. There is one for each of your guests and they are open-ended. They can return tomorrow, next year, or ten years from now."

"That's wonderful, but you should have given them out yourself. I know everyone would want to thank you personally."

"No my dear. Everyone is so tired now. Besides they are your group and I would prefer you give them at your farewell dinner tomorrow night."

"But Simon…"

"No arguments now," he said patting her hand. Then, taking another envelope from his breast pocket, he handed it to her. "For you, Madeline. You are always welcome, by yourself or bring your family, a friend, another group. There will always be a room for you here at Greystone Manor. If the hotel is full, you will stay in my residence."

Momentarily stunned Madeline stammered, "Simon, I don't know what to say."

"Please don't say anything, just promise to come and visit. Often. Now, about tomorrow. I've arranged for Global Tours to be here at ten o'clock. There's no need for bags to be out tonight. The coach will be available to leave whenever you are ready in the morning." Handing her a key, he continued, "I've arranged a suite for you tonight."

"Oh Simon, that's so thoughtful, but, after everything we've been through today, I would really rather not be alone. I'll just stay in Chloe's room tonight. Could you have housekeeping send up some extra towels?"

"Of course, my dear. I completely understand. I'll see to it right away."

Handing back the key, Madeline thanked him again and returned to the table. "The bus will be here at ten in the morning to take us back to London. We're not on a schedule, so don't worry about having your bags out tonight. There will be plenty of time after breakfast. We should all get a good night's sleep. I think we've earned it, don't you?"

Pushing back from the table and standing up, Jake, looking gray with fatigue, chuckled, "That's an understatement darlin'. I feel like I been rode hard and put away wet."

As everyone smiled and walked toward the door, Madeleine found Robbie. "Are you staying tonight?"

"No, lass. I've got to get back and tell the family about Violet before they read about it in the tabloids. Graham promised to keep it under wraps until I've broken the news. His Lordship's going to be heartbroken."

Madeline nodded her head in agreement. "I should go with you."

"No Maddie girl. You're about ready to drop and your people need you." Putting his arm around her, he whispered, "We'll sort it all out when you get back tomorrow."

"OK," she whispered back. "My rental car," she remembered. "Robbie, can you drive my car back to London? Simon will have Joe's car returned to Cheltenham."

Madeline and Robbie followed Chloe to her room. Housekeeping was just leaving as they went in to get Madeline's car key. "I'll be right back Chloe. I just want to make sure all the rental papers are in the glove compartment."

"Umm hmm," Chloe said with a sly smile.

Arm in arm, Madeline and Robbie took the lift back to lobby and walked through the conservatory, into the soft night air. As soon as they were out of the light spilling from the doorway, Robbie turned and took Madeline by the shoulders.

"Maddie," he started to say, then pulled her tight against his body and crushed her mouth with his. Her arms went around his neck and clinging to him, she kissed him back with equal ferocity.

When they finally separated, both were shaking with the intensity of what just happened. He took her by the shoulders again and choked, "Tomorrow."

Looking into his fiery green eyes, she whispered, "Tomorrow."

Friday, September 28, 9:30 AM

"Madeline dear," greeted Millie as Madeline and Chloe made their way through the dining room to join their group for breakfast, "Did you get some rest last night? With all the excitement yesterday, I thought I would never be able to get to sleep, but, as soon as my head hit the pillow, I was out like a light."

"Yes, Millie, thank you, I did. How about everyone else?"

As they took their seats, everyone was eager to know if Madeline had any more information. "I talked to Marty this morning and Kelly is doing much better. She's going to be transferred to University College Hospital in London this afternoon."

"Will we be able to see her when we get back?" Dolores wanted to know.

"We can certainly try. The hospital is just across from Euston Square, only a couple of Tube stops from Green Park."

"Well, I for one don't want to go home without seeing she's alright with my own eyes," said Marge.

"You bet," John chimed in. "I sure don't want to leave with the image of how we last saw her. She was in pretty bad shape."

Looking around the table, Madeline could just picture the group descending on the hospital en masse, demanding to see their precious patient. "Why don't I call as soon as we get back to make sure she's arrived and is settled in her room. We don't want to storm in and scare the staff to death."

"Yeah," Jake laughed, "The poor Brits would think we Yanks were on the war-path again."

Simon Grey stepped up behind Madeline's chair, smiled and said, "What's this about a warpath?"

"Oh, that's just Jake…being Jake," Madeline answered, good naturedly punching Jake in the arm. "You can take the cowboy out of Texas, but…"

"Ah shucks, Ma'am," Jake said, pretending to flinch as if she were going to hit him again.

"You know," chuckled Simon, "I've always wanted to visit Texas. I understand it's very large."

"Yup, that it is. Why I bet you could fit nine or ten Englands between El Paso and Texarkana." Standing up to shake Simon's hand, Jake continued, "Anytime you want to come, you've got a standing invitation at the ranch."

Simon accepted Jake's handshake, then looked around the table. "I know you're all anxious to return to London. Your coach should be here momentarily, but please, take your time. There's no need to rush."

Simon then took his leave to check on the coach while the group light heartedly finished their breakfast and returned to their rooms to finish packing.

The bellman's staff collected everyone's luggage and, loaded everything onto the coach, while the rest of the staff lined up outside the conservatory to say goodbye. Even the old bat who had been so rude to Chloe when they checked in, had a smile on her face.

The ride back to London was relatively quiet, everyone lost in their own thoughts, and when they arrived at Ascot House, Robbie and his staff were on hand to greet them and accompany them to their suites.

Robbie went with Madeline and Chloe and, as soon as the door was closed, Madeline asked, "How is Lord Hargrove? Have you told him about Violet?"

"Aye, first thing this morning. I didn't see any reason to wake him last night. Maddie, he's devastated. The poor man seemed to whither before my eyes."

"I want to see him, Robbie," Madeline said, turning back toward the door.

"Nay lass, he won't see anyone, not even David or William."

"I don't care. This is not his fault and I won't have him blaming himself for his daughter's vindictiveness."

Madeline was out the door before Robbie could stop her, so he ran after her and caught her at the lift. They rode up to the fifth floor, got out and went to Lord Hargrove's door.

Madeline knocked. No answer. She knocked again, harder. "Lord Hargrove, its Madeline Marlborough, I have to speak with you." Still no answer. "Robbie, use your passkey and open the door." When he hesitated, she touched his arm, "He might be in trouble. Please, open it."

Robbie put his keycard in the door and went in. "Your Lordship," he called. "Its Robbie come to see if you need anything."

Slowly he and Madeline walked down the entrance hall and into the living room. There they found Lord Hargrove, still in his dressing gown, sitting in a chair, staring blankly out the window.

Approaching with care, Madeline said softly, "Lord Hargrove?" When he didn't respond, she knelt beside his chair and took his hand. "Lord Hargrove, look at me, please Sir, look at me."

Gone was the impish English gentleman she had known, replaced by a shriveled old man with a haunted look in his eyes. He finally turned and looked at her without recognition.

"Sir, its Madeline. Please don't do this," she pleaded. "Its not your fault. There is no way you could have known what Violet was doing. And besides, she's a grown woman. She's responsible for her own actions."

"Aye," said Robbie, putting a hand on the old man's shoulder. "Violet has been jealous of her brothers and angry with me for years. What she did has nothing to do with you. If anything, the blame lies with us, not you. Please Sir."

A single tear slid down the old man's cheek and Madeline immediately pulled him to her, his forehead resting on her shoulder. She hugged him until she felt his arms go around her. "She's my daughter," he whispered.

"I know Sir, I know. And it's devastating when our children do horrendous things, but Clive, our children grow up and make their own choices. Violet made a bad choice, but it was her choice, not yours. She is responsible, not you, not her brothers and not Robbie. What she did, she did on her own and she must accept the consequences."

"But…"

"No buts. You know I'm right. Now," she said, pulling back and kissing him on the forehead, "Robbie is going to help you get dressed and we'll be very disappointed if you don't join us tonight for our farewell dinner."

When Lord Hargrove started to protest, Madeline stood up, bringing him with her, Robbie supporting him from the back, "I mean it. Eight o'clock sharp. Everyone wants to see you, especially the Talbot sisters," she winked.

Friday, September 28, 7:45 PM

"I still can't get over how well Kelly looked this afternoon," said Chloe as she came out of her room, fastening a gold and pearl hoop in her left ear. "Youth is a wonderful thing, you know?"

"I do indeed," answered Madeline, fluffing her silver curls in front of the mirror over the fireplace. "But I think we look pretty damn good for ladies of a certain age."

"Ha!" said Chloe, grinning at her friend, "We look pretty damn good for babes of any age. You ready?"

"Let me just grab my bag."

As Madeline ducked into her bedroom, Chloe called after her, "Do you think Lord Hargrove will make it?"

Returning with her evening bag, Madeline answered, "I certainly hope so. Let's go find out."

They decided not to tackle the stairs in their heels and met Marge and Millie in the lift. "Don't you look lovely this evening," greeted Millie as the doors closed.

"Thanks," said Chloe, "You two are quite the picture yourselves."

Obviously pleased, the sisters stepped out into the lobby and led the way to the private dining room, where Lord Hargrove and William stood at the door engaged in conversation with Jake and Suzie. Lord Hargrove look frail but dapper in his black tuxedo, but he was there, with his son at his side, laughing at something Jake was saying.

Suddenly a deep Scottish voice said over her shoulder, "You're a fetching lass, Maddie-me-girl. And who is your lovely friend?"

"Oh Robbie," Madeline smiled as he offered an arm to both women and escorted them into the dining room.

Dinner was an elegant affair, made even more special when Joe and Marty Dalton joined them. Marty went straight to Lord Hargrove and gave him a hug while Joe shook hands with William and David, reassuring them that what had happened to Kelly was between Clayton Andrews and the Dalton family. "Andrews used your sister, not the other way around. I'm just sorry she was caught up in his vendetta."

It was a delightful party celebrating both Kelly's safe return and new friendships that would last a lifetime. Madeline made a special presentation of the gifts from Simon Grey and made sure everyone knew they were from him, not her. When dessert had been served and champagne flutes filled, Joe stood and raised his glass. "Here's to our gracious host. Lord Hargrove, you have been so kind to all of us, we want you to know we appreciate your impeccable hospitality. And here's to all of you, the most amazing group of people Marty and I have ever met. But, most of all, here's to you, Madeline Marlborough, our very own fearless leader, the most brilliant and determined tour director in the world. You put everything together, figured out where Kelly was and saved her life."

With that, everyone stood and shouted, "Here Here!"

EPILOGUE

▼

Saturday, September 29, 7:30 AM
Chloe Gets a Surprise

Chloe awoke with a start and looked at the clock on her bedside table. God, it was seven-thirty already and she knew Maddie wanted to see everyone before they left for the airport. The Donovans, the Shepards and Marge and Millie were all going home today. She and Maddie were going to spend a couple of extra days in London before heading home and, of course, the Daltons would be staying a few days as well.

Throwing off the covers and heading to the bathroom to brush last night's party off her teeth, she knew Maddie wouldn't wake up on her own. They had partied way too late.

Everybody had a great time. After dinner, the celebration adjourned to their suite. What a kick it had been to open the dumb-waiter and find enough booze and munchies to supply a battle ship. David Hargrove had thought of everything and, at midnight, he sent up half a dozen pizzas.

At one o'clock the Shepards and Talbot sisters said goodnight and Chloe finally gave up, leaving Maddie and Robbie still talking with Jake and Suzie.

Chloe threw on a pair of jeans and a tee shirt and padded into the living room. Knocking on Maddie's door, she said, "Come on Maddie, you'd better hurry," then continued into the kitchen to find a tray with hot coffee and a basket of scones and croissants. "God bless dumb-waiters, every house should have one."

Chloe took the tray into the dining area, set it on the table, poured herself a cup of coffee and ripped off a piece of croissant. Of course Madeline hadn't appeared, so she took a sip of coffee, buttered her pastry and walked back to Maddie's door.

Popping the flaky piece in her mouth and licking the butter off her fingers, Chloe knocked three times and opened the door. Madeline was sitting on the bed, tying her sneakers. Just then the bathroom door opened and out came a very tall, wet Scotsman, wearing nothing but a towel and a grin.

"Morning Chloe. And a beautiful day it is."

The look on Chloe's face made Maddie and Robbie howl with laughter. Finally, catching her breath, Maddie said, "Oh Chloe, close your mouth. Your tonsils are showing."

0-595-33131-9